The Hidden Order

Tap into the wisdom

Liliane Grace

Published by Grace Productions
https://lilianegrace.com

www.lilianegrace.com

First published in Melbourne, Australia in June 2012 as
The Hidden Order – Can you see it?

This edition published in Melbourne, Australia, in August 2021

Sequel to *The Mastery Club*®
See the Invisible, Hear the Silent, Do the Impossible

A CIP catalogue record for this book is available from the National Library of Australia.

ISBN 978-0-6485624-4-3 (paperback)

Typeset in Adobe Caslon Pro

Artwork by Kimberly Djehanian

Printed and bound by Ingram Spark, Australia

Disclaimer:
The purpose of this book is to stimulate thought rather than to treat illness or provide advice.

The Hidden Order

Tap into the wisdom

Liliane Grace

WHAT PEOPLE ARE SAYING

"I loved your book and couldn't put it down. I loved that it made me think. I enjoyed this book as much as The Mastery Club and I'm already looking forward to reading it again. This is another magical book from Liliane 'The GREAT'." – **Ben Wagner, 12 years**

"i. loved. the. book! OMG i read it in one go i just couldnt stop reading it."
– **Stephanie Limm, 17 years**

"Kids are hungry for stimulating questions and ideas that expand their mind and awareness. They don't just want to be entertained – they also want to think. They want to know why the world is the way it is and how they can achieve their goals and find their true self.

"The Hidden Order is even more enjoyable than The Mastery Club. It was an enlightening experience reading it. We really liked the advanced concepts in this book that built on The Mastery Club, and the way that old ideas were reviewed. The timing was perfect – it reminded us of these concepts at a perfect time in our lives.

"The Hidden Order is an amazing book which we would recommend for every teenager and their parents." – **Jarrah (13) and Tahnaya (16) Wynne, co-authors of Meditation For Kids, By Kids**

"The Hidden Order is a fantastic read. So much food for thought (no pun intended) but even the food details! So deliciously described. It has made me want to experiment a million and one ways with salads and eat more nuts, seeds, legumes etc and make healthier food choices and definitely introduce raw apple crumble into our lives.

"Not only have you challenged my taste buds, my mind has expanded with knowledge, my soul is replenished, my heart is excited... You've shed light on topics I hadn't yet discussed in full detail with my daughter. We have now. You made the conversations about 'girl's stuff' come about so easily.

"I've had lovely little conversations after each chapter to ensure my child has grasped the concepts fully. Sometimes explaining things through examples and child speak. It is a fabulous extension to The Mastery Club..." – **Kym Fullerton; mother of Georgia Schumann aged 9**

ABOUT THE HIDDEN ORDER

"A lot of what I'm tripping over in life at the moment seems to have been taken directly from the pages of The Hidden Order. Funny, that! This is a beautiful, important, beautiful, important, beautiful, important book." – **Jenny Zimmerman, mother, writer, amateur philosopher and naturalist, chook-keeper**

"The Hidden Order is an extraordinary book that resonates and speaks long after the cover is closed for the first time. Brain-stretching, heart-stretching, it fires the reader up with 'Yeah, let's get to it NOW' and 'OMG, where have my thoughts been all my life? I read this book in an afternoon, plunging through it, as eager to absorb as a sponge in the desert, and it will take the next month to fully digest it all." – **Helen Patrice, author of A Woman of Mars: Poems of an Early Homesteader**

"Yet again, "besties" Nina and Natalie take us on a journey of the life we all want – not lived in fear and hesitation but with purpose and wisdom, and in the spirit of hope, exploration, imagination and adventure – where you can visualise, plan and achieve your own dreams, or put simply; if you can master yourself then you can master anything!" – **Ade Djajamihardja, Film and Television Producer**

"Beam me up, Liliane, it's magical... I've learnt so much without feeling as if I'm learning at all." – **Tom Zulu, Business Coach**

"If you liked The Mastery Club, you will love this even more! Liliane Grace has done it again! The kids are back and raring to rock your world with their courage and wisdom. Read it yourself first and then offer it to your children. Because if they read it first, they may leave you behind in the dust of their own evolution. It is not just a compelling read; it is profound and inspiring. I will be stocking it in my office for all my clients, regardless of their age. Congrats Liliane!" – **Ken Pierce, Psychologist, Speaker and Co-Author of The Dance of Bullying – A Breakthrough Tool for Teachers and Parents**

VI

DEDICATION

TO DR JOHN DEMARTINI, Philosopher and Behavioural Educator extraordinaire, whose deep questioning and tireless research have resulted in insights that are transforming lives all over the world, including mine. With this book, I salute your work and carry the torch with you.

FOREWORD #1

ABORIGINAL WISDOM has long taught that for every good spirit there is a bad spirit. There is always, everywhere, a balance of shadow and light, just as Liliane Grace explains in *The Hidden Order*.

Our lives are sometimes difficult and baffling, but if we turn to the ancient wisdom in our culture, we are often reminded of things we may have forgotten, like the fact that our hard times serve us and have greater purposes than we may be seeing.

In my case, my life took some very confronting paths but I am grateful for those times because they led to me being reunited with my Aboriginal family and becoming grounded in my culture. I could have decided that I was a no-hoper and given up, and either died in gaol or become caught in a life of petty crime, but my spirit called me to believe in myself and to create a life I could be proud of and celebrate.

I hope that my story, which inspired Liliane to create the Joel character, inspires you.

Jeremy Yongurra Donovan

FOREWORD #2

THE HIDDEN ORDER is a story for young people that offers a number of profound and deeply beneficial insights, many of which greatly differ from mainstream views held by society.

The ideas it presents about health, wellness and personal growth may be new or even unsettling for some readers, however, as an educator and researcher specialising in wholistic health, nutrition and wellbeing, I am particularly aware of the well-founded scientific and clinical research on offer in support of these concepts.

Cancer, for example, as presented in this story, is not necessarily the dis-ease it is widely promoted and accepted as being. There is a large and increasing body of research and evidence to indicate that it is actually a part of the body's own natural healing process, a process that is to be supported rather than suppressed. Methods of fasting, cleansing, juicing and wholefood eating, along with addressing the underlying emotional causes and spiritual wellbeing of an individual, are all important and effective strategies in healing every form of illness and dis-ease.

I hope this book not only entertains readers but also inspires them to embrace a more wholistic approach to health and wellbeing, including a wholefood lifestyle, and to gain an understanding that all illness and dis-ease in the body is a simple, yet intelligent feedback mechanism signalling the requirement for healing oneself on a physical, emotional and spiritual level.

Dr Kristian Ronacher (PhD)
www.drronacher.com

"Everywhere beneath the world's confusion there is an underlying order."

- Murray Gell-Mann, physicist (boy genius)

"If [God] is omnipotent, then every occurrence, including every human action, every human thought, and every human feeling and aspiration, is also His Work."

- Albert Einstein, physicist and mathematician

"Nothing is good or bad but our thinking makes it so."

- William Shakespeare (Hamlet)

"Is this real? Or is it just happening inside my head?"

Dumbledore beamed at him, and his voice sounded loud and strong in Harry's ears even though the bright mist was descending again, obscuring his figure.

"Of course it's happening inside your head, Harry, but why on earth should that mean it is not real?"

- Harry Potter and the Deathly Hallows, J K Rowling

SHAKE IT OFF AND STEP UP

A PARABLE IS TOLD of a farmer who owned an old mule. The mule fell into the farmer's well. The farmer heard the mule 'braying' – or whatever mules do when they fall into wells. After carefully assessing the situation, the farmer felt sorry for the mule, but decided that neither the mule nor the well was worth saving. Instead, he called his neighbours together and told them what had happened and asked them to help haul dirt to bury the old mule in the well and put him out of his misery.

Initially, the old mule was hysterical! But as the farmer and his neighbours continued shovelling and the dirt hit his back, a thought struck him. It suddenly dawned on him that every time a shovel load of dirt landed on his back, he should shake it off and step up! This is what the old mule did, blow after blow. "Shake it off and step up... shake it off and step up... shake it off and step up!" he repeated to encourage himself.

No matter how painful the blows, or distressing the situation seemed, the old mule fought panic and just kept right on shaking it off and stepping up!

You guessed it! It wasn't long before the old mule, battered and exhausted, stepped triumphantly over the wall of that well! What seemed like it would bury him, actually ended up blessing him. All because of the manner in which he handled his adversity.

– Author Unknown

CONTENTS

Chapter

*PS. Find the new Mastery Club Lessons! They're hidden
in the pages of this book.*

XVI

CHAPTER 1

It's On Again!

IT WAS A SWEATY-HOT DAY without even the flicker of a breeze. I was lying on my bed feeling hot and bored and tired – you know that heavy, lazy feeling like you can't even move a muscle? – when Mum's voice yelled out from downstairs, "Nat! Nina's on the phone!"

At that, my heart gave a leap and I jumped off the bed with the speed of an Olympic gymnast, threw my bedroom door open and thundered down the stairs to grab the phone from the hallway table where she'd left it.

"Hi! You're back!" I beamed. "How was it?"

"Phenomenal!"

It felt like ages since I'd heard her voice, which sounded as bright and full of energy as ever. "I was ringing to organise for you and the others to come over and stay at the farm for a few days," she said briskly. "Reunion of the Mastery Club! Time to set those New Year goals."

Typical Nina: straight to the point and busy organising. "Great," I said, still beaming, "I'll check with Mum. When?"

"Soon as we can get you all over here," she answered. "Find out how soon you can come and I'll call the others and get back to you. How was your family holiday?" she added, almost as an afterthought.

Images ran through my mind of swimming in the sea, sandy picnics, hot sleepless nights, fish and chips on the beach, walks in the pine forest… "It was pretty good. Katie and Evan drove me a bit nuts but they were okay. Some of Dad's family was there some of the time since it's his family's holiday house, and that was fun for a bit, but it was good when they left… to have the place to ourselves." My cousin Ella's face flashed before my mind. We'd had a couple of chats while we were at Sorrento together; she was nicer than I'd realised.

Never one to stay on the phone for long, Nina hung up to call the others and get this visit organised, and I wandered into the dining room to check with Mum about dates. It was a lot cooler down there than upstairs in my room. I could feel the sweat under my hair at the back of my neck starting to dry.

Mum had my secondary school textbooks out on the table and she was covering them with clear contact film. "Here," she said, passing me the scissors, "You cut, I'll wrap."

She placed a Year 7 Maths book on the pile on her right and picked up a Year 7 English book. My stomach felt a bit funny, looking at them. I'd been so conscious, at the start of last year, that it was going to be my final year at primary school, but then when Nina arrived unexpectedly in the middle of the year all those thoughts were driven right out of my mind and I became caught up in her mad plan to start a Mastery Club. A mad, wonderful plan. She'd opened my life up to such new ideas and experiences that I would never be the same again. Instead of feeling like I was just going through life reacting to all the things that happened around me, I now knew I was the creator of my life. It was like belonging to a secret society that walks the streets with hidden, magic powers that the people around you don't know you have – or know they have, in fact. Because this wasn't like finding a magical object that gave you power; this was waking up powers that everyone already has.

But I still felt a bit funny in the tummy when I thought about going to secondary school. No Nina, for one thing, and Clare would be at a different school this year. We'd been together since kindergarten, Clare and Sandy and Billy and me, and now Clare would be gone. That would feel weird. And the work would be harder, I supposed, more 'real study'.

"So how's Ms Nina?" Mum asked, busily folding and sticking.

"Good. She's back from that course she did with her parents. She wants to have us all over for a few days. Okay?"

"No reason why not. There's nothing on till you go back to school. Speaking of which, where will she be going?"

"She's not. You know, Mum, she's home educated."

Mum stopped what she was doing and stared at me. "Still? At secondary level?" She shook her head in mild disapproval. "I have a lot of respect for her parents and her aunt and uncle, but really… Are they doing what's best for her? Can they provide her with everything she needs on her own at home in the country? It's all right at primary level, that's a lot of learning through play, but at secondary…? How is she going to get an education?"

"She gets the kind of education that really matters," I said, cutting the shape of a geography book.

Mum narrowed her eyes. "What's that supposed to mean?"

"Well…" I felt a bit uncomfortable. "If you know how to set goals and achieve them, you can do anything you want."

"That's true, but there's a lot more to life than just your own personal goals. It's important to have an understanding of life that goes beyond your own little world."

"Rosie and Pete take her all over the place – apart from when they went to Nepal, but that was for their honeymoon. And just now she did that course with them that was supposed to be only for adults."

"What course was that?"

"Something about the mind…" I let my voice trail off, realising that I didn't really know anything about it myself.

"Mm," Mum gave her head another little shake. "I wonder… Still, so far so good. She's certainly a very likeable and capable young lady. Though I'm not sure that green hair is called for…"

"Her green hair is what makes her so special."

Mum looked at me wryly. "Now really, Natalie, think that one through. Are you saying that if she changed her hair colour she wouldn't be special any more?"

"It's not the hair colour itself," I argued, "although that helps. It's the who-she-is that chooses to go around with green hair that's special. She does it on purpose, to stand out, so she doesn't just blend into the crowd and be a nobody. She wants to be a somebody in her life. She wants to make a difference and grow, so she puts herself out there."

"Well, she certainly does that." Mum placed the geography book on the sheet of contact I had just cut, and pressed and tucked in silence for a moment. "So you're being invited to visit for a few days?"

"Yes. Me and Sandy and Billy and Clare. To set goals for the year," I added meaningfully.

"Tell the others I'll drive you all up there, if you like. I haven't seen where Nina lives yet. It's about an hour away?"

"An hour and a half," I said. "She thought Nuncle and Liz might take us in their friend's van again."

"Oh. All right. Well, whatever works. I'd like to see Rosie's and Pete's farm, but it doesn't have to be this minute."

By the time I called the others, Nina had already been in touch and either spoken to them or left messages, and the plan was falling into place. We'd have three days at her place in the last week of the summer holidays. Nuncle and Liz would take us and Mum would pick us up those lovely three days later. Excitement and anticipation began to bubble in my chest, rising higher and higher until I was just about dancing with eagerness. Four sleeps to go!!

CHAPTER 2

STRANGER DANGER

I OFFERED TO WALK OVER to Liz-and-Nuncle's house to save them picking me up, but really it was so I could see their place again. I hadn't been there once over the school holidays, even though I'd promised to stay in touch. Somehow, with Christmas and going away and stuff, I'd just never got around to it, which made me feel a bit bad because they were really special to me, even more than my own blood-relatives. (I felt uncomfortable confessing that, even just to myself. Should I love my blood-relatives more?)

Anyway, on Friday morning I shouldered my backpack, gave Mum a goodbye hug, yelled goodbye to my sibling-terrors, Evan and Katie, and headed out. Dad had already left for work so I texted a 'bye' to him while I was walking. It was a beautiful summer day, not too hot yet, though it would probably heat up quite a bit by the afternoon. The cicadas were already making their shrill noise.

Nina's aunt and uncle lived a couple of streets away from me but I'd never known that either they or their street existed until she turned up in my life. It's funny how people who are going to be really important to you can be living right under your nose and you don't even know. I looked around at the houses on either side of me as I walked, wondering if there was someone else behind those closed doors and curtained windows who might be about to come into my life. The houses were all just boring brick and weatherboard little boxes with driveways and cars and flowerbeds. (Like my place.) It was no wonder that Liz and Nuncle's house stood out a mile, once you knew to turn into the little lane that was actually a street and not someone's driveway…

Begonia Lane was more over-grown than ever – I almost shot right past it. I made a sharp turn into the lane, feeling the difference under my feet immediately. From flat, concrete pavement to something bumpy and uneven. Cobblestones? It was like coming into another world, a sort of old-fashioned magical world. Especially when you got to the end of the street and came to face-to-face with Liz and Nuncle's property, and you saw the colourful, turreted, oddly-shaped house sitting amidst vegie patches and chooks and hay bales. And right under your nose, a little trickling creek, of all things, that you had to cross by a tiny arched bridge.

A big smile was blossoming on my face as I stepped onto the bridge. I couldn't help it. I just felt happy here.

I walked toward the house through my memories of all our times here: meeting Liz and Nuncle, visiting when Nina had news that her parents were lost in a storm in Nepal, holding our Mastery Club meetings in Nina's upstairs attic room where she was staying while her parents were on their honeymoon; being a special guest when her parents returned home safely, and celebrating with everyone's families on the Slide Night. A street and house and family that had not even been a blip on my radar, as Dad says, had suddenly come full-focus last year.

I knocked on the kitchen back door and it was opened almost

immediately by a beaming Nuncle. His brown hair looked a bit greyer and his eyes seemed to twinkle more than ever but otherwise he was just as I remembered him. "Natalie!" he declared, "My goodness, you've grown!"

It was true. He didn't seem to be as tall as I remembered, but he was just as stout. Suddenly I was being drawn close and enveloped in a hug. His arms around me were warm and comfortable as he held me against his chest. I could smell coffee and something spicy.

Liz said laughingly from behind, "Let her take her backpack off!" And then I was standing in their sunny, colourful kitchen hugging Nina's Aunt Liz, her clear blue eyes glowing at me when she stood back. She was wearing old overalls like plumbers wear, but on her, the ex-model, they looked fantastic. A strappy yellow singlet under an old blue overall, and she could have turned heads on the catwalk. Man. Even in her late 40s with a bit of grey starting in her hair too.

"It's so good to see you," I said, and the three of us stood grinning at each other for a while before they poured me a glass of freshly squeezed orange juice and cut me a slice of home-made spicy fruit cake. I'd eaten quite a big breakfast, but everything they made always tasted so good…

I had to tell them my news, which wasn't much, just our family holiday and Christmas, while they bustled around packing bits and pieces to take, and then we went outside to the friend's van, loaded up, and Nuncle drove us out of there to Billy's place. He was in his driveway shooting baskets. We watched for a minute before he noticed us and stuck the basketball under his arm, scooping an old battered bag off the ground with the other hand and leaping into the van. His mum and stepdad were at work, he said, and his sister was staying with friends, so there was no-one to say goodbye to.

Sandy was sitting on the fence at her place. As soon as she saw us coming she jumped off the fence and darted to the front door. A moment later, as Nuncle pulled up beside the driveway, she was heading towards us with an old army backpack of her dad's hooked over one shoulder and yelling "Bye!" Then her parents were coming down the driveway and her gruff father was talking to Liz and Nuncle through the van window about the details of our visit, and her mother was smiling at us and waving goodbye as we pulled away from the kerb.

Clare's tiny unit is the back one on their block, so Nuncle drove down the driveway and I popped out to knock on the door. A big guy in a singlet was sitting on the steps of the next-door unit drinking beer. He waved the can at me while I stood waiting. Finally the door opened and Clare and her mum were there, arguing about something and saying hello to me at the same time. Clare was frowning and saying "Okay, okay," and grabbing her bag and making me go backwards to get out of her way, she was in such a hurry to get out of there.

"Sometimes being the only two people in the house is a bit much," she muttered, pushing past me to get into the van. I said hello and goodbye to her mum, who had bags under her eyes and kind of messy hair this morning, and followed Clare into the van. Clare's mum didn't come over to say hi like I thought she would. She just smiled the sort of smile you keep for visitors and waved from the front steps. I guessed she wasn't feeling that great, especially being a bit messy and Liz being a model and gorgeous in anything.

Now the van really felt full and it got noisy because everyone was talking to someone, and it also rattled and wheezed a bit. Nuncle put some music on – jazz, I think, and we let the streets roll on past us as we headed out of the suburbs and into the country towards Nina's farm.

Once again I was struck by how far away she lived. It seemed to take forever to get there. Suburban streets, highways, freeway, little towns, rural streets, and then finally we were turning onto gravel roads and really getting close.

"Awfully dry out here," Liz remarked, as we bumped past yellowing fields and shrubs and trees that were so dry they even looked crunchy. It was certainly different to our visit last spring when it had been lush and green everywhere.

We rattled across the cow grid and onto their driveway, pointing out the alpacas in the distance and looking for the house – there it was! surrounded by a wide verandah and trees and a vegie garden. I couldn't see Nina, which surprised me, but her parents, Rosie and Pete, were sitting close together on a loveseat and swinging slowly back and forth. They smiled and waved and stood up, calling for Nina, who burst out of the house a moment later as Nuncle parked and switched off the engine. She was grinning and green-haired as usual, but she wasn't alone. Someone was following her out, the screen door banging behind him. A boy. A tall, dark-skinned, lanky boy. I stared at him through the van windows, waiting for the others to climb down, and wondered who he was. He looked Aboriginal.

Nina was hugging everyone, especially her aunt and uncle, and introducing them to him, and when I finally stepped down I was in time to hear that his name was Joel and she had met him at the course and he'd been visiting them for the last couple of days. A stab of something like jealousy went through me. She wasn't *mine* – she could have other friends! I scolded myself. But some of the brightness seemed to have gone out of the day now that a stranger was here.

CHAPTER 3

No Flies On Us

NINA GRABBED ME in a bear hug and squeezed tight. Then, holding onto my hand firmly, she declared, "It's so good to see you guys! Are you hungry? I've made a totally awesome fruit platter."

I had to laugh, and we all followed her into the house where there truly was a mouth-watering display of fruit on the kitchen table. Melons, berries, mangoes, peaches, bananas, plums, grapes – there is no doubt that Nature has the most brilliant colour palette I've ever seen. I guess that's because it's the Grand Organising Designer that Nina's family talks about. And this lot was begging to be eaten. We all dug in, relishing the sweet juiciness.

The adults were hanging back a little bit at first, just talking to each other while we attacked the fruit. I sort of half-noticed Liz and Rosie in what looked like a quite serious conversation, very quietly, by the fridge. And Nuncle was watching Liz with a sober expression. A moment later he turned his gaze away and looked at Joel, who was standing back a bit too, kind of shyly, and something like sadness flickered across his face. It was weird. Then Nuncle sensed me looking at him, and he smiled and came over to the table, jostling between me and Clare to get at the fruit, and teasing us for being gluttons and not leaving any for him.

After we'd eaten and had rinsed plates and hands and faces, Nina beckoned us out to sit under the trees. There was a lovely breeze out here, and we collapsed onto the grass under the gum tree to gaze upwards, through patterned leaves, at the blue sky and out across the sun-hazed fields.

Joel was sitting just at the edge of where we had clustered together. He was older than us, maybe about seventeen. I could see the faint beginnings of a moustache on his upper lip. He looked awkward and I wished I could have been nice enough to be friendly to him and talk to him a bit, but really, honestly, I wanted him gone so it could be just us, our Club. I angled myself away from him a bit, not exactly turning my back on him, but not exactly making him welcome, either.

"So how was the amazing course?" Sandy asked bluntly. "Did it live up to your expectations?"

Nina rolled her eyes dramatically. "A-*ma*-zing," she said. "Insight after insight. Wasn't it?" she asked Joel, over our heads.

He nodded slowly.

"We went from about eight in the morning till about ten at night and really, we could have gone even later. It was all so fascinating."

Sandy eyed her quizzically. "Fourteen hours a day of schoolish sort of stuff? You must be mad."

"We already know that," said Billy.

"Mad is her middle name," Clare chipped in.

"Nina Mad Baxter," Nina murmured, trying it on.

"So. Tell us something about it. What was so amazing?" Sandy persisted.

Nina gave a sigh. She wriggled backwards and leaned against the trunk of the big gum tree.

"Where do you start?" She looked at Joel again. "Where do you start?"

"At the beginning?" he suggested.

"Brilliant. No. I can't."

"Why not?" I asked.

"Because the course was full of games and if I tell you about them, I'll spoil it for you if you ever do it. You see," to Sandy, "that's why we could go all day: it was *fun*."

"Well, that's different then," Sandy said. "What kind of games?"

"Games with stuff like balloons and mirrors and candles and music and juggling balls and bits out of movies and –"

Suddenly we were viewing this course we'd previously given no serious attention to with great interest. We'd just assumed that she was going to be sitting at a desk all day listening to some adult drone on. You mean there were grown-up courses that were actually designed to be *fun?* Why couldn't they design school that way?! I mean, kids are supposed to be fun-machines; we're supposed to learn through *playing*.

"But there was a lot of talking too," Nina added, as if she could read our minds. "*Lots* of talking. And some of it I didn't understand at all. Nuncle would have been right at home. There was heaps of quantum physics and stuff like that."

"What was your favourite bit?" Clare asked, ignoring all the big words.

"I hate to disappoint you," Nina said, "but it wasn't the games *exactly*. It was what the games got us to see, which is this way of looking at the whole world and everything so that it all fits together and makes sense and nothing is wrong. I know…" she paused, looking at us each in turn; "that sounds nuts, but the more you look into it, the more you get it. And there was this other idea we talked about a lot of the time that really got inside my head, this idea that nothing means anything."

"The Lessons Begin…" Sandy said in an ominous tone of voice.

"I liked the Lessons," I retorted, in case she put Nina off telling us more. "What do you mean, 'nothing means anything'?"

"Well, it's really more that we give everything all the meaning it has. Like, if I frown at you, you might think I don't like you, but I might just be worrying about something that has nothing to do with you at all, and I just happened to be looking in your direction while I was thinking about it. So we all go through our lives making up what everything means, and what we come up with isn't the real, absolutely true meaning, it's just how we're interpreting it and what we're making it mean in that moment."

Immediately I thought about what I was making Joel mean. A threat; a disturbance in my life; an interference. I could make him mean a new friend. But I didn't want to.

"We are absolutely one hundred percent convinced that our opinion of what's going on is the whole truth," Nina bubbled on, "but two people will look at the *exact* same situation and to one person it will be a good thing and to the other person it will be a bad thing. So then who's right? What's the truth?"

She answered her own question with a little bounce. "Nobody! Because unless you can see the whole big picture, you've only got a little bit of the truth."

"That's Nuncle's 'Good Stuff, Bad Stuff' Game," I said, remembering.[1]

"Yep. So we can make anything mean something empowering or something disempowering. We are the creators of our own reality!"

We sat in silence for a moment. A fly landed on my upper arm and I blew it away. It came straight back and headed for my nose, so I flapped my hand at it.

"Nuisance, right?" Nina said, watching me.

"What?"

"The fly. You're interpreting it as a nuisance."

---

1 Introduced in *The Mastery Club*, Chapter 32

"Flies *are* nuisances," Sandy proclaimed heavily. "That's a fact."

"I bet they're not to someone," Nina said. "Someone would see good in them."

"Yeah? Who?"

"Well, if you're a bird, flies are delicious meals for you and your babies."

"Yeah, if you're a *bird*, but they're no good to *people*."

Nina grinned her 'gotcha!' expression and said, "Here's the deal: if I can come up with three ways flies are good for people, will you agree that maybe a lot of what we think and believe might not be the whole story?"

Sandy looked at her with suspicion, sniffing a hidden trap, then agreed. "Okay, three ways flies are good for people, but they have to be *real* ones."

Nina nodded her head vigorously and said, "You're on; give me a sec." She closed her eyes, and sat in complete stillness. We were starting to get a bit restless, wondering if she'd actually fallen asleep, when she opened her eyes and said, "Number One: flies eat all kinds of garbage, road kill, and animals that die in the wild. If they didn't, there'd be a whole lot more bad smells and disease around."

"Yep, you've got to give her that one, San," Billy said. "Remember that speeded up nature film they showed us at school last year? You know the one with maggots eating dead animals?"

Clare shuddered. "Gross!"

"Yeah but it's true: they're incredibly fast at getting rid of dead stuff."

"Okay; one." Sandy stuck a finger in the air and looked at Nina challengingly.

"Number Two," Nina continued. "Did you know that in the olden days before we had antibiotics, people used to get infections and sometimes even die from little cuts?"

"That's insane!" Billy exclaimed. "What – *little cuts?*"

"Yep. But someone worked out that if you put maggots into the wound they eat all the yucky dead flesh without touching the clean parts, and people who would otherwise have died got better."

"Maggots! Ughh!" That was totally disgusting, but we couldn't deny it was a real 'good' from the flies.

Nina furrowed her brow; "Number three – did you guys learn in science about genetics?"

"Have we done genetics?" I asked the others. They shook their heads doubtfully.

"Homeschooling to the rescue!" Nina said brightly. "You see, to begin with, scientists worked out most of genetics using fruit flies because they have such short lives so the scientists could mate them and track the results over lots of generations really quickly."

"How do you mate flies?" Clare wondered.

"So?" Sandy crossed her arms. "What's good about that?"

"Well, genetics is the hottest thing in medicine right now, and some people reckon it's going to be the source of healing in the future – getting rid of asthma and deformities, repairing damaged brains and spines, and even wiping out genetic defects!"

Nina sat back triumphantly. "Whew! I believe that's three 'goods', Sandy. Thanks for making me think so hard – I might not have come up with all that without you pushing me." She gave a cheeky wink. "Will you admit now that a lot of our beliefs aren't very well thought through?"

Sandy was clearly torn between admiration and resentment. "Okay, you win that round," she said grudgingly. "But you can make anything mean anything!"

Nina laughed delightedly, "Exactly! That's the other side to 'nothing means anything', and I reckon it's even *better* this way. Everything *does* mean everything because everyone sees everything differently, and the only thing that stops us seeing it someone else's way is because we've got different information or beliefs." She propped herself up on her knees. "Now here's a question for you guys: How do you think we humans look to the flies?"

"Like giants or trees or something," I suggested, baffled, but Billy was way ahead of me.

"They'd be thinking we're bad news when we swat them or use fly spray," he said, flapping his hand at a blowie. "Go on, rack off. I don't want to kill you since you do actually have a good side..."

"Flies don't think," Sandy reproved.

"I know they don't think the way we do," Nina said, "but even amoebas know what they like and don't like, and flies are much smarter than bacteria. I meant, are we good or bad to them?"

The blowie started buzzing around Clare. She batted it away, saying, "I suppose to a fly our windows would be bad because they can't work them out and so they get stuck."

"This is just like that story Nuncle told us last year about the man and the horse,"[2] I mused. "Thinking something is good or bad, and then changing your opinion when you get more info."

"Exactly," said Nina. "When we don't understand something we call it 'bad' – whether we're a fly or a person. Okay; other side: how might we be 'good' to flies?"

"Garbage!" Billy declared. "Lovely, yummy garbage we leave out all over the world for them to eat!"

"That's gross," Clare said again.

He stuck out his tongue and pretended to lick the air. "Plus, they land on us to get a drink, so I guess we're just like big salty juice bars to them!"

"Ugh. Totally gross!" Clare shuddered. "But... that *does* mean we're good and bad, too, depending on how you look at us."

"Okay, I surrender," said Sandy. "You win – this time."

Nina gave her a big, warm smile.

---

2 *The Mastery Club* page 203

"But," I interrupted, in a dramatic voice, "if we didn't see *that*, if we've gone our whole lives thinking that flies are just a pain, how much more are we missing – right?"

"Now you're getting a glimpse of what that course was like for me and Joel," Nina affirmed. She glanced at Joel as she said this, and he looked up from the little pile of leaves he'd been quietly gathering and shredding.

Mastery Club Lesson #11[3]

What Are You Making It Mean?

* Nothing Means Anything… and… Everything Means Everything.

* Which means that we give everything all the meaning it has for us.

CHAPTER 4

BRAIN STUFF

"SO FLIES AND HUMANS *both* have a good side and a bad side, which is that Law of Polarity," Clare said.

"That's exactly right," Nina agreed. "*Everything* has a good and a bad side to it but most people label things just good or just bad. Like 'school is bad'," she looked at Sandy pointedly while she said this, "and 'mountain biking is good'," to Billy.

"It *is* good," said Billy.

"Yeh but I bet there are bad sides to it too. Like getting tired and falling off and skidding and punctures and getting lost."

"Okay, fair enough," he acknowledged. "Dad took me skiing last winter and there were, like, three ambulances on standby at the bottom of the hill, but Mum reckons there are *five* when they're in mountain-biking season, so she'll only let me go on the safest routes and events possible." He made a face.

"What about that huge bushfire last month?" Sandy demanded. "People died in that. And animals. What's good about that?"

"Well," Nina glanced at Joel. "The heat of the fire is the very thing that allows some seeds to regenerate, isn't it? Because otherwise they'd just stay dormant. And some species flourish when there are fires. For instance, this cute little native mouse that loves grass and openness, so when fires burn off the undergrowth, this mouse is really happy because the grass grows and it can get around more easily, which means it can eat more and have lots of babies. And then it's got less predators because they don't like the openness so they can't hide."

We were all staring at her. Clare even had her mouth open.

Nina grinned. "I just learnt about it." She threw a handful of dry leaves at Clare. "From Joel. Aboriginal people used to do regular burns to keep the land healthy. Didn't they?"

He nodded.

"So if your whole family dies in a bushfire, you can make that mean something good," Sandy said. (In the confrontational sort of tone that reminded me of their fight last year.) I held my breath.

"Boy, you always like to go for the tough stuff, don't you?" Nina said. "The thing is, if you believe death is the end, then you'll see it as bad. But if you believe it's the beginning of something else, it won't look so bad, will it?"

At once I thought of my Gran dying last year, and my feeling that she was not really gone, just not in her old body any more.

"That doesn't make death *good*," Sandy argued.

"I'm not saying that exactly," Nina said. "We must be here for a reason and life is great! Seems to me that this is one of those Old-Man-and-Horse issues: we humans just don't know enough to judge if something is good or bad. Life is so huge and we've each only got these eensy-weensy tiny perspectives on it."

Joel asked suddenly, "Have any of you ever had someone you loved die, and you dreamed about them later?"

"My nana died a few years ago and I dreamed about her a *lot*," Clare said, turning towards him.

"And how was she in the dreams?"

"Really happy. I always woke up feeling good."

"But that was just a dream!" Sandy retorted.

"Was it? Are you sure?" Joel met Sandy's gaze and she stared back at him, then faltered and looked away.

I had a funny feeling, watching him, that he'd experienced some things that none of us had; strange, amazing things.

"Yeah," Clare said wonderingly. "Maybe our lives are the dream and our dreams are the real stuff. I read a story about that once."

"And what do you mean by 'just' a dream?" Nina demanded of Sandy. "Didn't we just agree that we might not know the whole story?"

"Even if there's another life after this one," Sandy said heavily, "or even if this one is a dream life – which is a weird idea – it's still terrible when heaps of people die in tragedies, for instance. Kids losing their parents and parents losing their kids… How do you find the good in that?"

"It's true that we don't like to see anything good in situations like that, but there always is," Nina said quietly, in a tone that reminded me of Nuncle. I could just imagine that he had told her what she was now telling us. "You go and listen to people who've been through a major disaster and half of them see it as all-terrible, and the other half can see blessings in it. So if some of them can see blessings in catastrophes, maybe the blessings were always there, but the other people just aren't seeing them."[4]

"Like what though?" Clare wondered.

"Not everybody wants to be here, you know. Have you ever thought that life is too hard and it's not worth it?"

"Yeah, but not for long."

"Sure but if you *did* think it long and hard enough, you might end up getting your wish. Remember, we're all creators here."

---

4   I found a cool website that's all about this: www.thankgodi.com

"You mean if someone kept wishing they were dead, they might end up dead? That's scary," Clare said.

"I wonder what makes some people able to see the good in things while other people can't," I murmured.

"Well…" Nina began.

"Here we go," Sandy muttered, tossing a stone across the grass toward the love seat. "Ms-Answer-To-Everything to the rescue."

"There is actually a part of the brain called the Reticular Activating System," Nina continued, "but I won't tell you about it if you don't want to hear."

"*I* want to hear," I protested.

"Reticular-*what*?" Sandy spluttered. (Which I guessed was her ungracious way of saying, 'go on'.)

"Activating System – R.A.S. for short," Nina explained, "and it hones in on what we're expecting to see. Like, f'rinstance, have you noticed that when something new happens in your life, suddenly you see it all over the place?"

"Our Greek Islands cruise!" I exclaimed. "I keep noticing stuff about Greece or cruise ships on TV and every time I walk past a travel agent there's a poster about touring the Islands. I'm sure I never ever saw them before Mum started talking about it."

"Exactly," Nina agreed, "and your old thing with bullies, Clare. I bet you were tuning into them."

Clare nodded. "Yeah. People looked mean or cross to me when Nat and Sandy didn't even notice them."

"Mountain bikes," Billy said. "When I was going for that goal, I saw them everywhere, especially the one I wanted."

"Hey, have you got it now?" Nina asked him.

"Yep," Billy beamed. "Dad and I went out the day after that end-of-year school concert and bought my bike. It is *sweet*."

"That's so cool. I want to see it," she beamed.

"You ever coming back to the 'burbs? It's a bit far for me to ride all the way out here. Then again…" he looked around almost wistfully, "I wish I'd thought to stick my bike in the van. It would have been the best to have a ride around here. Much better than the streets at home."

"Bring it next time," Nina said. "I'll be heading your way now and then to visit Liz and Nuncle – or you guys – but other than that, I'll be here."

Not wanting to hear a reminder of the distance between our homes, I steered the conversation back to what she'd been talking about before. "So what does seeing something everywhere have to do with meanings or being able to see the good or whatever? I'm lost."

"Well, when you expect to see something, often you do. It's like someone who believes that no-one likes them. Wherever they go, they'll run into people who seem to not like them. But that might not be the case at all. It's just how they're *seeing it*." Her eyes flickered across to Joel, and he returned her gaze steadily for a moment, before looking away into the distance. And then she blushed. *Nina blushed.* She rushed on, leaving me wondering what they weren't saying.

"If you decide that you're an idiot, that Reticular Activating System bit of your brain goes, 'O-kay! Let me find some proof for you of that.' And if you decide you're smart, your R.A.S. goes, 'O-kay! Let me find some proof for you of that.' The more proof we link to an idea, the stronger it gets until it's a full-on belief. And then we're stuck. Unless we choose to change our beliefs and what we're making things mean."

She turned to Clare. "When you were feeling powerless, everyone looked like a bully to you. And they acted out their parts. Then when you changed how you saw yourself and the people around you, they had to either play a different role or just mosey on out of your life."

Clare nodded again.

"There's something like four hundred *billion* bits of info hitting our brains per second," Nina declared, "but we can only let about two thousand bits in at a time. So we miss out on *heaps*. We think we're noticing everything but we're just not. It's impossible. We'd go crazy if we had to notice everything. So the R.A.S. part of our brain kindly takes over and sort of filters everything we see so we'll only notice the things that we think are important or that fit with our beliefs."

"You are frying my brain," Sandy said, but not unkindly.

"This weather is frying me," Billy added. "Let's go inside."

We all stood up and brushed the leaves and grass off our backs and bums. I saw Nina glance at Joel for a second before leading the way to the house. He hung back momentarily, and then set his lanky body in motion after us. Billy was holding the screen door open. As we walked into the house he came in beside Joel and asked him something.

We passed through the kitchen for a glass of water. Nina's parents and aunt and uncle were sitting around the table and speaking quietly. They stopped talking when we entered. I don't like it when grown-ups do that. It makes me feel like something is wrong. But maybe I was just interpreting it the wrong way. Maybe they were all just tired. Or something.

"Hey, Joel," Nuncle said, leaning back in his chair and turning towards us with a warm smile. "You be ready to go in about twenty minutes?"

"Sure," said Joel. "Thanks. I'll get my bag."

"I've packed you a lunch to eat at the airport," Rosie said.

"Thanks," he said again. There was an awkward moment, and then he headed off to get his stuff and Rosie stood up to start organising our lunch.

In almost no time at all, we were standing outside by Nuncle's borrowed van and everyone was saying goodbye before he and Liz took Joel to the airport for his flight home. I was struggling with mixed feelings: relief that he was going and regret that I hadn't made a bigger effort; I didn't even know who he was or why he'd been visiting. I hadn't been friendly enough to ask him one single question about himself. He and Billy had had a good old chat while he waited on the verandah with his bag, but I hadn't paid him a squeak of attention.

And now he and Nina were having a last few words and she was even giving him a very quick sort of hug, and then Joel smiled down at her. A dimple appeared in his cheek and his face was quite transformed. It was an infectious smile, and I found myself smiling back happily and waving goodbye, as if to an old friend, as he climbed into the van. Liz and Nuncle came around giving us all hugs, and I told them I would definitely drop in soon for a visit. Definitely.

"We'd love that," Liz said.

Nuncle drove the old van away along the bumpy driveway, and we watched until they had disappeared behind trees.

And now, at last, we had Nina to ourselves.

Mastery Club Lesson #12

The Reticular Activating System (R.A.S.) is the part of your brain that looks for proof – or more of the same.

* It's determined to prove to you that you're right.

* Sometimes that's not very useful…

CHAPTER 5

SETTING OUR GOALS

LUNCH WAS DELICIOUS, as ever. We had lots of salads, the usual ones like tossed green salads and coleslaw, and some strange ones, like grated beetroot and carrot with sultanas and almonds and pecans in it. That was quite yummy. And there was another salad of apple and celery and walnuts in a dressing of tahini, which is a sort of sesame seed paste, blended with lemon juice. And a salad with hard-boiled eggs and steamed asparagus and tomatoes and baby spinach in olive oil and herb salt. I don't usually find salads very interesting or very filling, but by the time I'd tried them all I was as full as a goog.[5]

We helped clean up and then followed Nina to her room, with its big picture windows looking out onto the farmland hills and fields and trees. Everything out there was a bit yellowish but it was still good to look at, stacks better than the next-door house the rest of us had, living in the suburbs. The usual posters, and overflowing bookcase, and a half-finished painting, this time of

---

[5] There's a glossary at the back of the book so if you come across a word that looks strange to you, go and check it out. (NB. A goog is an egg.)

herself. Her face had been sketched in and she was staring out from the canvas, without a nose or mouth yet, her green hair with its pink fringe making a splash of colour already. I'd thought you were supposed to sketch in the whole face before you started filling in colours, but Nina is Different.

Her hand-written 'Master Yourself and You Can Master Anything' poster was on the back of the door, and there was another one in pride of place above it: *'What are you making it mean?'* I guessed that one was inspired by the Conscious Creation course she just did.

"I suppose you're going to pester us with that question all year?" Sandy asked, pointing to it.

Nina smiled mysteriously.

"So." Billy tossed himself onto her rumpled, unmade bed. "What are we going to do now? Come up with some new goals?"

"Yep. Anyone thought of any already?"

We all shook our heads, falling onto cushions and beanbags around the room, and then Clare said, "Well, yeah. I want to find some new friends. I'm going to be at a different high school from these guys," she told Nina. "It's the first time we've been apart since prep. I'm going to miss them so much."

She looked miserable as she said this, and I felt a pang too. Clare's mum couldn't afford the school fees where the rest of us were going, even though it wasn't *that* expensive, and I felt bad about it. Kind of guilty that I was going and she wasn't, and sorry for her, and sad. It was all a bit of a mess, but my parents hadn't taken too kindly to my idea that I shouldn't go to that school if Clare couldn't. So I was going.

"Hmm," said Nina.

"My goal is to start selling more of my pottery," Sandy said. "I want to save heaps so that as soon as I'm ready I can afford to leave home."

"Geez," said Billy.

"I know you think I should see my dad differently and get on with him," Sandy told Nina defensively, "but we're so different, it's really hard. I get on brilliantly with his brother, my Uncle Brendan, but me and my dad," she shook her head, "bad news. I wish my uncle was my dad, but no such luck."

"How about your mum?" I asked. "Do you get on with her?"

Sandy shrugged. "She's okay, but she's a bit of a pushover. She gives in to everything Dad says. We don't really have much to talk about either."

I thought about my parents: my hard-working mum with her home-based business and her efforts to be really responsible and teach us kids to be responsible, and my dad with his dreams and ideas and occasional bad investments. This year we were going to the Greek Islands to take the holiday he'd screwed up for us last year. I was so excited about this holiday, I couldn't wait! I'd never been overseas and only on a plane once, years ago, when I was really little. This was going to be *ace*.

"Well, sometimes the best thing is to move on," Nina said, surprisingly. I reckoned she was holding back from clashing with Sandy at our very first get-together in ages. I had been expecting her to say something quite different.

"You can always see it as an opportunity to become really independent," she added.

Sandy looked a tad relieved. "Yeah," she said.

They all turned to me and Billy. "What about you two?"

"My goal is to keep this Club going while you're here and we're there," I said. "But I don't know how we're going to do it. We don't know as much about this stuff as you."

"You know what you know," Nina said, looking into me with her penetrating grey eyes. "Are you going to invite some new people in? People learn best by teaching. You'll probably get much clearer on it all by teaching it."

I hesitated. Our group was special. Did I want a stranger to join us?

"Fresh blood," said Sandy. She rubbed her hands together with a ghoulish expression.

"It would be good to have a few more guys," Billy said; "no offence."

"Are you going to have meetings at school?" Clare asked wistfully, "Or can we make them after school so I can join in?"

"After school," I said definitely. "We'll swap houses again."

"Hey, drop in at Liz and Nuncle's occasionally," Nina said, "they'd love that."

"We will, for sure," I promised. "What about you? How are we going to have meetings with you?"

"Skype," Nina said. "We'll do it online. Have you all got computers with cameras and that?"

"Of course." Sandy looked scornful. "This *is* the 21st century."

"What about you, Bill?" I asked. "What's your goal?"

"Well… there's a mountain biking championship coming up… I was thinking about entering it."

"Yay, Billy!" Nina cheered.

"And I have to decide who I'm going to live with." His face darkened a little. "Dad wants me to come and live with him in his new place and Mum wants me to stay with her. I'm just going backwards and forwards at the moment, which is driving me crazy, but I can't choose."

We were all silent. I couldn't imagine choosing between my parents either. I don't think anyone could. Well, Clare didn't have any choice, she only lived with her mum since her dad had disappeared on them when she was tiny. And Sandy didn't seem to want to live with either of her parents. I could imagine how hard the choice would be for Nina, who totally loved her parents. Last year she'd had to face up to the possibility of losing both of them forever when they had disappeared for a few days in the Himalayas, and then she'd had the pretty good second choice of living with Liz and Nuncle, but still.

"What about you?" Clare asked Nina. "What's your goal?"

Nina was clear and brisk as usual. "One," she said, holding up a finger, "to stay in touch with you guys; two," another finger, "to be a professional youth speaker/motivator sort of person; three, to find something really outrageous to do that will put me right outside my comfort zone."

"You don't think becoming a professional speaker will do that for you?" Sandy asked drily.

"Yes, but you have to have lots of experiences to have material for your talks," Nina explained. "What about school goals, you guys? Anybody want to blitz the year?"

Sandy made a sour face. "Now, why would we want to do that?"

"For the fun of it!" Nina exclaimed, eyes sparkling. "To be ahead of everyone else. For the sense of achievement! To be relaxing and doing what you want while other people are still working and catching up."

"How are we supposed to do that anyway?" I asked. "We get set work each week so we can't go ahead of what they give us."

"Oh yeah," she said, "that's a bummer. It's much easier to charge ahead when you're home schooled."

"What a bummer," Sandy echoed, sarcastically.

"You don't know what you're missing," Nina told her. "Maybe there is a way? I don't know."

"Well, I guess I'll set a goal to up my marks," I said. "They could do with it."

"I'm going for an A in English," Clare said, "and maybe even a high C for Maths…"

"Good plan," Nina approved. "Hey, you," she said to me, "are you going to get more specific than 'up my marks'?"

I reflected on last year's report card. I'd had Bs all the way through, for every single subject, except Sport, where I got a C. "I'll go for some As," I said abruptly. "I'll tell you which ones when I've decided."

"Cool."

"So we're done?" Billy asked. "Everyone made a goal?"

We nodded, looking around at each other.

"Then let's get out of here. I want to go climb a tree or something."

Moments later we were bursting outside, running and yelling across Nina's farm, up trees, down to the dam, walking on fences, finding alpacas, and fighting for turns on the tractor. We didn't say another sensible thing for the rest of the day.

CHAPTER 6

JOEL'S STORY

NINA'S DAD PETE baked a spinach pie and roasted pumpkin for dinner, which we ate outside, on various chairs and cushions on the verandah. It was just lovely out there – except for the mozzies. There was always someone slapping. Finally Clare confessed that if she didn't go inside she'd be totally covered in red bumps, so we took our mostly-empty plates and followed her back inside.

"In one day here I've eaten as many vegetables as I do in a week at home," Sandy said, scraping the remains on her plate into the compost container.

"I love vegies," Nina said through her last mouthful.

"I don't usually, but here…" Sandy's voice trailed off.

Rosie came in with the empty casserole dish, banging the screen door behind her. "Hey, who's for some chocolate mud cake for dessert?"

"Did you say chocolate?" Billy asked, perking up.

"That I did. Pete is a dab hand when it comes to making chocolate cake," Rosie said. "I sure know how to pick 'em." She grinned at Pete, who had entered behind her with their bottle of wine and empty wine glasses. "They all want some 'mud'."

The cake was DELISH. It was served with a great big dollop of real cream and a big spoonful of strawberries, and after we'd eaten it, no-one could budge one centimetre. So we just crawled from the kitchen floor to the lounge room floor, and played board games all evening (which I hadn't done for ages), while Pete mucked about with one musical instrument or another in the background, and Rosie brought out her trusty camera and took a few snaps of us.

The sunset was pretty magnificent too. Rosie went out with her camera to capture it and we dragged ourselves to the window. We were struck silent by the fiery skies – a glorious spread of pinks and oranges in different shades as far as you could see. You don't get to use that word 'glorious' much in this modern world, but it certainly did fit that sunset. ("It doesn't really set," Nina told her mother reprovingly when she came back in. "You told me that; it 'eclipses'.")

At ten-thirty Nina's parents said goodnight and went to bed, and we started to gather mattresses (from Nina's room and the spare room) and couch cushions and blankets and pillows to make a huge bed on the living room floor.

"Hey!" Nina grabbed my arm. "Let's have a midnight Mastery Club meeting!" Her eyes were glowing with excitement. "Go on – let's! It'll be ages before we'll have another chance."

"Apart from tomorrow night," Sandy said, in her usual wet-blanket way.

"You mean you're staying another night?" Nina asked her, very straight-faced, as if she hadn't known.

Sandy threw a pillow at her and Nina threw one back, and our newly-made bed was soon unmade as we all joined in.

"Ssh!!!" Clare hissed over our screams of laughter, "we'll wake your parents up!"

"Now we have to do this all over again," I added, standing up out of the mess to survey it ruefully.

"You fix and I'll get candles," Nina said. "You can't have a midnight meeting without candles. And snacks." She widened her eyes mysteriously, and disappeared.

"Methinks she's been planning this midnight caper," Sandy said. "It's no sudden bright idea." She sighed and dragged someone's twisted sleeping bag out of the pile. "Okay, whose is this?"

Finally we had our massive bed re-sorted, this time with a hole in the middle for a bunch of candles and a tin of oatmeal biscuits that Nina convinced us were even better slathered with butter. And mugs of fresh creamy milk.

"Before we start," Clare said, lying on her tummy and looking up at Nina, "tell us about Joel. Are you two...?"

"No!" Nina exclaimed, blushing. "He's just a friend. He's way older than me. He's, like, seventeen or something."

"So you met him at the course?" Sandy said.

"Yes. He and I were the only kids – young people – there. Everyone else was grown-ups. So we kind of...gravitated together. And I don't even know why because really he's much more like an adult than a kid."

"And he's Aboriginal," Billy stated.

"Yes. His mother is white and he was living with her most of his life before he found out about his dad. She hadn't told him that his dad was Aboriginal. It's a pretty interesting story."

"Well – tell us," Billy demanded.

"Can you?" I asked. "Would he mind?" The image of lanky, dark-skinned Joel flickered through my mind; that quiet watching face with its broad nose and faint moustache.

"No. I told him I'd probably blab and he said I could tell you – some of it, anyway," Nina said. She reorganised herself on the pillows. "His mother brought him up. No dad. But he could never relate to his mum very well. He was always trying to find out who his dad was but she wouldn't tell him, or she'd say things but the story would keep changing – like 'he was Maori' or 'he was African'. Obviously he was dark because their skin was so different. So Joel just felt like a loner and an outsider all his life. He was teased a lot at school. The only thing she did keep saying was, 'He was bad news, so don't try to find out more about him.' It was like she didn't want to remember that part of her life."

"As if she could ever forget, having a son whose skin is so much darker than hers," Clare butted in.

"Exactly. See, she was making that time in her life mean that she'd made a huge mistake getting pregnant with Joel, so every time she looked at him, he was like this reminder of her mistake. Not a very nice way for him to grow up.

"Anyway, finally one day they had this big fight and she told him that his dad was an Aboriginal and had been in and out of jail for years and probably was in there now for all she knew. She didn't know or care. Joel was totally shocked. The kids at school had called him an 'abo' and he'd always denied it, because they'd said it like a taunt, and so he didn't want to be something that everyone hated. Now he was finding out that he was. So he was mad with his mum and mad with school and mad with his dad for being someone no-one likes and mad with him for being in jail."

We were all quiet then, watching Nina's serious face in the flickering light. Outside an owl called, right into our moment of silence.

"So his marks at school got way worse. They were never very good to begin with, but he started failing everything and not caring, so then he had all the teachers on his back as well. Anyway, he finally decided that he just didn't fit into this white world any more. So he starts trying to contact his dad, just to meet him and kind of 'face the enemy'. But his mum won't tell him what jail or what his real name is, because she'd given Joel her name. So he gets madder and madder and finally they have this terrible fight and she kicks him out. She throws him this piece of paper with his grandparents' address on it and slams the door in his face telling him to 'go and live with the people you belong with'. So he's out on the street by himself with one bag of stuff."

"Man…" said Billy, with feeling.

"How old was he?" I asked. I was beginning to feel very bad about not being nicer to Joel when he was here.

"Fifteen." Nina crumbled the last of her biscuit into her milk and swallowed it.

"Fathers really know how to cause trouble, don't they?" Clare said suddenly. "I mean, look at us: mine walks out on my mum when I'm tiny, Billy's dad leaves his mum, Sandy's dad is… hard work, Nat's dad messed up their holiday last year, and Joel's dad…"

"My dad didn't exactly leave my mum," Billy pointed out, to be fair. "She actually left him."

"Yes but that was because he wasn't doing a very good job of being a dad," Clare argued. "Or a husband. Or whatever. And when your dad went out with my mum over summer, it only lasted a tiny while and then she was crying all the time again."

"Your mother cries a lot," Billy said darkly. "That's not my dad's fault."

"Yes but she hadn't for ages," Clare frowned. "She just started again after they stopped going out."

"Methinks Clare is right," Sandy pronounced, lying on her back with her knees up. "Dads are difficult."

"So what happened next with Joel?" I asked. In my mind he was still wandering around the streets at night by himself with one bag over his shoulder, and I was feeling troubled for him.

"He lived with some other street kids for a bit."

"His mum must have been feeling really guilty," Clare interrupted.

"I don't know. He hasn't spoken to her since then. He's going to – he's working up to it," Nina said. "He saw some tough things, living on the streets. You know, fights and crime and people getting badly hurt and even dying. In fact, he was in such an angry state that he got pretty out of control and ended up in jail himself. He said he felt like his life was worthless so when the cops came he didn't bother to run away like the others. He just let himself get picked up."

We were lying on our stomachs now, the flickering candle light on faces that were all turned to Nina's.

"Anyway," she said, "there was this new strategy in the government to let young Aboriginal offenders go back to their communities and be disciplined by their own people, and since his grandfather was a pretty respected elder in his community, they arranged for him to go there. So the police called his grandfather who came down to get him and now he's living in that community. It's way up north. So suddenly, from being brought up in a white world, he's living just with his own people, the old way, in the bush."

"Geez," Billy breathed.

"His grandfather's on this mission to get young Aboriginals reconnected with their heritage, so he started to teach Joel the cultural lore. That's all their ancient wisdom that they pass on by word of mouth," she added. "No books," to Sandy.

"So how did he get to be at your course?" I asked.

"The guy who leads the course knows his grandfather and has been inviting him in as a guest speaker for the last few years to talk to everyone about ancient Aboriginal wisdom," Nina said. "So now you've got the whole story. Pretty much."

"It's like a rags-to-riches tale," Clare mused, "from misery to happiness."

"He didn't look that happy to me," Sandy disagreed.

"He looked very calm though," I said thoughtfully, reflecting. "Very inside-himself and quiet."

"He's still got quite a bit on his plate, like facing up to his mum again," Nina said, "and he hasn't said much yet about what it was like when he met his dad. Can't have been easy."

Once again I felt grateful for my simple home life and my mum and dad who fought occasionally but loved each other and were very there for each other. What a hard life Joel had had. I didn't envy him one bit.

Nina glanced at her watch. "Five minutes to midnight!" she crowed. "Everybody ready for our next meeting?"

Sandy yawned. "If we really have to."

Nina bounced on her pillows. "Of course we do!"

It had been such a long day already. I wasn't sure that I could stay awake much longer myself, but I forced myself to look interested and changed the way I was sitting to be more comfortable for whatever might be coming next.

CHAPTER 7

Spooky Stories in the Midnight Meeting

"Okay," Sandy yawned again. "So what's on the agenda, Boss?"

Nina glowered at her. "I'm *not* the boss."

"Mighty Leader, then."

"You *are* our leader," Clare burst out, before Nina could throw something at Sandy. "We don't know anything about this stuff. You teach us."

"Face up to it, dude," Billy agreed.

"But I don't want to be bossy. Am I bossy?" Nina asked.

"A bit," I allowed. "But it's okay."

Nina looked searchingly at Sandy, who stared back in her bulldoggish kind of way. "Is it?" Nina demanded.

Sandy sighed. "Yes. Okay. Go on. What did you want to do now?"

"I thought we'd go over the Mastery Club Lessons from last year." She was still looking at Sandy. "What do *you* think?"

"Do we have to call them 'lessons'?" Sandy asked, "that's so *school*." She grimaced.

Nina shrugged. "I guess I called them lessons because that's what they are. I don't have any bad meanings around school, remember."

"She has an answer for everything," Sandy remarked, and for some reason, that made us all laugh.

We each plucked another biscuit from the tin, and Clare said: "I think that's a good idea, to go over the Lessons. They've all blurred together in my mind. I can't remember what we did when."

"There were ten," Billy said helpfully.

"Brilliant." Sandy gave him a push with her foot, and he rolled over, almost into a candle. He gave a yelp.

"Order!" I scolded, grinning. "The first one was the day that pottery lady came to school and you talked to us about how everything is made of energy and you can make anything whatever you want. You can use the clay to make a gun or a rose and you can use your mind to make anything mean anything." I stopped in my tracks and stared at her. "That's what your course just now was about."

"So it was," Nina marvelled.

"That's right! You told us the story about the two guys whose letters got mixed, and the sick one got better and the healthy one died because they believed what was in the letters!" Clare added enthusiastically.

"Yeah, I remember," Sandy said. "We're supposed to focus on how we want things to be instead of how they are now."

"Because solids only look solid. It's really all just energy buzzing around and we can affect it with our thoughts. Okay," Billy said. "That was number one. What was number two?"

"Hold on," Nina said. "Do you want to hear a really crazy idea?"

"Not really," Sandy told her. "Okay, go on! I'm just kidding."

"Well, you know that *we're* not solid either. But that means who you think you are as well as your physical body. Your physical body totally changes every seven years – did you know that? Skin changes fastest, skeleton takes the longest, but you have a whole new body every seven years."

"Sweet!" Billy said.

"Then how come people have the same old illnesses year in, year out?" I asked.

"Because they hold the same ideas, and their ideas keep the physical pattern going. But what I was going to tell you is that no matter what you might remember from your life, no matter how clear the memory is, you *weren't even there*. If you go back far enough, not one single atom from your body today was there when it happened. So…" she rolled her eyes at us, "did it really happen?"

"Okay. You just fried my brain again," Billy said into the silence.

"Are you sure about that?" Sandy asked.

"Yep. We might not be able to see it with our eyes, but matter just flows around from place to place and comes together to make us for a few days or a lifetime – which, by the way, is nothing but a millisecond to the universe – and then flows off somewhere else and another lot comes. So we're constantly changing. Actually, I'm in you and you're in me and –"

"Ugh!" said Billy.

"That's weird," Clare murmured.

"So if no-one stays the same," I said, thinking aloud, "and if nothing ever really happens, then… what's real?"

"Good question," Nina said.

"How do you know what to believe?"

"Good question."

"What does anything mean?"

"What you make it mean," she said. Meaningfully.

"I think my brain will need about a decade to figure that one out," Billy commented.

"Oh don't worry," Sandy reassured him. "Nina will pester you about it till you get it."

Nina gave Sandy a poke in the ribs.

"She'll always do that," I told Nina, "always. Just ignore her. Be famous. It's your best defence."

"So speaketh the daughter of the lawyer," said Sandy. But she was grinning, and I suddenly realised that she loved her role as the 'problem person' in our group. She enjoyed teasing us and being difficult and getting all that attention. I'd never realised that before. And maybe she didn't either.

"Okay. What was Lesson Number Two?" Clare asked.

"Goal-setting," Billy said. "I remember that one. We had to choose what we wanted."

"Done!" Clare declared. "Next?"

"Hold on," said Nina.

"Here we go," Sandy grumbled, but she rolled her eyes with a hint of enjoyment.

"Did you know, there's this university," Nina went on, ignoring her, "that did a study of people and their goals, and they found that just having a goal in your mind is hardly effective at all. But if you write it down, tell a friend, make up an action plan, and agree that the friend can stay on your case about it, you're much more likely to achieve it. What does *that* sound like to you?"[6]

"A pain in the bum?" Sandy suggested.

"A Mastery Club," I said, bopping her on the head with my pillow.

"Exactly," Nina confirmed. "Which is why we're going to make sure we write them down and have an action plan before you go."

"Roger," said Billy. "What was Number Three?"

"Visualisation," I said, remembering our first attempts, with

---

6 Dominican University in California; study conducted by Gail Matthews, PhD.

Nuncle's help, at imagining our goals coming true, and my own visualisations of my family cruising in the Greek Islands. And that *was* coming true! This year. My stomach gave another lurch of excitement as I thought about it.

"Seeing the invisible," Sandy said, reminding us of our old Club motto. "And the new information is…" she trailed off expectantly, with a flourish of her hand towards Nina.

"… that the brain can't tell the difference between real and imagined," Nina announced, picking up on her cue seamlessly.

"That's not new," I objected. "You told us that already. That's why those basketballers who imagined getting baskets could get as many as the ones who actually practised."

"Yes but listen to *why*." Nina sat up excitedly. "Some scientists think that the world is actually a great big hologram. You know those images they make with lasers? People used to think the world was this big hard ball and if you cut out a piece of it and kept cutting and dissecting, trying to get smaller and smaller bits, you'd finally get to the tiny little pieces that the whole world is made of – the 'building blocks', they called them. Which is what 'atom' actually means: 'uncuttable'. But no matter how much they cut, they couldn't get to those building blocks because instead of getting smaller pieces they were just getting smaller wholes."

"Huh?" Billy asked. "Whaddaya mean, 'smaller holes'?"

"You know how if you tear a normal photo into six pieces, you get six different parts of the whole picture? Well, holograms are so cool and weird that if you tear one of them into six pieces, you get six whole copies of the original picture! So these scientists were finding that each little bit was a miniature whole – each piece had all the characteristics of the whole in it, and each of these little wholes was actually a hologram – just an image made out of light."

"Are you saying *we're* just holograms?" asked Clare with a shiver. "That's spooky. I know why you wanted to do this meeting at midnight now." She glanced over her shoulder into the dark shadows, looking for hologram-ghosts, perhaps.

"So that's partly why nothing's solid when you magnify it," Nina continued, "because it's actually an *image*. Get it?" poking herself repeatedly in the side of the head, "an image! So what you *imagine* when you're visualising is pretty much as real as the so-called real thing. So anything is possible. The world is your canvas."

"Did she just say something?" Billy asked Sandy.

"Yes," Sandy answered, "but it didn't make any sense."

Nina sighed.

"Then why can't I just walk through that wall?" Sandy demanded. "If everything's just light and images and imagined?"

"Because everything's light at different frequencies –"

"That's vibrations, right?" Clare interrupted.

"Yes. And things of the same frequency are of equal density, so they're solid to each other."

"Which is why, if we bang their heads together, it will hurt," Sandy told Billy.

"I'm much too dense for all this frequency stuff," he replied with a grin.

"It's not that complicated," Nina scolded, lying on her stomach again. "Nuncle explained it to me like this: light doesn't travel in a straight line, okay? It vibrates through space, and a fast vibration is a high frequency. Some physicists even say that matter is nothing but low frequency light – they actually call it frozen light – because if you go far enough into the microscopic, subatomic world, *everything's* made of the same stuff." She prodded Sandy. "The reason you can't walk through walls is because walls are the same frequency as your body. But your mind and imagination can go through that wall like a hot knife through butter because they're a *higher* frequency."

"Like Harry Potter and Platform 9¾," Clare said knowledgeably.

Nina gave her a perplexed look. "No, not like that at all. Honestly, you guys, there's no way human bodies are going through walls or levitating or anything like that. Ever. You can only do that sort of thing with your mind or your astral body, which is a sort of energy body."

"What sort of energy body?" Sandy narrowed her eyes.

"Rub your hands together like this," Nina instructed, sitting up again, and demonstrating. "Then gradually pull them apart… really slowly… and just feel what's between them."

"Wow!" I marvelled, as we copied her. "It's like a rubbery sort of…"

"Weird," Billy agreed, focusing on the space between his hands. "Springy…"

"You've got a whole body of that stuff," Nina announced. "You know how you can wake up from a dream with a sort of a bump? That's your energy body landing back in your physical body."

"Okay, enough!" Sandy exclaimed, burying her face in her pillow and covering her ears.

"So walking through walls is an imagination thing," Nina said, ignoring her. "Same with floating up when you think happy thoughts, like in *Mary Poppins*, but there really are some pretty out-there magical things that happen right here on earth with real people. F'rinstance, Tibetan monks who go into trances and then travel these amazing, impossible distances by taking huge bounding leaps!" (Here Nina bounced and gestured the vast distance with her arms, making the candles flicker wildly.) "And create these inner fires that make them so hot they can sit in a snowstorm and dry out *three sheets* that have been soaked in a freezing river —"[7]

"You seen any of that?" Sandy's muffled voice queried from inside her pillow.

"No; heard about it."

"Humph!" was the reply.

"The question is," Nina said, addressing the Sandy-lump, "are you open-minded enough to see something like that if it's happening right under your nose? Or will your R.A.S. think it's impossible and so you'll never see it? Maybe we really all are magicians, if we could just believe in ourselves enough."

---

7   'Lung-gom' is the Tibetan practice of travelling while in trance and 'Tummo' is the practice of the inner fire. Fancy being able to hold a cup of noodles in your bare hands *and boil them without needing a stove???*

Mastery Club Lesson #13

Everything is Light Vibrating at Different Frequencies

* Even matter is 'frozen light'... wow.

* So nothing is stuck or fixed or solid – it's all Energy.

* In our image-inations we can do anything. Maybe we have more potential than we have realised... more, even, than in our wildest dreams...

CHAPTER 8

MAGICAL ME

"IT'S TOO CRAZY for words," Clare said, wriggling deeper into her sleeping bag.

"But what if it *is* true?" I mused. "We only use a little part of our brain's potential. Maybe, when we use all of it, we will actually be able to do magic."

"Bingo," said Nina.

"And what if books like *Harry Potter* are there to stop us completely believing in the appearance-world?" I added. "What if they help keep our imaginations flexible?" For the first time in my life, I'd found a really good and honourable reason for reading so many fantasy books. I hadn't just been wasting my time; I'd been exercising my brain and imagination and kind of training myself in the truth – without even knowing it!

Suddenly, even though it was half-past midnight, I felt wide-awake.

Billy gave a huge yawn. "Do you mind if we finish this tomorrow? I mean, later today?" He'd been leaning up on his elbow and now collapsed onto his pillow, burying his face in it so that all we could see was his tousled black hair. "I'm having a bit of trouble concentrating…"

"Me too," Clare agreed, through a yawn of her own.

As for Sandy, she had begun to snore.

Nina and I looked at each other and grinned. We blew out the candles, and as the smoky fragrance wafted away and darkness took over the room, our friends sighed and muttered their way to sleep, and we continued smiling at each other in the faint light of the moon.

"It's great to be back together again, isn't it?" Nina whispered.

"Yes. I missed you and your crazy ideas."

"I just may have made up for all that time apart already," she chuckled.

"I reckon!"

"You see," she went on quietly, "I was right about you. You were ready for these ideas. You're the real magician. You brought me into your life."

"No. *You're* the magician," I argued, forgetting to whisper. "You were the one who set the intention of starting up a Mastery Club when you came to school –"

But she stopped me. "Nat. Don't you get it? You were wanting to do real magic before you ever met me. You didn't just come into my life because *I* wanted people to join *my* club. I came into your life because *you* wanted to do real magic, too. Maybe it was your wanting to learn real magic that made my family decide that I'd go to your school. We looked at about three schools, you know."

I stared at her, silenced. So I wasn't as stupid or powerless as I'd always thought? Somehow, in this great mysterious universe, my secret wishes had been working their own magic.

We lay on our stomachs in the darkness, gazing at each other and listening to our friends' breathing, and I felt filled up, somehow, with a kind of joy and gratitude. It was as if I'd been given a quick sneak peek into how the world works, that Grand Organising Design that Nina and her family talked about. Already the curtains were being drawn together again, and I'd probably go back to feeling small and not very clever tomorrow, but for a moment I had seen that there was something like greatness inside me, and that everyone had it.

It was your love of something, I realised dreamily. If you really loved something, and wanted it with your whole heart, you could make magic.

I reached out past the smouldering candles for her hand, and her fingers found mine. We squeezed hands and smiled, and the next thing I knew, someone was rolling into me heavily and the sun was blasting through the window and Rosie was knocking on the lounge room door and calling out, "Anyone for breakfast?"

CHAPTER 9

A Land of Milk and Rivers

"Yes!" Nina called out in reply. "Won't be long." She pushed her spiky green-pink hair out of her eyes and fixed us, each in turn, with her penetrating grey stare. "It is essential that we think of six impossible things before breakfast, in order to exercise our marvellous minds."[8]

"Never going to school again," Sandy said, stretching in her bag; "heaven."

"A world with no gravity where you just float around wherever you want to go by the power of your thoughts," I put in.

"Food that tastes like meat without having to kill anything," Clare said. Nina and I were both vegetarian, but the rest of them were meat-eaters. They liked the idea of not killing animals, especially Clare, who was a big animal-lover, but they couldn't seem to go without their meat.

---

8   With a salute to Lewis Carroll's Queen of Hearts, *Alice in Wonderland.*

"Winning the championship," Billy dreamed.

"Why is that impossible?" we asked him.

"Because I haven't been training enough and those other guys are twice as fit as me. I have to face the facts." He sat up and scratched his head, and I suddenly noticed how much taller he was getting, and that he was the only boy and the rest of us were girls. That sounds silly, especially as the four of us had hung out together since we were in preschool. Of course I knew he was the only boy. What I mean is… Clare and Sandy and I had always teased him for being 'a boy', and messy and smelly and stuff like that, but suddenly there was this other boyness about him, and I wasn't sure what it was. It made me think of Joel, though, and his little bit of a moustache.

"You have to *make* the facts," Nina scolded him. "Anything is possible. See the Invisible, Hear the Silent, Do the Impossible."

"Yes, ma'am," Billy saluted her. "And your vision, ma'am?"

"A world where everyone is doing the work they love," Nina said, "so that every morning they wake up electrified with looking-forwardness to their day."

"Is that a word?" Sandy asked.

"It's an impossible word," Nina pronounced.

"Ah."

"What about just putting your hand on someone and kind of downloading everything they've been thinking or everything they know," I said in a burst, "or on something like a book, and getting all the info out of it."

"Like in *The Matrix*."

"Yeah."

"That would be sweet," Billy agreed. "Now, don't you think we should go to breakfast and not keep your nice mother waiting?"

"You're just an endless stomach," Nina said in despair.

"I'm a growing boy," he replied, standing up over us and marching out to the kitchen.

A moment later we were all surrounding the kitchen table, which featured a big stoneware bowl that was filled with sodden muesli. At least, that's what it looked like.

"Bircher muesli," Nina explained, serving herself. "It's been soaking all night in almond milk and yoghurt and grated apple and nuts and berries and honey and –"

"Yummy," Clare said, grabbing a bowl.

"*Almond* milk?" Sandy queried.

"Yes, nut milk."

"How do you get milk out of nuts?"

"You blend them. With water and maybe some dates. Easy peasy. You can make milk from all sorts of nuts, and also oats and rice and chia seeds. Dairy is one of the worst things for humans to eat," Nina said. "Really, we shouldn't be drinking milk after we've been weaned. That's what milk was designed for: to help babies grow. You don't see animals drinking their mother's milk after they've been weaned, and we shouldn't either. It makes us congested and acidic."

Sandy narrowed her eyes. "What about the yogurt? That's made from milk."

"It's coconut yogurt." Nina took a big mouthful and chewed, regarding us with raised brows and big wide eyes, a bit of almond milk trickling down her chin.

The muesli certainly tasted good. In fact, it was delicious. Creamy and sweet and nutty and healthy.

It was already pretty hot, so after breakfast Nina's dad suggested that we grab our bathers and towels and squeeze into the back of the ute, and he drove us further up the road to their favourite river picnicking spot. Then Pete laid a picnic rug on the ground and sat down with Rosie and his guitar, and we stumbled away over the stones, exploring. Nina led us to the cubby she had made years ago that was still there, and we all crawled inside – and then right back out again when we found it full of spiders and other creepy-crawlies. "You city kids!" she laughed.

There was a rope hanging from a gum tree over the river, and Billy was the first one to grab hold of it and take a flying leap into the water. He landed with a huge splash and came up gasping for air. "It's fr-fr-freezing!!!"

"Mountain water," Nina said, following him in.

I couldn't stay in as long as them, I had to keep coming out again to warm up, and Clare only lasted a few minutes before she turned blue. Sandy's much tougher; she went for quite a long swim. But maybe she was just showing off. Then again, her dad's an army guy and he's raised his kids to be pretty tough.

By lunchtime we were all sodden and shivering. We tripped and dripped our way over the bumpy stones to our towels that were spread out in the sun, and slowly baked dry and warm. Then Rosie gave us salad and cheese rolls, and our conversation trailed back to the Mastery Club Lessons.

"It's all energy," Clare said, counting them off. "Set a goal, visualise it… what was the fourth one?"

"Treasure mapping," Sandy reminded her, "those posters we made with pictures and stuff of what we wanted."

"Our gold!" Nina crowed. "You know, it's interesting. Pirates have maps with just a cross for the gold and lots of warnings about the dangers on the way, and we make big detailed maps of the gold and hardly give a thought to the dangers on the way."

"Because you said we need to keep our eye on the gold – I mean, goal – and not get distracted by the obstacles," I reminded her.

"Yes, that's right. But the next Lesson was all about the things that can go wrong and what we need to do to deal with it."

"What *was* the next Lesson?" Billy mumbled, his face in his towel.

"First Force, Second Force, Third Force," Nina said.

"Oh yeah… What was that about again…?"

"That after you set an intention you'll probably experience some resistance, so that's when you have to get creative and resourceful so you'll pass the test and achieve it." She dug him in the ribs and he groaned. "Get that? With your Championship."

"Wha'wasnex'?" I asked hazily, but I didn't hear her answer; I'd fallen asleep.

CHAPTER 10

MORE NUTTY IDEAS

THE SUN WAS LIKE a deliciously warm blanket, and somewhere, very far away, I could hear birds and music and singing. I drifted in that lovely place for a while, until I became aware of something cool sprinkling onto my skin. I opened an eye and saw Rosie leaning over me. She smiled and continued trickling handfuls of sand onto my shoulder. I looked around and saw that everyone had fallen asleep, and she had been covering each of us with extra clothes, towels and sand.

Clare woke up then, and sat up with a little start. "Oh dear. Am I sunburnt?"

"No, I covered you all up in time," Rosie said. "But we'll head back now before it gets really roasty out here."

Clare examined her arms and legs and tried to look over her shoulders. "I totally forgot about sunscreen."

"We all did," I said, hearing my mother's voice in my mind – *'and remember to wear your sunscreen!'*

"We're not very into sunscreen over here," Rosie confessed. "We're sun-lovers."

"But it's much too harsh for our skin," Clare told her reprovingly. "You know – the hole in the ozone layer."

Rosie sat on the sand between us. "Well, there are studies that say the main reason we burn is a lack of fruit and vegetables in the diet. The sun is incredibly important for our health for oh, so many reasons! It's a preventive against cancer, for one thing, including skin cancer, whereas sunscreens can be quite cancer-causing."[9]

"Whoah," I said. "That's different."

"Yeah." Clare inspected her arms again.

"When I was a kid," Rosie said, "we used to live outside all summer and be quite fine. If you're healthy on the inside, your body can deal with a bit of sunburn. It's the chemicals in the sunscreen that confuse your body and cause toxicity."

"Truly?" I asked. I wondered what my mother would make of all that.

Around us, the others were beginning to stir. They joined in on our conversation about the sun as we packed up and headed back to the farm. Sandy was very sceptical – being red-haired, she was also prone to burning. Billy always went a deep tan in only a few minutes of sunshine.

"You know," Rosie said as we piled out of the ute with our stuff, "you can kind of trust your feelings about it. If people look and feel good with a tan, if they give off a healthy vibe, then it probably is healthy, whereas getting so tanned that you look leathery doesn't seem as healthy, and getting badly burnt hurts, so that can't be too smart either… Same as with food: you just know that fruit and vegies are wholesome and good for you. The colours and tastes are so vibrant. But junk food – it's so greasy and rich and sugared; it just doesn't have that healthy vibe."

---

9   When I got home I googled 'sun scam'. Check it out!

"I like that crunchy, fried taste, though," Sandy said.

"A bit of frying is fine here and there," Rosie replied, "but a whole diet of it is pretty dangerous for your health. How about chips for dinner?"

"Yeah, okay!" Sandy agreed enthusiastically.

And Rosie kept her word. That night she served up a big spread of potato chips that were divine. They were shallow-fried in coconut oil, she told us, and golden, salty, crisp. We ate them with sour cream and salad, and in the middle of our meal Sandy looked up, licking her lips, and said, "You can't tell me that there isn't *something* good about junk food – not that this is junky, Rosie, but you know what I mean."

"Of course not," Rosie smiled, "no offence taken, and your point is taken. For sure, junk food's quick, easy, convenient…"

"And there must be a bad side to raw milk," Sandy continued intently. "I mean, isn't that the Polarity Law?"

"It is. And yes, there is a risk of bacterial contamination and the milk doesn't last as long as the pasteurised stuff. But there's a health risk with drinking dead milk too, so we all choose which risk we want to take."

When we'd cleaned up, Nina took us for a twilight walk up their road to a lookout. It was really steep – we hadn't noticed how steep when we were in Pete's ute – and pretty soon we were all puffing.

"This is – a good reminder – of that – fifth lesson," Nina said in bursts.

"What was it?" Billy asked (the least puffy among us, probably because of his extra biking fitness).

"First Force, Second Force, Third Force," she said, stopping to rest for a moment. "One, set a goal – which was our idea to go for a walk; two, get your commitment tested – it's bloody hard, and three, have to build your character – and muscles – to deal with it."

"So why do you have to get tested in *everything?*" Sandy complained. She picked up a stone and sent it skimming off into the distance.

"Well, maybe not *everything,*" Nina said, "but the testing is the thing that makes you grow, isn't it? If life wasn't a bit hard, you'd just get flabby and selfish. They say that if you wake up without a problem you should get down on your knees and pray for one. Otherwise it could mean that you're dead."

"Ugh!" said Sandy. "They can keep that idea to themselves, whoever 'they' are!"

I giggled.

We trudged on in silence for a bit and then Nina beckoned us to follow her off the road toward the little fenced-off lookout. We climbed the fence and stood on the rails, gazing out into countryside that was gradually fading into darkness. A few lights dotted the land below us.

"I wonder what it would be like living in the bush or the outback all your life," Billy said suddenly, "and not having houses and cars and fridges and all that crap. Just nature. Just earth and animals."

"Weird for us, normal for Aboriginals, I guess," I mused. "I wonder how Joel is finding it. It must be hard going from houses and heaps of stuff to being outside all the time with hardly anything."

"They live in houses too," Nina said. "Partly in the bush and partly in a house. He said it was all a bit strange at first but he likes it now, especially the bush bit. He likes the quiet when they go bush."

We listened to the countryside quiet around us for a few minutes. It was very still. Imagine if those stars were your only lights at night… Imagine if you could never switch on a TV or a radio or a computer or use a telephone. Wow.

"Let's go back," Clare said, "I'm getting bitten again."

"Law of Polarity," I reflected , as we slid off the fence and started back down the hill. "What goes up must come down."

Nina's voice had a grin in it, as it came out of the darkness. "The upsy-downsy balance of life," she agreed.

"I can't believe that we kids are talking about this stuff," Sandy remarked. "It's too weird for words."

"She has us in her power," Billy intoned. He stuck his arms out in front of him like a zombie, and started to walk stiff-legged.

"Yes. I really must pick up a few bats while we're out here for my next spell," Nina murmured, looking around for bats without missing a beat. "And if you see a unicorn, let me know. I urgently need one for my next enchantment of you; you know, its blood."

Sandy began to walk like a robot next to Billy. "My. Goal. To. Destroy. Master." She swung her stiff arms around and set Nina in her sights, making after her with choppy lurching steps.

"No master here," Nina replied airily, looking around. "Just a nutty kid with an equally nutty set of friends."

"Saved," Sandy said darkly, dropping her arms.

"You want to look at why you're still so mad with me," Nina told her in a frank tone of voice. "It keeps coming up."

"What about you?" Sandy retorted. "Aren't you attracting it?"

"*Touché,*" Nina licked her finger and make a mark in the air. "One for you. Yep. Thanks. I'll look into it."

I'd been listening to that last exchange in surprise. At least now the little undertone of tension between them was out in the open. I wondered how it would play out.

"Beat you back!" Billy yelled suddenly, and he sprinted off down the hill.

The rest of us followed, and we arrived at the kitchen panting, in time to see Rosie pushing frozen bananas and mango pieces through her juicer to make fruit ice cream. Like everything else we'd eaten here, it was delicious.

CHAPTER 11

Last Day With Nina

I WOKE UP ON our last morning with mixed feelings. I felt heavy and sad that we'd be leaving today, and also unsettled and nervous at the thought of starting at the new school. That day was coming closer and closer.

Rosie and Pete asked us if we wanted to go to the farmers' market with them but we said no. We sat on the verandah with toasted sourdough bread and watched them rattle down the drive in their ute.

"We have to go back home today," Clare said, picking up on my thoughts, "and then school." She hugged her knees mournfully.

"I'm picking up a very low vibe," Nina said.

"Yeah… *really* low frequency," Clare moaned.

"Hey, we were here last year when we talked about that," I remembered. "What was that Lesson called? It was all about music."

"The Law of Resonance and Vibration," Nina replied, "popularly known as the Law of Attraction. They told us at the course that most people have that one a bit wrong. Most people think of the Law of Attraction as 'like attracts like', but actually –"

"Likes repel and opposites attract," Billy said.

"Exactly. We sort of vibrate in harmony with the things that are like us but we're also magnetically attracted to opposites – that's how we get our balance of support and challenge, I guess. Being supported feels good in the moment and being challenged doesn't, but we need both of 'em."

"That dam down there is being a powerful magnetic force at the moment," Sandy said, licking her buttery-honeyed fingers and gazing into the distance. "It's cool and wet and I'm hot and dry… Who wants to swim?"

"I'm in," Billy mumbled, through a mouthful of toast.

"What time is your mum coming to get us?" Clare asked me.

"About four, I think."

"Then we'd better get on with it!" Nina said briskly. "We've got to make sure everyone's goals for the year are watertight before you go."

"We haven't finished going over the last-year-lessons," Clare pointed out.

"New goals are more important than old lessons," Sandy said, "and dam-swims are more important than anything for city kids who have to leave soon."

Some ants were already crawling onto the sticky plates we had abandoned on the ground. Billy poked at a dish with his big toe, pushing it away from them, and the ants hurried after it. "I remember one of the last lessons," he said, picking the plates up suddenly, "It was the Wash-The-Dishes lesson. The day we left a mess at my place and you two," indicating Sandy and Nina, "had that fight."

Oh yeah.

"What was that about again?" asked Sandy.

"You thought Nina was being bossy," I began.

"I don't mean that," she flushed. "I mean the actual, you know, lesson."

"That we have to walk our talk," I said, hiding my surprise at her red face. "Not just keep all this stuff as great ideas in our heads, but do something about it."

"Right." She stood up abruptly and went to open the door for Billy, and we followed them into the kitchen to wash our breakfast dishes.

CHAPTER 12

ACTION PLANS

THE TENTH LESSON was 'Don't Give Up', and it was kind of funny because that was almost how we were feeling by now. We'd all wanted to keep the Mastery Club going and make new goals for the new year, but going over all that stuff had suddenly made it all seem really serious and hard work. Well, I was sure it didn't feel like that to Nina, who eagerly led us into her room and found paper and pens for us to write our goals, promising that we'd go for a swim right after that; but I could see that Sandy and Billy and Clare looked a bit restless, and I felt kind of muddled myself.

"Actually," Clare said to Nina as she received some paper and a purple pen, "you gave us those lovely Record Books for Magic at the end of last year. We can use those to write our goals."

"I didn't bring mine, but," Sandy said, plopping down on Nina's bed and twirling a red pen between her fingers.

"Me neither." Billy was gazing outside.

"I forgot mine too," I admitted.

"You can just copy it in there later if you like," Nina said. She sat on her desk with her back to the window and looked at us all through narrowed eyes. "Are you guys okay?"

"This is just feeling a bit like school," Sandy said. "You know, like homework."

"Oh." Her gaze drifted to me. "You too?"

"A bit," I confessed, feeling traitorous. "I want to do it but…"

"You've all just forgotten your whys," Nina pronounced.

"What?"

"Your goal-whys. Why you want your goal. If you don't really want it, it'll just feel like work."

"I think we need to go outside," Billy said, his gaze still glued to the window. "For a break."

Nina hesitated. "Okay…" she began.

"We've done a lot of thinking this weekend," Clare said kindly. "We do like the Club, but we're not used to it."

"Not used to thinking?" Nina asked, perplexed.

"Well, it's a different sort of thinking."

"It strains the brain," Sandy said, standing up and stretching.

"Maybe we can talk about it more down by the dam," I suggested, following the others out and drawing Nina with me.

She was very quiet and thoughtful as we traipsed across the farm and over a fence and down the grassy hill towards the dam. There were some great climbing trees down there. Billy and Sandy had shot ahead of us in a burst of energy, and we could see them already scrambling up a tree each while Nina and I dawdled after them along narrow paths through the yellow grass. For a moment we couldn't see Clare, and then she wandered out from behind a tree and went to sit by the water's edge. The sun was blastingly hot today; we watched her get up after just a minute and move to a spot in the shade of a tree.

"This is a good First Force, Second Force, Third Force for me," Nina commented.

"Why?" I asked.

"Well, I wanted to do the goals and you guys didn't, so I've got to grow in some way. I'm feeling disappointed." She turned her grey eyes on me candidly, and I felt uncomfortable.

"I'm sure we will soon," I reassured her. "We just needed a break."

"Don't try to make me feel better. That's *my* job." She plumped herself down onto a little hillock. "If I'm feeling bad it's because of what I made it mean. And I can change that."

"What did you make it mean?" I asked curiously, sitting next to her.

"That you guys aren't as interested in all this as me and maybe I really am just a pest. Like Sandy says."

"We really *are* interested in it. It's just… we're not used to doing so much of it," I finished lamely.

"Mum and Dad warned me not to overload you." Nina gave a laugh. "There were so many great ideas at the course and I wanted to share it *all* with you! They must have known this would happen."

"We can always do the next bit about the goals on Skype," I said, "if we don't get around to it."

"Yeah…" she cast about for a stone and flicked it towards the water.

A rustle of leaves and jerking branches caught our attention. Sandy and Billy were moving around in their trees and yelling and waving. We followed their pointed arms to the driveway, where the ute was slowly appearing in a cloud of dust.

"Don't give up," I said to Nina, with a shy smile and a gentle bump of my shoulder.

She smiled back. "I won't. I *did* set the goal of moving outside my comfort zone, so I guess it's a case of 'Ask and ye shall receive'!"

Nina didn't talk about any of her ideas for the rest of the day. We swam, moseyed around the property, ate lunch – a spread of delicious dips and cheeses that Rosie and Pete had brought back from the market – and then helped them with some chores, like mending a fence and taking hay to the alpacas.

At four o'clock on the dot my mum arrived. For a moment it felt strange to see her here. It was as if I had two lives and they had just collided. She climbed out of the car and walked towards the house carrying a big bag of apricots from our tree for Rosie and Pete and Nina, and looking around at everything. Rosie welcomed her in, offering a cup of tea, and we waved to her from the lounge room where we were playing a board game.

"Back to the real world soon," Sandy said flatly.

Clare clapped her hand to her mouth. "The goals!" she exclaimed. "We didn't finish them!"

Nina scooped up the dice and gave it a toss. "We'll do it on Skype." She looked up from the board at each of us in turn. "That is, if you still want to. Do you?"

"Yes, definitely," I said.

"Sure," Billy agreed, but I wondered if he really meant it.

"Yeah," Sandy said, "I guess."

"Of course we will," Clare said. "Sorry that we didn't get it done today."

"It's okay," Nina said, "it's *our* Club not my Club."

"But we should have a last Mastery Club meeting sort of *time* before we go," I said, suddenly struck by the immediacy of our departure and the unknown-ness of a future get-together. It wouldn't feel right if it all just trailed away.

"A ceremony!" Clare said, sitting up suddenly.

The others agreed. We abandoned the game and went to Nina's room where we sat on the floor in a circle. Nina put a candle in the middle and lit it, and the flame flickered faintly in the bright room.

"Let's link arms," I said, and we did it in that complicated way where your arms cross in front of your own body.

"To the future of the Weird Mastery Club of Nina and Co.,"

Sandy said solemnly.

"May it flourish," I declared.

"May we See the Invisible," Clare began, and we joined with her in the rest of our Club motto: "Hear the Silent, and Do the Impossible."

"May we live as Masters do," Nina said, "taking one hundred percent responsibility for ourselves and our goals and meanings."

"Okay! Okay!" Billy exploded, as if we'd all just been hassling him unbearably. "I'll go for being in the top three at the Biking Championship – all right?"

We grinned at him, eyes lighting up as the magic began to take hold.

"I'll ring my Uncle Brendan as soon as I get back and find out about the next pottery market," Sandy said, "and I'll get going with making more stuff."

"I'll be very positive about making friends," Clare promised. "I'll talk to four new people on the first day at school, whether I like them or not."

"Yay, Clare!" we cheered.

"And I'm going to write a sign about getting A for English and a high C for Maths and put it on my desk," she added.

I was beginning to feel left behind. "I'll decide on my A subjects by the end of the first week at school," I decided. "And I'll have the first Mastery Club meeting at my place on the first Friday night of the first week of school. Okay?"

"I'll check the Skype connection thing tonight and make sure I've got you all on my system," Nina said. "And I'm going to think up a talk I can give somewhere. I don't know where, yet… I'll research that."

We grinned at each other, and jerked our crazily interlinked arms up and down three times to seal the deal.

"There was one last thing I was going to say," Nina began, a little tentatively as we began to disengage. "It's something else from the course. Okay?"

"Okay."

"It's for us to be… kind of… *detectives* this year… on the look-out for order."

"Order? Whaddaya mean?" Billy asked.

She took a big breath. "Do you remember at the end of last year when Nuncle was talking to us about Divine Order and how often things look wrong and bad to us but it's all part of the G. O. D., the Grand Organising Design?"

"Yeah."

"Well, they were talking about that quite a lot at the workshop, and they were challenging us to be able to look past the appearance of chaos and mistakes and find the order. Most people don't see it, and that's why they get stressed and worried, but they reckon it's always there. A kind of Hidden Order. Masters can see it."

"How *do* you?" I asked, "see it, I mean."

"By looking for the balance," she said. "The fact of the matter is that life kind of balances us out over time anyway – if we get too cocky we're brought down, and if we get too down something happens to lift us up. But if we can *consciously* do it for ourselves, that's true mastery – and it's also a lot quicker that way, if you're interested in growing faster."

There was a knock at the door and Rosie called out, "Are you ready to go, kids?"

"Yes, just a sec!" Nina called back. "So… I was really hoping you guys would do that with me. Take on the challenge of looking for it – because we could help each other recognise it."

"So," Sandy intoned, "we are now also members of the Secret Society of The Hidden Order."

We linked up and shook our crazy arms again, and then tried to get up without letting go, which made Clare and Billy bang heads in the middle and nearly stumble into the candle. Nina snatched it away in time and blew it out while the rest of us giggled and deliberately fell over each other again. We gathered up our bags and pillows and made our noisy way to the kitchen and then outside, where we loaded up the boot of the car. Rosie gave each of us a hug, and Nina did too. As she wrapped her arms around me and brought her green head close, she whispered, "Thank you," and "See? You're a leader already," and then we were climbing into the car and waving, and Mum was starting the engine and we were turning around and heading away down the dry and crunchy driveway.

I craned my neck for a last view of Nina and her parents. They were standing arm-in-arm, waving to us. I felt a whole mixture of things: happiness and sadness and endings and new beginnings.

"Did you have a good time?" Mum asked.

The car rattled over the cattle grid onto the road and we told her about our picnic by the river and the alpacas and all the meals we'd eaten and Joel, Nina's new Aboriginal friend. But we didn't say much about our Mastery Club talks.

Review of the First 10 Lessons

1. **Everything is Energy and You Can Use Your Mind to Create Anything**

   ▷ so don't fall for appearances…

2. **Choose a Goal**

   ▷ it's how we grow.

3. **Visualisation**

   ▷ the brain can't tell the difference between real and imagined so be the Director of your own movie(life)!

4. **Treasure Mapping**

   ▷ make a map of your goal-treasure (gold).

5. **First Force, Second Force, Third Force**

   ▷ 1st = your intention; 2nd = resistance, problems, obstacles; 3rd = your response. (Will it be commitment and creativity or excuses and evasion…?) You build momentum when you Go For It!

6. **The Law of Polarity**

   ▷ everything has a positive and a negative side.

7. **The Law of Resonance & Vibration**

   ▷ you resonate in harmony with similar vibrations; your emotions determine your vibration.

8. **You Have to Become a New Person**

   ▷ you grow in the process of achieving your goal.

9. **They're Not Just Ideas**

   ▷ just thinking about them won't cut it; you have to act on them.

10. **Don't…Give… Up…**

    ▷ it's the darkest before dawn. Hang in there.

CHAPTER 13

New School Challenges

DAD WAS FULL of beans on my first morning at high school. "Enjoy it," he beamed, "your school years are the best!" He kissed me on the top of my head and gave me a high five before heading out the door to work.

Mum had made me a delicious lunch for the first day – usually I have to make my own. She tucked it into my backpack, worrying again about how heavy the bag was with all those new books and folders in it, and walked me to the corner bus stop. "Have a great day," she said. "I'd wait with you for the bus, but…"

But my little brother and sister were at home alone, supposedly getting ready for school but more likely making messes everywhere with cereal and honey and eating in front of the TV, which was forbidden on a school morning. I waved goodbye to her and waited for the bus.

It was a sunny morning and a few others were waiting too. I recognised my school uniform with its green and purple colours on a few other bods. Hanging around at the bus stop was another school uniform, a business suit, some grandmotherly clothes and a tight black skirt and stilettos office worker outfit – *how do they stand up in those shoes all day????*

When the bus arrived I climbed aboard and automatically scanned the faces for Billy's, since he took caught this bus when he was visiting his dad, but I couldn't see him. Then I remembered: he was going to ride his new bike to school to build his fitness for the Championship. Sandy came from a slightly different direction so she'd be on another bus. Clare was going somewhere else altogether. I thought of her, on her own this morning, as I found a seat between another student and her schoolbag and a businessman reading the newspaper.

I didn't feel like reading. I sat there, bumping along, squished between them while my thoughts zigzagged from wondering what lay ahead of me to remembering our time at Nina's, to distractions as new people climbed on board and I found myself staring at someone's tattoo or listening to someone's conversation on their mobile phone.

When we arrived at Harrison Secondary College, I picked up my heavy load and joined the throngs trudging up the driveway. This was a much bigger school than my primary school and I felt more anonymous than usual. I was never the kind of person who stood out, and I really didn't want to be, but at my old school, by Year Six most people knew me. Here, nobody did.

Except for Billy and Sandy. I ran into them as the driveway curved around the oval. Tall, lean Billy was half on his bike, resting his weight on one foot; the stubby figure of Sandy stood with hands stuffed into blazer pockets that weren't really designed for hands. I could foresee her pockets getting stretched and saggy before long. I called hi and they turned to see me.

"Well," Sandy said dourly, "another year in prison begins."

"Come on," I encouraged. I was determined to play my Nina-role well. "Let's at least *start* with a good attitude."

She rolled her eyes at me but said nothing.

We headed on towards the spread of buildings, Billy walking his bike beside us. "I mean, really," I said, a little uncomfortably, "Nina's right. We could just decide to make it a great year."

"You go right on ahead," she said, with a flourish of her hand, as if she was inviting me to help myself to a rich feast.

"I will." I shifted the weight of my backpack. "I don't like it any more than you, Sandy, but I'm not going to suffer all year."

"See you guys," Billy butted in, wheeling his bike off to the right, "gonna put this in the shed."

Sandy and I were in the same house but Billy had been allocated to another one, so that was another separation. She and I sat together in our homeroom listening to the welcome spiel and notices. Our homeroom teacher was Miss Walker, an enthusiastic young woman with long wavy hair and a smile that was almost too big.

We didn't see Billy until lunchtime, briefly. He was bolting a sandwich before hitting the sports field with some of his new friends. He looked pretty happy. Sandy had been speaking to a few other kids here and there. I was conscious of doing my usual shy thing and hanging back. I thought of Nina turning up at my school last year for the first time and standing in front of a sea of strangers, staring at us like we were all the lonely newcomers and she'd been there for ages. She had been so confident. I didn't feel like that at all.

Mathematics, English, Geography and an afternoon of Sport – swimming, which I've always quite liked. Our first English text was a novel about an Aboriginal girl who'd been part of the Stolen Generation – taken away from her family because she was a half-caste, and put in a mission. It seemed that whenever Nina introduced something to me, suddenly it was everywhere. (Was that my R.A.S. at work?)

At last the first day was over and I was home. I didn't properly relax until I'd walked up our driveway and into the house. I shoved my school bag under the hallway bench and went in search of something to eat. The house was empty, so I guessed that Mum was doing errands with Katie and Evan on their way back from school.

The phone rang while I was munching a peanut butter, sultana and celery sandwich. It was Clare.

"How was it?" I asked.

"Awful," she said. "I was so lonely. You?"

"It was okay. Sandy was pretty grim about it to start off but then she seemed to find quite a few people to talk to. She even ran into someone she knows from her pottery class."

"Oh. Yeah. Sandy's always okay."

"Did you talk to four people?"

"Sort of…" She was quiet for a moment and I waited. "Do teachers count?"

I grinned. "Only if you want to invite them over after school and stuff like that."

She gave a little giggle. "Well, I did talk to four kids but it was mostly things like 'thanks' when they held a door open for me or passed me the handouts or something like that. It wasn't exactly conversations."

"Maybe you needed to be more specific," I suggested. "You know how Nina is always going on about that."

"Yeah…"

"Let's see if we can make this year great," I said in a burst, trying again to live up to my intention. I just wanted someone to do it with me…

"Yeah," she agreed, "yeah, let's. Let's do a visualisation right now."

That took me by surprise. "Okay." I put the remains of my sandwich on the bench and hiked myself up onto a kitchen stool. "Do you want to do it? I mean, say something?"

"Let's just imagine ourselves with lots of friends, laughing and having a good time," she said. "You see yourself in your school and I'll see myself in mine."

"Okay." I closed my eyes and sat with the phone against my ear, which wasn't very relaxing. "Clare?"

"Yes?"

"I'm putting you on loudspeaker."

"Ok. I will too." We punched the buttons and put the phones down and I sat perched on the stool with my eyes closed. For a moment I created a flickering image of me and Sandy and Billy laughing at that spot by the oval where we'd met that morning. That felt nicer to see than Sandy's frown, but it faded pretty quickly.

New people, I told myself, and tried to summon an image of us with new friends around us. It's not easy to imagine people you haven't met yet, but Nina did it. She visualised herself with four new friends at her new school that turned out to be us. I saw a few blurry faces but they were gone too quickly to see who was who. The only one I really noticed was Miss Walker, the teacher, so that wasn't much use.

"How did you go?" Clare's voice asked through the loudspeaker.

"So-so," I said, opening my eyes.

"Me too," she said.

"Let's do it again tonight, before we go to sleep, and in the morning," I said. It was way harder believing in this stuff without Nina, I was finding.

"Yeah," she agreed.

"Hey Clare," I said, "thanks for suggesting it."

"Thanks for doing it with me," she said. "I didn't think Sandy or Billy would."

I thought back to Sandy's rolling eyes this morning, and Billy's distraction with sporting friends. Maybe it would be up to me and Clare to keep the Mastery Club going.

CHAPTER 14

TRAINING WHEELS FOR THE MIND

I SPENT A FEW minutes visualising again that night, and a few minutes the next morning. It was always difficult in the morning with needing to get up and get ready for school, and doors banging and little siblings yelling or crying and parents knocking on your door to ask if you're up yet, but at least I did it. I remembered Nina saying that it's not *our* power that makes things happen; we just open to the power by our intention and focus. So I hoped that would do and hurried to the shower.

Mum was looking a bit stressed already this morning. Her business phone kept ringing, which didn't usually happen this early, and she was trying to cook porridge and make school lunches and keep Evan and Katie on track. Dad had gone to work but Mum worked from home.

"The others are coming over tomorrow night, remember?" I told her as I buttered my toast. "For a Mastery Club meeting."

"What was that?" she asked, wrapping a sandwich with a

preoccupied frown. "Oh! Yes, okay," then: "Damn!" as the phone rang again, and: "Nat, would you check the porridge?" as she dashed out.

It was ready, so I served it up for Katie and Evan and then went looking for them. They were watching TV, illegally, so I switched it off and sent them to the table. They couldn't exactly complain to Mum, but they gave me some pretty dark looks.

"Why's your phone ringing so much today?" I asked, when she hurried back into the kitchen.

"I've got a client about to launch a website. It's the biggest one I've done so far and there are a few glitches. I really need to sort them out before they go live." She threw a desperate glance at the kitchen clock.

"Can I do anything?" I asked, though I only had a few minutes spare before I had to run for the bus.

She shot me a grateful smile. "You're a sweetheart, Nattie, but no, Ruth will be here any minute to take these two to school for me and then I'll be onto it. Have you filled the dishwasher?"

"Yep, apart from what's still being used."

"That's fine then. You go and have a great day."

I left the whirlwind behind me and trudged off to the bus. The new school was beginning to feel less strange now but I was still glad that the first week back was just a short one.

This last day, being Friday, seemed to go by pretty quickly. Sandy and I grabbed our bags and headed out to the front of the school to catch the bus to my place together. There were crowds of kids and teachers and parents everywhere, and buses lining up one after another. Billy turned up with his bike as we were climbing aboard. He was planning to race the bus to my place.

"I can only drop in for a bit," he called to us. "Some of the guys are riding down to the beach tonight for a swim."

"Can we come?" Sandy asked, with one foot on the step up into my bus.

"The *guys!*" he yelled, walking his bike away through the jostling crowds to get a clear start.

Sandy made a face after him and followed me to a seat. She was not very talkative today; just sat staring out through the window, so we jolted along in silence together, occasionally catching sight of Billy as he rounded a corner behind the bus or shot past us when we'd stopped to pick someone up or let someone off.

As we climbed down at my stop, he went tearing past, legs pumping madly and sweaty hair stuck to his red face. Sandy and I shouldered our backpacks and took off after him, but he beat us. He was sitting on the doorstep with Clare, gasping, when we came pelting up the driveway. Clare beamed and said hi, but Billy was panting too much to say anything, much less gloat about beating us.

Mum had left a bowl of fruit and some crackers and cheese out on the bench. We gathered around and dug in.

"So how's your school going?" Clare asked.

"Pretty good," Billy said, magically recovered at the sight of food, and stacking slices of cheese and biscuit and apple together.

"Okay," Sandy said. "How's yours? People treating you okay?" She said it with some of her old bulldoggish gruffness. Sandy had always been Clare's protector through primary school, though her strategies were quite different to Nina's. Sandy would front up to any aggressor with such a threatening expression and stance that they'd soon melt away; Nina was more for loving people. It was a style that had taken us all by surprise, but when she explained what she meant, it kind of made sense. And the fact was that Clare had been pestered by people until she took those new ideas on board.

"Let's get Neen on Skype," I said suddenly. "If Bill has to go soon."

"Why?" Clare asked him. I heard him explaining while I went to switch on the computer in the family room.

I dialled Nina and called the others over. They came, dragging chairs and squishing up next to me. In a moment Nina's green-haired face was there, grinning at us. She asked how school was going and everyone said their bit about it. It wasn't very easy for her to see us all because most of the time someone was getting bumped out of her picture.

"What are we going to do?" Sandy asked abruptly. "In these meetings?"

Nina hesitated for a second.

"Talk about our goals, of course," I said, "and how we're going with them."

"That's going to get pretty boring."

"The idea of a Mastery Club is to choose a goal that really inspires you and then do all the things we've been talking about so you achieve it," Nina said from the screen. "It won't be boring if it *inspires* you, Sandy, if it's a goal you really care about."

"And you're going to teach us some new stuff along the way?" I asked. It was her crazy ideas that inspired me.

"Well, that was the plan I originally had: to learn about how the mind works and all that while we're going after our goals. But is that what you guys want?"

"I do," I said. "Is something wrong?" I asked Sandy. "You sound upset."

Sandy shrugged. "I'm just sick of school already. I suppose I should be doing some affirmations," she said to Nina.

"Might help," Nina said quietly. "Think of them as training wheels for your mind. If you're in the habit of thinking something limiting, then doing an affirmation consciously for a while can help to break the habit. I'll be honest with you guys. I've been a bit lonely since you left. I don't want to go to school but I *have* been feeling lonely, which I'm not usually, so I've been saying affirmations like, 'I'm a great friend to myself' and 'My life is rich with friends' – things like that, over and over."

"Is it working? Has anything happened?" Clare asked with interest.

"I met this girl at the supermarket who's starting up a Drama class around here, so I'm going to join. And Joel rang."

I could have rung, I thought, but I'd been so caught up with starting at Harrison. In fact, we all could have rung. You just didn't think of Nina as someone who needed company or help or anything. She seemed so… self-sufficient…

"Once you take on this new way of thinking where you're more conscious, it starts to feel as natural as the old way was," Nina was saying. "I mean, you didn't have to talk yourself into believing the old way, did you? You just saw things that way. Once you really get the new truths, they're obvious and you can't see things any other way."

"Nat and I tried some visualisations about friends," Clare said.

"Did you?" Sandy asked, turning to look at us.

I flushed. "It hasn't worked yet," I said, and then felt stupid.

"You've got to talk to people," Billy stated, "if you want to make friends."

"Duh," Sandy retorted.

"Well, he's right," Nina's voice broke in. "We've got to imagine it *and* take action, do the inner work *and* the outer work. You know, when I first came to your school I'd been visualising having friends for a few weeks before that, and then I came up with this plan to find someone who would start a Mastery Club with me. I was so focused on looking for that person that I stopped feeling self-conscious."

Clare moved suddenly, trying to scratch herself on the nose, but she accidentally poked Sandy in the face with her elbow, so for a minute we were a muddle of 'Ow!' and 'Sorry' and 'Move over' and 'Sorry…'

"So are you going to teach us some more new Lessons?" I

asked, when we were more or less comfortable again. Beside me, Sandy sighed heavily.

"Really there's only ever one Lesson," Nina replied. "Which is 'what are you making it mean?' And if you don't like what you're making it mean, what do you want to make it mean? This stuff about how we perceive reality is A.May.Zing. Really. Think about it. There's no such thing as a set 'one-reality' that everyone experiences. It's all how we each see it, which comes down to what we're telling ourselves." She paused for a moment and then, when no-one spoke, went on.

"Scientists have discovered this thing called the observer effect, where the fact that they're watching an experiment affects how it turns out."

"How do they know? You can't do an experiment without being there," Sandy said suspiciously.

"I don't get it exactly. Nuncle told me they reckon that nothing can exist without being observed so things don't become real to us until we pay attention to them. Or to put it the other way around, whatever we focus on becomes real. Cool, huh?"

Nina's grey eyes were getting that shine to them again. "It was something to do with observing light," she continued, "and it would become either a wave or a particle depending on if it was being observed or not. Things are just… what did they call them…? probability waves – until you focus on them, and then they become particles. Something like that. I think it means that anything is possible until we make a decision about what something means, and then it narrows down to that one thing."

"So the more I think that I'm all alone and it's not fair that I'm by myself at this school, the more real I'm making it," Clare frowned.

"Exactly. And then it gets really weird because in other experiments, when they were looking for a particle they'd see a particle and when they were expecting to see a wave they'd see a wave."

"The old R.A.S.," I said.

"Yep. See, what they finally realised," Nina said with a little bounce, "is that light has a double sort of nature, it's both particle and wave, and we get what we're looking for. Just like you, Clare; you can be a loner or a leader – it's the same 'you' being either one, but you become what you decide you are. You can create 'lonely and alone' or you can think how great it is that you're free to start a whole new experience, maybe as one of the leaders at your school, and then create that reality. Like a butterfly Clare leaving the old patterns and habits in the cocoon…" She flapped her arms for a silly moment.

"More real magic," I murmured.

"Yes... So you see? We truly are the creators of our reality."

"This gets way weird," Billy remarked. "It must be what people mean when they say if a tree falls in a forest and no-one's there to see it or hear it, does it make a sound?"

Outside a car door banged. Any minute, Mum and the terrors would arrive. Or perhaps I shouldn't create that terror idea and just call them the siblings?

"What if we each think of a really stuck thought we've got and change it around this week?" I suggested. "We could blitz it with affirmations."

"Great idea!" Nina enthused.

"I'll do the lonely thing," Clare said. "I'll do training wheels about having heaps of great friends."

"I can't do 'school is great'," Sandy said flatly. "I don't want to."

"I've gotta go," Billy said. "I'll think of something and text it to you. Seeya, Nina!" And he dashed out, colliding with Evan and Katie in the hallway. I could hear them disentangling themselves.

"I'll get back to you guys about it too," Sandy said abruptly. "See you, Nina. Seeya Clare, Nat." And then she was gone.

Clare and I looked at each other and then at the screen.

"What are you making it mean?" Nina asked us.

Mastery Club Lesson #14

Af-firm-ations – Training Wheels for the Mind

* Whatever you focus on becomes real.

* If things aren't working out as you want, blitz your thinking by deliberately adopting useful self-talk.

* Choose simple phrases that feel good, like "I deserve to have what I love" or inspiring declarations like, "I am a genius and I apply my wisdom".

* The more you do it, the more comfortable it becomes, until that new statement is your new identity and your natural way of thinking.

CHAPTER 15

NEW PATHS

CLARE AND I promised each other to keep visualising and affirming that "I have lots of new friends and we get on really well" (Clare) and "I'm moving forwards in my life and loving it" (me). That was Nina's idea. She thought I was getting too hung up on how things had been in the past. I thought she was probably right. In fact, the more I thought about it, the righter she seemed. I was always trying to put things back to how they were before.

"What if something new and even better is just around the corner?" she had asked before we all quit Skype.

Something new *was* around the corner: my family's trip to the Greek Islands. That evening Mum and Dad spread brochures all over the table and started to talk about all the different excursions we could go on. I browsed through some of them, but when they started arguing about it, I went up to my room and left them to it.

Saturday morning was blue-skied and balmy outside, but inside the house it felt cold and dark. I ate my cereal standing in a patch of sunlight and then, on the spur of the moment, headed out for a walk. I don't usually like walking for no reason. Mum can do that 'go-for-a-walk-just-for-fresh-air-and-exercise' thing, but I find it too boring. I'd rather have a place to go.

Pretty soon I realised that I did have a place to go – I was heading for Liz and Nuncle's house.

I turned up Boronia Lane and the old familiar smile turned up on my face as I treaded over the cobblestones towards their crazy colourful house. As soon as I'd crossed the little bridge I saw Liz squatting in the garden. She was very focused, placing bits of something on the ground. As I came closer, I realised she was making a mosaic path. The sections that had already been laid were a beautiful swirl of colour winding between her vegie patches towards a little fountain centrepiece.

"That looks great!" I enthused.

Liz looked up and smiled. "Hello, Natalie. I'm glad you like it. I'm rather loving it myself." She leaned back on her heels to survey her handiwork then turned back to me. "How's the new school?"

"Okay," I said, sitting cross-legged beside her. "I'm in a class with Sandy but I've been missing Nina and Clare. And Billy's in another class."

"Ah… I gather you all had a great time at Nina's."

"Yes."

"The Mastery Club still happening this year?"

"Sort of." I picked up an iridescent blue stone and turned it to and fro in the light. "It's not easy with Nina being away. Billy's sort of losing interest and Sandy's always been… kind of in and out of it…"

She nodded and placed another piece. "Tricky…"

"Is Nuncle here?" I asked.

"On the phone."

I sat and watched her working. She had beautiful hands, I noticed; long, elegant fingers that moved deftly. "Are you going to make the path go all around the vegie patches?"

"Yes. With animal designs."

"Which animals?"

"Turtles to begin with. It's time to go slow…" she said enigmatically.

The back door of the house opened suddenly and Nuncle stepped out, saying, "That woman is driving me mad!" in a furious tone of voice.

Liz raised her face to him and must have made some sort of message with her eyes because then he saw me and stopped short. "Hello Natalie."

He smiled at me welcomingly but he didn't look his usual cheery self. They invited me in for a drink, and I accepted, but then I almost wished I hadn't. Liz stood up slowly, stretching, and Nuncle took a step towards her. "I'm fine," she said quietly, with a little shake of her head. He looped his arm around my shoulders instead.

We all drank a glass of apple juice and Nuncle asked me all the same things Liz had asked, and then we talked about my family's upcoming trip to the Greek Islands.

"You're going to love it," Nuncle said with certainty. "Especially since you had something to do with bringing it about."

I didn't stay much longer. There was a funny feeling there. I'd always noticed Nuncle's twinkling eyes but this time I found myself noticing the lines around his eyes. He seemed a bit distracted. And Liz was very dreamy, as if she wasn't all there.

I walked home more slowly than I'd left it.

CHAPTER 16

I'm Put on the Spot

ON WEDNESDAY Miss Walker asked me for 'a word' as everyone was leaving the morning meeting for the first class. She waited until most people had left the room and then she said, "I've heard that you and your friends set up some sort of club at your primary school last year. Something about the mind. Is that right?"

"Yes," I replied cautiously.

"I have something of an interest in the mind as well," she said, and flashed me one of her big, white-toothed smiles. "How would you like to lead a club like that here?"

"Oh I wasn't the leader of it," I said quickly. "That was our friend Nina."

"Well, maybe this could be *your* opportunity," she said, and waited.

I shifted my bag to my other shoulder. I'd told Nina I wanted to keep the Mastery Club going, and she'd told me that teaching the principles would help me learn them. But this felt quite a bit too scary.

"I thought I'd invite a few students who strike me as being

open to this sort of thing," Miss Walker said, watching me. "Not too many. We could meet in here or in the library at lunchtimes, perhaps. What do you think?"

"I'll think about it…" I said, with an involuntary glance at the door.

"Maybe you could jot down a few notes for me about what you covered last year?" she suggested, in the sort of tone that was more like a statement than a question. "If you don't have too much homework, that is."

"Okay," I agreed. I could do that and then maybe she could run it…

"Wonderful!" she said warmly.

The problem was that she was so nice. She'd been very friendly and encouraging since the first day of school. And she was pretty and seemed to be liked by most of the kids and teachers. So it wasn't going to be easy to say no.

I told the others about this unexpected request at our Mastery Club meeting on Friday, which was at Clare's this time, (around the dining room table where Clare's mother's computer was).

"Would you help me?" I asked Sandy.

"No thanks!" she said at once. "That can be your thing."

"And I'll be doing sport at lunchtimes," Billy added quickly.

"You better watch out," Sandy told him, "or you'll turn into a sportaholic like your dad's a workaholic."

"It sounds like a great opportunity," Nina piped up from the screen.

"I don't know…" I said. "What am I supposed to tell them?"

"About the lessons and the basketball experiment and visualisation – stuff like that," Clare suggested.

"But what if they ask me things I don't know?"

"Make it up," Sandy said. "They won't know the difference."

I looked at her darkly. "Very helpful."

"OK. That's sorted," she continued with a cheeky grin. "Now what are we doing today? I've got to get going early. My uncle's picking me up tonight to get ready for one of his exhibitions."

"Are you going to invite us this time?" I asked, still a bit cross with her.

"Maybe," she said, kind of closing the subject off.

"Before we do anything else I've got news," Clare announced. "I have a friend. Her name's Serenity and I've told her about our Mastery Club and she wants to join. Can I bring her next week?"

I'm moving forwards in my life and loving it,' I told myself silently. "That's great, Clare," I said aloud. "Sure. Why not? Time for the Club to grow, I guess."

Sandy shrugged. "What's she like?"

"Really nice," Clare said. "I think *you're* really going to like her," to Nina, on the screen.

"Groovy," said Nina. "It will be weird meeting her through Skype, but so what."

"I've got a training next week so I might not be able to come," Billy told us. "Maybe this should become a girls' club?"

"Maybe you should bring a guy," Sandy countered.

It was his turn to shrug.

"So," Nina said, "have you decided on your school goals, Nat?"

I had honestly forgotten all about that. You see, my Dad and his family are big on doing well at school. They're mostly barristers and lawyers, so getting top marks is Very Important. Sometimes that felt like too much pressure. I shook my head. "Have you thought of your outrageous thing?" I asked back.

"Yep. I'm going to visit the Aboriginal community where Joel lives. We arranged it on the phone the other day. I'll be going in winter for a couple of weeks. Rosie and Pete are always talking about understanding other cultures by living in their shoes and I really don't know anything about the Aboriginal culture at all, so it seemed like a good opportunity."

Wow.

"Sweet," said Billy.

"You two *are* going out, aren't you?" Clare accused.

"No, we're not! How can we be? He's up there and I'm down here. And he's way older. We're just friends."

"Well you're going to be up there soon," Clare persisted.

"We're just friends," Nina repeated firmly.

There was a key in the lock and Clare's mum stepped in. Their flat is very tiny; in only a few paces you can get from the front door to the dining room table (which is also her office where she does typing work for people), and then a few more steps to the kitchenette if you keep going straight, or a few steps to the bedrooms and bathroom if you go toward the left.

"Hi kids," she said, dropping her bag and a coat on the sofa. "I'll just creep past you into the kitchen."

"Hi Hazel!" Nina called from the screen, as Clare's mum came into view for her.

Clare's mother stopped, bamboozled. "Was that Nina?"

We all giggled and pointed.

"Well, hello," Clare's mum said to the screen. "How are you?"

"Pretty good, thanks. And you?" Nina replied cheerily.

"Oh, you know, busy," Hazel said vaguely. She gave a little wave and went into the kitchen.

We re-grouped around the screen. Billy snatched a glance at his watch, and I felt a pang of disappointment that he was maybe pulling out of our group. *I'm moving forwards in my life and loving it,'* I reminded myself again.

"You said our Mastery Club was going to be about doing real magic," Sandy said to Nina in a challenging tone of voice, but friendly. She was in a pretty good mood tonight since an evening with her uncle was on its way. "Well. How about it? How about some lessons in time travel or invisibility or making things appear and disappear?"

"We've been doing magic all along," Nina said promptly. "For instance, did you know that 'abracadabra' means 'I will create as I speak'? It was used as a healing blessing in ancient times."[10]

"Really?" I asked.

"Really. So that's affirmations. And we've done Time Travel – what do you think visualising is? That's putting yourself into the future in your mind."

"I meant the instant sort."

"You can be anywhere in your mind in an instant," Nina said.

Sandy narrowed her eyes sceptically. "I meant... oh, never mind!"

"And then there's Invisibility," Nina continued. "I was thinking we should introduce Invisibility this year."

Now we were all looking at her sceptically.

"Serious," she said, regarding us gravely. "What is it, after all?"

"Not being seen," Clare said.

"Exactly. And there are times when not being seen is the perfect thing to do. Like when it's someone else's special day and it's better to let them have the limelight."

"That's a pretty weak idea for a Mastery Club thing," Sandy said.

"Why?" Nina asked. "What if we each set a goal of doing something to help someone and not being seen while we're doing it?"

Put like that, it appealed to me. I'd always liked the idea of magic because of the good you could do just by secretly waving a wand. In theory.

---

10   The killing curse from Harry Potter sounded so much like those words that I did some googling and found out that Abracadabra is the Aramaic translation from 'avra kehdabra', which has several possible origins – Hebrew, Chaldean, Gnostic – and the meaning and words are slightly different in each. http://answers.yahoo.com/question/index?qid=20090909142128AA5ZePs

"They can't know you've done it, okay? So you can't get thanked. You've got to be invisible."

"Like what?" Clare asked. "Do what sort of thing?"

"We can't tell each other, can we?" Sandy said, "because then we won't be invisible."

"Unless we can be visible to each other," Clare argued back. "After all, we're the magicians so we can see through invisibility."

We all laughed.

"Okay. Brainstorm!" Nina said from the screen.

"Housework," I suggested. "Mum's always saying that she wishes the Shoemaker's Elves would visit our house. I could get up in the middle of the night and do some cleaning…"

"Boot polishing," Sandy grimaced. "Dad hates doing it."

"Mum's been dropping hints about getting the car cleaned for a while," Billy said.

"If you know someone who's sick you could leave some food at their front door," Nina added from the screen.

"The other day Mum was buying a coffee and when she went to pay, the girl at the counter said she didn't need to because the person who went before her had paid for hers as well!" Clare told us. "Mum was amazed. Apparently this guy is a regular who often does that."

"Picking girls up," Sandy said shrewdly.

"Nope. Mum thought that too, but he didn't even know whose coffee he'd bought," Clare said. "He'd gone by the time she turned up to pay."

"Speaking of going," said Billy, "I've gotta shoot."

"Shit! Me too!" Sandy exclaimed, jumping up.

"Hey wait!" little screen-Nina yelled. "I was going to tell you: I'll be at Liz and Nuncle's the long weekend in March. Want to meet there? On Saturday or Sunday afternoon?"

"Sure," I said at once.

"I can't," Billy said. "Going on a camping trip with Dad."

Clare said she probably could and Sandy said it would depend on the time because the pottery exhibition started that weekend too. But Nina wasn't finished.

"And my parents' Mastermind Group, the one that gave me the idea for our Mastery Club, is meeting that Sunday night at Nuncle's. You're all welcome to come to that as well."

"Bummer," Clare said. "We've got a family dinner that night."

"I can't either," Sandy said. "That's when Mum and Dad are coming to see the Exhibition."

"I'll come," I said. Wild horses wouldn't have kept me away.

Mastery Club Lesson #15

MAGIC!

Abracadabra: I will create as I speak!

Time Travel:

We can go anywhere in our minds…

Invisibility:

Doing something without being seen…

CHAPTER 17

ELF PATROL

MISS WALKER didn't waste any time following up on her idea. She gave me an extra special smile as soon as I arrived on Monday and said, casually, "Have you thought about it?"

"I wrote down some of what we did last year," I told her, avoiding her real question while I dug around in my school bag. I'd clipped the page to my English homework, since she was also my English teacher, so I gave her both things now: The Mastery Club 10 Lessons that Nina had taught us, and my answers to her questions about our literature text, that story about the Aboriginal girl.

"Thank you," she said eagerly, her eyes already scanning the Mastery Club page.

"I was just wondering," I said awkwardly, "how you knew about the Club?" (I'd been wondering that all weekend, as I sat with my Record Book for Magic, going over everything I'd written in it in coloured pens, and remembering things from last year that I had forgotten.)

"Your Aunt Kim actually," she said, looking up. "We attend the same Yoga Class."

"Oh," I said. My Aunt Kim was the only person on Dad's side

of the family who seemed to share some of my interest in these things. Or so I'd discovered at a family dinner last year. I wandered away to my locker while her gaze returned to the sheet.

Somebody gave me a smack on the back while I was stuffing homework books into my locker and pulling out the ones I needed for the first classes. It was only a light whack, but the surprise of it made me bang my head on the edge of the locker. "Hi Sandy," I said, rubbing my forehead.

"G'day," she said cheerily. "Good weekend?"

"Fine, thanks."

There was something almost unsettling about a Sandy-in-a-good-mood. I watched her sort out her books for a minute, still rubbing my forehead. "Looks like yours was good."

"I made a great new piece for the exhibition," she said. "My uncle showed me something really cool about working with glazes. It looks awesome."

This was a very strange and new Sandy. I was still standing there, staring, after she had clanged her locker door shut and sauntered away with her bag of books.

The bell rang, and Miss Walker called me over in the same moment. "This is wonderful," she beamed, indicating my Mastery Club notes. "I'm really impressed. I'll speak to those other kids now, the ones I had in mind for the Club, and we'll make a time for a first meeting. I'm so excited!"

There was nowhere in that speech for me to say, "But I don't really want to do it..." so I just kind of half-smiled and half-nodded, and scooted away to my first class.

And anyway, I guess, to be honest, part of me did. I was terrified of leading a Mastery Club on my own, but a little tiny part of me wanted to have a go.

Clare was sick so she couldn't come to our next meeting, which meant that we didn't get to meet Serenity. Anyway, it was a bit of a non-event of a meeting because the internet was down at Sandy's so we couldn't get Skype to work, and Billy kept getting text messages about sport things and bike rallies and stuff, so he was way distracted. When I asked him what his affirmation was going to be, since he hadn't texted it, he said, "Oh yeah!" and still didn't get around to telling us. In the end, since we couldn't get Nina on Skype, he nicked off and Sandy showed me her pottery.

She was working on a whole series of Australian animals and they were so good. They looked alive. Their eyes had a real life shine to them and even their fur looked real. And they weren't just sitting there; she'd made them crouching or digging or holding something between their paws. I was pretty impressed. Not just by the animals. Sandy herself was different. She came alive just talking about them. When I thought about the grumpy, stubborn, bulldoggish person Sandy often was, it was a very nice change to see her crackling with energy and happiness. But when I commented on the change, she just made a face and changed the subject.

I kept thinking about it, though, as I went home that night. How people come to life when they're doing things they love. Nina was an example of that, and Sandy with her pottery, and Billy with his sport. I wondered what would bring me to life like that? Did anything?

Mum loved her work, I knew that, but she often looked stressed as well, so it was hard to tell if it was a real love-aliveness thing. She had lots of energy but it was rushing-around energy; it didn't seem quite the same thing. Dad was a mostly cheerful, optimistic sort of a guy, and pretty bouncy with energy. Watching him tussle on the lounge room floor with Katie and Evan after dinner, I wondered if he loved his work the way that Sandy loved her pottery and Nina loved her crazy ideas. He often got stressed too, and he worked really long hours some days, and came home very tired.

I went to bed early that night and set my alarm for one a.m. I had decided to turn into a Shoemaker's Elf, since I couldn't think of another way to be invisible. I stuffed my alarm into a sock and then stuck it under my pillow – somehow I had to make sure that it would be loud enough to wake me, but muffled enough to not wake the rest of the family.

When it did go off, buzzing and vibrating right under my ear, I nearly jumped out of my skin. I smacked it off and lay there, heart racing with the shock of being woken up so abruptly when I'd been so deeply asleep. The last thing I wanted to do was to get up, but now was the perfect time.

Mum had a business client arriving in the morning right after we headed off to school, and the downstairs bathroom was a mess. Last night, as we were doing the dishes, she'd wearily mentioned that she'd have to get up extra early to have time to clean it before the person came because my mother *hates* anyone even seeing the bathroom if it's a mess. I didn't usually notice mess but she had pointed it out to me once in her efforts to make me into a good housecleaner: yellowish stains on the toilet from where Evan had missed his aim; smelly wet towels bunched up on the rack or heaped on the floor; slimy stuff around the plughole in the sink; hair trailing from hairbrushes and spilt water all over the bench part of the sink; smears on the mirror; dustballs in the corners on the floor; cloudy streaks all over the shower cubicle walls, and dark stains in the grouting between the tiles (that was mould)... Yuck.

I flicked the light switch on and stood there in the doorway of the downstairs bathroom in my dressing gown at one-ten a.m., staring at the horrible job I had set myself. The harsh light brought all the yucky, dirty details into sharp clarity. If Dad was set to cleaning the house he'd swan in there with an armful of evil chemicals, spray them around, and then escape, leaving them to do the work. But Mum was sticking to natural products now that she had watched some scary documentary about chemicals and their effect on people and the earth. So I had, in my arsenal, a big plastic bottle of white vinegar, a packet of bicarbonate soda, a couple of old rags, a little bottle of essential oil of lemon, and a pair of rubber gloves. Closing the door quietly, I locked myself in with the horror.

"Start with the cleanest bit so you don't spread the germs," Mum's voice advised in my mind. What was the cleanest bit? I looked around with a frown. Obviously not the toilet, that would have to be last… if I even dared to touch it at all. Maybe the sink?

I picked up the hairbrushes, one by one, and dragged a comb through them, pulling out tangled hair and fluff and dumping it into the bin. Then I put the brushes away in the basket where they were supposed to go. (Kids' hairbrushes were really supposed to be kept in the upstairs bathroom but they always ended up down here.) I pulled the gloves on and began to wipe up the puddles on the sink-bench. Then I went for the bit of hair in the plughole, and that was when I got my first shock. It wasn't just a bit of hair in the plughole; it came slowly, drawing a long trail of yucky, slimy hair after it. Mine and Katie's, I guessed, and all bound up with people's toothpaste spit and other gross things. I was gagging a bit as I air-lifted the horrible thing out of there and, dripping, over to the bin. Scattering bicarb soda everywhere was quite satisfying, and pouring the vinegar over the top of it was even fun, because it bubbled and sizzled in a fabulous acid-alkali chemical reaction. Then I had to actually scrub.

Cleaning the sink was easy enough, but when I tried to clean the mirror, I couldn't get rid of these little threads that kept turning up, and every time I wiped, more smeary marks appeared. So I gave up on that and went over to the shower. It wasn't really that bad because mostly the siblings used the bath upstairs and I used the shower in the bath upstairs, and Mum and Dad used the one in their ensuite, but because it was hardly ever used, it was often forgotten, and then dust and moisture and stuff would somehow make it dirty all by itself. Weird.

But cleaning it was no easy thing. I climbed into the shower in my dressing gown and slippers, but when I started using the vinegar – ugh! I had to open the shower door quickly for some air. Then of course the wet stuff started to dribble down my arm and make puddles on the floor, so I climbed out of there and took my slippers and dressing gown off – I was getting too hot anyway. I went back in with my rag and bicarb and vinegar and scrubbed as high as I could reach. The bicarb on the rag was getting really grey, so I kept throwing more and more on. Gosh. Dirt was huge. I began to wish I could just wave a wand. I guess that was why people like Dad used those chemical things – it was like waving a wand, but that was a kind of magic that did harm.

Maybe this invisibility-magic was doing me some harm. It was certainly depriving me of sleep, and was it good to breathe in vinegar?

When I'd scrubbed the walls I realised I had to do the floor, too, and I was just backing out of the shower cubicle on my hands and knees when the bathroom door opened and Mum appeared in her dressing gown. Her look of shock was only just matched by my look of surprise and disappointment.

"Nat!" she exclaimed, "what on earth –?"

"It was supposed to be a surprise," I grumbled, standing up and brushing the dust off my PJs.

For once, she was speechless. She wandered to the sink and looked at it in amazement, then at the shower, then at me.

"I haven't done the toilet yet," I said.

And then she opened her arms out to me and we came together in a big hug. There were tears in her eyes when we stopped hugging, and I felt like crying too, but I think it was tiredness.

"You sweetheart," she said, "whatever brought this on?"

"I just wanted to help," I said. I couldn't mention Invisibility Magic, that would have sounded too weird, and after all, my cover was blown. (So now I'd have to come up with something else for that challenge.)

"But in the middle of the night?"

"It was supposed to be a surprise."

"Thank you," she said. She reached toward me and brushed a loose strand of hair that was falling into my eyes behind my ears. "Just like the Shoemaker's Elves. A dream come true." She smiled at me gratefully, and then I sat on the sink and watched her clean the toilet and finish the mirror (you can use scrunched-up newspaper to clean a mirror – imagine that!), and then she walked me back to bed, arm-in-arm up the stairs, and tucked me in. She hadn't done that in a while.

CHAPTER 18

THE LAW OF CONSERVATION

THE LONG WEEKEND couldn't come too soon for me. Not only did it mean a bit of a holiday, it meant a Mastery Club meeting at Liz and Nuncle's with Nina – just like the good old days – and a visit to the adult mastermind group that had inspired Nina to start ours.

It had been a swelteringly hot summer but today was perfect autumn weather. The sun was shining, the sky was blue, it was warm enough for just a t-shirt, and there was a very pleasant breeze. We'd set our meeting for nine a.m. Saturday morning – it was going to be later but Billy's dad was picking him up to go on their camping trip at ten, so this way he could at least come for a bit.

"That's pretty late to leave," Sandy had remarked. "If you were going camping with my dad, he'd be dragging you out of bed at five a.m." (Sandy's dad probably forgets his kids are kids, not soldiers.)

Billy had shrugged. His father was more of a corporate

executive workaholic sort of a guy – he was probably trying to get in a bit of work at the office before they left on this father-son bonding thing he was doing in a belated attempt to reconnect with Billy. Their relationship had been struggling over the last couple of years since he'd split up with Billy's mum.

When I arrived at Begonia Lane, Billy was cycling towards me on his new mountain bike, and wearing a huge backpack. We walked up the lane together, and just as we were crossing the little bridge, Clare's mum drove up the driveway and unloaded Clare and Sandy. Nina came bursting out of the kitchen door, grinning from ear to ear. There was something different about her but at first I couldn't figure out what it was; then I realised that her hair wasn't as green as usual. It was more of a washy blonde with a faded greenness about it. Strange.

She hugged us all and admired Billy's bike, and we waved to Hazel who was heading straight off for an appointment. Then we clattered into the kitchen where Liz and Nuncle were slicing apples into a big casserole dish. They stopped chopping for hugs – this was one huggy family – and then shooed us out to start our meeting so that we'd be finished in time to have some raw apple crumble before Billy had to leave. *Raw* apple crumble???

"So where's Serenity?" Nina asked Clare as we went up the narrow, winding staircase to her old room in the attic.

"Her family has gone to some sort of music festival this weekend," Clare said.

"Oh well; next time."

And then we were back in the amazing room Nina had lived in for five or so months last year, the room that had been our Headquarters. Liz and Nuncle had left it set up as a bedroom but it had an unused, dusty feel to it. Nina was going to be sleeping here again tonight, so the bed was made up and the window was open, but it didn't feel very lived-in. Her posters and paraphernalia were gone and it felt kind of quiet and still in here. I sat on the window seat where a lovely view of their property and the streets around stretched below.

"Return of The Mastery Club!" Nina beamed, from the centre of the room.

"And the Secret Society of the Hidden Order," Sandy reminded her, stretching out on the neat bed.

"Okay! News, everyone: what's happening? How are your goals going?"

For a change, I jumped in first. "I've been doing my affirmation about moving forwards in my life and loving it," I said, "and that feels pretty good actually. And Miss Walker, my teacher, is organising that Mastery Club group for me to start, which is terrifying. And I still haven't made a decision about my schoolwork goals. Dunno why. I keep forgetting to think about it."

"Family news?" Nina asked, straddling a chair.

"Mum's business is booming and she's stressed out – oh! And I did the Invisibility thing. I cleaned the bathroom. And she found me, so that got screwed up, but she really loved it anyway."

"There's something interesting about you trying to be invisible," Nina observed, looking at me with her clear grey eyes. "You seem to be getting more visible this year. More 'in the spotlight'…"

I was digesting this when Sandy cut in: "Speaking of visible, what's with the fading green hair?"

"Just time to stop doing that," Nina said simply. "I've been green for a year. I'm going back to my own colour."

"Which is?"

"Blonde."

"So you're going to blend in with the rest of us, eh?" Sandy asked. As if *she* was the blending-in sort, with her fiery red hair and equally fiery temper.

"I'll find other ways to stand out," Nina smiled.

"Go on, then," Sandy pressed, "how? What have *you* been up to, Ms Mighty Leader?"

Nina gave her an evil frown but didn't take the bait. "You know how I wanted to do some official speaking engagements? Well, we had to give a talk in the Drama Group. To a match. They light a match and you have to talk till it burns down –"

"That must have been hard for you," Sandy said, "only a match-burning amount of time to talk."

"What was your topic?" I asked Nina, cutting Sandy off. About time someone did.

"The Law of Conservation," she said.

"Man!" Sandy rolled her eyes. "Those poor kids in your Drama Club."

"Maybe they'll turn it into a Mastery Club," Clare said, getting off the floor to sit next to me on the window seat.

"The law of what?" I asked.

"It's this law that nothing is created or destroyed, it just changes form. It's 'conserved', which in science means 'maintained', I think; kind of… 'kept the same'."

"Are you sure about that? Things are dying and being born all the time."

"Yes, but it just *looks* like that. They're not actually dying, they're just changing form – if you look at them at an energy level. The energy and particles that made one thing rearrange themselves into something else. Like a body becoming dust, I suppose. Dead people don't just 'end', right? they become something else."

"That's spooky," said Clare. "That means we're walking around on dead people."

"It's *much* spookier than that; we're *made* out of dead people," Nina grimaced. "Where do you think your atoms came from?"

"Ugh!!!"

"But," she added brightly, "before they were in dead people, the atoms that made us came from exploding stars. Pretty mind-blowing, eh?"

Stars, I marvelled. We were made of stars! And dead people...

"So everything just keeps changing form over and over again, which is the Law of Conservation; and that Law is why everything always has a good and a bad side – get it? Because they're 'conserved', so you can't ever get rid of either side."

"Everything? You mean physical things *and* idea-sort-of-things?" I asked.

"Yep, physical and metaphysical."

"This girl knows too many big words," Sandy stated. "You're so certain about this always-balanced thing but it sounds a bit far-out to me. I reckon there must be exceptions." And I knew she'd immediately be on the hunt for some examples where it wasn't true and it didn't work.

"Seriously," Nina said seriously; "no matter what you do, come up with anything that you think is better than something else and you'll find out that it's not."

"I accept the challenge," Sandy replied, holding her gaze.

"But things are getting better all the time," Billy said. "Well, some things are – with progress and technology."

"Like what?"

"Like... transport. It used to only be horse-drawn buggies and stuff like that. Now we've got jets and super-fast trains and rockets – all sorts of better stuff."

"So we think we're improving things because now we get places faster and more comfortably, but there are still negatives: pollution, traffic, noise, stress, traffic jams, jet lag, people working sixty-hour weeks with no time to just live..." Nina rattled examples off so quickly that I knew she'd thought about this one before.

"Okay, fair enough," Billy acknowledged.

"Yeah," Clare said knowingly, "modern technology is destroying the world. We should probably go back to the good old days before machines when life was simpler and quiet and in tune with nature."

"Not so fast," Nina said. "It wasn't that great in those cowboy days, either. I saw this show about American history once, and one episode was on the cities. Did you know that in New York City, around 1900, horses dropped two and a half *million* pounds of manure on the streets *every day?*"

"Shit!" Billy exclaimed, which I figured was an attempt at humour. Sandy gave him a little kick.

"And something like forty horses died every day, but they just left them to rot because that made them easier to cut up and haul away; so all those dead horses lying around created diseases like typhus and cholera and typhoid fever – something like 20,000 people a year died from it, just in that one city. And the sound of so many horseshoes on the cobbled streets was so loud that you couldn't talk outside."

"How do you remember all those facts?" Clare asked in amazement.

Nina gave her a surprised look and shrugged. "I dunno. Don't you find that things like that stick when they interest you? Anyway, when cars came along lots of people saw them as the great saviour that would get rid of all this horse-created disease and noise. So those people couldn't see the negatives about cars, and there are people today who can't see the negatives about horses, but they both have good and bad."

"But if you can't get rid of negatives, if we're always going to have an equal balance of positive and negative and we can't ever improve anything, what's the point of anything?" I asked, struck by the truth of her example.

"That's what I wondered," she said. "On the course they were saying that we evolve through making different forms. For example, you don't like how your bedroom looks so you redesign it, but it will always have good and bad bits about it. Life goes through this endless cycle of loving something and thinking it's the bees' knees, and then getting bored with it or sick of it and wanting something else. Like clothes – did you like your clothes when you were six?"

"Yeah, I suppose."

"I had this cute little overall with a duck on it," Clare burst out. "I so loved it. I wore it every day *and* to bed."

"Would you wear it now?"

"No way! Anyway, it wouldn't fit."

"Do you like your clothes now?"

"Most of them, yeah."

"Do you think you'll still be wearing them, or even *like* them, when you're eighteen – or eighty?"

It was like a little light bulb went off in my head. "So the very same clothes are good *and* bad, depending on how we look at them."

Nina nodded enthusiastically. "Through all your clothes, forever. And *everything* is like that! It's kind of like we're here on earth for the adventure of transforming things – and masters," she added meaningfully, "put their energy into what they'd truly love, and into grand visions, while everyone else puts their energy into whatever they want or need in that moment."

"So nothing is created from nothing and nothing is lost," I repeated slowly, trying to get these new ideas into my head. "Everything's just energy changing form all the time. And nothing is improved because you can't get rid of a thing's bad side; it just changes form."

"Yep. Like support or challenge: they're always in our lives in equal balance whether we recognise it or not. Sometimes it's our parents challenging us, sometimes it's our friends –" pulling a face at Sandy; "and sometimes it's our parents supporting us and sometimes our friends. But we never only get supported or only challenged; we always get a balance. You," she said, as Sandy opened her mouth to speak, "might have a mean old challenging dad, but I notice you have a very supportive and caring uncle."

Sandy shut her mouth again.

"If you go looking for it, you'll find the balance. The *Order*," she pointed out, with Meaning. "You challenge me," again to Sandy; "Natalie supports me. Equal balance. If you start supporting me – a strange idea, I know, but it might happen one day – someone will start challenging me – maybe Natalie! It's an invincible law of the universe. Everything's always in perfect balance no matter what we do. *So-o-o-o* – and this is what the course was all about – what if nothing is good or bad, it all just *is*, and we call it good if we like it and can understand it and use it, and bad if we can't?"

There was a long silence, then, "More fried brains, anyone?" groaned Billy.

"What did the Drama Group kids think of your talk?" Clare asked.

"Interesting," Nina said.

"Are you sure they weren't just being polite?" Sandy said.

"They asked me to do another match," Nina went on, ignoring her, "because they were *so* interested. I talked about roles, and how we each have every single characteristic under the sun but in different forms, which is why no-one's better than anyone else. They found that pretty interesting too, being actors, and we had quite a big conversation about how the same trait turns up in different people in different ways."

Hearing that gave me a pang of jealousy; *I* wanted to be in that Drama group and learning all of this stuff too. There was a tight, squishy feeling in my stomach. I looked outside for a moment, down at the garden. Liz was squatting there, working on her mosaic path again. The sunshine was glinting off the coloured pieces.

"Have you been invisible?" Clare asked Nina, and Sandy said, "Yeah, that's what I want to know."

But just then Billy's phone bipped and he read the message, which was from his dad, saying he would be here in half an hour, which reminded everyone that Billy had better share his news before he had to go.

"Okay," he said, from the chair he was straddling back-to-front. "I know it looks like I haven't really been part of this for a while, but I am doing it. My affirmation is just that I'm getting better at cycling every day and I'm in the top three of the Championship. So I've been saying that pretty much every day quite a few times whenever I'm out riding. I've got it taped onto my handlebars — in code so the other guys don't know what it says." He flushed a little. "They'd probably stir me."

"That's great!" Clare enthused, and I felt a rush of relief that he wasn't dropping out. It wouldn't be the same without Bill, even though he didn't say very much. Usually.

"And I'll probably clean the car for Mum for my Invisibility thing," he added. "Just waiting for a good time when she's not using it."

"How are you going with choosing family?" Nina asked.

He shrugged and looked away. "Dunno. Going camping with Dad might help me figure it out." After a moment he said, "I'm not actually looking forward to it very much."

There was a knock on the door and Nuncle looked in. "Anyone for some raw apple crumble with sweet sour cream?"

"Aren't those kind of contradictory ideas?" Sandy asked. "Isn't apple crumble usually baked till it's melt-in-your-mouth-soft? And 'sweet sour', Mr Vizar? Isn't that a bit weird?"

"Since when have you called me 'Mr Vizar'?" he asked. "I'm

Nuncle to you; or Max. Come and taste," and he held the door wide open.

"Hang on, we haven't done Clare or Sandy yet," Nina said.

"You can do me downstairs," Clare called from the doorway, already on her way out. "While we're eating…"

Mastery Club Lesson #16

The Law of Conservation

* Nothing is created or destroyed; it just changes form.

* This law encompasses physical things (like bodies) and metaphysical things (like our feelings – so we'll never get rid of anger for instance; it will just change form…).

* When we understand this principle, we begin to see that we are part of a bigger reality, a bigger system that is very orderly and intelligent and orchestrated by Love. There is purpose to life. Things are not random or chaotic or meaningless.

* Mastery is the ability to recognise this Order and the changing forms, and to consciously trans-form our lives.

CHAPTER 19

NO-ONE GETS THE BLUES AROUND HERE FOR LONG…

THE RAW APPLE crumble was delicious: thin slices of lemon-freshened apple (with the skin on) coated in a crumble of roughly ground nuts and seeds and chopped dates and sultanas and honey and that sesame seed paste called tahini. Then there was sour cream with maple syrup and cinnamon to dribble on top. It was divine. After tasting this, I didn't think I could ever go back to cooked apple crumble again.

"Why aren't you really fat?" Clare asked Liz and Nuncle, through a mouthful. "When you eat this great stuff all the time?"

In fact, eyeing Liz in her simple red dress, it struck me that she looked slimmer than usual, maybe even a bit too thin…?

"We eat at least eighty percent fruit and veg," Liz replied from the sink, where she was rinsing the knife and chopping board; "that 'stuff' is mostly water, you know, so it doesn't have many calories."

"But the cream?"

"Not a big part of our diet. And we don't eat much bread or

pasta and virtually never eat pastries. Just as much live food as possible."

"Don't you miss junk food?" Sandy asked. "I mean, this is nice, but…"

"Not at all. The more you eat live food, the more you develop a taste for it until everything else tastes kind of heavy and dense and even… dead."

Well, it was certainly true that this food was bopping with aliveness. I could feel the juicy energy of it going into my body. I eyed the last bit in the dish and wondered if I could ask for seconds.

"You see, when food is raw and whole, it delivers all the nutrients you need in perfect balance to your cells," Liz said, pulling up a stool between Clare and Billy. "The more processed our food is, the more difficult to digest and absorb, the more toxic, and the more likely we are to gain weight from eating it. White flour and white sugar are very stressful to the body, whereas foods like this are healing and nourishing."

"Tell them about the signatures," Nina said, and she began to scrape the last of the crumble into everyone's bowl, a tiny scraping each, to be completely fair. She pointed the serving spoon at a poster on the fridge, which showed a man and a woman sprouting fruit and vegetables from all parts of their bodies. Naked bodies. It was a bit embarrassing.

"Well, it's very simple; nature always is," Liz said. "Each food has its own sign-of-nature, or signature, and that signifies which part of the body that food was designed for. For example, apples: if you cut them across the middle instead of down through the top where the stalk is, you'll see a perfect five-pointed star. Any food that has a five-pointed star means that it's good for the whole body."

Nina's chair scraped on the floor as she leapt up and flung her arms out in the air and spread her legs apart – demonstrating that humans themselves are five-pointed stars, I realised after a moment. "That's why an apple a day keeps the doctor away," she said, sitting down again.

"Walnuts have a tough outer shell and a left and right hemisphere and they're all wrinkled, just like the brain; they happen to be great brain food," Liz continued. "Tomatoes and capsicums are red with four chambers, just like the heart; they're heart food. Carrots, if you cut them in cross-section, have a pattern just like the iris; they're good for the eyes. Celery's long and straight and has about 23% sodium in it, which is exactly the same amount of sodium as our bones – and it snaps like our bones do. Silverbeet and other veiny foods are good for our circulatory systems."[11]

This was amazing. I'd heard some of those things before but I'd thought they were just old wives tales or something; I hadn't realised there was actual truth in them.

"And," said Nina, "blueberries are good for you if you've 'got the blues', and sunflower seeds help you to feel sunny again."

Sandy regarded her sceptically. "Aren't you taking this a bit too far?"

"Nope. There's actual amino acids in sunflower seeds that help you feel good."[12] She stood up and began clearing the dirty dishes. "Now we have to get on with it because Billy's dad will be here any minute."

"He's here now," Billy said, with a glance out the window.

"We'll go and head him off," Nuncle offered, and he and Liz left the kitchen for some helpful (for once) adult chatter.

"Okay, well, my abracadabra affirmation," said Clare, "is: 'I have

---

11   Later Liz showed us a book called *Nature's Secret Messages: Hidden in Plain Sight* by Elaine Wilkes that had all this info and more.

12   The amino acid tryptophan is responsible for processing serotonin, which is the neurotransmitter that makes us feel good. Like the big words? I got them out of that book: *Nature's Secret Messages, Hidden in Plain Sight* by Elaine Wilkes – page 186!

lots of new friends and we get on really well', and that's obviously working because now I've got Serenity and actually I'm pretty happy with just her for now because we get on so well. And for my Invisibility thing I've been writing little notes to some kids at school who are kind of the outsiders."

She stopped suddenly and blushed a fierce red. "It's these kids who don't have any friends and they're not really my type either but I was feeling sorry for them, so I've been writing them little anonymous encouraging notes and slipping them into their bags when they're not looking."

"Wow," I said. We were all a bit dumbfounded. I mean, Clare used to be an outsider kind of person herself, not by us but by the rest of our old school, and she wasn't exactly the main centre of attraction at her new school, from what I had gathered so far.

"Like what?" Nina asked curiously.

"Like, 'Don't listen to the people who are teasing you. You've got great qualities. Believe in yourself.'"

"Wow," I said again. "That's really nice."

"It's quite fun," she said. "It feels good."

"What you put out comes back to you," Nina murmured.

"Sandy, tell your news," Clare said. She looked very pleased with herself.

"Um. Oh. Well. Affirmation. Haven't really thought of one yet. Probably just that I'm selling lots of stuff at the exhibition."

"It's already started, hasn't it?" I asked.

"Yeah. Friday night."

Better get on with it, I didn't say.

"And I cleaned Dad's boots but he didn't seem to notice. Didn't say anything, anyway."

"Maybe he was so surprised he didn't know what to say," Clare suggested. "Or maybe he thought it was your mum or one of your brothers."

Sandy shrugged. "Who knows? He never talks much to anyone."

Voices were approaching the kitchen-back-door of the house.

"I've gotta go," Billy said, standing up.

"Thanks for fitting it in," Nina said. "It wouldn't have felt the same without you."

"That's okay. Thanks for making it at a time I could come," he replied awkwardly. "And if you're talking to Joel ask if I can give him a ring."

"Okay," Nina said. "I'm sure he'd like that."

The door opened and Liz and Nuncle entered with Billy's dad, who Clare and Sandy and I had known for years, but hardly knew since he'd always worked such long hours, so we'd barely ever seen him. It wasn't easy to imagine him camping; in fact, it was strange to see him in jeans. He usually wore a suit.

"Hi kids," he said. "Been having a good time?"

"Yeah," we replied, and that was about where the conversation ended. So after a moment when it became obvious that no-one was going to say anything else very interesting, Billy started with his goodbyes, and in a short time it was just me, Sandy, Clare and Nina, standing outside in the sun after Billy and his dad had rumbled away, with his bike in the back of an expensive-looking Land Rover.

"Now," Nina said, rounding on us; "it's really quite perfect that Billy has left early because I have something to tell you and it's for girls' ears only. Come with me!"

CHAPTER 20

SURPRISING NEWS, SHOCKING NEWS

WE CLATTERED BACK up to her room in her wake, and as soon as we had all burst in, she dug into her overnight bag and then presented each of us with a sealed envelope with our name on it.

"What's this?" Sandy asked, turning it in her hands.

"Open it and see."

"Why not for Bill too?" I asked.

"Open it and see!!!" Nina exclaimed. "What's with you guys?"

I worked my finger into a loose corner and slit the envelope open raggedly. There was a card inside, heart-shaped and red. I drew it out and opened it. It was a hand-made invitation. I read it silently.

Dear Natalie,

You are invited to Nina's Red Tent Party, on the occasion of her 13th birthday, to celebrate her rite of passage into womanhood.

Date: Friday 13th April, 5 pm until Saturday 14th April 12 pm.

Venue: Liz & Nuncle's house

Please bring something yummy to eat and something that is a symbol of womanhood.

We hope you can come.

Love,

Rosie and Liz and Nina.

"What's the red tent thing about?" Sandy asked suspiciously.

"It's from a book about how women in biblical times used to get together in a red tent to do all their women's business, like when they were menstruating or giving birth."[13] Nina was sitting on the bed cross-legged, watching us. "Usually the only women who were invited into the Red Tent were the ones who already had their periods, but I don't know if you have yours yet and I wanted to invite you three because you're my best friends."

For a moment I wondered if Nina had any other friends, to say nothing of best friends. How had she gone for so many years on her own without friends? As for us, Sandy and Clare and I might have been best friends since we were toddlers, but we'd never spoken about periods before. I'd had my first one during

---

13   *The Red Tent* by Anita Diamant. She showed it to us.

the summer – just a bit of a brownish stain on my undies that had totally taken me by surprise. Mum had been quite excited and acted like it was all special; she even took me out for lunch, just the two of us, but I'd been a bit embarrassed about all the fuss. I hadn't had one since, but Mum had said it can be irregular at first.

"Well, I haven't started yet," Clare said. She looked at the rest of us. "Have you?"

"Just one little bit," I said. "In the summer holidays."

"Yeah, for ages," Sandy said. "So what?"

"So it's a special time," Nina replied earnestly. "Didn't you do anything special with your mum?"

"She wanted to make a fuss but I didn't let her," Sandy said. "It's embarrassing."

Oh… I had always thought Sandy and I were really different, but not in this, apparently…

"Older cultures have all sorts of rites of passage around becoming a man or a woman," Nina said, very informatively, "but it's just been totally lost to most of us in the west. Which they reckon is one of the reasons why there's so much crisis among young people – like drugs and graffiti and violence and even suicide. Rosie and I have been talking about it for a while, how it's such a big change in your life and deserves to be recognised and celebrated. She wanted to do a rite of passage for me, and the more we looked into it, the more I wanted to do it too."

For a moment I had a vision of Nina and Rosie curled up together on the couch in their lovely house in the country and talking about 'becoming a woman'. Maybe that was what my mother had tried to do when she took me out to lunch, only I hadn't really been very open to talking about it. I had kept changing the subject…

"But there's heaps of different ways of doing it," Nina was saying. "In some cultures it's a big event, like a wedding, which I definitely didn't want. And sometimes it's a religious thing, like the Jewish Bat-mitzvah, when it means they're ready to choose their religion for themselves, as adults, instead of just going along with it as they had when they were kids. But there's usually a party or a ceremony and gifts and special food and all sorts of symbolic stuff. Like your first pair of high-heeled shoes –"

"Ugh!" said Sandy. "Not for me!"

"Joel was telling us that to Aboriginals, a female's blood is considered really powerful and magical, and even dangerous for men. And in some cultures getting your period is the start of pretty much being an outcast every month for a few days, because you're considered unclean and you can't touch a male or even offer him food."

"They do call it 'the Curse'," Sandy remarked.

"Rosie said that has something to do with the Adam and Eve story, and being cast out of the Garden of Eden," Nina said. "I don't know. That's all a bit weird for me. I like the stories about rites of passage where it's a special occasion to honour and respect becoming a woman: how our bodies are changing and the first flow of blood when we get our periods, so we can now have babies and kind of keep life going on."

"Do you want to have babies?" Clare asked curiously.

"One day," Nina said. "I think it must be pretty special when it happens, don't you? When you're ready, I mean."

It all just seemed way too far off to be real to me. Having babies. Wow. That was way off in the future to me. Even just having a boyfriend wasn't very high on my list of priorities. I looked at the invitation again. "What do you mean by 'bring a symbol of womanhood'?"

"I don't know. Whatever that is to you," Nina replied unhelpfully.

"So what are we going to do?" Sandy asked, a little warily, "at this 'red tent party'?"

"Women's business," Nina said, with a mysterious expression.

And we were left with the mystery, because that was when Hazel arrived in her dusty white Suzuki to pick Clare and Sandy up. I reluctantly headed home as well, because Liz and Nuncle were taking Nina into the city for the afternoon.

I mooched around at home for the rest of the weekend, willing the time to pass until Sunday night, when I'd been invited to the Adult Mastermind Group.

"It's a what?" Mum and Dad asked, when I reminded them about it on Sunday afternoon.

"A Mastery Club for adults," I said. "It's been running for years. I'll know more after I've been to it."

"Fair enough," Dad said, putting his book down with a yawn. "If Max and Liz are at the helm, I'm sure it will be an enriching experience. What time do you have to be there? I'll walk over with you."

When we arrived, at quarter past seven, there were already a few cars in the driveway. We debated for a moment about going to the back-kitchen-door as usual, or knocking on the front door, but then someone climbed out of a car and went to the front door, so we followed them. They didn't bother knocking; just opened the door and walked straight in. We followed through the unusual house with its curvy passages and all-shaped windows, past the library room that was chock-a-block full of books, past the reading room, which was a sunroom full of plants and armchairs, past the staircase that wound up to Nina's attic room, and… into the kitchen where everyone was gathering. Dad and I gave each other The Look; you know, the roll-your-eyes 'we-might-as-well-have-gone-to-the-back-door-as-usual' look.

Nina bounced over through the crowd to hug me and shake Dad's hand, and I'm glad she did because I was on the verge of getting nervous with so many unknown adults. I was beginning to wonder why I'd agreed to come. These adults were noisy and obviously very old friends because they were making themselves right at home, opening cupboards and the fridge as if it was their place.

Nuncle came to say hi to me and chat with Dad, and Nina started to take me around and introduce me to everyone, which made me even more nervous because she told every person there that I was the first friend who'd joined the Mastery Club she started at school last year, and then they were all looking at me and shaking my hand and asking questions and making adult jokes like, "I hope our Club meets your standards!" which wasn't really very funny at all.

And then Dad left and we trooped into the lounge room with our cups of tea and dips and crackers and carrot sticks to munch on during the meeting. I looked for a spot where I could hide a bit and just watch. Nina was sitting on the floor and leaning against her dad's knees. She caught my eye and pointed to a beanbag in the corner, beckoning me to bring it near, so I dragged it over and sank into it next to her. Which put me slap-bang in the middle of the room, not exactly the hidey spot I'd had in mind.

When everyone was settled, Nuncle embarrassed me totally by saying, "Before we start we'd like to formally welcome our guest, Nina's lovely friend Natalie, who seems to have as great a hunger for these ideas as we have."

Everybody looked at me then and lots of voices called out "Welcome, Natalie!" I blushed a hot red and mumbled "Thank you".

"We'll start with our usual moment of meditation," he went on, and then again spoke to me, and I realised, in horror, that he was probably going to do that all night: single me out to explain what they were doing. Oh no!

"You know the visualisation you do in your Club meetings?" he asked. "Well, we like to start with a few moments of quietness while everyone concentrates on their breathing and brings their attention to their heart, to their feelings of love and gratitude."

"Okay," I said, wishing everyone would stop looking at me.

Nuncle gave me a warm and gentle smile, as if he knew exactly how I was feeling. I felt as if he was saying, *'Relax, Natalie, you're with friends who love you,'* and my embarrassed feelings melted away a little.

Pete switched a CD player on and some beautiful, restful music began playing, and everyone closed their eyes and sat still.

I closed my eyes too, and was instantly aware of my heart beating quite strongly. As my breathing slowed down, it seemed to grow calmer. I listened to the sounds of breathing from Nina and the people near me, and to the music (which sounded like a harp)… and I wondered how to bring up feelings of love and gratitude. I knew that I loved my family, but right now they seemed very far away, and just thinking about them didn't make me feel love. Should it have? I wondered about that… Okay then, what *was* I grateful for?

It didn't take me long to realise that, despite my discomfort, I was grateful that I was here, grateful that I knew Nina and her family. I remembered the warmth I had felt a few minutes ago from Nuncle, and the delight in Nina's smile that I was sharing in things that were so important to her.

At that, a feeling of love actually did fill my heart, and to my surprise, my eyes began to fill with tears. I blinked and shifted my weight, and the beanbag squeaked and sighed and I realised that maybe it hadn't been such a good choice of a seat after all. I spent the last few minutes of the meditation time with my eyes shut but distracted, trying not to move and almost holding my breath. It was a relief when Nuncle began to speak again.

"Liz and I would like to thank you all for your support during the last couple of months," he said quietly. "The tests have come in positive, so it does look like we have a tumour to deal with. We're welcoming the opportunity for growth that cancer brings, and would like to ask you all to finish your meditation by holding Liz in your hearts and minds, totally healed and whole again."

My eyes snapped open in shock. Cancer! Nina's beautiful and healthy Aunt Liz? Surely not!

Nina was looking at me with inscrutable grey eyes. She gave a tiny nod, and then closed her eyes again to join everyone in blessing her aunt. I searched the room for Liz, and found her sitting on the couch next to Rosie, both with eyes closed in still, calm faces. They were holding hands.

I made myself close my eyes but all I could think was, "Liz! Cancer…"

CHAPTER 21

IN MY WORLD, NOTHING GOES WRONG

BUT WHAT SURPRISED me even more was everybody's response to this news. When they opened their eyes to start the meeting, nobody seemed shocked or even particularly worried. A couple of people asked Liz questions about the tests she'd had and she answered them, and then a tall bearded man said, "In my world, nothing goes wrong," and they all grinned and raised their cups, saying, "Amen to that!" and "So be it!"

Nuncle caught my eye and, reading my shocked expression, remembered his task of explaining everything to me. "I'm sorry, Natalie," he said. "I've just realised this is all news to you. Liz has been diagnosed with cancer, as you've gathered. We've known about it for a few months now but we don't see it as a death sentence, as so many do. We choose to see it as an opportunity for learning and growth, and since all people are connected, our group has decided to all work with the issues it brings up for Liz in our own lives too."

"But how did she get it?" I burst out. "Liz, you're so healthy!"

"Now," Liz grinned, "but you didn't see me through most of my life, honey-bunch. As a model I was calorie-conscious but I wasn't eating very healthily. And it was a stressful life: I smoked, I drank; I lived at the hairdressers and nail technicians and make-up artists, so I was saturated in toxic chemicals all the time. It caught up with me, sweetheart. Put simply, my body needs to do a big detox and get rid of all that accumulated crap. In fact, it's very likely that all those chemicals were part of why I wasn't able to have kids."

"So no chemotherapy for you," a pink-faced woman with fluffy hair said.

"Nope," Liz agreed, "no cut, burn or poison for this girl. We're going the natural road all the way, even if I end up in a box."

I stared at her in horror.

"But that's not the plan," she said with a wink. "There are plenty of people who have cleared cancer out of their bodies through fasting and raw diets, and that's what I'm doing. Which is why I'm skinnier than I've been in years."

Now that I thought about it, I realised I hadn't actually seen Liz eating for a while. She'd prepared food for us but I'd only seen her sipping glasses of water with lemon…

"And then there's the emotional side of it," she added. "Whatever we feel is most missing becomes most important to us, and I felt ugly as a kid, so I was always working hard to look beautiful, hence the decision to be a model. And I was pretty angry with my parents for judging my choice of vocation. They thought I was flaunting my femininity, and I got all mixed up with guilt and defensiveness and resentment – a nice little cocktail of emotional toxins. So it's time to love myself and love them and do some healing."

"You know how our Club motto is 'See the Invisible' and all

that?" Nina said, "well, their motto is the idea that to a master or an alchemist, nothing goes wrong; so no matter what happens in their lives, they have the power to take what they've been given and transform it into something else."

"The alchemist, or master, transmutes base experiences into high ones," the bearded man affirmed. "It's the path of transformation instead of resistance and reaction."

"Exactly," said Nuncle. "You remember the story I told your Club last year about the Old Man and the Horse? Everything is part of a bigger picture – just something to learn and grow through; so we've chosen to support each other in seeing each challenge in our lives as an opportunity instead of a threat."

"The old 'what are you making it mean' lesson." Nina raised her eyebrows meaningfully at me.

"After all, if you change the way you look at things," Rosie pointed out, "the things you look at change."

I realised I'd been holding my breath, and let it out slowly. Everything they were saying made sense, but I still felt worried about Liz.

"And sometimes we need to travel these confronting and uncomfortable roads because they are somehow a part of our life purpose," an Indian man said. "Perhaps we will meet someone on this new path who is critical to the unfoldment of our journey."

"Or we'll come across some critical information," the pink-faced woman said, passing a sheet of paper to Liz. "You obviously know about hydrogen peroxide for bleaching hair, being a model, but did you know that you can take a dilution of the food grade version and use it for healing cancer? Apparently it tastes disgusting but it's been known to help reverse even the most aggressive cancers." [14]

---

14   www.oneminutecure.com

"Thank you," Liz said, reaching across for the paper. "You see, Nat? I'm learning, growing, being supported. I'll be fine."

"We call it The Law of Higher Good," Nuncle said. "Otherwise known as Divine Order. No matter how something looks, it's of service in our evolutionary journey."

Then they started to give examples of Divine Order in their lives: the child born with Down Syndrome that had unified a troubled family, the retrenchment that had resulted in a better job, the car accident that had caused someone to have to walk to work, making him fitter and happier; and for Nuncle, the marriage breakdown that had led to a more fulfilling marriage with Liz…

"Life is just a series of transformations to the master," the bearded man said. "Things happen in our lives, and we tend to judge them as good or bad, which is a natural human response, but then most people get locked into their judgements. What we're endeavouring to do here is to create our reality consciously, so as soon as we become aware of making a judgement that causes us to feel out of balance, we change how we're thinking about it so that we're viewing the issue as an alchemist would – or as a master would. Because in a master's world, nothing goes wrong. Instead of resisting experiences, a master sees each situation as a gift, and in doing so, transforms it."

I wondered how they did that. Did they use visualisation and treasure maps, the way our Mastery Club did? Or something else? Before I could spend much more time wondering, my question was answered. And, funnily enough, it seemed that one of the key things they did was to ask questions.

"The quality of your life is based on the quality of your questions, Natalie," Nuncle said, "so we're going to endeavour to ask some really good questions now to help Liz get into the core of the issue."[15]

Everyone was taking out notebooks and pens. Nina handed me some paper and a blue texta. Some of the questions reminded me of Nuncle's Good Stuff, Bad Stuff Game, like what was the benefit of having cancer, and Liz said things like 'a wake-up call', and 'time to stop and go slow and heal' – which reminded me of her turtle mosaic outside… but some of the questions were a bit weird, like identifying the characteristics of cancer that were upsetting. Liz said, 'its invasiveness'. And then she was asked to identify where *she* was invasive, and how that served other people, and she listed off times and places that she was pushy and took over.

My head was spinning. I couldn't relate to Liz being pushy, she seemed so nice, but when I thought about Sandy's pushiness I could see how it made Clare stand up for herself, and it had made Nina and Sandy sort out some of their differences, so I could understand that there might be some benefits in that sort of quality. But I was glad when the meeting came to an end and Dad turned up at the door to collect me.

15   A while after this meeting Nuncle lent my mum and dad a book about this technique because Mum was so freaked out about Liz and her cancer… but I'm getting ahead of myself. If you're interested, it's called *The Breakthrough Experience – A Revolutionary New Approach to Personal Transformation* by Dr John Demartini.

Mastery Club Lesson #17

'In My World, Nothing Goes Wrong'

* Everything serves.

* To a master, nothing goes wrong because everything is an expression of Divine Order – it's our job to find it…

CHAPTER 22

DANGEROUS IDEAS

I HADN'T INTENDED to say anything about Liz to Mum or Dad, but the next morning at breakfast it just came burbling out of me; how she had cancer and they were all okay about it and she was going to create her reality and get well again without any doctoring.

Mum was shocked through and through. "I think that's a very dangerous idea," she said, putting her cup of coffee down. "I can't imagine what they think they're on about. There I was, entrusting you to their care and you tell me this! It's absurd. It's crazy. They're insane. Natalie, I'm not sure that I want you to keep going with this Mastery Club."

I began to regret telling her.

"I haven't said anything about these ideas you've been learning because it seemed to be doing you some good." Mum started clearing the table with a restless energy. "But I've been a bit concerned that it's just not based in reality, that they're filling your heads with absurd ideas – Charlie! Are you aware of this?"

"What?" Dad called from somewhere in the house.

"The meeting at Liz and Max's house last night," Mum called back. "Liz has cancer, the poor thing, and they're saying that she should just, you know, close her eyes and imagine herself well or something. And not see a doctor or do anything responsible or sensible!"

Dad came in. "What was that?"

Mum said it all again, while I sat at the table feeling anxious and knotted in the stomach. Who was right? So much of what I'd learned from Nina and Nuncle made sense to me, but when Mum put it like this… I just wasn't sure anymore.

"Now don't overreact," Dad said calmly. (The Barrister) "They've got their heads screwed on over there. I'm sure it's not as crazy as you think."

"Why won't she go and see a doctor?" Mum asked me. "How can that hurt?"

"She's fasting," I said, "to clean out the toxins." But that just made matters worse.

"Fasting! That'll weaken her." Mum closed a cupboard door with a little bang. "How is she supposed to get healthy if she doesn't eat anything?"

"I don't know," I mumbled.

The phone rang then, so I jumped up to answer it, relieved that I could now escape the conversation, but it was Nina, wondering how I was after last night's meeting and hearing Liz's news. This was the first time ever that I wasn't sure I wanted to talk to Nina. Especially with Mum in the background all steamed up.

"Are you okay?" she asked.

"Yes…" I took the phone to the hallway and sat on the stairs. "Well, sort of. I'm still a bit shocked. And I told Mum and she's *really* shocked. I mean, is it really safe for Liz to not go to the doctor and have it cut out or whatever? That's what most people do."

"And then most people get cancer again because they didn't

get to the cause of it," Nina said promptly. "Did you know that something like the third biggest cause of death in the world is medical intervention?[16] There are heaps of cancer specialists who won't even allow their family to have chemotherapy because they know how dangerous it is."[17]

"But what if she dies?"

"She might die either way. She could die tomorrow, crossing the road."

"Yes, but…"

"Cancer's not such a bad thing, Natalie. People are scared of it because it's getting to plague proportions.[18] But that's because most people have been eating bad diets and getting exposed to lots of chemicals and having beliefs that don't serve them. Really it's a blessing. It's a wake-up call for Liz to clean the toxins out of her body, for one."

"But… should she be fasting? Won't that make her weak?"

"Fasting gives the body a great big rest from having to digest, which takes up most of its energy, so then all that energy can go to healing. The actual word 'fast' means 'make strong or firm' – something like that; not 'make weak'."

"But is that enough? Is fasting enough?" Even as I spoke, I realised that Nina was echoing all the things that Liz and Rosie had told her, just as I was being the voice of my mother's fears and concerns.

"It's a big part of the plan, but she's doing lots of other stuff too. She's stopped her consulting work so she can rest a lot, she's

---

16   It's called 'iatrogenic disease'. You'll find that 'ia' word in the dictionary.

17   www.RaveDiet.com

18   The 'war on cancer' has resulted in more people than ever getting sick with cancer and dying: http://www.naturalnews.com/032700_National_Cancer_Institute_Dr_Samuel_Epstein.html

lying out in the sun every day because the sun is a major healer, she's walking and doing yoga, she's watching funny movies with Nuncle because laughter is healing, and when she goes back to eating she'll mainly just eat raw foods for a while."

I changed the phone to my other ear. Mum and Dad were still talking in the kitchen.

"Most people wouldn't do all of that stuff," Nina was saying, "because they want to be able to just pop a pill and be better without changing any of their habits. But the body is a very powerful healer if you just support it. And then she's doing all the mind stuff too; she's visualising herself well and affirming that she's well and digging up beliefs that aren't serving her."

"I didn't really understand that," I confessed. "Was Liz saying that she was so mad with her parents for criticising her for being a model that she got cancer from that?" I'd been mad with my parents for all sorts of stuff. Did that mean I was cooking cancer too?

"Sort of. You see, if we have a big emotional reaction to something and we push it down instead of dealing with it, the stress of it gets locked into our cells and tissues and then later it comes out as illness. Which is why people need to get to the cause of things to really heal them, rather than just cut the sick tissue out."

"But people get angry all the time..."

"Yes, and it doesn't always lead to cancer. Sometimes it leads to stomach aches or headaches or backaches or skin rashes..." she gave a little giggle and then got serious again. "You know what? Some people have cleared up serious illnesses really fast just from getting an insight into what was causing it and making a change in their consciousness. Because when a true change happens on the inside, in the mind, it happens on the outside too – in the body."[19]

"But what if you don't find the insight?" I asked, still worried. "I know our thoughts are really powerful," I added, feeling like a traitor, "but is changing your beliefs really powerful enough to save your life?"

"You know how you can get people who drink and smoke and have terrible diets their whole life but they stay healthy? That's probably because they have great beliefs – they probably love life and love themselves. Love is the big trump card that can overcome anything – even chemo and surgery, I guess. It's just that our family likes doing things in holistic ways and getting to the cause. Hey, do you want to come over today and talk to Liz and Nuncle about it?" she asked brightly. "We'll be here all day. We're not going home 'til tonight."

"Mum doesn't want me to be in the Mastery Club anymore," I blurted. "She thinks the ideas are dangerous."

There was a little pause. "Oh." Nina's voice was flat and a bit strange. "So… are you going to stop?"

There was a longer pause while I sat with this problem. "No," I said at last. "But I might not come over today."

"Okay," she said. But she sounded funny.

---

19 Brandon Bays, author of *The Journey*®, and many others. Dr John Demartini has discovered the language patterns that indicate the 'cancer personality', and his Breakthrough Experience helps people trans-form…

CHAPTER 23

UPS AND DOWNS

THE REST OF that day was kind of strange. Mum was a bit calmer when I got off the phone so I guess Dad had said something that soothed her. But all day I felt this push/pull toward Liz and Nuncle's house, like I wanted to go but didn't. Then Clare rang to invite me to Sandy's exhibition with her and her mum, and I said yes, for something to take my mind off it. But I felt bad that I wasn't suggesting we invite Nina too, especially as she was just around the corner for a change.

I told Clare about Liz's cancer in a private moment when Hazel wasn't around – I wasn't making that mistake twice! And she was shocked too. But she said, quite confidently, "Liz will be okay. She'll face up to it and sort it out." I wished I could be so sure.

Sandy had been at the Pottery Exhibition all morning and was about to leave when we arrived. I didn't want to say anything to her in her moment of glory. She took us around and pointed out her stuff, which looked every bit as good and professional as the adult work. Her Uncle Brendan was a smiley overweight guy with a bald patch. He shook our hands and put an arm around Sandy's shoulder, saying, "She's made some great pieces, hasn't she?" and Sandy didn't even shrug his arm off. She just smiled and didn't say anything at all. I was gob-smacked.

Her parents had been to the exhibition last night, and her mum had bought one of her sculptures, a kookaburra. Sandy had mixed feelings about that. It's kind of weird when your parents pay you for something you've done – apart from pocket money for housework, of course. She felt like she should have just given it to them but her mum insisted. And someone else had bought something – she didn't know who but there was a big red 'sold' dot on a possum.

As soon as Hazel had dropped me off at home, I started thinking about Liz and Nina and all of that again, and the uncomfortable feelings started churning around. Then on Tuesday Miss Walker came up to me first thing and said she'd arranged for me and those other kids to meet in the Library, Study Room A, at lunchtime on Wednesday – tomorrow!! – so I was stuck. And just at a time when I felt the most mixed up about being in a Mastery Club myself.

I grabbed Sandy and Billy at the caf during recess and told them Liz's news. (I felt a bit uncomfortable doing that, but I needed someone to talk to about it, and I was pretty sure Nina's family wouldn't mind. After all, the others had been invited to the adult mastermind group too, so they would have been in the know by now if they'd been able to be there.)

They stood stock-still in the middle of the noisy caf, staring at me.

"Man," said Billy, "that's a bit of a shock."

Sandy dug her hands into those straining pockets. "Does she seem okay?"

"Yes, she seems fine. But I had this big blow-up at home when I told Mum. She reckons the Mastery Club ideas are dangerous, and she doesn't want me to do it anymore."

"Dangerous?"

"Using your mind to heal instead of going to a doctor."

A boisterous group of kids went charging past us, bumping into me roughly as they passed.

"Come here," Billy said, and he led us out of the rowdy caf to a bench outside. "You know that story Nina told us about the two men whose letters got mixed up and the one who was sick got better and the one who was well got sick? Well, the other day Terry told me that something like that actually happened in his family ages ago. His grandfather had been sick so they went to the doctor and had some tests and the tests came back saying he had cancer, but the grandfather also didn't speak much English, so he couldn't really understand what the doctor was saying. He just kept nodding like he understood but he didn't.

"So then he and the grandmother went home from the doctor's and she never told him that he had cancer. She knew he hadn't understood it properly, so she made up some other thing like he'd had a virus or something and he was fine now, and she sent him out to mow the lawn. And every time he said he was feeling a bit funny, she said 'You're fine', and gave him a job to do. And twenty years later he's still okay. He's had all sorts of other ills, but no cancer."[20]

Sometimes I'd wondered about Nina's stories, and how true they were. It was good to hear this and know that it could really happen, that the mind really could have such an effect. So then maybe… maybe Liz would be all right?

Sandy squatted down to retie her shoe. "I know her ideas are pretty weird and out there," she said, "but I wouldn't stay in the Club if I didn't think there was something in it."

I started to feel like a bit of a traitor, and suddenly I saw that

---

20   Based on a true story – but this is not medical advice!

Sandy and I had changed places, just like Nina had said we might: Sandy supporting, and me doubting and challenging. It was a shock.

The bell rang for the end of recess but we didn't move. "Maybe we can do one of those Invisibility things for Liz and Nuncle," Billy suggested.

"That's a great idea," I said. "Let's talk about it on Friday with Clare. And hey, thanks for telling us about Terry's grandfather."

"By the way, how was your camping trip?" Sandy asked, turning to look at him.

Bill shrugged. "Okay. Dad forgot to bring matches *and* the can opener, so that was a serious screw-up, especially since just about every meal was out of a tin."

I grinned. Typical.

"But it was all right. Someone turned up late at night and lent us some stuff. The place we went to was ace. We did this really long hike way off the beaten track and ended up near an inland lake. *So* quiet. The tallest trees you've ever seen. Yeah, it was nice there."

The second bell rang and a passing teacher gave us a raised-eyebrows 'aren't you meant to be going to class?' look, so we got up slowly and headed off. But I was feeling better.

Nuncle rang that night and had a long talk with Dad on the phone. Then with Mum. I could hear her saying, "Of course you must do whatever seems right to you…" when I went into the kitchen for a glass of water. I dawdled a little bit, and she said, "just concerned that Natalie will –" and then she saw me and took the phone into her office. I hate that. I hate knowing people are talking about you as if it's none of your business. So then I stood right outside the door, trying to hear what she was saying, but I could only pick up the odd word.

Dad came past and saw me there. "Eavesdropping, eh?" he said.

I flushed. "Well, she's talking about me."

"With the door closed," he said, "which probably means she wants some privacy."

"But it's about me," I argued.

"Parents have the right to sort out their concerns about a child without the child's involvement." Dad opened the door to the kitchen and gestured for me to go in. "Sometimes it's better that the child doesn't witness parents going through their agonies of doubt and confusion. Parenting ain't easy, mate. You kids don't come with an instruction manual, you know."

Closing the kitchen door behind me, he opened the freezer door with a conspiratorial wink. "Ice cream?"

"Sure." I grabbed a couple of spoons and bowls.

"What your mother is really worried about," he said, as he dug into the chocolate ice cream with a big serving spoon, "is that you'll start thinking that you don't need to take action in the world to make things happen, but you can just, what do you call it? visualise, and then poof! it'll land in your lap. Life isn't like that."

"I know." I climbed onto a stool. "Our Mastery Club is about taking action too. We're always talking about what we can do."

He passed me a bowl and started to fill one for himself. "It sounds to me like Liz is doing lots of sensible things. I know her approach isn't mainstream but it may well work. And she can always change her tactics."

The ice cream was delicious. Chilly to the teeth but delicious.

"Miss Walker's asked me to start a Mastery Club," I said. "For school kids."

"Really?" Dad looked at me appraisingly. "Are you going to?"

"The first one is tomorrow. She kind of sprang it on me. Kim told her about our Club, would you believe? They know each other from Yoga classes."

"Indeed? Kimmie? Well, tell me how it goes," he said. "I'll be interested."

So Dad wasn't going to stop me doing Mastery Club stuff. And I guessed Mum wouldn't either. She was just a bit freaked out.

I scraped my bowl and let the last spoonful of ice cream melt into my mouth. And then I started worrying about what I would do in that meeting tomorrow at lunchtime in the Library, Study Room A...

CHAPTER 24

Study Room A
& The Land of Take-
What-You-Want

I MET MISS WALKER in the library at ten to one. She smiled at me cheerfully, not noticing how terrified I was feeling (damp hands, heart about to jump out through my throat, shaky legs…), led me to Study Room A and unlocked the door. There was a table in the middle of the room with eight chairs pulled in around it. Miss Walker put a stack of paper and some coloured marker pens on the table and began to examine the room.

"Shall we leave the chairs around the table?" she asked me, with a thoughtful look on her face.

"I suppose so." I put my Record Book for Magic on the table and then picked it up again and hugged it to my chest.

"Just tell them a bit about what you did in your Club," she said, with an encouraging smile.

We sat at the table and waited for the others. Three of the walls were glass so everyone in the library could look in. I felt very self-conscious. My palms were sweaty and my mouth was dry. Nina would have eaten this up but I just wanted to run away.

The first person to arrive was a very studious Asian boy with glasses. His name was Mark and he was in Billy's homeroom – at least, I thought so. He sat down and began to read a book. In his wake was Tom, who I recognised from my homeroom, a gangly boy with big ears and a loud, clumsy sort of manner who seemed to be a bit of a loner. Tom perched on the edge of the table and started talking to Miss Walker, then he wandered to the glass wall and knocked on it to get someone's attention, and then was back to the table again. While he was all over the place, Petra, who reminded me of how Clare used to be at our old school (shy, with downcast eyes), slunk into a seat and sat looking down at her lap. Miss Walker was glancing at her watch when two Year 8 girls called Holly and Bree burst in, chatting and giggling. My heart sank. Shy, nervous kids were easy to talk to; it was these confident ones who were scary.

It was hard to tell if the last person who came in was a boy or a girl, except for the school uniform dress. She was tall and thin, with very short fair hair and a flat chest. Long fine fingers kept playing with a long blonde fringe. Kat was the name, I discovered. She took the last seat and looked at me intently through the wispy fringe.

"Thanks for coming," Miss Walker said. "I've invited each one of you specifically because of things you've said or interests you've shown, or because I think you would particularly benefit from being part of this group. Some of you know Natalie, from 7B. She's going to share with us her experiences of being part of a Mastery Club." Miss Walker turned to me expectantly.

Everyone was looking at me expectantly.

I swallowed. "Hi," I said, and licked lips that were as dry

as if I'd been in the Sahara all day. Everything I'd planned to say had gone right out of my mind. They say that when you're really enjoying something, time speeds up, and when you're not enjoying something, it goes really slowly. I knew that for sure now. I could just about feel the seconds tick tick ticking past…

What will I say? I asked silently, desperately, although I didn't know who or what I was asking. As if in answer to prayer, Clare's voice came to me: *About the lessons and the basketball experiment and visualisation – stuff like that.*

So I just opened my mouth and launched in. I told them about Nina coming to my school last year and wanting to start up a Mastery Club where we learnt about our minds and we set goals and achieved them. I told them about visualisation, and how the brain can't tell the difference between something that is real and something that is imagined, which is why those basketballers were able to get pretty much the same result from just imagining shooting perfect baskets as the team that actually practised every day.

They were pretty interested in that. Holly and Bree started to talk about trying visualisation with their netball team.

"So what have *you* done with this?" Mark asked, pushing his specs up his nose.

Miss Walker couldn't contain herself. "Natalie visualised her family going to the Greek Islands for a holiday – and they're heading off this July!"

They all stared at me in amazement. Put like that, it sounded like sheer magic. But I'd had to grapple with my fears and doubts, I'd had to visualise regularly, I'd had to affirm, I'd had to take action with a treasure map and learn Greek and make Greek sweets… And, it seemed, my Gran had had to die…

I was thinking about that when Petra said, "So are we going to be a Mastery Club and, sort of… imagine some goals?"

"That's what I was hoping you'd be interested in doing," Miss Walker said eagerly. "We could inspire the whole school! What do you think?"

"Yeah," Tom said. "There's this ace computer game I want."

"But what happens if two people want the same thing, like to be Team Captain?" Holly asked. "Or if two teams want the same trophy," she and Bree exchanged glances, "and they're *both* visualising for it? Who gets it?"

"Yes," Mark agreed. "If all kids started using these principles someone must get disappointed."

I was stumped. I'd never thought about that before. Billy and Clare and Sandy and Nina and I had each wanted such different things. I flushed, brain racing.

Miss Walker stepped in. "I imagine it must go to the person or team who most deserves it through their level of commitment and the actions they take," she replied confidently.

"What about my brother, then?" Bree argued. "He gets straight As all the time and he never does any work."

"Just lucky," Holly pronounced.

"When people love doing something or have mastered it, they unleash greater ability," Miss Walker said, "and sometimes it looks effortless."

Holly and Bree exchanged doubtful glances.

But what would Nina say about who wins out of several? I wondered, as my brain darted here and there searching for the answer. And again my brain answered, with just one little word: *"Order".*

"And…" I said cautiously, "there's this other principle in the universe that everything is working perfectly, no matter how it looks. So if two people are visualising and only one of them gets it, it's probably because it wasn't right for the other person to get it."

"So how do you know if the thing you want is right for you?"

Kat asked in a slow, lazy voice.

"Because you love it," I said simply, thinking about Sandy and her pottery. "But maybe you won't know for sure until after you get it and you realise it's not exactly what you want. Or you might start going for it because you're really sure you want it, but not get it and not understand why until later." I wasn't sure where that answer had come from. By now, all I wanted was for the bell to ring and let me out of this torture-chamber. Out of the corner of my eye I saw Sandy skulking around in the library and watching us. *Make it up,* she had said. Well, I was doing that all right!

"You'll never get two athletes doing exactly the same preparation to the same degree," Miss Walker pointed out. "One will want the trophy more and see their dream more clearly. They'll feel they deserve it more, train harder, be more disciplined, fear success less, listen more to their trainers... They're the ones who win. But if you're trying to achieve something that you think you *should* without really valuing it yourself or really committing yourself, you're much less likely to be successful."

"So then I don't have to bother with schoolwork anymore?" Kat drawled.

Miss Walker answered her tartly. "Being at school is a big part of your lives until you're seventeen or so, and I'd suggest that you're best off doing whatever you can to be successful here. Find a way to make this important to you or you're in for a tedious few years."

Nina had said something like that to me once. Suddenly I had a brainwave. "There's this thing called First Force, Second Force, Third Force," I told them, "where your First Force is your effort to achieve your goal, and then the Second Force is what happens, like maybe not achieving it or obstacles and delays. Your Third Force is what you do next; if you give up or keep going for it." I stopped, and then added in a rush: "You have to kind of trust that the things that stop you are part of the process.

If you fail at something, it's probably so you'll smarten up your skills and that, and then try again."

"Good point, Natalie." Miss Walker glanced at her watch. "We're almost out of time. I'd like to propose that you each choose a goal of some sort and that we trial this Club for the rest of the term – there are only a few weeks to go – and then you can decide if you'd like to keep meeting next term. What do you say?"

"Okay," Tom agreed, and the others nodded or said yes. So then we went into the choosing phase. Holly and Bree had netball goals, of course, and Tom wanted his game. Petra said she'd have to think about it and Mark said something about a chess championship. Kat looked at me sideways and said she might go for a holiday in Bali. I had a funny feeling when she said that, like there was something I was forgetting.

Then the bell went and everyone vamoosed and Miss Walker congratulated me on 'a good first session'. I escaped in relief, only to have someone grab my arm. It was Sandy, curious to know how it had gone. I felt a little dart of anger that she hadn't wanted to help but had the time to spy.

"It was okay," I said, "no thanks to you."

I think my dart found its home. She looked away, and this time I felt a pang of guilt.

"They asked me all these questions I didn't know the answer to," I said. "I'm not Nina; I don't know!"

"You're not supposed to be Nina," Sandy said. "You're supposed to be you."

When I got home I looked at the phone. Ring Nina? I was torn between wanting to tell her how it went and ask her questions – kind of 'report' to her, as my leader – and reluctance to speak to her at all… because then we'd be sure to start talking about Liz… So I didn't, and I felt bad all evening.

That night Mum asked me to read the siblings their bedtime story since she had a lot on her plate. When I sat on Katie's bed she handed me *The Magic Faraway Tree* by Enid Blyton. (This series is almost sacred in my house. Mum loved them when she was a kid and I loved them when I was little and now the siblings were into them too. They're about some kids who stumble upon an enchanted forest and a magical tree that is connected to all these fantasy lands, and they have some pretty kooky adventures.)

When Katie handed me the book, it was open at the chapter about the Land of Take-What-You-Want. Figures. Ever since Nina had come into my life with her new ideas I'd found myself bumping into those ideas, in one form or another, all over the place. Or maybe it was my R.A.S., just noticing connections…

As I read about the children and Silky and Moonface getting into trouble in this crazy land, I was reminded of the conversation today in Study Room A. Could people have whatever they wanted? What if they wanted stupid things or things that weren't good for them? What if the things they wanted caused problems for other people? What if people did get absolutely anything they wanted whenever they wanted it? That sounded good, but as Jo and Fanny and the others in The Faraway Tree were finding, getting what you wanted could actually be quite disastrous.

CHAPTER 25

THE YIN-YANG OF IT ALL

THE NEXT DAY at school Miss Walker treated me to a sunny smile as soon as I arrived in our homeroom, and then for the rest of the day I kept running into those kids from the Mastery Club. Tom careened into me in the corridor between classes and gave me a huge conspiratorial wink. Petra stopped me in the girls' toilets to nervously say that she was thinking of making her goal a mouse. (Her mother hated mice and didn't want any in the house, but Petra had always wanted one. Did I think she could go for a mouse? I said, I supposed so…)

When I went to check some books out at the library, Mark was already in the queue with a pile of books in his arms. He indicated the two at the top – one was about the brain (he was planning to research things like visualisation, or 'mental rehearsal' as they described it in sports psychology, he informed me), and the other had an image of the Eastern yin-yang symbol on its cover. You know, that circle divided in half by a curvy line and one side is black with a white dot, and the other side is white with a black dot?

When he took a step forward to borrow his books, he dropped the lot. We both knelt to pick them up. The yin-yang book had fallen open on a page with another picture of the symbol and some words in bold; they jumped out at me as I reached for the book: "*...the ancient Chinese understanding of how things work. The outer circle represents everything, while the black and white shapes within the circle represent the interaction of two balanced energies, called 'yin' (black) and 'yang' (white), which cause everything to happen.*" I stood up slowly with the book open in my hands, still reading, "*They are not completely black or white, just as things in life are not completely black or white, and they cannot exist without each other.*" Wow! The Law of Polarity. I closed the book and handed it back to Mark with respect and a bit of anxiety. At this rate, he would soon know more about it all than me...

I didn't see any sign of Bree and Holly but Sandy reported that she'd overheard them talking about visualising with their netball team. And Kat kept turning up everywhere. She didn't speak to me at all, but I just kept noticing her here and there. Sometimes she'd be looking at me through that long blonde fringe, and sometimes she was absorbed in something else and didn't see me at all. But when she did, she never smiled or waved. Just looked at me. It was a bit weird.

That yin-yang symbol followed me around for the rest of the day too. I found myself doodling it on my book, or thinking about the words I'd read. Especially the words 'and they cannot exist without each other'. So nothing could be only good or bad, just as Nina had always said...

That afternoon I rang Nina as soon as I got home. She answered immediately, almost as if she'd been camping by the phone waiting for me to call.

"Hi," she said, warmly, but without her usual eagerness; kind of a bit warily.

"I've realised what's bothering me," I told her, walking upstairs with the phone. "It's that, ever since I met you, I've sort of thought of you and your family as perfect, you know. Like people who are masters and don't have problems like the rest of us."

"That's crazy," she said at once.

"I know." I went into my room and closed the door. "But I guess I was so shocked about Liz being sick because it sort of broke that idea. I guess I wanted you all to be perfect."

"We *are* perfect," she said, shocking me again. She waited a moment – for dramatic effect, then giggled and said, "We're perfectly balanced with good and bad sides to us. That's the perfectness. If we were just all one side we wouldn't be perfect at all."

"But most people think being perfect is being all good," I said. I was sitting on my bed gazing at the little magic/meditation table squished between my bed and the wall, with its candelabra and crystals and velvet cloth. Funny how that stuff didn't seem so important to me anymore. I supposed I'd found more powerful magic in my own head.

"Yes, but being all good is a fantasy," she said. "No-one can be like that, and life would end if it was."

"How?"

"Well, if there were only females and no males, *finito* the human race," she said. "*Kaput*. We need both."

"Yes… that's obvious, but…"

"There's no buts. We need both sides all the time because the opposites together create things and hold the balance. And anyway, what would be the fun of being all-good-perfect? You might as well not bother to be here."

"I think it would be *more* fun," I argued. "Life would be much easier, for one. You wouldn't have to worry about schoolwork or friend problems or parents fighting. And you wouldn't get sick."

"But all of those things are how we grow."

"But if you were all-good-perfect you wouldn't *need* to grow."

"Everything needs to grow, Natalie," Nina said. "Even the universe is growing. It's expanding and evolving all the time. Everything goes from seed to full potential. And anyway, how boring would life be if you weren't growing? Nothing to do and nowhere to go? Yuck!"

I realised I was frowning. I changed hands and held the phone to my other ear.

"So Liz is a perfect person with great parts and messed-up parts and she's growing by sorting them out," Nina said. "Hey, how did your Mastery Club at the school go? Have you done it?" The eagerness was right back in her voice now.

"Yes, yesterday. It was…" a grin broke out on my face, "good and bad."

Nina laughed. "Really? How unexpected."

Grinning even more, I told her all about it, describing the kids and what I'd said and what they'd asked me.

"But I was really stumped with this question: what if lots of people want the same thing and there's only one of it, like the netball trophy or being team captain?"

"It's very simple," she said. "People want stuff but sometimes what they want is a fantasy because they're not really prepared to do what it takes to have it, for instance. Like being a famous actress when they're too scared to say boo and aren't doing any drama training or anything like that. That's a crazy impossible goal for that person. You can't achieve an illusion, but they'll probably beat themselves up for failing at it. But if they *really* want something and it's a true goal and not a fantasy, and they really do stay committed to it and take action, they probably will achieve it eventually."

"So does that mean that someone who doesn't get their goal didn't want it enough or try enough?" I asked.

"Probably. Or maybe they weren't ready for it. Maybe it wasn't right for them yet or maybe there's something else that's better for them coming around the corner."

Gosh. I had said that. In fact, between us, Miss Walker and I had given pretty good answers.

I told Nina what I'd said about Order and the Three Forces, and she said, "You see? You were thinking me and Liz are masters but those kids in your Club probably think you're a master. After all, you're going overseas. That's pretty big."

As she said that, I realised why I'd felt uncomfortable when Kat shared her goal of going to Bali. Last year Nina had encouraged us to start with simple things. I'd only set the Greek Islands goal after I'd already seen some magic happen… My forehead creased in a worried frown for a moment, and then I thought, It's okay. I'll tell her next time. I'm not perfect. And then I thought, with a smile, I mean, I am perfect: perfectly messed-up.

"Looks like you've mastered the Law of Stepping Up," Nina said.

"What's that?" I asked.

"You know. Taking on a big new challenge even when you don't think you can do it."

"But that's what we were doing all last year too. All goals are like that."

"Yes. I just thought of that name now, though. What do you think of it?"

The Law of Stepping Up. "I suppose it gets followed by the Law of Crashing Down," I said.

Nina laughed. "Only if you get cocky and big-headed about it."

No fear of that. I was still pretty nervous about Stepping Up.

"Actually, going after a big goal always brings up your worst fears and your feelings that you can't do it," Nina said. "I was really scared, at first, about going to your school last year and starting up the Club."

"Truly? You didn't look scared at all."

"I was though. I was telling myself over and over to relax, and that I was there with a purpose, and the right kids would turn up to be my friends and do the Club with me. And I'd been visualising it for ages, so that helped too."

"Natalie!" Mum knocked on my bedroom door. "Have you done your homework? I'd appreciate a hand in the kitchen."

"I'm on the phone," I called back. "I won't be long."

"Okay," she said.

"Was that your Mum?" Nina asked.

"Yeah."

"How is she…? About the Mastery Club?"

"She hasn't said anything else. And Dad's okay about it."

"Good…" Nina said. "Well, I mean, I'm glad, since nothing is good or bad."

"Talking the truth about things gets very tricky, doesn't it?" I reflected. I mean, if you couldn't say anything was good or bad without meaning it was good-and-bad or bad-and-good, then talking was no longer a simple thing. Nuncle's game had warned us about the illusion of describing things as good or bad last year, but I hadn't really got it then.

"Yeah. It sure keeps us on our toes," Nina agreed.

Mastery Club Lesson #18

The Law of Stepping Up

✳ Committing to our growth brings expansion and challenges.

✳ It can be uncomfortable but it's always valuable.

CHAPTER 26

SERENITY
(BRINGS UPHEAVAL)

ON FRIDAY WE MET at Clare's again for our Mastery Club meeting, and to meet her new friend, Serenity, at last. When Sandy, Billy and I arrived at Clare's place, she and Serenity were in the tiny kitchen making drop scones for us. They didn't have to wear uniforms at their school, and Serenity was wearing a pink-and-orange tasselled headscarf, dangly bead-and-feather earrings, a rainbow-coloured top that she'd obviously dyed herself, purple genie-pants and some orange sparkly ballet flats.

"Oh hi!" she beamed as we turned up in the doorway. "I've been wanting to meet you guys for ages! Clare has told me all about you!"

Sandy, who used to be Clare's kind of protector at school, just looked at her, and Billy was a bit taken aback too. So I said hi for all of us. Clare was bustling around with plates and marmalade and honey and jams and butter, and organising us all stools at the bench so we could eat the drop scones. Which were delicious.

And Serenity talked pretty much non-stop the whole time. Before long we knew that she lived with her mum, her dad came and went – 'they have these terrible fights and he goes and then he's back and they're as close as anything. It's true love: they can't live together and they can't live without each other…"

Was that true love? I wondered. It sounded passionate, all right, but was passion true love?

And she had four younger brothers and sisters who were just adorable and *so* annoying. The other day Felix got into her jewellery box and she was still looking for bits. And her mother was the most amazing dressmaker with her own brand, and they often went to festivals and markets on the weekends to sell her stuff.

When I was finally able to get Serenity to stop talking so I could ask her if she'd set a goal, which was the whole point of the Club, she said, "Yes. World peace."

I was a bit startled by that.

"I don't want anything for myself," she said, "people are too egotistical – no offence – and it's all this self, self, self that makes all the problems in the world."

"Then why did you want to join a Mastery Club?" I asked, "since it's for kids who want to achieve things?"

"Oh I do want to achieve things!" she said with wide eyes. Green eyes flecked with yellow, and a bit of sparkly green eye shadow too, I noticed. "I want to achieve world peace."

"All of our goals so far have been so… *'self'*," Clare agreed.

"Let's get Nina on Skype and start our meeting," I suggested, a little flabbergasted. While we were waiting for the computer to warm up and the connection to be made, I asked Clare how much she had told Serenity so far, and if they'd been over all the Lessons and stuff we'd done.

"Yes, most of it," she said. "Serenity has already made this really cool treasure map for her mum's business."

Which baffled me even more.

Serenity was obviously very excited about meeting Nina on Skype. Her first words, when Nina's fadey-green-headed image popped up in front of us, were, "Hi Nina! I've been so looking forward to this! I bet we're soul mates!"

For some reason, I didn't feel threatened by Serenity at all.

Nina welcomed Serenity into our Club with a friendly smile, and asked everyone how they were going with their goals. I was very curious to hear what Serenity would say about hers. How do you set out to achieve world peace if you're a twelve or thirteen year old girl?

Billy reckoned he was on track in his training schedule and Sandy had sold another couple of pieces at her exhibition, so she was rapt. Nina's dad Pete had organised for her to give a little talk about our Mastery Club at a business breakfast, which maybe could mean the beginning of her career as a professional speaker! (Although she said she wasn't being paid.) I said that my goal of keeping our Mastery Club going was working out, and I'd unexpectedly started another Club, the one at school – at this Billy and Clare asked how it had gone, so we side-tracked on that for a bit.

Then I told them that I had never said what I wanted to focus on with school stuff and I was getting clearer about it. My conversation with Nina about not being able to achieve an illusion, and what Miss Walker had said about your goal having to be important to you, had made me realise that while I wanted to do reasonably well at my school subjects, they weren't where my real interests lay; I was fascinated by everything Nina taught us and I wanted to understand *that* stuff. *And* I didn't want to drift through school anymore; I wanted to finish my school years feeling like I'd achieved something that mattered to me. I was beginning to suspect that running the Mastery Club was part of this new intention, even though that still terrified me.

Nina's smile was particularly warm when I shared all this, and I knew she was also remembering our conversation last year when she'd said that I could plan on contributing so much to school that I fell in love with being there.

Clare announced that since she had achieved her goal of a friend she was now choosing another goal, which was also world peace. And that was when our meeting became very interesting.

"Great!" Nina said cheerfully. "I thought we'd make our goals smart today, guys, since I don't think we've talked about that before."

"Smart?" Sandy queried.

"Yes. S, M, A, R, T. It's an acronym, you know, where each letter stands for something. S is for Specific and Simple, M is for Meaningful and Measurable, A is for Achievable and Action-oriented, R is for Responsible and Realistic, and T is for Timed and present Tense. So the idea is to make sure your goal fits into this SMART thing." She looked at Serenity and Clare innocently.

"So… your world peace goal, guys, how can you make it specific?"

"Specific?" Clare looked baffled. "What do you mean?"

"Well, it's a bit too general at the moment."

"It's a bit too big, too," Sandy interrupted. "How can *you* ever achieve 'world peace'?"

Clare sighed, as if she'd known all along that she'd have to explain this to us. "Well, *obviously* we can't achieve it by ourselves but it's a much more important goal than just doing better at maths. It's the sort of goal you'd work on for years and years."

"Sounds like a recipe for giving up to me," muttered Sandy.

"In that case, that's a mission, not a goal," Nina said. "It's like a life purpose or something. Goals are specific things that you can tick off your list, and missions are big – they're your life dream. So what do you want to have for your goal?"

Serenity twisted a strand of her brown hair. "Hmmm…" she said thoughtfully.

Clare looked from Serenity to Nina and back again.

"I think," Serenity announced, "that I'll work on being very peaceful myself. And being really kind to my brothers and sisters and mother." She looked at us each with her big green eyes. "Yep, I'll be a living example of peace and positivity. Clare?"

"Okay…" said Clare, a little doubtfully.

"There's just…" began Nina, and then she stopped herself. "Never mind."

We spent the rest of our time checking our goals against the S*M*A*R*T checklist.

S meant that they had to be specific and simple, which was pretty straightforward. M meant that your goal had to be measurable, like, 'make $200' not 'make a lot of money'. It also stood for 'meaningful' – in other words you had to be doing something that mattered to you. A stood for Achievable and Action-oriented, so that was a check that you had a clear action plan for achieving it (or at least for achieving the first step). R stood for 'realistic', which meant your goal was not a silly fantasy, and 'responsible', which meant that *you* were taking responsibility for your goal and not expecting it to land in your lap or expecting someone else to achieve it for you. And T meant you had a set date for achieving it or doing it. *Commitment!!!* You also had to put your goal in the present Tense because the brain only knows 'now'.

Nina made us 'SMART' all of our goals step-by-step. She went first:

Nina:

S – Specific and Simple: give an inspiring talk at the business breakfast.

M – Measurable: when, where and what had already been

agreed on; Meaningful; yes.

A – Achievable: yes; Action: start planning her talk.

R – Responsible and Realistic: yes.

T – Timed: it was already booked for the 5th May.

Affirmation (in present Tense): "It's the 5th May and I am confidently giving a great talk to the business breakfast people, and they are loving it."

Sandy:

S – Specific and Simple: sell two more pottery pieces by the end of the exhibition and make two more by the end of the April school holidays.

M – Measurable: counting to two is easy; Meaningful: yes.

A – Achievable: yes; Action: visualise two more 'Sold' stickers and make a time with her uncle to go to his studio and make two more pieces.

R – Responsible and Realistic: yes.

T – Timed: by the end of April.

Affirmation: "It's the end of April and I have sold two more pieces and made two more."

Billy:

S – Specific and Simple: enter the next mountain biking competition.

M – Measurable: yes, he had to submit an entry form by the due date; Meaningful: yes.

A –Achievable: yes; Action: go onto the website and get all the details.

R – Responsible: yes; Realistic: yes.

T – Timed: the deadline for entering was in two weeks.

Affirmation: "I am submitting my entry form on time for the Wilderness Youth Mountain Biking Competition."

Natalie:

S – Specific and Simple: run a much more interesting next

Mastery Club meeting at school.

M – Measurable: hmmm… tricky to measure. Maybe people's comments after it? Meaningful: yes.

A – Achievable: yes; Action: think and plan something over the weekend.

R – Responsible: yes; Realistic: I hoped so…

T – Timed: by next Wednesday.

Affirmation: "It is Wednesday 16th March and I am running a great Mastery Club meeting and everyone is getting heaps out of it."

Clare and Serenity:

S – Specific and Simple: "Be kind to our family and anybody who crosses our path." (Serenity's words).

M – Measurable: count the people? Meaningful: yes (part of their mission for world peace).

A – Achievable: of course! (according to Serenity); Action: 'turn the other cheek' if people were mean.

R – Responsible: yes; Realistic: yes.

T – Timed: every day…

Affirmation: "I am the spirit of kindness, patience, and forgiveness."

At the end of this Sandy confessed that this was the first time she had really enjoyed a Mastery Club meeting. Serenity said she had had an *awesome* time and was *so* excited about being part of a Club that was living life so consciously instead of just drifting along.

Billy reminded us that we were going to come up with an Invisible thing we could do for Liz and Nuncle, so we had to explain who they were to Serenity and what was happening for Liz right now, and all about the Invisibility thing.

"I love this!" Serenity glowed. "It's totally all about kindness! How about if we bake them a cake?"

"That's a great idea except that Liz is on a water fast at the moment," I said.

"I was thinking we could do some weeding for them," Billy suggested. "Maybe Nina could find out when they're not going to be there and we could sneak over."

"Okay," Nina said. "But it might not be so easy for me to sneak over."

"You do the scouting and we'll do the sneaking and weeding."

"Deal," she agreed. "I'll get back to you."

"I'm so excited about being in this Club!" Serenity beamed. "It's the best, Clare, even better than you said!"

Mastery Club Lesson #19

SMART Goals are:

S = Simple and Specific

M = Meaningful and Measurable

A = Achievable and Action-oriented (what's your first step?)

R = Responsible and Realistic

T = Timed (and worded in present Tense)

CHAPTER 27

DANGEROUS ATTITUDES

IN ENGLISH Miss Walker started a discussion about spirituality. She asked how many of us went to church or some other religious institution, maybe a synagogue or a mosque. A bit under half the kids put their hands up. I gave my hand a little half-hearted waggle (we went to Church for the major things like Christmas and Easter).

Then she asked those people to share what it meant to them, and they said things like 'being part of a spiritual community' and 'making Jesus the most important thing in my life' and 'keeping old traditions alive'. I was quite surprised by some of the people who I'd never in a million years have guessed were religious. A lot of kids said they weren't into religion but some of them did believe in God or some sort of spiritual side to life. I supposed I fitted best into that category, and I thought about telling everyone the meaning of God that I'd learnt from Nina: the Grand Organising Design or Designer.

But then Miss Walker read us a bit out of the book about the Aboriginal girl's spiritual beliefs and someone said that those cultures were kind of Stone Age and superstitious and ignorant and lots of people made agreeing sorts of noises. Miss Walker looked at us closely and asked, Why did we think that? Had any of us experienced indigenous culture? Had we lived in an Aboriginal community? Were we close friends with an Aboriginal or Islander? No-one said yes; not one person. (I thought about Nina, soon to visit Joel in his community, and wondered what that would be like…)

"Ah," she said, as if that explained everything. "Then how did you arrive at the conclusion that indigenous cultures were outdated and ignorant? Or have you been taking on ideas you've heard without thinking about them?"

"Well, things like serpents eating the world or spitting it up or something isn't very realistic," someone said.

"But perhaps it's symbolic," she said. "Maybe it's a way of explaining things through imagery."

"My family owns a big farm," a girl called Ruby said, "and whenever we've hired Aboriginals they've been really unreliable. They just nick off whenever they want to."

"Walkabout," a boy said.

"And they don't have school so all they learn is hunting and stuff like that," someone drawled.

Miss Walker came around her desk and sat on it. "What if I told you that they actually have a very sophisticated and intuitive understanding of the world, and of their part in it? There was hardly any crime in Aboriginal societies; they had their own systems of law and order that were respected by their communities. And their way of teaching children was done through play and observation of nature, rather than school – surely you like the thought of that!"

"I hope my mother never hears me say this," the class clown said, "but you can't learn *everything* through play."

We laughed, while he added, sliding down his seat comically, "She's told me that *soooo* many times…"

"School is supposed to prepare you for life," Miss Walker pointed out, "and that's exactly what indigenous peoples were traditionally doing: they were preparing their children for *their* lifestyle. Aboriginal children are brought up learning to read the signs of nature because Nature provides their food, their shelter, their defence systems, their entertainment… It's literally their classroom.

"Our Western science makes all its greatest breakthroughs through observing nature, you know, but most of us don't have the first clue, and maybe our disconnectedness from the land is at the root of many of our modern ills. Depression and other forms of mental illness, for example, can be greatly helped by simply going for a brisk walk outdoors…"

Those words, 'signs of nature', reminded me of what Nina and Liz had said about signatures in nature; that certain foods signalled what part of the body they were for by their very shape and colour, and things like that. I wondered if Aboriginal kids were learning the same sort of thing… and what school would be like if subjects like this were part of the curriculum… I could just imagine the sort of school where kids were taught the Mastery Club lessons and how to heal themselves instead of having to go to doctors… how cool that would be!

Miss Walker opened another book. "This is an Aboriginal story about the Creation time when the gifts of awareness were given to man," she said, putting the open book in front of a kid called Jake, and pointing to a passage with her finger. "Read here, please."

"The first gift was the gift of hearing," Jake began, "so that people could hear the song of all the elements around them, like the movement of a dragonfly's wings or of water in a stream far away."

Miss Walker murmured 'Thank you,' and passed the book to

the girl sitting next to him.

"Then they were given the gift of smell so they could smell the changing seasons and the wind and the rain and where food was," Sara continued, and Miss Walker moved the book to the next person.

"Then they were given the gift of taste so they could taste their food, all the animals and plants that were sac – sacrificing their life for humans," George read.

Miss Walker set the book in front of Sandy, who read, "And then they were given the gift of sight, but as soon as their eyes were opened, they judged everything." Sandy paused for a moment and looked sideways at me. I knew she was thinking that this could have been a story that Nina or Nuncle told us…

"Keep going," Miss Walker said.

"They saw the spiky fruit and thought it looked dangerous so they neglected that medicine," Sandy read; "they saw the prickly echidna and judged it as dangerous and they avoided it."

"Thank you, Sandy," Miss Walker said, passing the book to me.

"The gift of sight was meant to be our greatest gift so we could see and appreciate the beautiful world," I read, "but it became a means for judging everything, and we neglected our feelings and our other senses."

Miss Walker thanked me and closed the book. She looked around the class thoughtfully. "That doesn't sound too ignorant to me…"

People were shifting in their seats and glancing at the clock. For a moment, I closed my eyes and just listened, paying attention to my first gift… A desk was creaking behind me. I hadn't noticed it before. Someone gave a faint shout somewhere outside.

"What I would like you to think about," Miss Walker's voice said, "is the degree to which you believe that your culture is superior. Indigenous people have a different set of values to

Westerners. Following arbitrary clock-time isn't as important to them as being able to sense changes in nature, for instance. But Westerners have made themselves the dominant culture and they tend to impose their values on everyone else. I want you to think about that."

"In my family," Sandy said as we walked out of English, "my dad is the dominant culture. He imposes his values on the rest of us. I wonder what he'd say if I asked him to think about that."

"Go on," I encouraged.

She gave me a withering look.

That Wednesday the school Mastery Club members all turned up on time. Mark said he was spending ten minutes every night visualising himself winning the chess championship. His research had found lots more examples of people who used mental rehearsal to achieve things. Tom said, "Oops…" – he'd forgotten all about it. (I gathered that Miss Walker had reminded him about our meeting at the start of lunchtime; he'd forgotten all about that too.) Holly and Bree were determined to see their traditionally losing netball team win this season, and they had actually started visualisations with their teammates already. Petra shyly revealed her goal of a pet mouse, and I told Kat that it would be best if she started with a simpler goal that she could set and achieve in a short space of time, rather than a big thing like a trip to Bali.

"But I've already got it," she said flatly.

"Really?" I was so startled that I just stared at her.

"Yes. I'm going with my folks during the April holidays."

"Goodness!" Miss Walker said. "That was quick. What did you do to bring that about?"

"I just thought about going to Bali. In my mind," she said in a sort of, 'What, do you think I'm dumb?' tone of voice. "You know, like you were saying. Visualising."

A little warning bell was ringing inside me. Something didn't fit.

"Was this a long-time planned family holiday or a sudden idea?" Miss Walker asked.

"It's been talked about for ages but it just suddenly got decided," Kat said, a trifle defensively, and I realised that she'd probably already known the trip was going to happen when she set her goal last week.

Miss Walker glanced at me and I sensed that she was thinking the same thing. How to succeed at your goal: set a goal that you know is sure to happen…

"Time to choose a new goal then," Miss Walker said brightly.

"Hmm… I'll think about that," Kat murmured. (And we would be on her case this time.)

Last weekend when I was planning what to do in this week's meeting I had decided to introduce the SMART system, so for the rest of that meeting we worked on making everyone's goals SMART. Kat finally decided she would set a goal of raising one hundred dollars for spending money while she was in Bali. Everyone did seem to enjoy this, so I guess I'd achieved my goal of running an interesting meeting.

"It's a bit like doing magic, isn't it?" Holly said, when we were talking about visualising goals as an action step.

"Yes," I burst out. "That's one of the things that got me in. I've always liked reading books about dragons and wizards and stuff like that, and I thought my life was pretty boring by comparison. So learning about the power of the mind and how the brain works and deliberately creating your reality is pretty cool because it's the kind of magic you can do in your ordinary life." There I was, saying the exact thing that upset my mother.

"What do you mean, 'create your reality'?" Petra asked. "Reality is just here already."

"That's what we think," I said, remembering our conversations at Nina's farm at the end of summer, "but actually everybody has different ways of seeing things, and different beliefs, so we're all living in our own worlds, in a way. It looks like one big shared reality but actually it's lots of individual realities."

Miss Walker leaned forward a little. "Two people can grow up with exactly the same parents and childhood circumstances and one reacts by dropping out of school and becoming a drug addict, and the other responds by working harder than ever and becoming a leader and business person. Why do you think that is?"

"Because of luck," Bree declared. "One of them probably had better luck growing up."

"Maybe. But what causes luck?"

"Nothing," Bree said. "It just happens to you."

"Maybe. And maybe we are each creating our reality in each moment of each day just through the way we talk about our experiences to ourselves," Miss Walker said, "and where we put our focus, and how much we want something and commit to it. Maybe we create our own 'luck'." She drew quotation marks in the air as she said 'luck'.

Last year Nina and Nuncle had been my teacher of this stuff; this year it seemed that my English teacher was playing that role. She certainly seemed to have been thinking about things like this for a while. I wondered if this was another aspect of the Law of Conservation – that no-one is missing, they just turn up in other forms. But then who was playing that Nina/Nuncle role before *they* turned up in my life? I was stumped by that question.

At dinner that night Dad asked me how the school Mastery Club was going. Mum pricked up her ears.

"What 'school Mastery Club'?"

"Nat's teacher has asked her to lead a goal-setting club," Dad explained, passing his plate for more casserole.

"I hope you're not talking to them about 'creating their own reality'," Mum said reprovingly. (Honing right in on my uncertainty, like a bee to nectar.) "Because that still troubles me."

"Why does it, Mum?"

"Because no-one lives in a vacuum all by themselves. You can't just 'create your reality'. You're part of a bigger system. Mentally ill people have that illusion, that they're Jesus or Napoleon or something. I don't want you to be deluded like that."

"Well, the way we do it it's not about being deluded." I dug around in my casserole for the sweet potato. "It's about being aware of how we're thinking and changing our thoughts so we're really responsible. Like, for instance, I was getting all worried about things so I started doing this affirmation that 'I'm moving forwards in my life and loving it', and it really helped."

Dad gave me his 'I'm impressed' look, kind of a raised-eyebrows-nod-with-a-thrust-out-bottom-lip.

"That's very good, Natalie," Mum said in surprise. "Very constructive. But you do realise that there are some things that we can't change no matter how much we try to believe the opposite?"

I frowned a little, wondering what to say to this.

"And the other thing that bothers me," she added, "is that people who may be victims in some way will be blamed for their circumstances, as if they've brought them upon themselves. And then no-one will want to help anyone because they'll think, that's *their* problem, they just need to change their thinking. So if people are starving or in pain or being killed by a mad dictator, they'll just be abandoned by the rest of us who are thinking, 'Well, they created that reality'."

Katie and Evan had been secretively rolling peas to each other across the table during this conversation, and now a pea shot past Evan into Mum's lap, so she was onto their game and began to tell them off for playing with their food.

I was determined not to run to Nina for answers. While Mum scolded the siblings I wracked my brain for ways to answer her, but my brain wasn't very helpful. All I could think of was that if people took responsibility for the things that happened in their lives, then they wouldn't be victims. But could that be true with the big scary things that happened in the world that seemed to be out of our control? Or even with the little everyday things that happen and seem to have nothing to do with us?

CHAPTER 28

WEEDS AND WAR

OUR FRIDAY MEETING became a secret working bee at Liz and Nuncle's house, because Nina had let us know that they'd be out. We met at the street end of Begonia Lane with our gardening gloves and trowels. Serenity was with us, and full of admiration for the unusual house, the little bridge, the vegie gardens, the chooks…

As we headed towards Liz's vegie patches, it felt very strange to be on their property without their knowledge – kind of like trespassing.

"I don't feel very invisible," Billy said. "Do you?"

"Sh!" Clare hissed.

"Why are you whispering?" Sandy hissed back. "There's no-one here."

"Neighbours!" I jerked my head towards the fence. "They're probably great friends. If they catch us snooping around…"

Sandy saluted me: aye aye, captain; and we knelt down around the patch with our tools.

"Whatever you do, don't dig up her vegies," I warned in a low voice, so of course then she had to pretend that she didn't know what was what and kept alarming me by nearly pulling out carrots and stuff like that.

I hadn't been back to Liz and Nuncle's place since the adult mastermind meeting when I'd found out about her cancer, and there was a big mixture of thoughts and feelings going around in me as I dug and pulled at the weeds. Liz's mosaic path had progressed, I noticed. The turtle, her symbol of slowing down, was finished, and she had begun work on a caterpillar; it lay on a large green leaf that had a big bite chewed out of it.

We left an hour later with bags of dirty weeds (to not leave any clues), grimy faces and hands, and a good feeling. Billy had even thought of sweeping the path clear of all our dropped bits of weed and soil so there was no sign that anyone had been there.

"Wouldn't you love to see their faces!" Clare chortled as we crept away up Begonia Lane.

And we kind of got to, the following night when we were meeting at Billy's dad's place and Nina turned up.

"What are you doing here?" I asked in surprise, seeing her greenish-blonde-haired self appear at the front door behind the pizza-delivery man.

"Mum and Dad are going out with Liz and Nuncle tonight," she beamed, "so I set this up with Bill because I knew you guys were coming here. And, by the way, they are *so* baffled about the vegie patch! It was the first thing they said when we got to their place tonight. They haven't got a *single* clue. Everybody gets their Invisibility badge!"

We all beamed at that, and hoed into the pizza with great satisfaction. Serenity had lots to tell Nina as we ate, and she just listened, chewing. Billy's dad, John, joined us to eat and I noticed Clare eyeing him a bit warily. After all, her mum had gone out with him over the summer but it had ended up with them calling it off and Hazel crying.

"Man, it's good to be here in the same room instead of trying to see you all on a screen," Nina said, when John had excused himself from the pizza remains and disappeared into his study. "So how are the goals going?" She looked at Serenity and Clare as she said this, and I was also curious to know how well they were achieving peace in their world.

"Terrible," Clare said frankly. "The more nice I try to be, the more mean I seem to get. I've been so mean to Mum – much more than usual."

"You've just got to try harder," Serenity urged her. "The ego is a very powerful thing and it doesn't want to give up its control over you. You have to try hard to let your kind nature through or there'll never be peace on earth."

"The harder you try, the meaner you'll get," Nina said.

"What? Why?" Serenity asked, startled.

"Because you can't cut yourself in half. Everyone's got meanness in them. It's like trying to always be positive. You can't. It's all part of being human. And anyway, being mean can be useful."

"Being nasty hurts people," Serenity objected. "It's war on a small scale."

Nina looked at Billy. "Where's the bathroom, Bill?"

He pointed.

"You have an opportunity to lecture someone and you're about to go pee?" Sandy demanded.

Nina grinned and stood up. "Follow me," she said; "all of you."

She headed to the bathroom and we squeezed in after her. It was surprisingly neat for a male-only place, especially one that had Billy in it (although he did live at his mum's most of the time). The sink area was quite tidy with shavers and deodorants neatly lined up, and a fairly clean hand towel. I guess I was particularly noticing all this, having just cleaned our bathroom.

(Was that my R.A.S. at work?)

Nina pointed to the mirror. "See yourself?"

We crowded together and stared at our reflections. Serious eyes stared back at me. There was a little perplexed frown on my forehead.

Sandy said drily, "And your point is…?"

"That the world is our mirror, and everyone out there is a reflection of us. And that usually we criticise other people for things we don't like in ourselves, so they're just waking us up to the part of ourself we're rejecting. For instance…" She looked at Sandy sideways. "You'll like this. The owner of the health food store in our town is the biggest know-all. Every time we pop in there to buy something he has to stop us and give us this great long lecture about something or other. He drives me up the wall! So Mum's been making me own the know-all part of me."

"Not too hard for you?" Sandy asked with a big grin.

Nina smiled back a little sheepishly.

"Actually!" Sandy almost pounced, a gleam in her eye, "I have just the perfect Invisibility Challenge for you, O Mighty Leader!"

Nina narrowed her eyes and waited. Sandy traced a pointed finger across her lips with a zipping noise. "Silence. A day when you don't speak – at all!" She sat back triumphantly.

Nina shook her head in pity. "What do you think I'm doing when I'm at home all by myself day after day when you kids are at school and Mum and Dad are out?" She mimicked the zipping action.

For a second Sandy looked put out, then she said, "It's easy when there's no-one around, but can you shut up when there are people around – especially when they're talking about one of your favourite topics? Huh?"

"Okay," Nina allowed, "more difficult. All right…" she narrowed her eyes again, "I accept your challenge."

Sandy smiled like the cat that's had the cream.

"Yes but don't do it *now*," Serenity objected. "I want to know what you mean about being mean."

Nina looked at Sandy and shrugged helplessly. It was Sandy's turn to narrow her eyes. "Okay, fair enough; another time."

"I know there are times when I'm mean," Serenity said, looking troubled. "I feel *terrible* about them. So I don't want to 'own' meanness. I want to transcend it. I want to be more kind, not more mean."

"I'm not saying you should be more mean," Nina said, "just that if we look at ourselves really honestly, we know that we've all got kindness in us *and* cruelty, and there are benefits to both of them… F'rinstance, being kind can be helpful but sometimes it isn't – like when your parents are over-protecting you, right? And sometimes being mean is helpful – like when someone makes you do something you don't want to do, but it's what you need to do."

"Like our cycling coach," Billy said with feeling. "Mean as they come, but it's doing us good…"

"Exactly. He'd be no use to your team if he was nice."

"That's different," Serenity disagreed. "That's a game. It's not real life."

"All the real life examples you would ever want are in your own life if you go looking… People mostly don't want to see this stuff because they just want everything to be nice all the time. But for real life we need to be *whole*, which means owning it all rather than madly trying to cut half of ourselves off."

An image of the yin-yang symbol flashed into my mind, with its light and dark sides neatly dove-tailing together.

"It's all the splitting of things that causes problems." Nina said, dropping the toilet lid and sitting on it, "whereas if things are kept whole, they're okay. It's true all over the place. Like with food – you take away the whole grains and end up with white flour or white sugar and that's toxic to the body and really unbalancing, but if you keep it whole, it's got all the bits in it that balance each other out and your body can process it better."

"The splitting up of parents causes problems too," Clare said with a grimace.

"Sometimes they're better off apart though," Billy disagreed.

I looked at him in surprise. So things must have been getting quite a bit better for him with his new stepdad.

"Could we come out of the bathroom now?" Sandy asked, her back against the door.

"You don't like it in here?" Nina enquired, all innocence. "Don't like the associations with...?"

"That's right," Sandy said firmly, squeezing out of the room and waiting for us in the hallway.

"Actually bathrooms are very balanced places," Nina said, as she came out. "You know, the yuck side of life and the cleaning yourself up side of life. Very balanced."

Sandy gave her a bit of a push, and Nina bumped into me, giggling.

"Seriously," she said, walking backwards up the hall. "Wars happen because people are making themselves right and better and other people wrong and worse instead of respecting both sides equally – both sides of themselves and both countries, or whatever. People out there," she waved a hand towards the street, "only attack us because we've got attacking energy going on inside ourselves in the first place. Otherwise they wouldn't. You wouldn't attract it if you didn't already have it in you, sort of thing. Does that make sense?"

"That's what you said last year when Clare had all those bullies on her case," I said. "And when she owned up to her mad feelings they just disappeared."[21]

"Exactly," Nina agreed. She stopped in Billy's doorway, blocking

---

21 Check out *The Dance of Bullying, a breakthrough tool for teachers and parents* by Ken Pierce and Alice Bailey.

the way. "The point of all this is that if we love and appreciate our whole selves, and other people's *whole* selves, there wouldn't be war. It's just a sign that we're not doing that because, honestly and truly, do you think if you really loved and appreciated yourself you'd want to go to war? You go because you're all embattled inside."

"Hang on a minute," Sandy objected. "I thought you said everybody had every quality, like that hologram-thingo, and so we *can't* get rid of fighting, and now you're saying that people can get to a place where they don't have upset inside themselves and they won't want to go to war. Sounds like a contradiction to me!" And she crossed her arms with a particularly bulldoggish expression.

"No, it's just that… uh…" Nina stopped talking, and frowned in thought. "You know what? I think you're right; that sounds wrong."

We goggled, never having seen Nina stumped like this before.

"I'm going to have to think about this one, guys; I'm not sure."

"She's not sure," Sandy crowed, as if this was music to her ears. Nina poked her tongue out at her.

"Well, *I* wouldn't go to war!" Clare argued.

"Maybe not to some other country to fight but you probably do go to war with your mum."

"Yes, but I wouldn't *kill* my mother! I just argue with her."

"It's a kind of war; it's still fighting," Nina said, "and stress can kill, you know – it definitely makes people sick. In fact, I think I heard somewhere that stress kills more people than the military…"

"Could we come out of the hallway now?" Sandy asked with a long-suffering sigh.

CHAPTER 29

THE NATURE OF NATURE

NINA BACKED INTO Billy's room and plumped herself onto his bed. "But anyway, war's part of the divine order."

"That doesn't make sense to me," Serenity declared, sitting on the floor right under a poster of these very warlike game characters.

"Ever been sick?"

"Sure."

"But you got better, right? How do you think that happened?"

Serenity shrugged. "Mum uses these natural remedies…"

"We do too. But the point is that the flu, or whatever it was, didn't just get tired and give up; your immune system *fought* against it and your white blood cells *killed* all the bugs. If they didn't, you'd die. So, children, are we all grateful that they do their job and go to war against all the viruses and bacteria we pick up every day?"

We nodded humbly.

"Fact is," she blasted on, "there's war going on all the time, from that tiny-teeny microscopic cell level right on up. If our bodies weren't killing bacteria in the millions every day, we'd die for sure. Then there's the human level." She was really getting into this; I could see that old light in her eyes… "If you don't like yourself at times, put up your hand."

Nina's hand shot up and the rest of us gave a little wave.

"If you argue with your parents or your brothers and sisters, put up your hand."

This time, all hands went straight up.

"If you fight with friends now and then…" Nina deliberately didn't look at Sandy. We stuck our hands in the air again.

"If your parents argue with each other, or with their friends or neighbours, put up your hand…"

"Okay, point taken – can we stop with the putting-our-hands-up bit?" Sandy exploded.

Nina continued: "Would you agree that there's competition between corporations?"

"Cities, too," Billy said. "My dad was just telling me yesterday that Sydney and Melbourne have been arguing about who's the best for over a hundred years!"

"Which brings us to wars between countries, the thing everyone's so upset about these days, right?"

"But all of this doesn't make fighting *right*," Serenity said.

"Who says it's right?" Nina replied. "It just *is*. The point is to stop fighting that fact and learn from it – no pun intended."

We were silent.

"So that's war from the micro level up!" she said, "and then it starts to get a bit weird, because scientists reckon our moon was created billions of years ago from planetary war – not like in Star Wars; they just mean planets smashing into each other. In fact, the Hubble telescope once found these two distant galaxies, one really huge and the other one much smaller, and believe it or not, the big galaxy was eating the little one, just absorbing billions of planets and stars like we'd eat a big dinner. *Aaaand* our very own sun is destined to eat this li'l ol' planet Earth up one of these days."

"Nuncle told us that last year," I said slowly, remembering. "So if war is everywhere, then maybe it really is part of the Order, too."

"Yeah. I mean, if this stuff has been going on from the micro level to the macro level over billions of years, what makes us think it's wrong?"

"How do you know all this?" Clare demanded.

"I grew up with it, remember? Mum and Dad and Liz and Nuncle talk about this stuff all the time. I was going to those mastermind groups with them since I was a toddler. Other families talk about ball games and what's on TV, and my family talks about the meaning of life... In fact, they started off *arguing* about it because they were exactly like you, Serenity; they just wanted peace. Big time. My Mum and Dad are hippies from way back."

The photos I'd seen of Nina's parents on their wedding day flashed through my mind – her mother had been wearing a simple cheesecloth dress; and there was hardly anything plastic in their house at all, it was all natural stuff.

"In fact, I remember the day they understood this because Mum was telling me that everything is made out of this one fundamental energy that kind of vibrates into different forms, and then she started talking to herself and saying, 'So if everything comes from the same energy, you can't just make one part of that energy good and another part bad... they're all parts of the whole. So... if you can't cut the G.O.D. out of the picture, then where is GOD not? Must be that the G.O.D. is also in wars and meanness."

"That's too weird," Serenity frowned.

"She was shocked, too, but how is it weird?" Nina asked. "Think about nature. Nature's a pretty wild place if you really look at it. There's heaps of killing and decay and all sorts of things going on there that we think are yuck."

"Like spiders that mate and then *eat* their mate," Clare said with a shudder.

"Yeah – that's a great example. And did you know that plants have got friends and enemies too? That's why organic gardeners do companion planting – it's to plant the ones that get on with each other together and keep the other ones away from them."

"Whoah," said Serenity, startled. "Mum does companion planting but I never thought of it like that."

"And then there's bird calls," Nina continued; "they're designed to either attract a mate or protect a territory, right? Birds are constantly telling any others in the area to keep out of their hunting grounds or there'll be trouble, and they're constantly on the watch for moths and insects and lizards and snakes and mice, and they'll eat 'em like that!" She snapped her fingers. "And all *those* creatures are eating smaller ones." She surveyed us calmly with those grey eyes. "No peace in nature."

I didn't know about the others, but I was feeling really full, like my brain had eaten too much. A phone started ringing somewhere with a very jazzy ringtone. It was cut off suddenly and we heard Billy's dad say, "Hello?"

"Hey, have you guys heard the story about the boy and the caterpillar?" Nina asked. "This boy cuts the butterfly's cocoon to help it out, and the poor baby butterfly just flops out and dies because it needed the struggle of squeezing out of the cocoon to make its wings strong enough to fly."[22]

"I get all this stuff you're saying," Serenity said earnestly, "but maybe we're here to *master* our meanness and create a Golden

----

22　We humans do that too, I realised. We squeeze and struggle out of the birth canal when we're getting born – unless you've had one of those births where they cut the mother's stomach open and lift you out, but I guess there's a difficult side to that too...

Age of peace and kindness and happiness."

"And break all the laws of nature? Honestly, Serenity, nature is about growth, not happiness. Everything grows but *nothing* has a one-sided, happiness-only experience of life. Not one single thing." Nina cocked her head and spoke with a strange sort of Indian accent that reminded me of Rafiki in *The Lion King*: "Ancient wisdom teach: the more you pursue happiness, the less likely you find it. Mastery is in being whole. Yes, mark my words, children!"

"Ancient wisdom, no less!" Sandy scoffed from Billy's desk chair. It was one of those swivelling office chairs, and she'd been slowly rotating while Nina was talking. But I wasn't in the mood for her mockery.

"You got a problem with that?" I demanded. "It's pretty clear that Nina would know more about ancient wisdom than you – or any of us!"

"Nope," she said airily, swinging around on the chair. "Just thought we needed to slow her down a bit before poor Serenity gets fried."

"I'm okay," Serenity said, still frowning, "I'm just thinking."

"You know Mother Teresa?" Nina said in her usual voice.

"She's the little old Albanian nun who helped lepers and outcasts," Clare put in. (She did a project on Mother Teresa once.)

"Yeah. Well, people say she's a saint but apparently there were some not very nice things going on as well – like physical abuse in her orphanages, and her homes for the sick were really dirty, and they wouldn't give pain relief because it's supposed to be a blessing to suffer like Christ..." Nina raised her brows at us. "And she was involved with a few shady characters, like corrupt business people who took money out of ordinary people... You don't hear about that side of her much. Doesn't sound so saintly to me."

"No..." Clare was obviously quite taken aback. "There was

none of that in the books I read when I did my project on her."

"But suppose she *was* saintly," Nina continued, narrowing her penetrating grey eyes. "Well, think about this – this will blow your mind: For Mother Teresa to be a saintly giving person, someone *has to be* sick and downtrodden and needy. You can't have one without the other. She wouldn't have had her purpose in life if there weren't desperate people who needed her. So desperate people must be part of the wholeness and divine order too."

"Wow." I was stopped in my tracks. "I always thought that hunger and stuff like that were… you know, signs that the world was sort of 'broken' and needed to be fixed."

"Of course they are!" Serenity said. "*You* wouldn't want to be hungry and poor and crippled so why should it be right for anyone?"

"We might not *want* to be," Nina replied, "but that doesn't mean it wouldn't be serving us – or those people – in some way; just like the butterfly needs to struggle to be strong. That's why we're being Order Detectives."

"Just one moment, Miss Detective," Sandy said, stilling her chair and fixing Nina with narrowed eyes, "you're saying that we *need* sick people and criminals and stuff like that because without them we couldn't have saints or healers or law-makers?"

"I'm saying that they fit together into a whole," said Nina, making a circle with her hands, "Because in this universe you can't get halves; only wholes. Except that most people don't see the other half."

"What, so we'll never get rid of crime and sickness and all that? Just always have breakdowns and disasters?" Billy had been tossing a tennis ball from hand to hand; now he dropped it into his lap.

"That isn't right!" Serenity declared. "Life has to be about getting better."

"But who says Divine Order isn't right?" Nina answered back.

"Because it's… yucky," Serenity objected. "It's cruel."

"You know that scientist, the one in the wheelchair?"

"Stephen Hawking," Billy said, picking the ball up again and starting to toss it.

"Yes. They reckon that him being stuck in that wheelchair was a blessing for him and for the whole world. Because it freed up his time so he could purely focus on thinking and coming up with brilliant insights about how the universe works."

Serenity shuddered. "Well 'they' don't know what it's like to be stuck in a wheelchair. They wouldn't say that if they did."

"Actually, I think it's true," Billy said. He set his sights on the rubbish bin next to his desk and aimed… the tennis ball landed neatly in the bin and boinged around against the sides. (I was impressed.)

"Dad was watching a doco about that Hawking guy once," Bill continued over the noise of it, "and I walked in when he was saying that there was a part of him that was frustrated because he couldn't play with his kids the way he wanted to, but there was another part of him that was pretty okay about it because his favourite thing was thinking. Now, *that* I don't understand," he added under his breath.

"So war is part of the order," Sandy said with a frown.

"Yes, strange as it sounds. Hey!" Nina said with a bounce. "Have you ever asked your dad why he's in the army?"

Sandy looked at her blankly. "No."

"Well! Why don't you?"

The front doorbell rang then, just as Sandy said "Okay, I will," as if she was taking up a major challenge.

It was Clare's mum, Hazel. She was standing on the doorstep looking flushed and dishevelled. She said hi to all of us in a very distracted sort of way and then took Clare by the arm, and as they walked away into the darkness, we heard her saying, "Your dad is here."

Mastery Club Lesson #20

Where is G.O.D. not?

* It's all part of the Order…

* We are here to grow, not to be happy. (That doesn't mean we can't enjoy our lives; the point is to grow in responsibility… which means we become much more empowered and much more likely to create fulfilling lives.)

* Even war is part of the Order; conflict plays a role in evolution.

CHAPTER 30

AUNT PAT TO THE RESCUE

I COULDN'T HELP wondering what was going on at Clare's house as the rest of us were picked up and headed home that night. She hadn't seen her father since he left when she was two years old. Clare thought her mum was still a bit in love with him and that was partly why she'd never married anyone else and why she cried a lot. But I didn't hear from Clare for a few days and I didn't want to seem like a sticky-beak by ringing her too soon…

On Monday morning I was surprised to see Billy leaping on board the school bus. He dropped heavily into the seat behind me, and blurted, "Bike's being serviced" in answer to my questioning expression.

"Oh." I twisted around in my seat. "Hey Bill, did you ever ring Joel?"

"Yeah. I tried a coupla times. He wasn't there."

"Did you leave a message?"

"Yep."

"Bummer." Was Joel going to be one of those typically unreliable Aboriginals? Or was he just on different timing, as Miss Walker said?

I turned around and watched the door to the bus jerk closed.

With a rattle, the bus heaved away from the kerb and we headed towards school.

"I don't expect there's much internet or phone lines up there," Billy said from behind me. And then I could hear music, so I knew he'd plugged into his iPod.

Joel made me think about Nuncle, for some reason, and Nuncle made me think about Liz. I hadn't thought about her for a while, and now I wondered how she was going. I could just see her kneeling next to her mosaic path and carefully placing the colourful pieces. Suddenly I shut my eyes and visualised Liz smiling and radiant, telling us that she was all healed. No more cancer. She was clear. Nuncle had his arm around her and his eyes were sparkling, and Nina was cavorting around saying, "See?"

There was a smile on my lips when I opened my eyes.

Wednesday was supposed to be the last school Mastery Club meeting before the term holidays but Miss Walker was away sick, so it was cancelled. Clare rang after school that day and asked if I'd stay over on Friday night because her mum was going out to a meeting and she wanted some company. She'd asked Sandy too, and Serenity, but not Billy; this wasn't going to be a Mastery Club meeting – just a girls' night.

So on Friday evening Mum dropped me 'round with my sleeping bag and stuff. Sandy was already there and she and Clare were sitting with Hazel and another woman at the dining room table that doubled as Clare's mum's working station. They'd pushed her computer and files to the side and were eating sultana scones off a very old-fashioned-looking blue and white plate.

"This is my Aunt Patricia," Clare said. "Mum's sister. They're going to the meeting together."

"Hello," I said, taking a seat.

Aunt Patricia offered me the plate of scones. She had large-boned hands and broad, ringed fingers. "And you're…?"

"Natalie," I said, accepting a buttered scone. "Thank you."

"Another one of Clare's friends in that magic club I was telling you about," Hazel told her sister. "You know kids – how they love fantasy and magic."

Patricia didn't say anything, but I noticed that her lips tightened a little. She smiled at me and put the dish back on the table.

Serenity arrived then, wearing her usual colourful hippie gear, and was soon chatting away to Aunt Patricia, asking her questions, telling her things… We discovered that they were going to a religious meeting of some sort. Hazel didn't seem very keen on the idea.

After they had left, Clare told us that her aunt was worried that Hazel would fall back in love with her dad, so she'd come to try and save her soul or something.

"What *is* happening with your dad?" I asked curiously.

She flushed a little and got busy stacking up the plates to carry them into the kitchen. "Oh, he's been dropping in a bit this week. He wants to patch it up with Mum."

"Wow. That's good news, isn't it?" I asked, picking up the blue dish.

"You'd better leave that one there. Aunt Pat will have a fit if it breaks. It's heirloom." Then she sighed. "Oh. I don't know. It's not how I expected."

We followed her into the kitchen.

"Why not?"

"Well… he's actually still with someone else… sort of… and it turns out he's got three other kids. We're not really sure why he's here. He told Mum that he misses her and he wishes he never left…"

"Some time to discover that!" Sandy exploded.

"Yeah… Ten years later…" Clare stacked the dishes in the machine. "He gave me an iPhone so I can stay in touch with him from now on, and he reckons he's going to pay the bill."

"Tricky," Serenity pronounced. "Sounds like he's keen, but can you trust him?"

"Exactly," Clare agreed. "Aunt Pat reckons no. She was here in a flash when she heard he'd been around. She does *not* like him at all. I don't know the whole story – they're not telling me, which is pissing me off."

"Do *you* like him?" I asked.

"He's pretty fun," Clare confessed. "We've been laughing heaps – just about wetting ourselves, actually. But he's also a bit unreliable. I can see that already. He says things and then doesn't do them. Mum's been telling him to forget it, it's over, go back to your other family, but I can tell she loves having him here, too. It's a bit of a mix-up, to be honest."

I was so used to my ordinary family with my down-to-earth, efficient mother and my devoted father that it was hard to imagine what it would be like living in that sort of situation.

"I totally get it," Serenity said with a sigh.

We had macaroni cheese for dinner and watched two movies. "Anyone for another movie?" Clare asked as the second one ended.

"Nope, I'm half asleep already," I mumbled.

"Okay." She lifted her arm majestically and pointed the remote control at the TV, and with a little spark, the lights and sounds were extinguished and the screen went black.

"That's just like magic, isn't it?" I reflected sleepily. "I reckon people who've never seen technical inventions would think that was definitely magic."

"Yeah," Sandy's muffled voice said from inside her sleeping bag. "I guess when you don't understand the science behind something, you think it's magic."

"Do you understand the science behind remote controls?" I asked.

Her head emerged and she gave me A Look. "No, but I know it's there. I know it's not a miracle."

"Speaking of miracles," Clare said, shaking her sleeping bag out, "Aunt Pat reckons she's had a few of them since she turned religious. She's been quoting all this Bible stuff at us."

"There is only one Temple that the Great Spirit has ever been in," Serenity said unexpectedly. "And that's the human being. Great Spirit never made any other church or temple or mosque. They're all man-made."

We looked at her in surprise.

"That's why I like your friend Nina, even though she has some strange ideas. She obviously understands the idea of honouring your body temple."

Which started me thinking about the Red Tent Party... next Saturday... and that I had to bring a symbol of womanhood. I had no idea what *that* was going to be.

CHAPTER 31

SYMBOLS OF WOMANHOOD

HAZEL DIDN'T say much about her religious experience the next morning, and Aunt Pat had left the night before – with her precious blue dish. We made ourselves cereal for breakfast and mooched around in our PJs until nearly lunchtime, when the doorbell rang. At that, we girls shrieked and tried to hide – we were in the lounge room and the windows look straight onto the front so we were sure whoever it was had seen us. Hazel went to the door carrying her breakfast (a cup of coffee), and a moment later a man put his head around the door straight into the lounge room, and we all shrieked some more and dived under our doonas and sleeping bags.

It was Clare's dad, and he *was* really good-looking – even I could see that. He was all those things you hear: tall, dark and handsome. When he smiled, his eyes crinkled up with lots of laughter lines, and you felt like smiling back straight away.

"Caught you out, have I?" he asked from behind the door in a lovely deep voice. "I won't come in, don't panic! I was just dropping by to see if Clare and her mum wanted to come out for lunch today."

Hazel was still holding the door handle; she had a small frown on her forehead, like she was trying to figure out what to do. She eased the door closed, driving her ex back out, and went to stand on the front step with him where we couldn't hear what they were saying.

"Ba-boom!" Serenity murmured mysteriously.

We went back to giggling and being silly, but I think we were all a bit distracted by his arrival. Relationships between men and women sometimes seemed very complicated.

The Saturday of Nina's Red Tent Party seemed to arrive suddenly, even though I was thinking about it and sort of worrying about it every day. "What's a symbol of womanhood, do you think?" I had finally asked my mother, when, by Thursday, I still couldn't think of anything to take.

"Gosh!" she looked at me in surprise, "that's unexpected. Why?"

"We have to bring one to Nina's party."

"Oh…" Mum smiled and shook her head a bit, then went back to pulling washing out of the machine. "That family really does give you some new experiences." She stood up with the basket. "Here's a symbol of motherhood: laundry." She grinned, and started to head outside to the washing line.

"*Womanhood*, Mum," I sighed, following her. "And I'm not exactly going to take our family laundry with me." Mothers!

"Okay… well… make-up? Take a lippie – that's easy."

I made a face.

"Lingerie?"[23]

"Mum!"

"Okay, all right." She shook out one of dad's shirts and started to peg it upside down. "Women are often associated with round,

23   That's sexy nightwear, and it's pronounced 'lanjeree' in French, although most English-speaking people call it 'lonjeray'… Mothers!

curvy shapes – you know, the round pregnant belly, breasts… Maybe you could take a round stone or a shell or something like that…?"

Now she was getting warmer, but I still wasn't inspired. I went to sit on the swing and watched her pegging.

"A cup, Nat," Mum suggested; she was on a roll now. "Receptacles are symbols of womanhood. You could take a pretty cup."

A cup or a stone might have been spot-on symbols, but they hadn't felt special enough to me. So I had headed off to the mall – I'm not usually that into shopping – and wandered around for ages, finally finishing up in a beautiful-smelling shop with crafts from all around the world. And that was where I found my gift.

We arrived at Liz and Nuncle's house on the dot of five o'clock. Sandy and her mum were just getting out of their car, and Clare and Hazel drove up as we climbed out, so we waited for them and then all walked to the house together. I was wearing a skirt and feeling quite strange because I usually hang out in jeans, but Mum had pointed out that if this was about being a woman, I should wear something more feminine. Clare was wearing a dress too, but Sandy was in jeans as usual.

Liz answered the door, wearing a divine, long-sleeved, midnight-blue felt dress with her hair up in a loose knot. Strands of her fair hair hung on either side of her lovely face. She didn't look sick at all, although she was definitely still on the thin side. She welcomed us into the warm kitchen, into an exotic aroma of incense and spices, and invited us to put our meal contributions on the kitchen table, which was already packed with mouth-watering dishes.

Rosie, in an elegant deep pink and yellow beaded sari, was stirring something on the stove as we entered. She put the spoon down and the lid back on and turned to greet us, calling for Nina, who burst in, beaming, a second later wearing a dress for once, a red, full-skirted, gypsy-like dress with black polka dots and a black belt. She looked totally different – even her hair was changed; the green had all but faded. For a moment, I felt a bit sad. It was as if we were facing a new person.

All the mothers drifted over to Liz and Rosie, and we could hear them asking discreet questions about this Red Tent Party from where we stood, gathered around Nina, feeling strange and awkward. Nuncle was nowhere to be seen.

"He's been banished," Nina told us with a grin. "He's not allowed back until tomorrow afternoon."

After about twenty minutes Serenity arrived with her plump, good-natured-looking mum and three little kids in tow. Serenity looked like an American Indian in a long sandy-coloured suede dress with dangly sleeves and tassels around the bottom. It was one of her mum's designs, she said, twirling. Her mother gave all the other mums business cards, and looked like she was going to settle in for a chat. My mother is very good at picking up cues. She noticed Rosie and Liz exchange glances, and said loudly, "Well, I guess we mums had better go and let these young ladies get on with their party."

Finally it was just us.

"This way!" Nina was sparkling as she beckoned to us to follow her. "Welcome to my Red Tent Party!"

CHAPTER 32

ENTERING THE RED TENT

THE LIVING ROOM had been transformed. There were red saris pinned around the walls and the couches had been arranged in a circle so that it really felt like we were entering a tent. A round red, orange and yellow rug bearing the pattern of a sun lay on the floor, and there were candles literally everywhere, on every mantelpiece and windowsill and coffee table. A fire was crackling in the fireplace, and all up, it was magic.

Sitting cross-legged in a pile of cushions at the edge of the rug, with her eyes closed and a basket of flowers in her lap, was the pink-faced woman from the adult Mastermind Group. She opened her eyes slowly as we came into the room.

"This is Marina," Rosie said, "a long-time friend of ours." She introduced everyone and Nina solemnly presented each of her guests with a flower from the garden and a pin so that we could attach it to our hair or clothes. Then we sat on the floor in a circle, and Rosie welcomed us officially.

"Our purpose this evening is to make Nina's journey from girlhood into womanhood a conscious journey," she said, smiling warmly at each of us in turn, "and to sanctify it; to make it holy, sacred. As females, we belong to a Sisterhood of Women that goes back hundreds of thousands of years and extends across the world into all cultures. We are sisters because we share the experiences of bleeding, of being able to bring new life into the world, of raising children and of nurturing people in general, and of being very connected with earth and moon, with the rhythms of nature and the wisdom of intuition.

"From what we understand, the Red Tent was a safe place where women could share their learnings, insights, and experiences with each other. So we are deliberately creating a symbolic 'red tent' in which we can share stories and experiences and connect with that sisterhood, and in doing this we're paying conscious attention to the journey into womanhood, and marking it out as special and an important journey, rather than letting it pass as if it's just any other day."

She smiled at Nina, who smiled back, and they held each other's gaze for a moment, and then Rosie reached around behind herself and brought out a basket that was full of instruments, which she placed in the centre of the room on the rug. She lifted out a hand-made drum and settled it into her lap. "We're going to start with a song. The words are very simple, so do join in."

As Rosie began beating the drum rhythmically, Liz and Marina picked up a rattle and rhythm sticks, and the three of them began to sing:

> *"O Nina, celebrate Nina,*
> *Sing it with an open, joyful heart.*
> *O Nina, celebrate Nina,*
> *Sing it with an open heart."*

It was really nice and really different, and the rest of us added our voices as we caught on.

Then they started again, "O Woman, celebrate Woman, sing

it with an open joyful heart. O Woman, celebrate Woman, sing it with an open heart." I could see Sandy looking a bit uncomfortable with this singing stuff, especially with it being so sort of *meaningful* rather than just music in the background. She was even more uncomfortable the next minute, because they started to sing the song for each one of us, and she was sitting next to Nina. "O Sandy, celebrate Sandy..." we all sang, and I couldn't help grinning at her hot red face.

Clapping hands or shaking rattles, we sang for Clare, for Serenity, for Marina, for Liz, and then I had everyone looking at me and singing "O Natalie, celebrate Natalie," and I was feeling this bursting feeling inside myself which was a mixture of embarrassment and pleasure and wonder. Then we sang for Rosie, and when we'd finished we put our instruments down and burst into a spontaneous happy applause for ourselves and each other.

"We have a plan for tonight and tomorrow morning," Rosie continued. "We're going to begin by sharing stories about our changing bodies and our experiences of menstruation. When Liz and I were little our mother never discussed any of that with us, and we grew up with some very strange ideas about it all," she threw a laughter-filled glance at Liz, who nodded emphatically. "We felt awkward and uncomfortable about the changes we were experiencing and we had to uncover the meaning in it for ourselves. Our mother just gave us some pads and tampons and sent us to the bathroom to figure out how to use them ourselves because she was embarrassed about it.

"So we want to share stories to make this whole process normal, so that *you* don't feel alone and uncertain, and to recognise its importance in our lives. And then we'll pause for some delicious Moroccan pumpkin soup – thank you, Liz, and alternate between talking and feasting for the rest of the evening. We have a huge and scrumptious banquet, thanks to everyone's contributions."

Nina went first, sharing how she had felt when she had discovered that she had her first period, and really, she had taken it much more seriously than any of us (me or Sandy, I mean). Nina was using home-made cloth pads and washing them out herself, instead of the shop ones, and she had even gone outside to sit by herself among the trees in the moonlight to say a little thank-you prayer for this change in her life.

Clare still hadn't had her period so she didn't have much to say except that she was even more curious about it now. Serenity told us that she and her mother had spent a few hours talking about 'women's business' and eating chocolate, all wrapped up on the couch together in blankets. Sandy shrugged and said she hadn't paid much attention to it, and I confessed that Mum had tried but I'd felt uncomfortable about it and had changed the subject.

Marina said she'd had many years of very painful periods so to her it *had* been a curse, until she had begun to understand the connection between our bodies and our emotions, and gradually it had become an easier experience for her. Rosie revealed that she had thought something was wrong with her when she got her first period. She'd been expecting it because she knew about all of that from Liz, but she'd been expecting bright red blood, and so when it started all brown, she'd been quite worried. Liz reminded us that, while she'd had periods, she'd never been able to have children, which had been a source of sadness for her for years. There were a few funny stories about getting your period unexpectedly and having to go through a day at school or work hiding a dark patch on your backside, and how it felt to suddenly have bigger breasts and start wearing a bra...

And that set us off into a conversation about appearances, and how much pressure there was on girls and young women to look a certain way.

"Buxom in the 1800s," Marina said, "and skinny these days."

"I don't pay any attention to that sort of thing," Sandy declared. "I am who I am and people can take me or leave me."

"Well, good for you," Liz said. "It's not that easy for plenty of girls and women. There's always some part of their body they're not happy with." She bubbled up with laughter; "It's the old bum-face dilemma!"

"The what?!" we asked.

"It's something that every model knows," Liz laughed. "When your bum looks great, your face is too fat. But when you get your weight down and your face is perfect, you lose your bum! We all used to moan about it in my modeling days."

"Can't escape that balance of good and bad!" Nina chuckled.

"Truly?" Clare asked, amazed; "I would've thought that models know they're stunning – because you are!"

"Not necessarily!" Liz was quite adamant. "They're often women who *don't* feel beautiful enough, and that's why they dedicate their whole lives to beauty – they're trying to improve themselves. And thank you, Clare," she added with a smile.

"I remember when I first met Liz, I thought she was a bit over the top on the clothes-and-appearance thing," Marina said, "but I've come to appreciate the care she takes – and to take a bit more myself."

"I think it's really nice to take pride in how you look and put some effort into it," Serenity agreed. "I love dressing – maybe because Mum makes clothes and she's really creative, so I've always had a lovely big choice."

"Lucky you," Liz grinned.

"I love expressing myself through clothes too," Rosie said, "but all the same, one of the reasons we decided to home educate Nina was to keep those superficial messages about appearance at bay. We wanted her to be free to follow her interests and express herself however felt right to her without peer pressure."

Well, they'd certainly succeeded there!

Nina grinned and rolled her eyes dramatically. "It was a bit of a shock, coming to school for the first time last year and seeing all these girls trying to look the same. You know, the 'in' girls. And then there was this balancing group going, 'It's not your appearance that matters, it's who you are *on the inside*' – which is a great message, but I reckon there are some girls who kind of take refuge in that, and if they're overweight they take this position that, 'You've got to accept me for who I am on the inside' even though they might actually feel better if they were a bit lighter. What do you think?"

We agreed there were pros and cons both ways, and that some girls had natural advantages in their shapeliness and clear skin, while others faced challenges in those departments, and none of us could believe that there were some girls and women who thought they were so overweight that they went so far as to make themselves puke out every meal! – and so often ended up looking like skeletons.

"They must really feel bad about themselves," Clare said with feeling. "I can't imagine what they must see in the mirror – like, where's all this fat that they're trying to get rid of?"

"Yet another R.A.S. thing," Nina observed; "we see what we believe rather than what's really there. Yeah, it's sad."

"And dangerous." Liz pointed to a picture of herself on the wall from her modeling days. She was wearing a pair of smart white pants with a halter neck top, a wide-rimmed sunhat and very high heels, and looking straight at the camera over one bare shoulder. "You see how skinny I was there? They put a lot of pressure on you to not gain weight – actresses too – until all you can think about is food… It's pretty easy to fall into that eat/vomit cycle, I can tell you."

"Did you?" Nina asked bluntly.

"No, I managed to hold it together, but I had friends who did it hard. They were stunning and yet constantly felt not good enough."

"There's a lot of truth in that statement that it's who you are on the inside that matters," Rosie said. "If you're full of fun and spirit you'll look beautiful even if you're overweight or not so attractive. I remember a girl at school who was quite solid and plain but she was the life of the party."

"Roxanne," Liz said, nodding. "But I agree with you, too, Neens; sometimes it's easier to make other people wrong than to get our body looking the way we want it to."

"The fact is that, no matter how we look, everyone has parts of their body they're satisfied with and parts they're not," Marina put in, "and because of the Law of Conservation, there'll always be –"

"– a balance of positive and negative!" we chimed in. And all laughed.

"Here's another balancing thing," Liz said thoughtfully; "Maybe because I've had a career where appearances are everything, I feel particularly respectful of people who don't care about them at all. Like those Aboriginal women elders you see with their wild hair and big bellies and mismatched, brightly coloured clothes. I like that freedom to just be themselves… I guess that's what's showing up in the women and girls who are very comfortable being more fleshy and curvaceous."

There really was no such thing as just black or just white, I mused. Anything you thought was a positive had something negative in it, and anything you thought was negative had something positive in it, just like the yin/yang symbol showed, with its white dot in the black part and its black dot in the white part. The more you thought about it, the more balance there was.

"While we're on this topic, ladies," Rosie said, "you are all looking divine tonight."

She was mostly right; it was only Sandy who hadn't done anything special, and she really didn't seem to care. ("As soon as girls start talking about clothes, I'm outta there," she said emphatically. "Anything but jeans looks really strange on me, and I don't feel comfortable.")

My cousin Ella was right into clothes and she did always look very stylish. Mum and I had been a bit critical of some of her clothing choices at times, but I had to admit that a little part of me had also often felt envious of how striking she always looked. I'd spent most of my life in jeans and blue t-shirts, which are good clothes for hiding in, but since this was my year for being more visible, maybe I'd start to change that…

We stopped for soup, which was delicious. There was also a beetroot soup and red grape juice, all symbolic of the 'blood of menses', we were told. I could see that Sandy found the association a bit distasteful; she was eyeing the redness warily, but she had some of everything, I noticed, and even scraped out her bowl…

After the soup we sat again in our circle, and the conversation turned to boys.

CHAPTER 33

REAL RELATIONSHIPS

NINA STARTED it off by asking Liz how old she was when she had her first boyfriend. "Hmm," said Liz, turning to her sister thoughtfully, "Twelve?"

"About that," Rosie agreed. "You were an early starter. I was sixteen, and it was Nina's dad," she told the rest of us. "We're childhood sweethearts."

Clare, of course, confronted Nina about Joel, who again said he was only a friend. "He's too old for me," she defended, "and I don't want a boyfriend yet. But I do like him and I sort of feel more aware of boys in general than I used to…"

I knew what she meant; I was nowhere even near being interested in having a boyfriend, but I was starting to notice boys more. Billy flashed through my mind as I said that, but I figured that was just because he was my only real boy-friend. You know, a friend who is a boy…

Sandy and Clare were the same as me, and Serenity said she'd had a few crushes but no boyfriends yet. Marina said she hadn't been interested in boys till she was at university, and then she'd had a couple of boyfriends, long stretches without any, then got married and divorced – a bit of everything.

In a pause in the conversation Clare suddenly said, "Why is it so hard for my mum to keep a man, do you think?" And that started the grown-ups off for quite a while. It turned out that Liz had had lots of boyfriends over the years, really lots. She was quite a specialist in 'running away from relationships', she said. Nuncle was the first man she had stayed with for more than five years – they'd been together for twelve years now, and she knew she was settled for life with him, but he'd had to work quite hard in the early years to keep her from running off whenever they hit a problem.

"Well, you were lucky then," Clare said, hugging her knees. "You got a man who wants you so much he sticks around through the hard times, but my mum can't seem to find someone like that. They're always disappearing on her."

"Our beliefs come into play here," Marina said. "What's your mother thinking? It's very likely that something happened in her childhood that set up a belief like 'men leave me'."

"Oh!" Clare said with a start. "Her dad left when she was little."

"Bingo. We tend to reproduce the experiences that we found hurtful. It's part of the healing process."

"How? Doesn't that just make it worse?"

"It's like Marina said," Liz explained. "We unconsciously look for someone who reminds us of the person we feel hurt us when we were little because we need to heal the wound, and the new person helps by bringing the issue to the surface."

"But how?" Clare repeated. "How do you heal it?"

I noticed that Serenity was sitting very still, gazing into her lap where her fingers were playing with the fringe of her Indian-ish dress.

"Healing something means making it whole," Liz said slowly, "so when we're feeling pain, it's usually because we're not seeing the wholeness, we're seeing part-ness. We put all of our attention on how we feel we were hurt, and we stop noticing how we were loved, or how the difficulties served us.

"In my case, my father had wanted a boy and he got me, a girl – and a very girly girl at that. And then I chose a career that disappointed him and moved overseas, which disappointed him. Over time he closed off from me... I couldn't seem to do anything right for him. And then I kept the pattern going with my boyfriends. I didn't intend to, but it just seemed to keep happening... so every time I felt that I was disappointing a fellow, I left him – before he had a chance to leave me. As if that would make it hurt less!" Liz gave a short dry laugh.

I had shot a quick, involuntary glance at Sandy when Liz was talking about her father's rejection; I wondered if these stories would help her get on better with her dad. I wondered, too, what beliefs I had made in my childhood that would affect *my* adult relationships...

"So there I was for years: stuck on how my dad rejected my femininity and not acknowledging how very supportive he was in other ways," Liz continued, "or how that rejection made my femininity so important to me that it even kind of gave me my career." She stopped and turned her blue eyes to Clare. "Am I confusing you?"

"A bit," Clare confessed.

"The bottom line is this," Marina said; "we think we're attracted to someone because they're good-looking or sexy or intelligent or fun, but it's also because they're a match with our story, with the part of us that's out of balance. And eventually that part comes to the surface and all hell breaks loose. If we don't understand this dynamic, we might leave and go looking for a better match – but we'll always run into that same issue, just in different clothes, until we've handled it, because it's itching to be healed. It's like having a role in a play that we perform over and over again until we get it – until we understand and appreciate our life exactly as it is. And *then*, paradoxically, it becomes exactly what we want…"

"That's it," Liz nodded. "If you can get to the place of feeling gratitude for your situation *exactly* as it is, you can really unleash some magic. It's quite extraordinary."

We were quiet for a moment, reflecting on this, and then she added: "You see, when we feel hurt, all we can see is our point of view. Once we're able to see more points of view, like how their behaviour gives us an opportunity to grow, we see that they are just playing a role in our story and *we* are playing a role in their story, and the whole thing becomes less painful. Honestly, girls, if you can get that there are no ideal relationships, only real ones, and that real relationships take work, you'll be way ahead of the game. And if you're lucky enough to have a partner who wants to grow, you can work through the issues together. That's where I've been very blessed with Max. He's prepared to talk through the uncomfortable stuff – me yelling at him and crying and carrying on."

I stared at her in amazement. Liz yelling? Crying? Carrying on?

"He's quite a bit older than me," she grinned, "more mature! But even if the other person isn't mature or just isn't there, if you ask yourself some good questions, and if you give honest answers, eventually you'll get past the judgements to the love."

She had been using questions to heal her cancer, I remembered. It seemed weird that questions could heal; you'd think it would have to be something more 'solid' than that, like medicine. But as I was having this thought, I reminded myself that everything started in the mind, with thought, and then it got layered with emotion, and then it ended up in the body or out in the world as a behaviour. Or so I had been learning since meeting Nina.

Clare was frowning. Rosie reached across our circle and laid her hand over Clare's.

"You're carrying on your mother's story to some degree," she said in a gentle voice. "You've probably got some thoughts in there about not being wanted because your dad left when you were little, too, right? It's incredible how precisely we will reproduce the issues that have caused pain," she said with a sigh. "But you see, he was probably struggling with his own childhood patterns and just doing his best. It wasn't about you. It was about him. And him leaving has made love very important to you, hasn't it?"

Clare nodded, flushing. Serenity bum-shuffled closer to her and looped an arm around her shoulder.

"It takes a lot of courage and honesty and willingness to heal our childhood hurts," Rosie said quietly. "Not many people are up for it. It's much easier to keep reacting and blaming and running away – or to go into a kind of numbness where you pretend it doesn't matter and you build a thick shell around you. Don't do that, sweetheart. Remember the process you went through with the bullies. This is the same. Find out how it's serving you that your dad left, how it's a blessing."

"Could we have a toilet break?" Sandy asked, and I really could have swatted her for being so insensitive. Hadn't she seen the tears glinting in Clare's eyes?

"Of course," Rosie said, keeping her hand on Clare's and her gaze locked with Clare's. "Let's have a group cuddle and then go eat our next course."

We stood up stiffly, shook out our legs, and linked arms in a tight circle. I looked around at each face: Clare, Sandy, Nina, Rosie, Liz, Marina and Serenity. I had never been as close to anyone as I now felt with these people – these women and young women… It felt odd to think of myself as a young woman, I still felt like a kid, but I supposed I was becoming one. And in some cultures I'd already be considered a woman now that I'd started bleeding. That felt weird.

We went back to the kitchen table where there was a true feast of spinach pie and salads and baked vegies and dips and buttered corn bread and a plate with olives and artichokes and dolmades and another plate with sushi and California rolls.

"What a spread!" Marina marvelled as we tucked in.

"It's a great symbol for the variety of relationships life offers us," Liz agreed, "the spicy ones, the sweet ones, the juicy ones…" She winked, and popped an olive into her mouth – which made me realise that she was eating again. There was only salad on her plate, but she was still eating.

"And all the variety *in* relationships," Serenity remarked unexpectedly. "The ups and downs and liking and not liking… My parents can get pretty dramatic with each other some of the time, but they hang in there through the hard stuff, so I suppose that is true love."

"You've named it, girlfriend," Rosie said with a smile; "there are plenty of couples that stay together quite unconsciously, building those protective shells around themselves, but the ones that keep communicating and doing their best reap the rewards. True love is the liking *and* the not-liking, not some fantasy dream of an only-nice relationship or a soul mate who will just have nice qualities. That's an illusion, if ever there was one! But the beauty is that the more challenges you work through with your partner, and the more you appreciate even the qualities you don't like that much, the richer and stronger the relationship becomes."

We sat around the table with our loaded plates, and as we began to eat, Nina asked exuberantly, "So, hey, did you all bring your symbols of womanhood?"

It turned out that we were going to look at those next.

CHAPTER 34

TREASURES OF WOMANHOOD

"I'M SO FULL I feel like I'm going to have a baby," Serenity groaned, cradling her belly as we settled ourselves back in our Red Tent on the gorgeous rug.

"Nowhere better!" Rosie teased.

"Is that your symbol?" Nina asked, grinning. "Very appropriate."

"No, this is." And she handed Nina a parcel wrapped in tissue paper. "Happy birthday."

Nina gave her a lovely smile and began to open the wrapping. She drew out an embroidered bag. It was black with multi-coloured threads woven through it in a striking pattern.

"It's made by women in South America," Serenity said. "And bags are containers which are symbols of womanhood. And most women carry them, so..."

"Thank you," Nina said warmly. "It's beautiful."

"There's something inside," Serenity added, and Nina unzipped the bag and lifted out another small package, which turned out to be silver hoop earrings.

"Thank you! They're lovely." Nina pulled out the earrings she was wearing and put the new ones in. She turned her head from side to side, modelling them for us. Then she said, "I hadn't meant for the symbols to be presents, you know."

But it turned out that we had all done that. Sandy had sculpted a Venus; she'd actually googled symbols of womanhood and found these little clay figurines that were supposed to be it, and then made one. We passed it from hand to hand, admiring the smoothly-formed, round-bellied woman, and then Nina sat it in the centre of the circle, where it stayed for the rest of the evening.

Clare's gift was a bottle of natural skin lotion. It came wrapped in a piece of brown paper with what looked like crayon squiggles on it. When Nina smoothed the paper out, the squiggles turned out to be a poem.

"Oh, don't read it aloud!" Clare protested, but Nina did.

> *"Girl to woman is my destiny.*
> *For now, I am a maiden,*
> *young, shy, and*
> *bursting with possibility.*
> *Ahead lies womanhood:*
> *tears and laughter,*
> *hope and despair,*
> *madness and fears,*
> *and, above all,*
> *love."*

Nina crawled across the rug and gave Clare a hug. Then she hugged Sandy, who was taken by surprise and didn't resist, before crawling back to her spot. I handed her my gift with two hands; it was heavy. She looked at me with grey quizzical eyes for a moment, and then began unwrapping.

"I know your family already has salt lamps," I began, as the orange globe was revealed, "but this one's roundness was what caught my eye."

"It's perfect," she said. "It will go on my bedside table." She gave me a kiss on each cheek ('a Greek kiss') and plugged it in. A soft orange glow joined the candlelight and firelight.

"And the light is the other symbol," I added. "Because you bring light."

Nina smiled. "I'm going to cry in a minute," she said.

"Nowhere better," Rosie smiled back.

Marina had made a stained glass artwork of a black woman's naked shoulder and breast against a vibrant colourful background. The woman was holding a flower up to her chin. It was very impressive.

"I'm bursting," Nina said, and there really were tears in her eyes. "I'll hang this in my bedroom window at home."

Liz brought out a box and a bottle. It was dark grape juice, and the box revealed eight etched wine glasses. "Symbol of womanhood, of course," she said, holding up a glass, "and something for you to celebrate this moment and all the other moments that are coming." She unscrewed the bottle and began to pour. We waited, mesmerised by the liquid as it bubbled into each glass, and then toasted Nina, toasted us, and toasted womanhood.

"And there's this," Liz continued, passing Nina a soft package. When the paper fell away, Nina shook out a vibrant turquoise dress with a black lace bodice.

"It's beautiful," Nina marvelled. "I'll feel like a goddess wearing this."

"That's the idea," Liz said. "You've been my daughter too, all these years, Nina. I'm so grateful to Rosie for sharing you with me. I don't think I've ever said it to you, but I want you to know how much you have meant to me all these years. All the cuddles you've given me, the times you've stayed over... that you've let me look after you and give to you as I never could…" she stopped, tears falling from her eyes.

Nina was crying too as she pressed close to her aunt for a long hug. For once she was without words, but her eyes said everything when she finally pulled back and sat looking at Liz, holding hands.

And then it was Rosie's turn. "You know how much you mean to me," she said to Nina, "you've made me grow more than anything else in my whole life. You've challenged me and terrified me and comforted me and made me laugh and made me think. I'll always be grateful to you.

"I have three things for you, my lovely Nina: this photo book which is a record of your life from the womb to now; this scarf, which is a symbol of womanhood because women have used scarves for aeons to protect ourselves and our babies and to carry food and goods, and for spiritual reasons; and this pendant of the moon."

It was an opal crescent moon on a fine silver chain. As we passed it around, admiring it, Nina read a little docket that had been tucked into the package: *"The moon reflects the sun's light and represents the appearance, growth and disappearance cycles of life, death and rebirth."*

"Also symbolic of the mysterious shadow side of life," Marina added, "with its fears and darkness."

"Thank you, Mum," Nina said, reaching toward her mother. They held each other in a long hug, and we sat waiting. I wondered how Sandy was feeling, since she wasn't close to her mother. Her face was a bit flat, sort of empty and expressionless.

"I know you're probably all still full," Liz said, "but we do have a few sweets to finish with."

At that, Sandy sat up, shaking off the flatness and saying brightly, "Always room for sweets!"

Liz grinned. "Stay where you are and we'll have them right here."

And a platter of fruit kebabs, fruit cheese, chocolates and chocolate sauce appeared. After that the only thing that was said for a while was 'yum' and 'mmm…' as we dipped the strawberries and bananas and pears into the sauce and then popped them into our mouths.

"Okay, I'm definitely having a Red Tent Party," Clare decided, licking her fingers.

"Well, Nina, it's been a night of treasures but you haven't told us what womanhood is to you," Marina said, when we were down to scraping the last bit of chocolate sauce out of the bowl.

"That's true," Nina said. She looked around at us all. "It's this: it's love and friendship and support and honesty and givingness and kindness. And it's all those things you talked about in your poem, Clare – crying and feeling lost and a bit crazy at times and doing your best to live your full potential. I feel so rich right now I could burst."

"We're all bursting with you," Serenity assured her solemnly, and we exploded into laughter.

"Yes. Was this a plan to give us the experience of being pregnant?" Clare asked, leaning against some cushions and patting her stomach. "I can't move."

"Maybe that's exactly what you should do," I said. "Maybe we should go for a midnight walk to walk some of it off."

Rosie and Nina exchanged glances. "Well, actually," Nina confessed, "I was hoping you would all join me for a medicine walk in the morning. On the beach. At dawn."

"At dawn!" Sandy exclaimed in horror.

"At dawn."

"Are you nuts?"

"It's the best time of day."

"That means we'll have to get up at four or something."

"Maybe not four, but early," Rosie agreed.

"Four-fifteen should do it," Liz grinned.

"What's a medicine walk?" I asked.

CHAPTER 35

NINA'S BIRTHDAY MEDICINE

IT SEEMED AS IF I didn't fall asleep until the early hours of the morning, so when Rosie knocked on the door of Nina's old attic bedroom at 4.15 a.m., I felt like I had to drag myself to consciousness from a long way away. It was dark outside, and that made us whisper as we dressed.

Liz and Rosie were standing in the kitchen, where the light seemed too bright, having hot drinks. Everyone looked bleary-eyed… except for Nina who was bright and bursting to go. Liz offered us a glass of freshly squeezed orange juice, and that helped a bit. She was packing a picnic basket with leftovers from our feast for breakfast. I went to hold the fridge door open for her as she brought things out, and noticed pictures of an African-looking boy on the door. Two were those posed school pictures; in one he was about twelve, and frowning; in another he was seventeen and staring straight at me with a stern expression on his face, like a challenge. And next to it there was another picture of him – at least, I thought it was him – holding a toddler in his arms and looking much more relaxed. I wondered who he was. Maybe an African person Liz and Nuncle were sponsoring?

We piled into the van that Liz and Nuncle seemed to borrow for all of these group adventures and began the half-hour drive to the beach. There was hardly anyone on the road and we were all pretty quiet, still half-asleep.

When Liz had parked, she and Rosie shouldered backpacks and Rosie gave us each an incense stick – a kind of torch to use as we followed them through the darkness along a sandy path. It was lovely to watch the burning orange point ahead of me, and to smell the fragrance that was wafting around just in front of my face. The air was cool and I was glad of my coat and hood.

We gathered in a shadowy knot close to the water, the rhythmic sounds of the sea just a few steps away from us, washing up on the shore and receding, washing up and receding.

"I wanted to do a medicine walk because to me, growing up is about becoming more conscious and more responsible," Nina told us, "and what I've read about these walks is that you walk really consciously, seeing everything as a symbol, as if it's a message exactly for you, and nothing is chance or random or coincidental. You see absolutely everything as meaningful. I thought it would be nice to do this because you'll each be getting your own personal messages at the same time."

I glanced at the faces around me. Clare was interested, Sandy inscrutable as she gazed into the distance, Serenity looked, well, serene.

"Let's sit for a moment and gather our energy and just feel the morning and the earth," Rosie suggested. So we sat on the cool, hard sand, and closed our eyes and listened to the waves steadily rolling in and trickling back, in and back, and felt the breeze play with our hair.

We seemed to be sitting there, still and quiet, for ages. I opened my eyes a crack to find out what was happening. Everyone was still sitting with eyes shut, except for Sandy who was drawing patterns in the sand with her finger. She looked at me and raised her brows as if to say, 'bit weird, eh?'

The faintest pink light was showing in the east above the cliff top. I put my hands flat onto the sand on either side of me and closed my eyes again, feeling the stillness of the sandy earth. It reminded me of times I had leaned against a big tall tree in a forest, and felt the tree's ancient stillness, as if it was patiently waiting while we humans rushed about here and there doing all the things we thought were so important, and meanwhile the tree and the earth knew that nothing was as important as just being.

I was becoming aware that my breathing had harmonised with the tide when Rosie asked softly, "Ready to walk?"

Without a word, we all stood up and brushed the sand off our backsides and legs. She and Marina shouldered the packs and we headed off into the dark on the lumpy sand.

"What did you mean by a message?" I asked, coming into step with Nina.

"Whatever it means for you," she said. "I'm not really sure either. I haven't done this before, but I think it's like, you just notice what you're noticing. What you notice and what I notice will be different. For example, I've been really noticing that breeze while we were sitting back there. So I guess a conscious walk is asking, what does a breeze mean to me?"

"What does it?" I asked.

"It makes me think of movement and change. The wind stirs things up and refreshes everything. After I've been for a walk in the wind I always come home crackling with aliveness and alert and clear-headed. I love it. So maybe the wind is a message for me to move and get out of stuckness and get a fresh perspective… Or maybe it's just saying that I'm going through a time of change." She looked at me with those thoughtful grey eyes. "But someone else would probably have a totally different interpretation. What have you been noticing?"

A bird flew overhead at that moment and we both glanced at it and then grinned at each other.

"What are you two talking about?" Sandy asked, as she and Clare and Serenity joined us.

"What things mean," I said.

"Well?" Nina asked me. "Is it the bird? What do birds mean to you?"

"Freedom!" Sandy declared. She raised her arms and ran off a little way like a gliding bird, then turned back and looked at us sheepishly.

"That Sandy don't feel free," Nina observed. "You know how she never told you guys that she was doing pottery? When she expresses herself, she feels like she has to hide."

I pondered this as we walked towards the sheepish Sandy, who was scuffing at the sand with the toe of her shoe, hands stuffed into her pockets.

"Birds are my totem," Serenity said, when Sandy was in earshot. "There was a whole tree of magpies warbling away like crazy as I was being born – I had a home birth and there's this great big gum tree right outside the bedroom. Mum said they kept their song up during my entire birth, so we decided to make them my totem."

"A totem! " Clare marvelled. "That's cool."

"So what do birds mean to you?" Nina asked her.

"I think they're amazing creatures," Serenity said. "One minute they're on earth dealing with practical things like feeding their babies and building nests, and the next minute they're soaring through the clouds, in the grandness of space, far from the little ordinary details of life."

I pondered that too, as we walked on, sand underfoot, dark

salty sea at one side and cliffs at the other side, the pinkish sky, and no-one to be seen but us... What did birds mean to me? I loved early morning birdsong too, and watching birds in flight. But I'd always been nervous walking under the pine trees on my way to school when I was little because I'd heard that magpies might swoop down and peck my head. The yin/yang of birds.

"How's it going, girls?" Rosie asked as the three women joined us.

"Good," we said.

"Are you prepared for the swamps and crocodiles?" Liz joked.

Sandy regarded her with one raised eyebrow.

"Rain's been forecast," Marina said. "Hopefully it will wait till we're finished, but if it comes, it comes."

"Yep. You just never know what will be part of the journey on a medicine walk," Liz agreed, and moments later we found ourselves clambering over slippery rocks that demanded all of our attention.

Suddenly everything was light! It was as if someone had thrown a switch. One minute we were walking through early morning half-light then suddenly we were in full light. We stopped walking and turned around, admiring the scenery in its new clothes, this lovely, soft, greyish, morning light.

"I'm getting hungry," Sandy said as we stood there. "I didn't think I'd ever be hungry again after that feast last night, but I am."

"Seems like a good time to stop for a bite," Rosie agreed. We knelt on the sand and shared leftover fruit and spinach pie, a strange breakfast but it was delicious.

Then we headed off again. Nina and Serenity began to collect feathers and stick them in their hair. After a bit they looked like two American Indians – very fitting for a medicine walk.

I had been wondering what the time was all morning and finally I realised I had stopped thinking about it and was just walking. A couple of women strode past us really fast. They gave a short wave and called, "Morning!" Soon they had disappeared into the distance. A little later we passed a weathered-looking fisherman. His dog came to sniff us, tail wagging.

"Symbols, symbols," Nina murmured, patting him, and then again as we picked our way through some smelly seaweed. The sun had cleared the clouds now and we were all feeling pretty warm. We began to take off our jackets and tie them around our waists.

For a while Liz walked alongside me, not saying anything. The pressure to ask built up in me, and finally I said, "How are you going – health-wise?"

"Well, thank you, Nat," she said after a moment. She looped her arm around my shoulders and gave me a little hug. "I've been through some pretty yucky patches with the detoxing I've been doing – really sick and tired, but I seem to be getting past that now... So... doing my best to learn and not fear, to surrender without giving up, to choose what I want without trying to control everything."

"That sounds very tricky," I said, "balancing all that."

"Yes. Life can be tricky." She dropped her arm, which made walking easier again for both of us, but more solitary.

Later we stopped for a brunch, a mini-banquet of the bits and pieces that remained. When we'd finished, Marina delved into one of the packs and brought out some homemade chocolate eggs. "Since Easter is close," she said. "They're feminine symbols, after all, and Easter is a rite of passage too. A death and a rebirth."

"Very fitting," Rosie commented.

One by one we lay on the sand and gazed into the sky, feeling the ground below us. Rosie's voice came from some-where nearby; "Life used to revolve around the changing seasons, the moon and women's fertility cycles. Now that we have electricity, that's all changed. We mostly live in defiance of nature, but doesn't it feel good to tune into it? I often wonder how much damage we're doing ourselves by getting out of harmony with nature..."

Another balancing, law-of-conservation thing, I realised. The wonders of electricity – how easy it made life, and then this damaging side of it. I had often got up in the middle of the night to go to the loo and discovered my mother still in her office, working. And in the morning she'd be in the kitchen when I got there, with bags under her eyes, and I'd wonder how much sleep she could have had.

Rosie organised us all into a tight bunch and took a few photos, and then Liz took the camera from her so that she'd be in some of them, and then a young man walked past conveniently ("No coincidences!" Serenity chirped), and took a picture of us all together.

"A new woman walks on the earth," Rosie chanted as we set off again. She began to click her fingers in tune with her song; Liz and Marina joined in.

Sandy came to walk alongside me and Nina. "So what are you making this walk mean?" she asked Nina bluntly.

"Well… I've been thinking about the past, when I was little, and how I'm leaving that behind in a way but also carrying it with me," Nina replied. "And thinking about the future and what I want to create in it."

"What *do* you want to create?" Clare asked from behind us.

Nina smiled, saying nothing.

"She's not telling," Serenity announced. "She's holding it inside as a vision."

"And what's the meaningness of not having green hair anymore?" Sandy added. "Can't be time to be ordinary!"

"No; time to be invisible," Nina said mysteriously. "I'm going to gradually fade away…"

"Yeah, right," Sandy scoffed, giving her a little push.

Nina giggled. "Okay! It's because Liz's cancer woke me up that it's probably not the best idea to be dousing my head in chemicals all the time. And anyway, real wizards don't need to stand out.

They do all their magic with their minds. I kind of like the idea that you just can't tell which of the ordinary people on the street know their own power and which are just living unconsciously. It's being an invisible wizard."

I'd had the exact same thought about strangers in the streets but I couldn't imagine Nina being anything but very noticeable, whatever colour her hair was.

Most of us needed the loo by now so as we walked on, we kept our eyes peeled for a toilet block. "I think we passed one a little while ago," Marina said at last. "Bush wee, girls."

Clare made a face. We took turns disappearing into the shrubs, and then someone realised that this was the turn-off-the-beach point. It was sad to leave the sea behind but lovely to be sheltered from the sun and be surrounded by trees. In one place we had to walk single file through some lovely tea tree scrub. It looked like a fairy glen – beautiful. In another place we struck a thousand buzzing insects and later, unexpectedly, a little patch of pine forest that smelt divine.

Finally we arrived at the car park again, and climbed into the van for the homeward drive just as rain began to pour from dark grey clouds.

Mastery Club Lesson #21

Honouring the Feminine
& Tuning In

✳ Everyone, male and female, has both a masculine and a feminine aspect.

✳ We honour the Feminine in us when we tune into Earth and Nature, when we connect with the pulse of Life, when we listen to our intuition...

CHAPTER 36

SUPERWOMAN LEARNS HOW TO CREATE TIME

SECOND TERM seemed to take off at a great rate. Clare arrived home and found that her mum and dad had had a big fight while we'd been at the Red Tent Party, and her dad had disappeared again. Hazel was in good form; she reckoned that she'd finally said what she'd needed to say and she was finished with him now, but Clare felt cheated and angry.

Miss Walker organised the Mastery Club to start again and I suggested that we do a short visualisation every time we met. It wasn't very easy because other kids kept staring through the glass at us, and once someone even knocked on the door to ask what we were doing, but it was good to be building our focus week after week. I think it was those quiet moments on the beach that put it in my head to make sure we did some regular visualising. So much of modern life was just constant rushing; I'd really enjoyed that stillness.

Nina had given her talk at the business breakfast and it had gone down really well – she'd been booked to speak at another one! It was really weird sitting at my desk at school knowing that at that very moment she was standing in front of a roomful of business people talking about Mastery Club stuff! Really weird…

Out in the world there were demonstrations in the Middle East and in Europe and a big earthquake in the Pacific. It seemed like everything was happening at once.

At my place, Mum was getting more and more stressed, trying to complete a whole lot of website projects before we went overseas, and worrying about going overseas now that there was unrest in Europe. Katie and Evan had been sick with at least one of them home from school for the last two weeks, so Mum was way behind in her work. Finally one night she said to Dad, "Take everyone to the park! If I don't have some space to myself I'll go mad!" When Mum talks like that, nobody argues, so we hot footed it out of there and left her in peace to cook dinner. Dad drove us to the park, and then sat in the car on his iPhone.

"Are you going to kick that ball or just carry it?" I asked Evan as we walked onto the oval. He frowned at me but dropped his brand new soccer ball to the ground and gave it a bit of a kick.

Katie ran at the ball and gave it a strong kick herself; then darted away.

"Hey!" yelled Evan, tearing after his property.

"Come on, get the ball!" Katie called over her shoulder, jabbing at it with her foot again.

Seeing he wasn't going to get near it, Evan slowed down, casting a furious glance after Katie.

"Katie!" I shouted, "be fair!" It was funny how you turned into a parent as soon as you were in charge of little kids.

Katie stopped the ball with her foot and threw it to Evan, who beamed and started dribbling it. Then Katie ran into the line of the ball again, snatching it away. Evan threw himself to the ground in a tantrum.

I glanced at the car but Dad hadn't noticed anything. His head was down – reading a message or texting, I supposed.

"Katie!" I scolded. "Don't be so mean."

"He's a sook," she said contemptuously.

"He's still not well," I reminded her. "Come on, Ev, get up. Katie will let you have the ball."

"She won't," he sobbed, drumming his feet against the ground.

"Yes she will," I said ominously. "Won't you, Katie?"

"Who wants the crummy old ball anyway?" Katie scoffed, tossing it in the opposite direction. Evan gave the ball a sideways glance and then looked up at Katie. I knew what he was thinking: would she beat him to it again?

"I won't get it," she said airily. "I'm going to the swings." And she marched away into the early evening mist.

I squatted down next to Evan, who still had his face on the cold earth – Mum would have been scolding him to get up right now, this minute! "Ev," I said, "you know your book about the Knights of the Round Table?" This was his all-time favourite book, a birthday present from Nana earlier this year.

He didn't answer, but lifted his head and began to sit up. Tears were scrawling their way through the dirt on his face.

An idea was dawning on me, a Mastery Club idea. "Those knights don't let their annoying sisters get to them," I said. "They're strong and brave, and they're on quests to do really amazing things."

Evan looked at me, perplexed.

"What if you were an Invisible Knight?" I continued, getting caught up in my own idea. "What if you were secretly a real knight but you had a knight suit that no-one could see? You could be Evan the Unstoppable – Evan the Great Knight who never lets his sister get him down!"

He didn't reply, just swiped the back of his hand across his nose. But a moment later he scrambled to his feet and marched away to pick up his ball, and suddenly I realised who had been my teachers before Nina and Nuncle and Miss Walker turned up: it had been the characters in my fantasy novels, people like Dumbledore and Gandalf and Aragorn… No wonder I had loved those books.

When we got back home Liz and Nuncle were sitting in the kitchen with Mum, who was in tears. "Liz always seems to turn up when I'm due for a cry," she sniffed, blowing her nose.

"You just crossed my mind," Liz said, "and we were only around the corner."

"I've been thinking about you two myself," Dad said, shaking hands with Nuncle. "I wouldn't mind another chat, Max."

"Any time," Nuncle said with his warm smile. "How are things, Nat?"

"Good thanks," I replied, hovering in the doorway.

"How about you blokes get the little ones ready for bed and Natalie and I will help Beth finish cooking," Liz said, standing up. Mum started to protest but everyone else was moving into action.

"This smells good," Liz said, stirring the pot. "Ratatouille?"

"Yes." Mum hadn't even stood up, and looking at her, I could see how very tired she was.

"I'll set the table," I said, and started to get the crockery out.

"Will you stay and eat with us?" Mum asked Liz politely.

"Thanks, but no thank you. We've got some soup on ourselves, so we'll need to head off in a mo and rescue it," Liz said, putting the spoon down and checking the rice. "This is all nearly done." She came to sit at the table again and took Mum's hand. "You know, there's nothing wrong with asking for help. I tried the Superwoman thing for a while, too, and look where it left me."

Mum nodded, sniffing.

"Natalie's a great resource for you." Liz's tone was quite tender as she sat gazing at Mum. "She's quite a treasure."

I paused at the door with my armful of dishes and cutlery.

"I don't want to burden her, it's not fair," Mum said. "She's just a child."

"A young woman, I'd say," Liz said gently. "And it will be worse for all of them if you get sick."

Mum nodded again, and sniffed and laughed and cried a bit at the same time. Then she got the hiccups and we all started to laugh. I took the dishes to the dining room and came back into the kitchen quickly.

"The thing with stress," Liz was saying, "is that you'll never get rid of it or avoid it altogether, but I've come across a strategy that works like a charm to get the stress out of things. I was catching myself saying, 'I have to do this, I need to do that' all the time, and I was constantly feeling pressed and hurried. So I changed what I was saying to 'I'd love to wash the dishes now, I'd love to answer my emails, I'd love to clean the bath…'"

Mum and I burst into laughter – how absurd!

Liz grinned. "It works. I relax and I feel like I have heaps more time. I gather that 'I'd love to' actually calls on a higher brain centre than those 'have-to, got-to' thoughts."

"I'd love to go to bed and sleep for hours and hours and hours," Mum said.

"Why don't you?" Liz replied, serious again.

Mum looked at her.

"Go on. Go to bed. We can serve this lot, can't we, Nat?"

"Sure," I said.

"I've got work…" Mum trailed off, pointing in the direction of her office.

"Early in the morning when you've had a deep, refreshing sleep," Liz told her. "Go on."

"Good night, Mum," I said encouragingly, and opened the door for her.

Mum hesitated for another moment and then said to Liz, "We should be helping you, not the other way around."

"You *are* helping me. Letting me give to you. Feels good," Liz replied, holding her gaze.

"Thank you," Mum said finally. She gave Liz a brief hug, and then me, and went to her room.

"And what would *you* love to do?" Liz asked me, as the men came clattering down the stairs with Evan and Katie after their bath.

"My homework," I said gravely, "I'd love to do my homework."

Mastery Club Lesson #22

* 'I'd love to…' is powerful time-making magic.

* Instead of activating the primal, reactive brain it activates the neural cortex – your evolved, new brain!

Brain Talk

Do you…

Love to

Choose to

Desire to

Want to

Need to

Should/Ought to/Supposed to

Got to/Have to…?

Notice how they each make you feel…

CHAPTER 37

OWNING IT ALL

I EXPERIMENTED with that 'love to' idea and it actually worked. When I said 'I'd love to do my homework', I felt much more like doing it than when I told myself I had to do it. I don't know if Mum tried it out but she did seem to calm down a bit after that, and Dad seemed to help her more. Anyway, before you knew it the school holidays were here and we were onto our last few days in Melbourne before flying to Europe. OMG!!!!

The Mastery Club came to my place for a last meeting before I left. It was the first time Serenity had visited. (She loved my crystals). It was also a cold, grey day and I was secretly delighted that we'd soon be flying out of here to warmth and sunshine. But I didn't say anything – I didn't want to rub it in.

We had to connect with Nina on Skype because she was getting ready to go and visit Joel in the bush, and as we crowded around the computer, I wondered if the others would keep meeting while we were gone. Somehow, I doubted it.

"Travel wishes first," Nina said, looking at me from the screen. "Create a brilliant time, Nat."

"Thanks. You too," I grinned. And then I changed the subject to everyone's goals. I didn't want to dwell on this amazing adventure I was about to have because Clare would have loved to do something like this and there was no way Hazel could afford it. She was frowning, like it upset her to even think about it.

"You first for a change," I said to Nina, "we know you're doing this comfort zone thing of staying with Joel and his people, but how are your other things going? Like the talk you gave at that business breakfast – what was it like?"

Nina rolled her eyes. "Man. Scary."

"What? The great Nina!" Sandy scoffed. "Surely not!"

"You try it!" Nina retorted. "All these men and women in suits sitting and staring at you. I had a stomach ache and diarrhoea the day before it –"

"Ugh! Too much information," Sandy grimaced.

"– and my legs were shaking and I kept going blank."

"Sounds like she was outside her comfort zone," Clare giggled. "This is such good news. Now we know you're human after all."

Nina made a face, but Clare couldn't have uttered a truer truth. Suddenly I didn't feel so bad about my nerves before that first Mastery Club session at school.

"Let's keep this show on the road," Billy interrupted. "I'm going to have to shoot soon. So – my goal's on track. Going on a mountain biking camp these holidays to learn techniques like racing strategies and jumps; we ride most of the time so I should get pretty fit. And there's that Championship race I've been visualising for at the end of it."

Bill already looked pretty fit, I thought, gazing at him. He was really tanned and shooting up much taller than the rest of us. And his voice was getting deeper. Every now and then he squeaked or even lost a word altogether, but on the whole his voice was much deeper. So while we girls had periods and bigger breasts to deal with at this puberty time, guys had their own issues with breaking voices and changing bodies.

"Very cool," Nina said, but she was looking at me when she said that, not Bill.

"Is it in the mountains?" Serenity asked. "I love the mountains."

"Yeah."

"I'm going to visit my Dad," Clare said suddenly.

"What?" I turned around to look at her. "I thought he was gone."

"He is gone. But he rang and it's arranged. After all, I have my own relationship with my father," she said, jutting her chin in the air. "Just because *Mum* doesn't want to see him any more."

"Good luck," Sandy said darkly.

"What's cooking with you?" Billy asked.

"Nothing much. Just the usual."

"Did you ever ask your Dad why he's in the army?" Nina enquired.

"Yes I did," Sandy said, giving nothing away.

"So what did he say?" Nina persisted.

"This stuff about wanting to serve his country and protect people."

"By killing *other* people," Serenity mocked. "No offence to your dad, but that makes no sense."

"Hang on, Serenity," Nina interrupted. "So," she said to Sandy, "your dad looks after other people the way you want him to look after you."

Sandy stared at her and then shrugged. "In my dreams."

"In your visualisations, maybe," I suggested.

She ignored me. "Anyway, Serenity's right. Save a life in this country, kill one in that country. Makes no sense."

"Nuh," Billy contradicted; "they try to kill as few people as possible to save as many people as possible. Unless they're nutters."

"The problem is that you're both making him wrong for having different values and beliefs to yours," Nina said, "and if you make people wrong for being different, then pretty soon we end up at war."

"But if people's values include killing other people then it doesn't seem to me that we should let them succeed," Serenity objected.

"You can't change everyone at once. It's like…" Screen-Nina cast around her room as if she was looking for an example; her eyes focused back on us. "Like this: right now on this planet there are cave people, nomads, farmers, city-livers, techno-heads and multi-billionaires all living here at once. You've got people whose idea of solving problems is to shoot them, and other people who do everything they can to avoid fighting. And the plain fact is that everyone has the right to grow up in their own time, just like how everyone's a toddler and then a kid and then a teenager and then an adult and then an old person… It's something we learnt about on the course – that everyone evolves through these different stages and different values, and just because we're at level six, for instance, does that mean we can't let other people be at level three?"

"In that case," I said triumphantly, "if we all let everyone just be, there wouldn't be war, would there!"

"Nope," Nina replied, "that would never happen because you'll never get the whole world letting everyone else be. There'll *always* be someone who wants to conquer and control other people, and there'll always be people like Sandy's dad who just want to protect. So the world is this mishmash of people who want to protect others balancing out the people who want to control others, etc. etc.."

"So war goes on forever," Sandy said. "Great."

"Hey," I exclaimed, "remember when we were at Billy's and you said that if people really love themselves they don't want to fight anyone, but also that everybody has every quality and you can't get rid of fighting? You were going to find out how we can have both of those."

"Yes!" Nina turned her head suddenly and called out, "Pete!" A moment later she said, still looking away, "Would you explain that thing we were talking about the other night?" and then her father's waist appeared on the screen next to her.

"Well, hello, all!" he exclaimed, bending down and peering at us. "Now, what thing was that, Neen?"

"You know, how everyone has all traits, good and bad ones, but you only go to war out in the world if you're at war inside yourself."

"Remind me."

Nina frowned in thought. "Well… can you ever get to be so loving inside yourself that you would never go to war? If war out there is always going to happen, then that must mean that people will always have conflict going on inside them."

"Ah." Pete looked around for a chair and pulled one close. "You know how music is organised in octaves, which are a series of eight notes?"

We nodded. Being a musician, Pete always explained things musically.

"Well, think of it like this: every time we judge something and then find the order in it, we've completed an octave, a cycle; in physics, Max would call it a quantum. But that doesn't give us a pass into paradise; we'll judge something else straight away – there'll be something new that we get all het up about. As soon as we own it and see the Order, we've completed another cycle and we get our *next* lesson. So we'll never sustain a state of peace for long because conflict is as much a part of the Divine Order as peace; war and peace form a whole together. But in the meantime, the faster we own our judgements and turn them to love, the faster we evolve… although that only means evolving into the next conflict, since this cycle of judgements and learnings goes on into infinity. Does that help?"

It did, but it went against everything I'd ever heard or thought. So much for heaven.

"And that," Nina added, "is backed up by science. It's not just our opinion."

I looked at Sandy.

"So we'll always have war," she said.

"In one form or another," Pete agreed, "because we'll never be in complete inner harmony. There'll always be something irking us. Like," he looked at Nina with mock severity, "I thought you said you were going to hang out the washing. It's still sitting in the basket and it's getting smelly. We're going to have to rewash."

Nina blushed. "Sorry, Dad, I totally forgot. I'll do it as soon as we finish this."

It was a very weird moment, seeing Nina being told off, even if it was done so nicely.

Pete farewelled us and disappeared, and Nina murmured, "Oops…" (about the washing) and then burst out with, "Hey! Do you want to play a game that we learnt at the course?" Her face suddenly grew bigger as she leaned closer to her webcam. "It's called the 'I Am That' game. Every time you see someone who's behaving in a way you don't like, you say to yourself, 'I Am That', and you see if you can own it."

"Why?" Sandy asked flatly.

"To evolve ourselves faster!" Nina glowed. "See, the whole purpose of life is Love. If we're putting people up on pedestals or down in pits we're not exactly loving them. Loving people is being equal with them and having them in our hearts. Besides, if you judge something, you're going to end up doing it. So if you can own it instead of judging it, you're safe!"

"I thought we were supposed to be being Order detectives," I reminded her.

"It's all part of the same thing," she said. "The Order is in seeing that you attract problems because of your own judgements; the Mastery is in changing your thoughts because then you're deliberately and consciously creating your reality instead of just reacting to things."

We were silent, digesting this.

"At the course they told us this very way-out story about a Jewish woman in the Holocaust who was standing in a queue with Nazis all around her, and machine guns, and sniffer dogs," Nina said. "She's about to be deported to a concentration camp, and she's thinking about these kinds of ideas and suddenly it occurs to her that being trapped is only one interpretation. She can fall in with the group belief that they're all trapped and maybe about to die, or she can hold a whole new idea. Like, that this is just a dream she's having and the *real* her doesn't have to stay in the dream. So she chooses that idea, and she turns around and walks out of that line, past the sniffer dogs and Nazis with guns, and she goes home and stays there safely for the rest of the war. And no-one even sees her go."[24]

"Wow! That's true invisibility," I marvelled.

"I don't believe that story," Sandy said flatly. "That's crazy."

Nina shrugged. "Doesn't matter if you do or you don't," she said. "I find it hard to believe too, but what if it's true?"

"You and Nuncle told me that when I changed I wouldn't even see those bullies anymore," Clare said slowly. "And I didn't. Maybe they weren't even seeing me anymore."

"Yep. The old R.A.S. to the rescue. If we believe people are out to get us, that's what we'll see and if we don't need people to bother us we won't bother attracting them. And, since the world is our mirror, if all we see out there is parts of ourselves, we're less

---

24 *The Indivisibility of the Infinite*, John Hargreaves, Mulberry Press Calif. 2003

likely to feel hostile to it all. Enter the 'I Am That' Game, folks."

"I've gotta shoot," Billy said. "We just look for where we do what they're doing? Okay, I'll have a stab at it. See you guys after the hols. Have a good one!"

"Cool – you too. And hey, you can own good things too," Nina added as he stood up to go. "If you see someone who's brilliant at something, you say 'I Am That' about that too. Seeya, Bill!"

"Good luck at the race!" we called after him, then turned back to the screen.

"Who else wants to play?" Nina asked.

"I will," I said, wondering what Mum would think of this latest Mastery Club challenge. *Masters reckon life is kind of a game if you can see it that way,* I imagined telling her. *'People take everything so seriously but really life is the game of creating your own reality.'* She didn't look convinced; in fact, she looked alarmed. I wiped that image away.

"I'll think about it," Sandy said, also standing up.

"But seriously," Serenity said, "don't you think the problem is them-and-us thinking? If we just had the 'us', if all people saw themselves as Earthlings instead of different nationalities, we wouldn't need to protect people against other people…"

"For sure," Nina agreed; then she added in her innocent voice, "but that won't happen until we meet other life forms and they get to be the 'enemy'. Then we humans can all be the 'us' and aliens can be the 'them'. You know, because of the Law of Conservation…"

Mastery Club Lesson #23

I Am That

* The World is our Mirror. When we can own what we see in the mirror, we are on the path to Mastery.

* 'I Am That' means that we own all the reflections we see, the 'bad' and the 'good'…

* The Order is in seeing that we attract attack because of our own judgements.

* The Mastery is in owning our judgements and changing our thoughts because then we're deliberately and consciously creating our reality instead of just reacting to things.

* Loving people is standing equal with them rather than above them or below them; standing equal puts them in our hearts…

CHAPTER 38

SANDY RUNS AWAY

MUM HAD STARTED packing and there were clothes and lists and stuff all over the place. I decided that I'd escape the chaos and walk around to Liz and Nuncle's to say goodbye. The Greek grandmother, who I hadn't seen for ages, was out in her garden when I turned into Begonia Lane. She recognised me and waved and called "Yassu tikanis!" And I even remembered the right word to say back: "Kala", and she beamed.

Liz's mosaic had progressed some more. The caterpillar was finished and a butterfly was emerging from its cocoon with shimmering colourful wings. I stood gazing at it for a while and then headed towards the kitchen door – and was surprised to hear the sound of crying. The door was open. I stopped stock-still, uncertain whether to go on, and then a voice that sounded for sure like Sandy's gave a great big sniff and said, "I'm never going back!"

There was a quiet moment, and then Nuncle said gently, "Things often aren't as bad as they look. We'll sort this out," and at the same moment, Liz came up from behind me and said brightly, "Hello Natalie! I thought you'd left."

I turned towards Liz and inside the kitchen there was the sound of a chair scraping on the floor, and Nuncle appeared in the doorway.

"We go on Monday," I said. "I was just dropping in to say 'bye." I swivelled back towards Nuncle. "Is Sandy okay?"

"Sandy's here?" Liz asked, taking her gardening gloves off and banging them together.

"Just arrived," Nuncle told her with a meaningful look in his eyes. "Come in, Natalie, perhaps you can help."

Sandy was sitting at the kitchen table with a grubby, tear-lined face. She sort of half-scowled at me – obviously not wanting to be seen like this, but I was here now.

"What's up, San?" I asked, pulling up a chair next to her and trying to hit the right note of sympathy-detachment that wouldn't offend her.

She gave a big sniff and wiped her nose with the back of her hand. Liz put a box of tissues on the table for her and Sandy grunted her thanks before taking a few and blowing.

"I was rude to Mum," she said at last. "She never stands up to Dad and I'm sick of seeing her be so wimpy. And then Dad heard us arguing and he came in and tore strips off me and I was so mad I just pissed off. They can suffer and wonder where I am. I'm not going back." She cast an angry sideways glance at me. "Same old, same old. No breakthroughs here."

"I'll make some tea," Liz said, standing up.

"Have you ever read *The Lord of the Rings*?" Nuncle asked, as if we were just having a social visit.

"Saw the movie," Sandy muttered. I had too – we'd seen it together.

"Do you remember Wormtongue, the advisor to King Theoden?" Sandy shrugged. "Sort of."

"He took the easy road," Nuncle said. "Lies and trickery and deceit. Remember Aragorn?"

"Of course," I said. I'd had a poster of that handsome ranger on my wall for a while…

"Upright. Upholds his values. He takes the hard road."

"So?" Sandy asked in that bulldoggish way of hers.

"You're taking the hard road," Nuncle said. "You're sticking to your values. You've got high standards for everyone and when they don't comply, you feel frustrated. You want your mother to value herself. You want your father to treat the two of you with respect."

Sandy looked at him hard, like she couldn't quite believe what he was saying.

Nuncle pointed to the picture of the African boy on the fridge. "See that picture of the boy?"

We nodded, looking at it.

"That's my son," Nuncle said.

Liz brought the snapshots and the tea to the table, and Sandy and I studied the young brown face in surprise.

"His mother is African-American. We met at university and were madly in love. But things happened… we argued… she told me to leave. And I was so self-righteous at the time that I did. I thought she'd come around; *I* wasn't going to give in. But she never came around and I've hardly seen my son since he was a boy. He took her part and didn't want to know me. He has his own son now. My only grandson, and I've never met him."

"Green tea," Liz said, passing us each a cup and sitting down. "So what are you saying, Max? That there's a fine line between walking the hard road of sticking to your values and being self-righteous?"

"Something like that," Nuncle grinned, his eyes twinkling. "Liz keeps me on the straight and narrow."

"You'd have been a great dad," I said with feeling.

"Yeah," Sandy agreed. "How come the good ones miss out and the… other ones get kids?"

"That's how it looks to you," Nuncle said, "but what if it's all perfectly in order? I gather that you Mastery Clubbers have tasked yourselves to find the Order in the universe."

"Yeah. S'not easy to see it," Sandy muttered.

"No. You're right. That's why most people don't. Are you up for looking?"

She sighed, glanced at me, sighed again. "Okay."

"Good on you. First question, then: what are you judging him for?"

"Being mean," she said at once.

"Mean," Nuncle echoed.

"Yeah. Always making people wrong. No-one can ever do anything right for him."

"Ah. Critical."

"Yeah."

"So who do you criticise?"

It was so obvious that we all burst into laughter.

"Any benefits to being critical?" Nuncle continued, taking a sip of his tea. "How do you think it serves you to be critical of your dad, for instance?"

"It makes me see him clearly," Sandy said. "I used to think he was pretty cool when I was a kid. Now I can see how he hurts people around him. He doesn't hit us; it's just his way of talking to people and making them feel small and useless. I don't want to be like that."

"So you get to clarify your own values. Good," Nuncle said. "How does it serve you when *he's* critical of you?"

"Makes me strong, I suppose" she said reluctantly (and not looking at me). "I get this fighting feeling inside myself that *I'm not going to take that from you!*" (I guessed that she was remembering all the times Nina had told her that her clashes with her dad were making her strong.)

"Is there anyone he isn't critical of?" Nuncle asked.

"My brothers. The sun shines out of their bums," Sandy said.

And her eyes glittered with tears.

"What if he wasn't critical of you? What if he admired every single thing you did?"

"As if!" Sandy snorted, dashing a hand across her eyes.

"How would things be different?" Nuncle persisted.

"I suppose I'd be softer," she admitted. "But I don't need him to admire everything. Just to not be so hard."

"Yes, that would be nicer," Liz agreed. "More comfortable for you for sure…"

Sandy looked sideways at her.

"But would you have such a drive to prove yourself and grow if you'd always been admired and coddled? Maybe you wouldn't have found sculpture? Maybe you wouldn't have met us or joined the Mastery Club?" she added with a cheeky wink.

Nuncle nodded. "And besides, nothing is missing. Who *does* admire you?"

Sandy shrugged.

"Lots of people," I put in. "We all admire Sandy for her pottery."

"And her acting. I seem to remember watching a pretty convincing Lion last year," Nuncle said.

"Let's go back to what you said about your father making people feel small," Liz interrupted. "Do *you* do that?"

I looked at Sandy while she frowned in thought. "I don't think so…" she said.

Nuncle glanced at me; I must have wriggled or something. "Natalie?"

"Well, I'm sure it's not deliberate, and it's definitely not as badly as your dad does, but you *do* do it a bit…" I said cautiously.

Sandy stared at me for a moment, and then shrugged. "I suppose so."

"Your story isn't that different from mine," Liz said, keeping her blue eyes steadily turned toward Sandy. "The old fatherly disapproval. I so wanted my Dad to love me for who I was, and support me in what I was doing. But he nagged and criticised and dropped hints until I just moved out and started to ignore him. I resented him for years, Sandy, until I realised that he *was* loving me – by challenging me. We humans think of love as just the supportive stuff, but it's both. We want to freeze-frame life on the 'nice side', to have everyone support us and be nice to us, and we forget that it's through the combination of challenging *and* supportive experiences that we grow. We truly need both."

"People who fall for get-rich-quick schemes," Nuncle said, picking up a bundle of promotional brochures from the kitchen table and giving it a short, sharp shake, "want the pleasure of wealth without the pain of doing the day-in, day-out hard work of earning and saving. Goodbye to you!" He dumped the brochures into a box under the table that held containers for recycling.

My father had been reading that exact same advertising at breakfast this morning! And Dad *was* a bit like that, I reflected. He did work hard every day, but he was always looking out for a short cut...

Liz topped up our cups with some more green tea from the pot. "It's not easy doing this kind of work, Sandy. It takes real responsibility and self-discipline. But you've turned up here so we're trusting that you're up for the 'whole truth'."

She looked straight at Sandy with her beautiful blue eyes. "We live in a world of people who are addicted to happiness and pleasure. People everywhere dig their heels in and resist anything that's uncomfortable like crazy, but the more we resist it, the more entrenched it gets, and the fact of the matter is that it serves us. What if you try appreciating your dad's disapproval? Blessing him for disapproving of you..."

"Blessing him!"

"Yes. Declaring the whole situation sacred and orderly. I've been doing a lot of that with the cancer: blessing my body and declaring it orderly and whole. Even blessing random people as I go around shopping and doing errands. Just being a giver of blessings… makes me feel great. Instead of seeing your Dad as a problem figure in your life, what if you see him as a gift; as something incredibly special waiting to be understood?"

Sandy frowned. She lifted her feet onto the chair and hugged her legs. Her eyes were dark and cloudy.

"You want a clue to finding the Order?" Nuncle asked gently. "It's simple, Sandy: the Order *is* the discomfort. We want to make our discomfort wrong and get rid of it, but our discomfort pushes us to make better decisions. Over and over again it's the people who struggled with something who create the breakthroughs."

We were all watching Sandy, as she sat there, hunched, chin pressed to her knees.

"I've been seeing quite a few health practitioners since I was diagnosed with cancer," Liz said, "And you know, really often it's the people who've been sick, or had someone close to them who was sick, who come up with new healing therapies."

"And often it's the people who felt they missed out who strive harder than anyone else," Nuncle added. "You *are* getting something out of the conflict, if you can just see it."

"It's just that it makes life so hard!" Sandy burst out. "I hate it at home and I hate it at school. There's nowhere that I'm happy."

"Yes, there is," I said. "Doing pottery with your uncle."

"Except for there," she grunted.

"And here," I pointed out.

She gave me a funny look.

"What if you were able to appreciate the comfortable things and the uncomfortable things equally, without needing to have more of the comfortable things?" Nuncle asked. "I wouldn't ask that of just anyone, but a Trainee Master…?" And he smiled his warm smile.

Sandy cracked the tiniest smile in response.

"Shit happens," Liz said bluntly, "to all of us. We can make it a tragedy or use it to grow. Most people think that their emotions happen to them – out of their control. But you know that's not true. The power is in here, in what you're saying to yourself." She tapped Sandy gently on the chest. "I wonder how your Dad would respond if you didn't get pissed off and sulky with him; if you just went, 'Okay, that's a mirror. Where am *I* being mean? Where am I making people small?' and then do something about it in *your* life. Maybe he'd change." She shrugged. "Could be."

"What's the order in you not getting to be a father?" I asked Nuncle.

"Well, the thing is, I *do* get to be a father," Nuncle replied. "It's just taken a different form. I've put a lot into Nina over the years, and I sponsor young boys who are in trouble or about to be. I've spent quite a few years now doing that. I bring them here or take them out or visit them; just spend time with them, listen to them. And being there for you guys last year was pretty special to me, too."

"But don't you miss your own son? Wouldn't you have preferred to bring him up yourself? Don't you want to meet your own grandson?" I insisted.

"Seeing Joel shook me up for a bit," Nuncle admitted. "My son's name is Josh and they're both dark-skinned, so their likeness brought up some more pain, and that galvanised me into making another attempt to connect with Josh. I'm hoping he'll respond – still waiting on that one. But who's to say I haven't brought him up in a way? My *not* being there has had an influence on his childhood, for sure. You know what we were saying about pain serving us? From what his mother has told me, that young man has got a big heart. And then, not having kids of my own to care for has given me the time to be there for a whole lot of young people. My friends who are parents get so tied up looking after their own kids, running them here and there, that they don't have much time for anyone else."

"Besides," Liz said, "if Max had stayed married, I'd never have met him. And if his wife had let him connect with his son, he'd probably never have come back to Australia with me. But there still is hope that they'll reconnect. We're going to the States later this year. We'll keep that door open, and see if some day Josh decides to step through it."

Nuncle reached across the table and covered Sandy's hand with his own. "We so want life to be easy and abundant and to always be loved and loving, but life is a process, and it's the process of being challenged that has us grow. A charmed life that's just a series of perfect 'frozen' moments wouldn't serve us at all."

"But it would be much nicer," Sandy grumbled. "I still don't want to go home."

"Why don't you call Sandy's parents and let them know she's safe?" Liz suggested to Nuncle. "Max is amazing with people," she said to Sandy and me. "He's so calm. He always gets his way – well…" (exchanging glances with Nuncle), "almost always!"

Nuncle gave Sandy's hand a squeeze and stood up. "I'll call from the study."

As he left, Liz went to the fridge to start making lunch. "I think what Max was saying before about Wormtongue and Aragorn is that you have a choice," she said, taking salad vegetables out. "You can opt for the easy road of complaining and arguing and rebelling and making your dad wrong and you right; or you can discipline yourself and take the harder road, the road of looking inside, owning the things you've rejected, and appreciating how the difficult things are serving you."

Sandy was silent. I watched her sitting next to me, hunched, her arms wrapped around her knees, feet up on the rail of the chair.

Liz put a big ceramic bowl on the bench and then came back

to sit at the table with us. She laid one hand lightly on Sandy's knee. "When I first learnt about the cancer I was really scared," she said quietly. "One morning, very early, I came in here and sat at this table by myself, and I made myself go and look for all the blessings. Honestly, girls, it didn't take me long to see that the tumour was making me go inside and ask myself what really mattered to me. It was making me pray again, reach out to the Great Spirit and ask for guidance. It was making me appreciate Max and Rosie and all the people I love way more. It was making me less reactive to trivial stuff because that just didn't matter by comparison with living and dying. It was making me conscious of my beliefs, like my story that my father had never loved me for who I was, which was not true at all. It was making me slow down and really look at each petal, each leaf in the garden, instead of rushing through as I'd been doing." She gazed outside. "The rain had absolutely bucketed down earlier that morning; I still remember the raindrops on that tree over there – they were clinging to the branches like fairy lights."

We followed her pointing hand to the silver birch tree outside, and then back to Liz. Her clear blue eyes met ours steadily. "I filled a page with blessings in just a few minutes, and I was moved to tears of gratitude. It became so clear to me that our challenges are gifts; they're blessings in disguise, Sandy, and yours are too."

"I never thought of it that way before," Sandy mumbled. "I kind of knew he was making me stronger but I felt angry about it. I wanted to be able to be strong *without* him being mean. But I guess it doesn't work like that."

Liz erupted into laughter. She stood up, shaking her head. "You've hit the nail on the head, honeypot." Returning to her chopping board, she began to slice carrots. "Wow. If only the rest of the world could see it so clearly. We want the skills and depth of character without the pain and hard work that generate them."

She laughed again. "How absurd. But... that's how the world operates. Most people find it easy to be grateful for good times and sunny days and friends, but how many are able to be grateful for trouble, bad weather and hostility? Yet that's how we grow."

Sandy said nothing; we sat quietly, mesmerised by Liz's knife rapidly chopping the carrots.

"So! Back to you, Sandy," she declared, tossing the carrots into the salad bowl and starting on cucumbers. "Your difficult dad has helped you to grow stronger, become independent, become brave because he was scary to you, develop acting skills –"

"What's that got to do with her dad?" I asked, startled.

"Creativity and artistry are often stimulated by turning inward," Liz replied, "and turning inward often happens because we're feeling troubled in some way." She tossed the cucumbers into the salad bowl. "All the 'bad' stuff you pin on him has to be balanced by equal 'goods', Sandy, but we're not trained to look at things that way, so most people don't see them. And not only that," she added, pointing the knife at us, "but he let you work all of this out for yourself, so you don't have to be obligated to him or to anybody – and isn't that kind of how you like things to be? Has it ever occurred to you to thank him for that?"

Sandy just shook her head. I could almost feel her brain rearranging itself as she saw the old things in this new way. (Mine was doing a bit of that, too.)

A door closed somewhere in the house; Nuncle had finished his phone call.

"Mind you, most of the people around you will want you to complain," Liz warned, planting a tomato on the board, "because that makes *them* feel better about their own pain. But mastery is in honouring the whole, not the part; the pain and the perfection. Back in the '70s, the writer Erica Jong said something really good about this: 'A terrible thing happens when you finally take responsibility for your own life – nobody to blame.'"

"Indeed," Nuncle agreed from the doorway. "Terrible because most people rely on complaint and blaming so much that they feel naked without it."

He had arranged for Sandy to stay the weekend… She was amazed and I was a bit envious – a whole weekend with Liz and Nuncle! She'd sleep upstairs in Nina's attic bedroom and be looked after by them for two whole days.

I stayed for lunch and then reluctantly got up to go. Nuncle beckoned me to him. "Do you mind if I play father to *you* for a moment?"

I shook my head and he put an arm around my shoulders, drawing me close to his chest, and placing the other hand gently on the crown of my head. "Travel safely, Natalie and family," Nuncle said softly, "may this journey be blessed in every moment and every way, and may you come home to us safely."

Liz moved closer and planted a kiss on my cheek. And then the two of them held me in a warm hug. Moments later, a chair scraped away from the table and Sandy joined us. One of her hands snaked around my back and she whispered, "Have a great trip, Nat."

When I looked back at them from the door as I was leaving, Sandy stood between Liz and Nuncle, all arm-in-arm, and her face was calm.

Mastery Club Lesson #24

Taking the Hard Road

* Taking the time to face the mirror, own the reflection, and act on the learnings is not easy. But…

* the hard road builds our character, and…

* doing it hard now makes life easier later, whereas doing it easy now can make life harder later…

CHAPTER 39

FLYING TO GREECE!

ON SUNDAY NIGHT I was so excited, I hardly slept. We had to be at the airport at four for a six o'clock flight, and Monday seemed to really drag while Mum raced to the shops for last minute things and repacked bags. The more stressed she got, the more good-natured and humorous Dad got, which sort of helped and sort of made things worse.

Nina and Clare rang to say good-bye. I mentioned that Sandy was at Liz and Nuncle's, and they both said they'd ring there, which made me wonder if I should have blabbed… Nina was packing for her trip to Far North Queensland to visit Joel, and also pretty excited.

Finally we were on our way to the airport, and then piling out of the taxi with our wheelie cases and looking for the right queue. I didn't realise it then, but this was just the beginning of queues… It took us an hour or so to work our way through the queue to have our luggage weighed and stamped and passports checked before we could queue up to go through the security barrier. Katie and Evan were fascinated by all the security guards sternly watching us and our hand luggage as it bumped along the conveyor belt through the scanners, and especially by the people who were pulled aside to be searched. (I was fascinated too, but I was trying to act grown-up, like I'd seen it all before.)

We got through pretty easily and went to buy some juices, which were yum. Mum had a bag packed full of things for the siblings to do on the twenty-two hour (!) trip, but she ended up buying another couple of things at the airport newsagent. We went to sit in our area by 'Gate Six' to wait for our plane to board, except that Mum wouldn't let us sit. "You'll be sitting for hours and hours soon," she said; "walk!" So she and Dad took turns minding our bags while the rest of us marched around the walkway, staring at everyone and everything.

Our plane started boarding on time. We joined the queue and had our passports checked again, then followed everyone along a funny kind of walkway to a narrow doorway where we were greeted by a beautiful Asian woman in an elegant long dress. This was actually the entrance to the plane. We squeezed along the narrow aisles, hunting for our seats. Evan found them: three by the window and two across the aisle in the same row. So then Katie and Evan started arguing over who'd have the window seat, and Mum told them off for blocking the way (other passengers were backing up in the aisle behind us), and gave the window seat to Evan. Katie plumped into her seat and sulked. But not for long: she discovered that we each had our own TV screen on the back of the seat in front of us – how cool!

It seemed to take ages for everyone to be seated and for the doors to be closed and the crew to do their safety demo but at last the plane was taxiing down the runway. Evan kindly sat as far back in his seat as he could to give Katie and me a good view as the plane took off. And then we were leaving Australia behind and swooping into the sky like a bird!

When we could only see sky, we turned our attention to our screens and soon figured them out. Then we each picked a different movie to watch – for once, no arguments about that! – and settled down. Mum and Dad thought this was wonderful. Dinner came on trolleys and I was fed first, being vegetarian – a 'special' meal. It was really fun opening all the lids and little packets to see what was inside. I had white rice with spicy beans and vegetables, a bread roll and margarine, a salad of tomato, cucumber and lettuce mix, and fruit salad: two types of melon. The others got chicken and rice and the same stuff. It was pretty delicious and lots of fun, but after that the plane started bumping – 'turbulence', Mum said, and I started to feel sick.

I watched another movie to take my mind off it and then fell asleep, only to be woken by Katie and Evan climbing over me to go to the toilet. I figured I might as well go too, and we all trailed down the aisle after Mum and took turns in another queue. The toilet was very cramped and when I flushed, I wondered where everything went – into the air? – and then didn't want to think about that any more… I think Evan was in there so long because he was trying all the buttons and looking in all the compartments. We heard the loo flush a few times.

The lights in the plane had been turned down low when we bumped our way back to our seats, and half the people were watching their screens while the other half were trying to sleep.

And then the long, long night began. I slept in fits and starts, with Katie's head on my shoulder, half-hearing Mum talking across me to Evan from time to time. At midnight the lights came on for another dinner, which was really weird. Dad explained that we were sort of going back in time. The meal looked good but I was too tired to eat. By now Evan was finally asleep so Mum saved his meal, and mine, for later. Katie was wide-awake, putting hers away like some eating champion.

And then we had arrived at Bangkok airport and were disembarking into the hot black night with our overnight bags. It was really humid and airless. We had to walk an endless distance along corridors and travelators to get from 'Arrivals' to 'Departures', and when we finally got there the queue became backlogged near the top of an escalator so everyone getting off the escalator was jammed into the people in front of them. Some of the passengers got pretty cranky about that. I thought it was funny, popping out like cooked toast on top of the people in front, but it was 'dangerous and very poor design', Mum said. The Aussies behind us criticised the long, slow, snaking queues as well. It wouldn't have been so bad if it wasn't so hot and we weren't so tired. There didn't seem to be any air circulation at all and it took ages to get through the security check thing.

Finally we climbed aboard our plane for the second leg of the trip. This time it was a jumbo and there were no individual screens, just one main one. (Katie was Not Impressed.) We were seated four in the middle, with Dad across the aisle from us. A very large Greek man sat across the other aisle from me, his hands resting on his big round belly.

Dinner arrived *again* – still going back in time! Vegies and bread – I didn't even know what it was; we were all too tired to eat. The seats could be pushed further back in this plane than the last one, and soon everyone was sleeping – or trying to. I managed to get a few good chunks of sleep in between rearranging myself in that awkward little space. Eventually the cabin lights came on and the air stewards began to move along the aisles, opening our blinds, and pretty soon breakfast was being served. It was a juice, 'frittata' (which was a yummy, herby potato thing), grilled tomato, zucchini (for breakfast!), bread roll or croissant, yoghurt, pawpaw, pineapple and melon.

And then the captain announced that we were nearing Athens

and would be landing soon! It would be twenty-seven degrees in Athens today and the time there was eleven a.m. It was Melbourne's yesterday. We had truly time-travelled…

CHAPTER 40

A LAND OF RUINS

AS WE WENT to collect our luggage, we noticed a few people rushing into little glass rooms – 'smoking rooms', Mum said, and we could see those poor addicted people in there puffing away like mad after all the hours on the plane when they hadn't been allowed to smoke. Ugh.

We came out of the airport to a view of distant blue mountains and trees. It was cloudy and warm outside. "Ah…" said Mum, beaming. At last: her dream holiday.

We found our bus pretty quickly and when the driver boarded he didn't even ask us to pay, so we travelled for free. I couldn't imagine that ever happening at home. As the bus headed along the freeway we passed signs we recognised, like 'IKEA' and 'Ericson' and 'Factory Outlet' but there were lots of signs in Greek too, that we couldn't decipher at all. The countryside from the bus windows was a bit like the Australian scrub, and very dry. Rows of bushes were planted here and there in small, odd-shaped areas. I wondered who they belonged to and what was growing there. The land looked messy. Now and then we could see houses in the distance – they were white or yellow or brown, and they all seemed to have balconies.

More and more apartments appeared as we approached the city, and they were mostly quite dirty-looking. Athens seemed very run-down. Our bus stop was Syntagma Square, and then we had to look for the metro, which took us a few stops until we were only two streets from our hostel, according to Dad's map.

"Oh dear," said Mum, as we turned into a narrow, dirty street, rolling our cases behind us. "This looks dodgy."

"All part of the adventure," Dad replied cheerily.

The entrance to our hostel was quite smart, and bearded Vassily at the front desk was very welcoming and lovely. He gave us a big old-fashioned key and directed us upstairs to the first floor. Our troubles began at the door to our room. The lock was loose and it took quite a bit of wiggling till we could get it to unlock. As soon as we stepped into the room, we sank into floorboards that were broken and sagging. Evan and Katie went straight to the tiny balcony to peer down at the noisy street below while Mum took an inventory of our room's faults.

"The floor is filthy. Half the lights don't work. We look onto the main road so there'll be lights and traffic noises all night. And the beds aren't very comfortable," she pronounced, lying down on one.

"Ah well, you wanted to do this bit on the cheap and lash out on the cruise," Dad said comfortingly.

We were very hungry so we left the hostel and headed back into Athens to explore the Acropolis and other ruins. On the way we stopped at a street stall and bought big golden delicious apples and bananas, and then some yummy cheese and spinach pastries at a tiny deli sort of shop, as well as some nuts and dried fruit for later. We ate the fruit and pastries as we walked. Evan began to point out all the police in town. There seemed to be lots of them. And lots of down-and-out looking people.

"What's that lady doing there?" Katie asked, pointing to a solid woman sitting on the ground with her legs sticking out and a paper cup standing in front of her. She looked at us with a flat expression.

"She's a beggar," Mum whispered. "Don't point."

"Ohhh," said Katie, staring over her shoulder at the woman as we walked past.

The first sight of the Acropolis in the distance was impressive. When we asked a Greek man for directions to it, he replied that we should catch the little train that went up the hill as it was steep and they needed the money since Greece was in crisis, so we did. The streets were really narrow here. I kept expecting us to turn into a main road like at home in Melbourne, and we never did. There were dogs sleeping all over the place, and cats running across the streets and the rooftops. Katie even spotted a tortoise!

All the pictures I'd seen in books and on brochures and television documentaries came real in front of my eyes as we arrived at the top of the big flat hill. There were lots of different broken-down buildings but the one that really caught my attention was the Parthenon, which was this vast structure of mostly whitish columns. Some of it was being restored and there was scaffolding around it, which took away from its ancient-ness a bit, but it was still way cool, and the view from that Acropolis was ace.

"A temple to the goddess Athena," Dad said as we approached it, "where young virgin maidens your age would have been put into service, Nat, and maybe even sacrificed..." He raised his brows at me.

We took stacks of photos, posing next to those grand columns. (Evan had to do something different, so Dad took photos of him balancing on big blocks and rocks and showing his muscles.) It wasn't easy to get a clear shot because there were people everywhere – hundreds and hundreds of tourists taking photos and reading guidebooks and slithering on the broken ground.

Mum and Dad read from their tourist guide as we wandered, and tried to load us up with some of that information too, but the siblings eventually raced ahead and I was drifting into daydreams, imagining myself in ancient Greek times wearing my tunic, or whatever Greek people wore, and flitting into temples to pray to the gods…

It was really hot. When we finally came out we bought freshly squeezed orange juices and went to the toilet (which you had to pay to use), and then walked back down the hill, stopping to look at all the little tourist stalls. There were heaps of them, all selling t-shirts with funny sayings and other souvenirs like key rings and bottle openers and jewellery. Evan started asking for things and Mum started saying no. I had a feeling there'd be quite a bit more of that before this trip was over.

We got back to the hostel and collapsed on the hard beds for a while and were woken by Mum and Dad at six-fifteen to go for dinner at the tavern Vassily had told us about. It wasn't easy waking up – our bodies were still on Melbourne time and just wanted to sleep… but the spread of food on offer at the tavern woke me up. There was quite a vegie delight for me: spinach pie, okra, eggplant, cannellini beans, lima beans, stuffed capsicum, roast and mashed potatoes, some tiny pasta things, and rice and spinach, carrots and peas… The others ate lamb and raved about it. Poor ol' lamb…

When we were leaving, my attention was caught by a particularly raucous group at a table near the door. A tubby Greek man with sparkling eyes was waving a book that said 'Plato' on the cover over the head of a girl who had a blue streak through her black hair. She was trying to grab the book and slapping at his arm and they were both laughing and talking at once in Greek. I stopped in my tracks, staring. Was this Nina and Nuncle or was I going nuts? I had no idea what these two were saying but I could just hear the Nina and Nuncle I knew chortling, "Nothing is ever missing!" Katie and Evan had to come back for me; I was so struck I hadn't noticed the rest of my family going on without me.

We returned to our hostel and discovered that smoke from Vassily's cigarette was floating right upstairs and under our door into our room, but we couldn't open the windows to let the breeze in because then we would also let in the mosquitoes – and the noise. And it was *so* noisy! Not the whirr of traffic speeding past but acceleration and braking, because our hostel was situated right on an intersection, so there was lots of horn tooting and shouting and motor bikes and other general noise. Evan had kicked his sandals off and in seconds his feet were black. Mum fussed and fumed about the poor quality, deceptive marketing, etc. etc., and Dad just shrugged and smiled, which made her madder.

I decided to escape all of that by listening to my iPod in bed, so I climbed onto the top bunk for some peace and quiet by myself. I fell asleep and woke up in the middle of the night, all achy and uncomfortable. Those mattresses were like planks of wood.

"Did I wake you up?" Mum whispered.

I propped myself on my elbow and looked over the edge of the bunk. She was sitting in the doorway of the tiny bathroom – the only light that worked was in there – and reading.

"No… What time is it?"

Mum checked her watch. "Two-thirty a.m." She looked tired. "The ship will be nicer, I'm sure."

"Ancient ruins and modern ruins," I grinned, "we've seen them all."

Mum gave a sudden smile. "It's funny how you dream about something for so long and then it never turns out how you expected…"

"Law of Polarity, Mum," I murmured, lying down again. "Everything has two sides. It's all in perfect balance…"

CHAPTER 41

CRUISING THE ISLANDS

WE SPENT ANOTHER day sightseeing around Athens and then a night at Port Piraeus in a nice, cleaner place with pretend marble tiles and air conditioning. Mum was much happier there.

And the next day – man! *That* was exciting. The ship was HUGE and there were masses of people waiting to go aboard. There was all this security stuff again – we had to have our photo taken and use a hand sanitiser before we were allowed on board.

We found our cabin (number 457), which was so cute with its bunk beds and everything all tucked away neatly. Then we went exploring and got lost heaps of times before we figured out the basic layout. (Well, we kids did; Mum kept getting lost on that ship throughout the entire cruise.)

As the ship began to move away from the shore, we were all summoned on deck for the emergency drill – with bright orange life vests on! That was fun. "We're Life Boat Number One," Mum told Evan and Katie earnestly. "Remember that, okay?"

"Yeah, yeah," said Evan, pulling away. He'd seen another boy.

We ate lunch on the top deck where there was a smorgasbord

and a swimming pool, and you could sit outside and gaze at the sea. I had never seen so much food in my life. I saw people piling up their plates really high, and then going back for seconds... and thirds... It was like, because it was free, they couldn't control themselves and ate far more than they needed – or even wanted to, I reckoned. No probs seeing the positives and negatives to free food, then!

Katie called me to look at some amazing food sculptures. Fish and animal and people's heads had been carved out of watermelons with the pips for eyes. We trailed around the tables gazing at them all in admiration; I could imagine Sandy appreciating these... After lunch some crazy people got up and started dancing on deck.

"Why don't you go and join them?" Mum asked, relaxing on a deck chair.

I stared at her, horrified.

We arrived at our first island that evening – Mykonos, which was beautiful from afar and awesome up close with its white buildings that all seemed to have blue roofs and doors, and a kind of blending effect of earth and rock and sea. And so many cats! We followed the cruise crowd, winding our way through the narrow streets past all the little shops ('boutiques', said Mum) and past outdoor restaurants where wooden tables and chairs were set under hot pink, flowery, vine-like plants that spread over rafters. There were cats everywhere, and Evan tried to pat every single one we passed. The rock-paved street finished at the top of a hill where some big white windmills ruled. We paid to use the toilet again, took lots of photos, and then I sat on the rocks listening to the waves and watching the 'sunset' with Mum while Dad followed the endlessly-energetic siblings around. It was just lovely.

Lights started to come on in the town after the sun had 'set', and we walked back slowly, popping into art galleries and admiring the romantic candle-lit tables at the outdoor restaurants. I saw Mum gazing at them dreamily, and was sure she would have gone there for dinner with Dad if it weren't for us kids. Instead we shared some cheese and spinach pastries to last us till we got back to the ship, and Mum bought a pair of earrings and a scarf for herself, and a t-shirt for Evan that said 'Made in Greece'. Katie and I hadn't decided what we wanted yet. Dad started making mysterious comments about those Greek guys called Plato and Socrates. I had no idea what he was on about.

After dinner the crew was introduced and we learnt that there were twenty-seven nationalities on board between the crew and the passengers – France, UK, India, USA, Canada, Australia, Argentina, South Africa, Brazil, Chile, Colombia, Uruguay, Russia, Ukraine, Serbia, Slovenia, Romania, Italy, Greece… and more! A conversation started between my parents and the adults sitting near us about different countries and their different cultures and customs.

"Did you know that it's rude to eat everything on your plate in Eye-ran because that would be like saying you weren't given enough to eat?" an American lady informed us. "The leftovers are for the beggars so if they eat everything they have nothing to give."

"Not an excuse you can use," Mum said smartly to Evan, who had been paying attention for once. "No beggars where we live."

"And the Chinese don't say thank you to family members," the lady's professor-ish-looking husband commented, "so thanking them is considered an insult."

"Goodness!" Mum exclaimed. "Why?"

"I suppose it looks like you're not trusting them to take care of you," he said with a shrug.

"We are all so different," Mum agreed. "I like people to look me in the eyes when they're talking to me, but I believe the Australian Aboriginals consider eye contact to be rude."

I thought of Joel, and how his eyes often seemed to slide away. So that was why…

"And we like to eat all quiet and nice," the American lady said, "but some Japanese house guests we had once – well! Have you ever! Such loud eaters, and they rush at their food and gobble it. I was shocked through and through, but apparently that's considered a compliment to the host. You know, a sign of their enjoyment of the meal."

Mum looked at Evan with warning eyes, and he smiled sweetly at her, planning to eat 'Japanese style' from now on, no doubt…

There was a song and dance show starting at ten-thirty p.m. but Mum said we had to go to bed. I objected, and she finally relented and let me stay up with Dad but took the other two to bed. It was pretty entertaining; they got some guys out of the audience and dressed them up as women and had them do the can-can, which was really funny. When we crept into our cabin an hour later, Mum and the siblings were fast asleep.

I crawled between the sheets of my bed and lay there in the dark listening to everyone's breathing and the sound of the sea, and was hugely struck by the realisation that my visualisation at Nuncle's last year had come true. The holiday I had just dreamily imagined in my mind was actually happening. I really was the sculptor of my life (Lesson #1). I'd set a goal (Lesson #2). I'd visualised it (Lesson #3). I'd treasure mapped it (Lesson #4). I'd dealt with my fears and resistance (Lesson #5). I was right now experiencing the positive and negative sides of the holiday (Lesson #6). I'd changed my vibration (Lesson #7). I'd become a new person (Lesson #8). I'd put the ideas into action (Lesson #9). And I hadn't given up (Lesson #10).

Lying there, I realised it was time to set another big goal.

CHAPTER 42

MUM STARTS JOINING DOTS…

I WOKE TO THE SOUNDS of voices in our cabin. Katie and Evan were chattering excitedly and Mum was saying, "Ssh, ssh," over and over as she tried to get them dressed and out before they woke me and Dad up. I peered over the edge of the bunk and Evan called out "We're going on deck to see the sunrise!"

"Sh!" hissed Mum.

"It's really 'sunsight'," I told him sleepily, remembering what Nina had said about 'up' and 'down' being illusions since we were living on a rotating globe and not on a flat earth. "Okay. I'm coming."

It was beautiful – just-right cool and the sky was pink. Lights were still showing on the island of Patmos as we approached. We ate breakfast on the sundeck so we could keep watching the island as we drew closer. (Cereal, toast, eggs, hash browns, pastries, fruit salad, yoghurt, juice – oops! Over-ate again… must be more careful who I judge…) Dad pointed out the monastery of St John high up on a hill.

We went from ship to land by tender, which is kind of a motorboat, and then headed off to explore. Patmos was a small island, much less touristy, it seemed to me, though it was still early in the morning – the shopkeepers hadn't finished setting up for the day when we arrived and started browsing. We wandered around, looking at all the souvenirs and stuff for sale, and then sort of drifted along the main road away from the shops at the port. Mum commented that the stonework of the buildings was different here – white rock with darker stones embedded in it, and this time there were heaps of dogs instead of cats. Evan and Katie ran from dog to dog until we realised we had actually crossed the entire island and were on the other side at the beach! The siblings were much happier playing about on the shore than looking at shops, so we stayed there for a while.

"Tell me, Nat," Mum said, stretching her legs out on the sand. "That day last year when you made baklava; you said that had something to do with us going to the Greek Islands. What was that?"

Was it safe to tell? Would she blast me for trying to 'create my reality'? I gazed out at the ocean, searching for the right words. "Everyone in the Mastery Club had picked a challenge to take on," I said at last. "And I picked a holiday here."

"But why?" she asked, baffled. "Whatever made you think of this?"

"I saw the brochures on your desk and I knew this was where you wanted to go… So when Dad had to cancel the holiday, I decided to take it on."

She looked at me with troubled eyes. "You mean you think that you brought this about, with your visualisations?"

I nodded, suddenly full of doubts. *Had* I had anything to do with it?

Mum looked at Dad urgently, and then back at me. "But Natalie, it was Gran dying that allowed us to afford this holiday."

"I know," I said. Once again Mum was voicing all my own private fears and doubts. I scrabbled in the sand at my side, wondering if there was anything to this idea of creating your own reality. Were we all just deluded? Was Nina leading us down some crazy path to insanity?

"Then… how can you say it was you?"

"Oh it wasn't *me*," I replied with sudden relief. "It was the G.O.D. I just held the vision and started to learn a bit of Greek and made a Treasure Map of us all here. Sandy wanted the part of the Lion in the school play and she was given the Munchkin Mayor, so she held the vision of being the Lion and started learning those lines. We didn't *make* those things happen, we just kept visualising them and working towards them…"

"What G.O.D.?" Mum asked with narrowed eyes. "Is this a religious thing?"

"It stands for Grand Organising Design," I explained. "Or Designer. It just means that everything in the whole world is this really orderly intelligent system and we humans are part of the Order. And our thoughts aren't just invisible nothings, they're real forces that can affect other people and even things."

Dad cocked his head at Mum. "Can't argue with that."

She frowned at him. "Since when have you subscribed to those ideas?"

"Just been doing a bit of reading lately," he said. Nuncle's books, I realised with an inward smile.

"Our thoughts can't affect things," Mum declared. "That's absurd!"

"Studies are out showing that they do," Dad said.[25]

"Things are just energy," I reminded her. "And our thoughts are energy. And there are heaps of examples of people who

---

25   Eg. *The Intention Experiment* by Lynne McTaggart.

thought something and it came true."

Dad gave a tiny nod.

"Well, maybe that's so in some instances," Mum said, still frowning, "but you can't surely believe that your thoughts affect big things, events that involve lots of people or – or health issues like cancer?"

"Why not?" I asked. "Lots of people have healed themselves with their minds."

"But Gran dying just then and providing the funds for this trip – do you really...?"

"We have this motto," I told them; "'See the Invisible, Hear the Silent, Do the Impossible'. It means that no matter how things look, hold your vision. So I just kept visualising that we were on this cruise even though I didn't have any idea how it might happen. I didn't visualise Gran dying!"

"Of course not," she said, "I didn't mean that."

"Gran was ready to go," Dad said simply. "Maybe at some level there was a kind of agreement between her desire to move on and Nat's desire for the holiday. Maybe their visions kind of meshed..."

That was a thought. I looked at my father with new respect.

"If people only had to think about what they wanted and it came about, everyone would be doing it," Mum pointed out. "And that certainly isn't happening!"

"Because most people are thinking all mixed-up thoughts about what they want and what they don't want," I said. "So they get mixed-up results. And they're not taking consistent actions – they do a bit and then they give up." I didn't exactly know where this was coming from; it was as if bits of all the conversations I'd had with Nina and Nuncle and Liz over the last year were coming out of me.

"*And* because life is set up so that we get a balance of what we want and what we don't want," I added. 'If we just got everything we wanted we'd all get fat and lazy and take things for granted. So we also get some challenges to make us grow."

"Listen to that, honey," Dad told Mum. "You want the kids to grow – I think this Mastery Club is delivering that for our daughter. I wouldn't be too worried about it."

"Some things won't change, no matter what people might believe," Mum said stubbornly.

"Guess that will be so for you, if that's what you believe," Dad said. And he winked at me.

Mastery Club Lesson #25

Absence of proof is not
proof of absence

* Some things won't change, no matter what people might believe… and some people won't believe, no matter what things might change.

* The masses have to see something to believe it, while the masters believe and then it appears.

* Remember: your R.A.S. delivers what you believe and expect…

CHAPTER 43

I PLAY THE
'I AM THAT' GAME

WE WENT BACK to the ship for lunch and ate too much again. After lunch we lay around on the sundeck and played in the pool (which was filled with fresh seawater each morning), and that afternoon we arrived in Turkey. It was pretty amazing to be in a new country, just like that. We shared a taxi to the ruins of Ephesus with some Texans (who really did say 'y'all', just like in the movies). It was a hoot. They were heaps of fun and did lots of bargaining with the driver, a Turkish man with rotten teeth who ended up driving us for half the price he had originally asked. The Texan minister's wife was the leader of the negotiations – we were all very impressed.

It was like going back in time, wandering down the wide dusty road of Ephesus with its huge crumbling amphitheatres and intricate carvings on the bits of buildings that still stood. The usual cats and dogs sprawled in the shade or wandered around. Katie and Evan were over ruins (to be honest, I was too), so we went through it pretty quickly and then dawdled along the souvenir stalls. One man was cheerily selling 'genuine fake watches'. There were lots of nice things, like bags and jewellery and embroidered tablecloths, but these salespeople were very pushy, getting right in our faces and urging us to look at their stuff. A swarthy man with a cigarette propped between his yellowing teeth, great big sweat stains under his armpits and masses of curly black hair escaping from the neck of his shirt, thrust some leather handbags right in front of Mum. "Look!" he insisted. "You buy? Very good quality. The best!"

Mum wrinkled her nose – he really stank – and smiled politely. "No thank you," she said. But he kept trying, and suddenly I remembered my Mastery Club homework: the 'I Am That' Game.

I had been staring at the man in disgust, I realised. "I was doing a 'them-and-us' – making myself better than him just because he was poor and a bit dirty… (well, a lot dirty). Could I 'own' this pushy, smelly man? Was there anything of him in me? It wasn't a comfortable idea. I just wanted to get away from him but I made myself look. He must have felt me looking at him; he turned away from Mum, who was still politely refusing to buy his stuff, and kind of leered at me. I walked on quickly, flushing. But then we had this little panic when we couldn't find Evan, so I had to stand on the spot hanging onto Katie while Mum and Dad retraced their steps. I returned my gaze to that salesman, who was now badgering another tourist to look at his wares.

Serenity was right. There was no way we could have world peace if we turned our noses up at people, like I had been doing with this man. But would she have been able to love him and 'own' him? And could I? Could I make myself equal with this rude man instead of better than him? Was *I* pushy and dirty and smelly?

"Stop squeezing my arm," Katie whined, and I loosened my grip a bit. She immediately wriggled free and dashed away.

"Come back here!" I yelled, rushing after her.

"Make me!" she taunted, darting towards a display of nicknacks.

"You are *not* supposed to run off!" I fumed, seizing her arm again. "We've already lost Evan. How would you like to be lost here with all these strangers?"

"Ow, you're hurting me!" Katie whimpered.

"I am not!" I denied, heart sinking. There it was: the forcefulness. And of course I had been dirty and smelly in my life. And rude. And tried to talk Mum into giving me things or doing things for me that she didn't want to do. I *was* him after all, or at least, no better than him.

We spied Mum and Dad through the crowd, walking back to us with a tear-stained Evan firmly held between them. "I want to go home," Katie sobbed, "I'm sick of this." She wriggled free of my grip again and ran towards them.

We all went to bed early in preparation for our bus tour on the Island of Rhodes, and when the bus arrived the following morning, Evan and Katie climbed aboard eagerly, trying several seats before deciding they had found the best spot. It was quite nice to be up high in an air conditioned bus since it was such a hot day, but the driver was very boring, pouring facts at us in an endless stream, and the scenery was mostly just dry countryside. I fell asleep, only waking up when we arrived at yet another ruin. "Do I have to get out?" I asked, when Mum shook my arm. "I'm tired."

But she didn't want me to stay in the bus by myself, so I had to trail after them. I went, feeling sulky. Dad was giving Evan a shoulder ride, so he was happy, and Mum had bought Katie a bag, so she was quite chirpy too. I dragged my heels, squinting in the glare. The toilet queue here was really long and the person taking the euros actually went into your loo after you'd been and checked it. What a gross job!

From the ruin we went to watch one of the last genuine pottery families making stuff on the wheel the old way. I had to admit that was pretty fascinating even though I was still being grumpy. Mum bought a few dishes, including one with really delicate paintwork. We'd watched them working on it with these fine little brushes. There was no way I'd have such a steady hand!

Then we were taken to the Old City, which was the oldest inhabited medieval town in Europe. Our guide led us through narrow, cobble-paved lanes with tall, fortress-like buildings on either side, and gates and archways. When he told us that we were in the Street of the Knights, Evan was suddenly way interested; he shot me a conspiratorial glance, obviously remembering our moment in the park. Dad bought him some souvenir coins, which he clutched protectively for the rest of the day.

I trailed along after the others, gazing at the buildings and imagining myself leaning out of a window in ancient times to talk to someone in the street – maybe my lover, who was about to go to battle… I had to admit that being here was pretty cool, and edged a little further out of my grungy mood.

I was stopped in my tracks by the sight of several brown-skinned children about Evan's age who were sitting on the kerb playing small, colourful accordions with puppies asleep at their feet and begging cups or bowls in front of them. I was shocked. Little children begging? Why weren't they in school? What was the government doing in this country! Katie and Evan were dumbstruck too. We stood there, staring.

One child dragged her puppy by the lead to speak to another child, paying no attention to the fact that its feet were splayed in all four directions as it tried to resist her. An American tourist was horrified and chased after the girl to tell her off. I didn't get to see what happened because our tour guide had turned a corner and we had to run to catch up, but those kids stayed on my mind for the rest of the day.

The island of Crete was next on the schedule but we kids absolutely refused to go and visit another ruin. "But it's a Palace," Mum coaxed.

"You and Dad go," I said. "I'll mind these two." And, amazingly, she agreed. So the siblings and I spent the day wandering around the ship and eating from the smorgasbord. (We'd have spent it in the pool but we needed someone older with us to supervise; luckily it was cool and cloudy so we didn't care too much.) Without Mum there to supervise, Katie's lunch was all from the dessert bar… I was about to lecture her but decided not to. I'd had enough of playing mother.

Mum and Dad made us dress up for dinner that night because we were eating in the restaurant instead of the buffet, and when I went to the loo I discovered that I'd got my period again. Luckily Mum had brought some pads just in case, but it made us a bit late.

There was a napkin-waving performance by the waiters while we were eating – a bit weird, but apparently it's traditional on cruise ships. Then Dad took the 'billy lids' to bed and Mum and I sat in one of the lounge areas and listened to music and watched people dancing. (She had been quite affectionate all evening since I'd whispered that I thought I had my period, and this time I hadn't pushed her away.)

"Thanks so much for looking after the kids today," she said yet again, giving my hand a squeeze.

"That's okay," I said. "It was a true win/win."

She smiled. "Yes. No ruins for you and freedom for us… It's always the way with the eldest child – I am too, remember? First you're the apple of your parent's eyes, the centre of attention, and then suddenly along come brothers and sisters and you're pushed to the side, and *then* you're expected to look after them!"

I shrugged. "It's not as if you ask me to very often." I'd been four when Katie was born. I remembered the fuss about her, and feeling like I wasn't special or important any more. And then Evan had come only two years later, and Mum had had even less time for me. She did ask me to help out occasionally, but I wasn't on duty all the time, like poor families where the kids my age had to stay home and work in the fields or mind little kids, and couldn't even have a life. The beggar children came back to mind…

"No, I wouldn't do that to you," she said. "And anyway, there are two sides, as you were saying the other night," she added with a grin. "You lost some attention but you gained some company – and some freedom because I was so busy looking after them."

And that comment reminded me that I could be looking for the Order in being a beggar child instead of seeing it as wrong. I wondered again what that could possibly be…

There was a very elegant-looking elderly woman in a black dress sitting across from us at a little round table. She had pearls around her neck and on her wrists and big diamond rings and very fluffed up hair, as if she'd spent most of her day at the hairdresser. She looked rich and bored. The heavy, waistcoated man sitting with her also looked bored. He was staring at the dance floor but didn't seem to be seeing it. There were two glasses of wine on the table in front of them and every now and then one of them took a sip, but neither one said a thing.

Mum followed my gaze. "They're a very wealthy couple who cruise all year long," she whispered to me. "Or so I've heard."

Looking at them, I could just imagine that lady turning up her nose at Vassily's dirty hostel, and probably thinking we weren't worthy company since we'd stayed there, but she was obviously not having nearly as much fun on her trip as we were. I could just imagine Nina demanding of her: *So what are you making it mean?* I smiled at that, and then was struck by the realisation that maybe life for those beggar kids wasn't as bad as it looked to me… maybe begging was a step up from something else… although I couldn't imagine what.

Our next and last stop was Santorini, where we would have two whole days before we began the long journey home. It's a volcanic island, which Evan thought was pretty cool. ("Will it blow up while we're here?" he kept hoping.)

You could see the different layers of rock on the cliff face as our ship approached, and narrow lines that Dad said was a road zig-zagging its way to the top of the cliff where the township sprawled, glinting white in the sun. Pretty soon we were on that road in a bus. Some of the tourists had chosen to climb the five or six hundred steps to the town, and some had gone on donkeys. ("Donkeys!" Katie had screeched. "I want to go on a donkey!" But "too dangerous," Mum had said firmly. "The cruise people don't recommend it.")

Our guide was a cheerful woman called Helen. "Half the women in Greece are called Helen, and the other half are called Maria," she laughed. Evan was hanging onto every word when she told us that the island had twenty craters that were still active and occasionally smoked. "But they only erupt every few thousand years, so the residents feel quite safe." ("I wish it would blow up while we're here," Evan said. He was serious too, the nutter.)

The bus rumbled along the highest and narrowest part of the island – we could see the ocean on both sides, far down below! There were almost no trees on the island, so no shade, and the domed houses and churches were white to reflect the sun, with blue roofs and doors. Mum oohed and ahed and took photos of *everything*.

"Santorini is a live geological museum – geologists and volcanologists often come here to study it," Helen said. "Lots of couples come too, for their weddings, as it's considered one of the most romantic – though expensive – spots on earth. Much of the graffiti is love messages."

When we were unloaded to wander through the sun-baked town of Ea, shopkeepers offered us pistachios, one of the local crops, and sesame-and-honey-coated peanuts. They were yum. Dad ordered one third of a traditional Greek breakfast: a coffee called 'frappée' – which means cold, shaken, with ice cubes and a straw, in a glass. (The other two thirds were a cigarette and a newspaper, according to Helen.) I scraped up my courage to say, "Yassu tikanis" to the shopkeeper, and he beamed at me, replying, "Kala, kala!" and gave me a free piece of baklava!

It was a very beautiful island, and jam-packed with tourists. We wandered through the town, finally arriving at a popular cliffside street where masses of people were setting up tripods and saving spots on the low stone walls or at the outdoor tables of restaurants to view the 'sunset', which was supposed to be quite famous. This time Dad suggested we eat on the island instead of on the ship, and Mum said there was no way we'd get a table now – they'd all be reserved, but he insisted that we give it a try, and soon we were sitting at one of those tables with iced juices and wine, watching all the activity around us and the changing colour in the sky. (It turned out that he'd booked the restaurant from the ship for a surprise. Mum was very happy.)

Our meals took ages to arrive and Evan and Katie were getting restless and irritable, so we left Mum and Dad in the restaurant and squeezed our way back through the crowd to watch the 'sunset'. People actually burst into applause and cheering when the golden-orange disc finally disappeared from sight. (Am I that too? I wondered. Could I 'own' that dazzling beauty? Nina had said to own good things as well…)

When we crossed the little street back to the restaurant, our meals had finally arrived. Mum and Dad had seafood, the siblings had fried fish, and I had risotto with Mediterranean vegetables.

It was all pretty tasty but the waiters were kind of arrogant and didn't seem very interested in us at all. And the bill must have been spectacular, if Dad's raised brows and silent refusal to show it to us counted for anything.

Back to the ship for the night and then it was our last day on Santorini. We found a beach of black volcanic sand. "Will it blow up?" Evan asked. "Dork!" I said. It was very hot though, so we spent most of the day in the sparkling ocean. Then we explored the town of Fira until it was time to go, when we reluctantly joined the end of a very long queue for the cable car that would take us back down the cliff-face to our ship.

It took us nearly an hour to slowly make our way to the cable car 'station', where a gum-chewing young man wearing a singlet that showed his big muscles directed us into one of the cars; moments later we took off with a jolt.

"Look!" I gaped, pointing to the stunning view above us as Fira appeared on the top of the island, lit up like fairyland; Katie nudged me, pointing way below us to where four cruise ships poised silently in the dark blue sea, also lit up. We kept looking from the town, at the top of the cliff, to the snaking steps against the rock face, to the jewelled ships in the dark ocean. It was a magical end to a pretty amazing holiday.

CHAPTER 44

CAN'T ESCAPE THE GOOD STUFF, BAD STUFF

MY FIRST IMPRESSION, when we arrived home, was of how much space there was in Australia. The streets were so wide and spacious after all the narrow, cobbled lanes on the Islands. And there were no more queues! (Apart from a traffic jam on the freeway when we were driving home in the taxi…) It was also freezing cold in Melbourne after our summer in Europe.

I was busting to catch up with the Mastery Club members to hear everyone's news and tell mine, but we just couldn't get it together in that first week of school. Clare wasn't answering the phone for some reason, and Nina was apparently still at Joel's.

Sandy and I caught up as soon as we saw each other at school. Sandy wanted to hear all about our trip and I wanted to know how her weekend with Nuncle and Liz had gone, which now seemed so long ago. (She looked somehow different, maybe taller, or slimmer… or something.) So I told her snippets about my adventure, and she said things at home were 'a bit better now', in usual Sandy cryptic style, which didn't reveal much at all. I got the impression that she'd had a pretty good time at Liz and Nuncle's, though. Billy waved at us as we were coming out of the caf, and jogged over.

"How did you go?" we both asked at once.

"Third," he grinned, and we gave him a high five. "Got a mate who wants to join the Club," he added. "I met him at the camp."

"Great!" I enthused. Now Bill would be less likely to lose interest.

Our turn for a slide night, I decided, as Dad and I sat clicking through hundreds of pictures that evening. We made up an invitation and emailed it to the others; within minutes a reply popped in from Clare: 'I'll be there', but when I emailed straight back to ask her where she was and what was her news, there was no answering message. Strange.

On Wednesday the school Mastery Club met and Miss Walker asked me to tell them all about our trip. We'd had about ten meetings by now so I was way more comfortable talking to these guys. They were surprised about the beggar kids and by how many beggars there were. I told them that in Athens a young girl had approached us with a piece of scrawled paper telling a sad story in broken English about her mother being sick and her brother needing an operation and her father dead, and could we spare a few euros? We did, and a few minutes later ran into another girl with exactly the same scrawled-on-paper story. The long-time travellers on the ship had said it was a racket and not to fall for it, so we'd started to look the other way whenever we saw one, but that seemed so mean – what if it was true? They certainly looked poor and miserable.

And then there were the poor-looking people who sat on the side of the road selling souvenirs. We'd looked at their displays at first, but they were mostly such crappy little things that we didn't want to buy them. It had felt so mean to be ignoring all those people, but, as Dad had said, if we gave to all of them *we'd* end up beggars!

"Besides, encouraging beggars gives them a reason to turn that behaviour into a serious business," Miss Walker said. Her next sentence horrified us: "Little children in India are actually deliberately blinded and crippled to make them into more heart-rending beggars."

After I'd talked about my holiday, we updated everyone's goals. Kat had been to Bali during the school holidays (she'd raised seventy-five bucks spending money in the end, which had been plenty); Mark was doing even better than usual in his chess competitions, and he was sure that was because of his visualisations; Holly and Bree were still having mixed results – some wins and some losses on the netball court; and Tom kept forgetting to do anything about his goal. (Miss Walker was getting a bit frustrated with him.) But Petra surprised us all.

"I've been visualising that I have a mouse," she said, her gaze sliding here and there between us, "and Mum is still dead against it. But over the holidays a new family moved in next door to us, and they've got just about every animal under the sun – including mice. So I've been over there just about every day playing with their mice!" She was so rapt that she forgot to be shy and looked at us all right in the eyes.

"That's an even better outcome," Mark said in his usual sensible way; "Now you don't have to clean the cage."

"Oh, I wouldn't have cared about that. But they've got guinea pigs and cats and dogs and birds and fish and turtles and chooks!" she beamed. "It's a *zoo*. Mum is Not Impressed – she's already been woken up by the rooster. It's awesome."

"But at least she doesn't have to have pets in her house," Miss Walker smiled. "Well done, Petra. So what is stopping you from getting focused on your goal, Tom? Why do you think you keep forgetting?"

He turned the palms of his hands to the ceiling with a comical shrug.

"Well, you do want it," she pressed, "it *is* important to you, right?"

"Yeah," he agreed.

"And it's a pretty specific goal and a specific amount of money that you need to earn…"

"That's S and M," Mark said, ticking them off on his fingers. "I think the problem is with the A and R." He pushed his glasses up his short nose. "I think Tom's Action Plan isn't happening."

"*Our* Action Plan is happening," Bree interrupted; "we're practising and visualising and still losing lots of games. I don't think this stuff works."

"It's not our fault," Holly added. "It's Jane and Emily and Rosanna and those other kids that don't turn up to practice. And you and me are the only ones visualising so it's no wonder."

"Hold on," Miss Walker said, "let's just finish with Tom first."

He looked at her expectantly.

"What's your Action Plan, Tom?"

"Jobs around the house to earn money," he replied.

"Are you doing them?"

He made a goofy face.

"Ah… Can't get paid for what you don't do."

"I did one job, but Mum didn't have any cash on her and then I forgot to ask for it. And lately I keep forgetting."

"Maybe you could get creative and come up with another way to earn some money."

"Like what?"

"Well…" Miss Walker cast about; her gaze settled on me.

"Any ideas, Natalie?"

"My friend Billy mows lawns," I said.

Tom shook his head. "Mum wouldn't let me."

"You could walk dogs in your neighbourhood," Holly suggested.

"Mum wouldn't let me. She panics about everything. She'd worry that I'd get bitten."

"Wash cars," I said. "That's safe."

"But I'd have to knock on people's doors. Seriously, she's the most panicky person in the world."

"What about your Dad, can't he help?" Mark asked.

"No dad. He died."

"Oh. Sorry."

We were all stumped.

"Weed gardens or look after people's pets while they're away," Bree said.

Tom just looked at her.

"Why don't you ask your Mum to come up with an idea for you, then?" Kat asked in her lazy, drawling sort of voice. "If she's going to get in your way all the time, she might as well help. I mean, if you're trying to save for your own stuff, that's good for her."

"Yeah," Holly said.

"I'll try that," Tom promised, and then added: "If I remember."

Miss Walker sighed. "How about making a *commitment* to remembering? No-one said this was going to be easy or that the game would just drop into your lap. You have to take action! It takes inner work *and* outer work. Are you visualising that you've got the game?"

Tom looked rueful.

"Well, there you have it. If you're not committed to it, how can you expect to achieve it?"

"But *we're* committing to winning netball matches and we keep losing," Bree objected. "Well, we've won some, but only against the worst teams and only by a goal or two."

"And we're visualising every day, aren't we, Bree?" Holly stated.

Bree nodded, and the two girls stared at me and Miss Walker defiantly.

"You've got to just hang in there," I said, remembering how

Sandy hadn't got the part she'd wanted until the last minute; and I'd had to wait for months before our holiday was a reality. "Sometimes it takes a while. Especially if you've got a whole team to deal with, and everyone else's thoughts."

"Yes. Would they be open to visualising as well?" Miss Walker asked.

"We talked about it and some of them said they would, but no-one really is," Holly said. "And half of them don't turn up to practice and a whole lot of people are really negative. Some of them are talking about dropping out, even."

"Maybe you'll end up with a more committed team," Miss Walker said optimistically.

The girls shrugged. They weren't convinced that anything was going to work, but even so, after everyone left, Miss Walker told me she was very pleased with how the Mastery Club was progressing. She had spoken to the School Principal about starting another group this term, and she wanted me to give them an introductory talk too. As I walked out of the library, I wondered how Nina was going with her 'youth motivational speaker' goal – it looked like I was becoming one without even having chosen it!

When I got home from school, Mum was crouched in front of the television with her hand over her mouth and shaking her head from side to side, saying, "Oh God, oh God…"

"What is it, Mum?" I asked.

"Tsunami," she replied, eyes glued to the screen. "In the Pacific. They've been having more earthquakes and now there's just been the most horrendous…"

I looked at the TV where fuzzy images of torrential waves showed people and even cars being washed away by the powerful tide. The camera screen kept getting splashed and you could hear muffled voices and screaming and splashing. A voice yelled, "Look out!" and there was a grinding noise, but the camera jerked away and we didn't see what had happened.

"Whole villages… gone," Mum murmured.

When I went upstairs to my bedroom, my eye was drawn to Nuncle's Good Stuff, Bad Stuff game, in its box on my bookshelf.

The Grown-Ups Get Into It

IT WAS QUITE AMAZING because at short notice pretty much everyone was able to come around to our place for the slideshow. A tanned Nina arrived first with Rosie and Pete and a huge green salad that had avocado and bits of orange in it, and a scattering of roasted seeds all over the top. (Nina had flown back home from Far North Queensland with Joel – who was in Melbourne to see his mother, she said, with a meaningful expression as they entered. "How was it?" I asked, busting to know. "A-May-Zing," she mouthed. "Tell you later.")

Sandy was hot on their heels with her mother, between them carrying a potato salad and a big Pavlova; her father was away on army business. (It wouldn't be untrue to say that Sandy looked quite happy and relaxed without him in tow.)

Billy had unexpectedly brought his friend Rick, the one he'd met at the mountain biking camp who was interested in our Club. He was a really fit-looking guy with streaky blonde hair. Both fathers followed them in, Billy's dad, John, with drinks, and Rick's dad whose name I didn't catch, with a plate of cold chicken pieces. ("Mum and Terry said sorry they couldn't make it; they'll drop in another time to see the pics," Billy called over his shoulder as he led the others into the dining room.)

Liz and Nuncle rang the doorbell next; they were carrying a big Greek salad and a plate of spanakopita, those cheese and spinach pastries that Mum and I loved, in keeping with the theme. Oh, and a book for Dad.

Finally Clare and Hazel arrived with Serenity and her mother, whose name turned out to be Shanti, or something like that. They'd brought a macaroni cheese and a curried rice dish between them, as well as some of Serenity's little siblings who we hadn't been expecting. Katie and Evan fronted up to examine these guests, and Mum and I exchanged glances, hoping they'd all be friends…

The house was bursting full and noisy as anything. Mum rescued her roast vegies and roast lamb from the oven just in time, and everyone started to load up their plates.

I grabbed Clare's arm. "So what's happening?"

She glanced around the room for a second, located Hazel at the other end, and turned excited eyes to me. "Dad wants me to live with him part of the time. Same problem as you now, Bill!"

Billy rolled his eyes. "Good luck then!"

"Safety in numbers?" Sandy asked, indicating Rick with a little jab of her head.

"You told me I should bring more guys," Billy grinned.

"Hope you don't mind me gate-crashing," Rick said with an easy-going smile, and I noticed that I actually felt quite relaxed about him being there. Not threatened at all. Maybe I was getting over that…

"But does he know what he's getting himself into?" Sandy asked no-one in particular.

I turned to Rick. "Billy said you're interested in joining the Mastery Club. Are you?"

"Sounds pretty cool," Rick replied. "My dad's into the sort of stuff you guys have been talking about so I've kind of grown up with it too."

"You should meet Nina then," Clare said, looking around. "Where is she? It's much harder to find her these days without the green hair…"

"Are you kids going to serve yourselves or just block the way?" Dad demanded playfully. "I'm hungry!"

By the time we'd finished piling our plates, almost every seat in the lounge room already had an adult in it. I was about to suggest we kids go up to my room when Sandy's mother raised a glass of wine and said, "Well, it's great to have you all safely home, what with all the earthquakes and tsunamis and political unrest going on everywhere."

"Hear, hear," a few voices said; and, "Yes, welcome back."

"My sister's been trying to get me to join her church," Hazel declared, "but really, these disasters just confirm my reason for walking away in the first place. I don't want to come down all heavy, but with so many disasters so close together it's been preying on my mind. I mean, why does God let such bad things happen to good people? You know what I mean? If He really is out there, why doesn't He show a bit of might? That famous might…"

"Free will, honey," Mum called from the dining table, where she was scraping the last of the potato salad onto her dish.

"You know what Pat thinks?" Hazel called back. "That these disasters *are* God's might: punishment for our sins…" She rolled her eyes. "That's a bit extreme for me, but gee, I remember singing hymns like, 'Lord, take away all our cares and heal all our woes', and we sure could do with a bit of that. Seriously: why doesn't this supposedly powerful God help out?"

I was again about to suggest to the Mastery Club members that we take our food up to my room when I saw Liz give Nuncle a gentle kick on the leg and make warning eyes at him. He gave her one of his twinkly smiles and opened his mouth to speak, but just then Mum came over from the table, saying, "We'd just be puppets having our strings pulled, Haze. Much as I don't like the mess free will makes, I must say I prefer that to being a puppet."

"Didn't someone say God is dead?" Dad wondered aloud. "Who was that – Nietzsche?"

"I think we should leave God out of it," Mum reproved. "Our problems are well within the realm of human ability to solve. How do they put it? There isn't an energy crisis or a food crisis anywhere on this planet – it's just a crisis of unwillingness to help others." Shaking her head, she went to sit on the floor. Dad tossed her a cushion.

"Just to play devil's advocate," Nuncle said, "what if there's no crisis at all? What if everything's in perfect order and the only crisis is a crisis of ignorance – that we can't *see* the order?"

Liz rolled her eyes and shook her head at him silently; Nina grinned at me from her spot on the floor. I gave up on any plans to take us kids upstairs and joined her.

"How can that possibly be?" Mum asked, a little edgily. "It's obvious to anyone that the world is in trouble: starvation, dictatorships, environmental disasters left, right and centre…"

"That's because you're viewing the whole thing through your values," Nuncle replied. "We all do that – whatever matches our values is good and whatever doesn't is bad – but what if *all* values are 'good', for want of a better word; what if they're all acceptable to God? The values of a mad, violent fundamentalist as much as yours, my dear."

Mum put her fork down and stared at him, speechless.

"If we ask ourselves what God's values are, so to speak," Nuncle continued evenly, "we have to acknowledge that God isn't pro-life, or at least he's not attached to preserving it in any particular form; Creation includes death at every level and in every form – cell death, species death… God, or the Grand Organising Design, as some of us like to term it, allows it all and accepts it all; it's all part of the Divine Order."

"God: the ultimate anarchist," Dad mused. "I've always been struck by the irony of warring countries both praying for victory to the same Deity. Does God play favourites – or is that prayer a pointless exercise? Perhaps He/She/It doesn't care who wins…"

"Oh, really!" Mum exploded. (Just then there was a thump from upstairs that would usually have sent her running, but she didn't budge; she had Nuncle in her furious sights.)

"Maybe they're praying to different Gods – maybe there are a few out there," Sandy's mother put in cheerily. "Maybe ultimately it's a battle of the gods and we're just pawns." She looked at Sandy. "I'm just joking. Don't tell Dad I said that." Sandy stared at her, and she gave a little laugh and looked away.

"Ah, as the ancient Greeks would have us believe." Dad dipped his head; "You have a point."

"And yet most religions refer to One God," Nuncle said, "and science refers to One Energy. It seems that they're talking about the same thing."

"Gosh, this *is* a serious conversation!" Liz exclaimed. "Shall we pick something a little lighter?"

"So Max, you're saying that terrorism and war and natural disasters that destroy thousands of people and their homes are good or part of some kind of plan?" Mum asked in horror, totally ignoring Liz.

"Let's take that tsunami," Nuncle said; he was settling in. (Liz gave a sigh.) "To us it's terrible because we judge it from the high value we place on survival and comfort; to the earth, it's a natural phenomenon, a 'burp', neither good nor bad… After all, do you worry about the billions of bacteria you kill every time you shower or brush your teeth? It's all a matter of perspective."

"But bacteria isn't conscious," Mum pointed out.

"How do you know?" Nuncle asked.

Mum stared at him for a moment, and then shrugged and gave a little toss of her shoulders.

"It's certainly a fair comment that the earth will look after itself to the end," Rick's father agreed. "No matter what we humans do to ourselves and each other, the earth will come out on top. It'll just get rid of us if it has to, to keep its own balance."

"Indeed." Nuncle shifted in his seat. "Look at it this way: one hundred years ago there were only about a billion people on the planet; today we've got seven billion. And in the last century we've had World War I, the Spanish Influenza epidemic that killed fifty million people around the world, the Great Depression, World War II, the Korean War, Vietnam, cancer, AIDS, and terrorism like 9/11. Never before in history have so many people died, and never before have so many been born. There are heaps more of us than ever, so, somehow, more death is linked to more life – and war is a big part of the dynamic."

Mum frowned.

"This is a principle known as the Law of Conservation – the kids have been learning about it in their Mastery Club," Nuncle said cheerfully. (Liz rolled her eyes again and looked as if she wanted to disappear.) "The First Law of Thermodynamics: you can't get rid of anything because it just takes a new form, and since you can't get rid of anything, there will always be a balance of opposites. For example, it becomes politically incorrect for parents and teachers to hit kids, so kids hit each other – or their parents. Violence in some form will be maintained throughout time, but society lives in fear and judgement of it, and in reaction to it."

"But it seems so wrong!" Hazel declared.

"Look at it this way: if there's One God – or One Energy, depending on your perspective – then where is God not? It must all be God, or all an expression of that perfect Order. With that perspective we can transform instead of merely reacting."

This was all sounding very familiar. It was fun to be ahead of the adults for once.

"Oh, my sister would have a heap of trouble with that one!" Hazel exclaimed, shaking her head. "That makes the Devil a part of God too!"

"Indeed," Nuncle smiled. "Going back to war, has it occurred to anyone that while we've been having all this trouble with global terrorism, bad as it appears, that we haven't had a major war for a long time? If there's a conservation of war, that could be the present form of it; instead of millions dying we have only a few thousand around the world. But nobody is grateful to terrorism for saving millions of lives, because they don't see its part in divine order. Nor do most people recognise that a good number of our most valuable discoveries and inventions have come out of war, out of that effort to conquer the other side."

BIG silence.

"Any food left?" Serenity's mother asked brightly from the doorway. "I was just sorting out a little altercation upstairs… What are you all talking about?"

CHAPTER 46

THE SMORGASBORD OF LIFE

"OH DEAR," Mum said, starting up.

"Relax, it's all sorted. Wow. This looks yummy." She began to scoop food onto a plate. "Carry on, I'll pick up the gist."

"We've gone straight to the meaty stuff," Hazel said. "My fault – sorry. We're talking about God, of all things."

"Lovely," Shanti said. "A favourite subject of mine."

"I think what Max is saying," Rosie offered, "is that if you look at the whole big picture, we need all value systems. They all balance each other out and if everyone had the same values, well, there's no point in being clones of each other. Besides, there are some jobs that would just never be done. I couldn't imagine being an accountant or a butcher, for instance! So thank God for those people."

"Exactly," Nuncle agreed. "Nature is healthiest when there's great diversity. Look at monocultures – they're the most susceptible to pests and disease. It just doesn't make sense for everyone to be the same. We need the variety."

"Of course," Mum said emphatically. "I *love* cultural difference."

"So long as those other cultures don't challenge your core values too much, I imagine, Beth," he said. "And I'm exactly the same; female circumcision, cutting off thieves' hands and cannibalism are a little too diverse for me, but they're perfectly normal in many places and times. And even the great Plato couldn't imagine a society without slavery."

Mum frowned again.

"I would have thought that the pinnacle of evolution would be to arrive at a united consciousness that doesn't create war; just love," Shanti declared, sitting on a seat Dad offered her with her dish of salad and curry.

"And at that moment we would blink out of existence," Nuncle replied, snapping his fingers. "When we can sustain true love, it's curtains for the human race. If you'll excuse a moment of physics, matter can only exist when those polarities are kept at a distance from each other. As soon as we unite them in a moment of true unconditional love, the positive and negative charges cancel each other out, we become pure light, and matter disappears. Light and matter are two forms of the same fundamental energy, but with them it seems to be an either/or situation – you can't have, or be, both simultaneously."

"Fascinating," murmured Dad.

"So, on this planet at least, for life to express through form we'll always have conflict of some sort. It's factored into the system because life itself is produced out of the interaction of those polarities. And conflict, no matter how much we dislike it, is how we grow. Weren't some of the most difficult times in your life when you grew the most?"

I noticed a look pass between Sandy and her mum, but I couldn't read the expressions on their faces.

"But you can't expect people to abandon their values," Mum argued. "That would be inhuman!"

Nuncle cocked his head. "Or an expression of profound unconditional love."

"How so?" asked Hazel. "I'm with Beth."

"Well, if God is the ultimate example of love, and God holds all values equal, then maybe our task is to find a way to do the same. Maybe true love is like the light that gives rise to all the colours of the spectrum, one that holds *all* perspectives and *all* values, rather than a monochromatic preferential sort of view. When light passes through a crystal it fractionates into a range of beautiful colours, and perhaps we get attached to blue or green or yellow ideas, but what if those are merely parts of the whole truth?"

"Interesting," Rick's father said thoughtfully. "Has anyone here heard of Buckminster Fuller? He was a real genius – inventor, philosopher, designer, writer; he won a Nobel Peace Prize. Bucky pointed out that we are each mini Universes – we're actually comprised of the same chemical elements as the Universe, and in the same proportions – and he put forward the idea that humans are effectively 'experiments'. We're as unique as our fingerprints, and each person's way of dealing with life is a kind of test case of possibilities, some of which will continue and some won't…"

Mum shuddered and Hazel gave a short, incredulous laugh. "Like we're in some sort of science fiction story? How awful!"

"Or how wonderful," Rick's dad countered. "To be the heroes of our own adventure story! And practical for the Earth because Nature always has a back-up plan – which I guess is what you're saying, sir."

"Max," Nuncle said; he was obviously enjoying himself.

"In Fuller's view," Rick's dad continued, "the current 'you or me', 'good or evil' separatist perspective just doesn't work today. He specialised in viewing the human condition from a non-judgemental perspective, and he came to believe that every human being is important, and that no individual or species is superior to another.

"Our bodies are a great example: we're each made up of millions of cells and tissues and organs, each of which exists individually, and we couldn't survive as individuals without all those sub-realities and contributions; no one cell or tissue or organ is more important than another."

"Well, of course," Mum said, but she looked uncertain, and I must say that I got a bit lost in that waterfall of words...

"You know what woke me up to this?" Nuncle asked. He was in his element, I could see. And when I looked around the room, everyone was following the conversation: Hazel and Mum with their disturbed expressions, Sandy's mum looking curious, my Dad and Billy's and Rick's with interest, Rosie and Pete and Liz with a kind of reserved enthusiasm.

The Mastery Club members were listening closely too. Sandy was sitting with crossed legs quite near to Liz and Nuncle, eating steadily but all ears; Clare and Serenity and her mother were frowning slightly as they digested this information along with their dinners; Billy and Rick had been talking among themselves but were now paying full attention. Nina, of course, was delighted.

"I heard about this concept in all sorts of different places in my uni days," Nuncle explained. " Plato, Leibniz, Jung, Bucky –" with a nod to Rick's dad; "they all talk about Divine Order, the extraordinary degree of intelligence in the design of the entire cosmos. It's *so* intelligent at every level.[26] Nothing is wasted and

---

26   If that seems like a mad idea to you, start to look for evidence of it. Did you know that the solar system is a replica of an atom? Think about it: you've got a central sun/nucleus and lots of electrons/planets revolving around it. There's a new field called molecular astronomy that goes into this. Also every single body part reflects the whole body. You can link the spine to every organ, the ear reflects the spine, the sole of the foot is connected to every part of the body... It's way too orderly to be random. And if you're up for some spookily perfect numbers, multiply 111,111,111 x 111,111,111 and see what you get. If you use a big enough calculator you'll end up with 12,345,678,987,654,321. How cool is that! Einstein said that mathematics is the language that God speaks, and when you get answers like that one, you might get a glimpse that you're listening in to His/Her/Its Conversation...

nothing is an error. It's self-correcting and self-balancing, and there are patterns of Order from the smallest microcosm to the grandest macrocosm.

"So I began to wonder if, in fact, the dynamics of our everyday human lives that we view as chaotic and full of mistakes were also orderly but we just don't have a big enough picture yet to see it. The idea appealed to me, but trusting that it was orderly wasn't enough – I had to be convinced. So I went looking for it…"

"And?" Hazel prodded.

"Well… I'm Jewish by birth," Nuncle continued, "and like many Jews, I lost family in the Holocaust and was harbouring resentment against Hitler and the Arabic Nations. But it was the realisation that these characters had power over me – *decades* after the war Hitler still caused me to feel physically upset – that made me decide to consciously address this issue in my life. And in the process of doing that, I saw a symmetry between those opposing groups – you know, the Jews with their 'Chosen People' ideology, and the Nazis with their 'Perfect Aryan Race' claim, that utterly floored me. I began to wonder if the two groups were magnetically attracted together to balance out each other's form of superiority…"

"Interesting," Dad mused; and Mum said, "That's alarming!" at the same time.

"And there's the extraordinary mirroring, fifty years on, of Israeli soldiers with machine guns and German Shepherds patrolling the barbed wire of Palestinian internment camps… the old principle that you become what you judge began to haunt me," Nuncle continued.

"One day I was pondering the fact that Jews are among the highest achievers in every nation where they live, and I was struck by the balancing factor of their perennial persecution and trouble… I could just imagine a booming voice speaking to them from on high – if you'll excuse the traditional God image – and saying, 'All right! You want an end to persecution – fine. But in that case, surrender all your momentous achievements as well. The two travel together. You can have both… or neither."

"What a dilemma," Rick's dad murmured.

"But how are those things a sign of order?" Mum demanded.

Nuncle's dinner was half-touched. His plate sat balanced on his knees, cutlery abandoned, as he said, "Most people live out a belief in chaos and randomness and being at the effect of things. They go through life asking, 'Why did that happen to me?' but they don't really look for the answer and they are rarely prepared to see their part in it. If we live by principle, trusting in Order, we go looking for the relationships between things – we ask, 'How did I create that? What is this showing me about myself? What can I learn from this? How best can I respond to this?' We take responsibility."

"But people don't choose to be hurt," Mum argued. "Who would choose to be killed at war or crushed by a dictator or – or drowned in a tsunami!"

"No-one," Nuncle agreed; "*consciously*. But unconsciously we choose the experiences that will cause us to wake up and grow and fulfil our purpose."

"Or to look after ourselves," Liz said with a sigh. (I guessed she was thinking, 'If you can't beat 'em, join 'em.') "Weight, for a very simple example. No-one consciously chooses to gain weight but people often do out of the unconscious need to protect themselves. Or cancer… that's a wake-up call, believe me."

"Our conscious minds are only responsible for some two percent of our thoughts and feelings and actions," Nuncle told us. "You're absolutely right, Beth. If life was a smorgasbord of experiences, no-one would wander along the table with their plate in hand choosing bankruptcy, divorce, abuse –"

"Sickness," Liz added, "childlessness – or problems with children…"

"They'd choose the ideal body, the ideal partner, the ideal job, the ideal kids, etc., and then give themselves no stimulus to grow. We go through life seeking what supports our values, and we often get it, but we also attract what challenges our values – by the Law of Magnetism."

"Because the banquet is supervised by our silent partner, the Grand Organising Design, who tosses in some of those other aspects to make sure we have a balanced diet," Pete said with a laugh. "Since you don't grow on dessert alone."

"It's not quite like that," Rosie disagreed. "The outer is just a mirror to the inner. If you're feeling worthless and beating yourself up on the inside, you'll attract someone on the outside to do the same to you until you wake up and see what you're doing and value yourself more."

"Did someone say dessert?" Billy asked into the quiet.

Mastery Club Lesson #26

The Law of Unconditional Love
or A Valuable Lesson

* The G.O.D. values everything and everyone.

* True Love = appreciating the whole.

* True Love is a balance of support and challenge from the smorgasbord of life…

Mastery Club Lesson #27

The Law of Magnetism

* We resonate with (and seek) similar values – that's the Law of Resonance & Vibration[27], and

* we also attract that which challenges our values (by the Law of Magnetism: likes repel and unlikes attract) for the purpose of growth…

* But the hidden, mystical truth is that, because we have a dual nature, light and dark, a desire for growth and change as well as a need for comfort and familiarity, we attract both, and then we get to choose which one we follow. And…

* all experiences offer us both benefits and drawbacks whether we label them 'supportive' or 'challenging'.

* Remember this: What you think about, you bring about.

---

27   See *The Mastery Club* (Book 1 in this series).

CHAPTER 47

O THIS YIN-YANG WORLD!

IT WAS JUST AS WELL that Billy spoke up then because the atmosphere was getting a bit intense. There was a burst of light-hearted chatter and laughter and bustle as everyone helped to clear the tables, stack the dishwasher, make tea and coffee, and bring out the dessert. While this was happening I went to the loo and ran into Liz and Nuncle in the hallway. "She asked!" he was saying in self-defence. Liz looked a bit fierce, but then they saw me. We smiled at each other a little awkwardly.

On my way back, I ran into Mum and Nuncle in almost the same spot. "Are you saying that we shouldn't help anyone because they've created their problem and so we should just – just leave them in it?" Mum was demanding.

"If there's something that you feel drawn to do, by all means do it," Nuncle replied. "We're here to do what we love, Beth, what inspires us. I'm talking about the paradigm we hold. If we view something as broken and problematic we get emotional and reactive; if we view it as an orderly dynamic, we stay centred and take responsible and useful actions. And operating out of that paradigm, we can create a transformation."

"What's a paradigm?" I asked, and they both noticed me standing in the doorway.

"Your worldview," Nuncle explained. Then he leaned over and gave Mum a peace-making kiss.

Finally everyone was back in the lounge room to watch the slides from our holiday. Seeing those pics really brought the whole trip back – excitement at the airport, arriving in Athens, the ancient Acropolis, the awesome cruise ship and our cute cabin, the islands and their stunning views... and also the exhausting flights, the yucky hostel, the beggars, the dirty toilets, eating too much, the pushy salespeople, the zillions of tourists and the queues, queues, queues! Hm. It was very balanced.

I made a point of describing the unpleasant side to Clare, who'd had stars in her eyes (along with me...) at the thought of my holiday in the Greek Islands.

"Yes but it was *mostly* good, wasn't it?"

"Well, there were lots of bits that weren't much fun but it was definitely worth it." I turned to Nina. "What about your holiday? Joel! How was it? What happened?"

"Really interesting and *really* different," Nina beamed. "Lovely and warm – a great escape from winter over here. It was like being in another world! Everyone sleeps in really late and then sloooowly they get up and sit around and talk or paint... No rushing around like in Melbourne; it's too hot."

"Not that you do much rushing around in alpaca-land," Sandy said.

"Not as crazily as you guys do," Nina agreed, "but I usually get up early and I'm always doing things. I'm not a go-slow kind of person."

"Noticed that," Sandy said wryly.

"Who did you hang out with?" I asked.

"Sort of everyone," Nina said. "The kids were really shy at first and then they hung around me like anything – and the things they got up to! I saw one kid *grab a spider* and go off trailing its web like a fishing line, and then – get this: he throws the spider into a water hole and a minute later he's pulling on the web and literally pulling a little fish out. It was unbelievable."

"Ugh!" Clare shuddered.

"And they can get up a tree so fast it makes you dizzy. I came outside one day thinking, what's that noise? It sounded like a flock of sparrows but it was this bunch of kids. They're like wild birds. It's all quiet and then a bunch of them will suddenly appear and literally run up a tree and sit up there eating fruit and chattering and then suddenly run down and disappear completely. One minute they're there, the next minute they're gone."

She dissolved into laughter. "Oh there was this so-funny thing that happened! They love footy – they're all good too. They've got amazing co-ordination and balance. They can siphon petrol out of a car *while it's moving*, and you see even really little kids up on rooftops. Anyway, one day a bunch of us headed off in a tip-up truck to a footy match."

"A tip-up truck!"

"Yes – they pack as many people as they can into whatever vehicle's available, and that's what it was this time. So all the women were sitting in the back and the guys were in the front, and everyone's talking at once so it's way noisy. Anyway, while the men were driving and talking to each other, this kid was playing with the button that makes the tray tip up and down, and every few metres he was dropping a few of us off the back, but none of the guys noticed! So there was this trail of angry women yelling and chasing the truck but no-one in the cabin could hear over the noise of the engine. They must have gone a kilometre or two before they realised we were missing. It was hysterical!"

"Sounds wild," Sandy said. "So what was the bad side? Huh, Miss Even-Steven?"

Nina grinned at her. "Dirty. Basic. Really crowded – there were…" she counted on her fingers, "about ten, no – thirteen people living in Joel's grandmother's house. And it looks like stuff gets trashed really quickly. There are broken things and old shells of cars everywhere. I was pretty shocked at first but then Joel explained that they're so used to being in nature and dealing with real things like trees and rocks and earth and animals that money doesn't mean much to them. It's like, if they break a spear or run out of food they just make more or hunt for more or share stuff, so money's kind of irrelevant.

"F'rinstance, they don't want houses the way we do, with separate rooms and that. I heard about people who knocked all the walls of the house out so they could sleep together, and who cooked kangaroos in their houses right on the floor – or took windscreens out of their land rovers so they could fit a mattress in the car. That's them doing what feels right for them, but for me it was a bit uncomfortable."

"Just checking," Sandy said.

"What did you do over the hols?" Nina asked her.

"Camping. With Dad. *Again.*" The word 'again' was loaded.

"And was there a good side to your camping trip?" Nina enquired innocently.

"Of course, Teach," Sandy replied, mirroring her wide-eyed innocence, "swimming, no schoolwork, pizzas, an outdoor cinema, hanging out with friends…"

"Sounds great," I said, and she shrugged.

"Did you take pictures?" Clare asked Nina.

Nina made a face, and Rosie, who was passing with a cup in her hands, paused for Nina's reply, grimacing. "Yeah. That was another of the difficult things. This girl asked me if she could look at my camera – I mean, Rosie's camera," Nina said guiltily, with a glance at her mother, "and while I was talking to someone else, she wandered away with it and it was missing till the day before I was leaving when Joel tracked it down. But by then it was wrecked. So… no pics to show and no more camera."

"Bummer." I'd been looking forward to pictures. Guess I'd have to go there myself… Now, that was an idea…

"By the way, you think *you've* got problems with school!" Nina poked Sandy on the arm, "but they've got all this pressure to be like us whites and be able to read and write and stick with a job and look after things; stuff that hasn't been important at all in their world for thousands of years. We read books; they read nature. If I was lost in the desert I'd be a goner in two seconds flat, but they can read nature and be totally safe in it."

She wrapped her arms around her knees thoughtfully. "I don't get what makes one better than the other but there's this mad need to turn them into us. We white people are so taking-over-ish that they have to learn our ways to stand a chance, but we aren't doing anything much about learning their ways. I reckon there should be two-way learning: the Aboriginals teach white people bush-survival skills so we can appreciate all their knowledge, and we teach them Western-world-survival skills; that way everyone can succeed in both worlds."

"If they want to," Rosie murmured, before moving on.

Clare grabbed Nina's arm. "You haven't told us the important news! How were things with Joel?" And she winked suggestively.

Nina narrowed her eyes. "I've already told you: he is simply A Friend. Got that? A Friend. And anyway, there are about three girls up there who are soft on him."

Clare and Serenity giggled.

"Speaking of which, Joel is in Melbourne for a week. How

about meeting next weekend at Liz and Nuncle's to catch up on his news?"

"Good plan," Billy said, and he started to fill Rick in on Joel's story.

CHAPTER 48

NO JOKING

"SO, SANDY," Nina asked in her innocent voice, "have you come up with any areas of life that are only good or only bad?"

Sandy, who was sitting cross-legged on the other side of me, said smugly, "I have actually: torture. Don't tell me you can find something good in that."

"Oh yeah… That's a hard one. I don't totally get that one…" Nina glanced around the room as if looking for someone, and then turned back to us. "But here's an interesting thing I've heard: did you know that North American Indian tribes used torture as an *honour?* It was saved for their bravest captives as kind of a last opportunity to show courage and rise above the flesh and grow closer to Spirit. And I guess some of the Aboriginal rites would look like torture to us," she added thoughtfully. "I must ask Joel about that…"

"Saved for their *captives*," Sandy remarked drily; "still sounds like a punishment to me. I bet they didn't do it to their best warriors."

"I don't know," Nina said honestly, "but a lot of what their warriors did would be torture to me. And you know how hard they train Marines and people like that – having to run long distances carrying heavy packs up and down hills and through obstacle courses in pouring rain or heat waves! That all sounds pretty torturous if you ask me."

"Training," Billy said to Rick with meaning, and they gave each other a high-five.

"Has your dad done any of that?" Clare asked Sandy. She nodded.

"Plus," Nina added, "torture comes in many forms –"

"My mother tortures herself with guilt," Clare grinned. "Does that count?"

"Sure. And that's a good point: some people get hugely tortured for a few minutes or days but other people get tortured in smaller ways for their whole lifetime, like living with people who constantly put them down. Or that guilt thing, or fear."

"Somehow guilt doesn't seem as awful as physical torture," I said. "I'm still finding it hard to see that there could be any good in things like tearing off people's fingernails or stretching them on racks or burning them – ugh! The only maybe-possibly-good thing about it could be if it makes you able to do mind over matter, like those American Indians."

"Well, if you punish yourself over something for your whole life and so you never live up to your potential, that's like a lost life," Nina said. "But I totally know what you mean. I guess the bottom line is that if you believe the Universe is intelligent and orderly and nothing is only one polarity, there must be a blessing in it somewhere. Have you guys seen *The Deer Hunter?*"

"Heard of it," Billy said, standing up. "Back in a sec."

"I watched it with Mum and Dad," Nina continued. "It's a classic old movie – really slow and goes for *ages*. There's a torture scene in it that's pretty horrible, but you could see that for the main character, going through that was an amazing wake-up call to appreciate life more. Before that he was always drunk and didn't seem to have any purpose to his life, and after it he was totally transformed."

"What about people who don't get transformed?" I asked. "What about the ones who die or are maimed? What could be the good in that?"

"Then it comes back to Order. There must be something going on in their life that makes that on track for them," she said.

"Like balancing out past lives," Serenity said thoughtfully. "Maybe it's their karma."

"And there's also blessings for the rest of the world."

"Like what?"

"Well, if you hear about someone being tortured, doesn't that make your heart open up to them?"

"Sure. I feel like just about killing the torturer –" Sandy stopped mid-sentence.

"Fancy…" Nina murmured; "a spot of war-ishness on your part?"

"Are you saying that when someone is being hurt and we feel for them, that that's a good side to torture?" I asked doubtfully.

"Sort of," Nina said. "It's like when that 9/11 attack happened and suddenly everyone wanted to be closer to their families and appreciated them more – especially the people who narrowly escaped losing each other. " She raised her pointer finger in a moment of inspiration; "*Plus,* it's hard to know the whole truth about anything looking at it from the outside. I might think you look much more happy than you really are – or much less, and you might think that about me, so maybe even really horrible experiences aren't as bad to the person having them as they look to the person watching… Especially if they've grown up in that sort of world."

Sandy looked at me. "Whaddayou think?"

"She tried hard to show both sides," I pronounced, in my best Judge-and-Jury voice. "Points for that, at least. And the thing about Order and the Law of Polarity makes sense to me, even though it's so hard to see it sometimes, so maybe there is a good side to it somewhere…"

"I was going to phone a friend," Nina said, "but he's a bit caught up." We looked across the room to where Nuncle was engrossed in conversation with Rick's father.

"Okay, I'll let you off the hook this time," Sandy said kindly, "but… have you done your Invisibility challenge?"

Nina made a face. "I have to admit, I'm finding it very difficult to do that silence thing. I mean, it's easy enough on my own, but when I'm with you guys I want to be able to talk to you, and when I'm at the Drama Group – well, there's no point going to a Drama Group if you can't talk…"

"Failed!" Sandy declared, in a very satisfied tone.

Nina bowed her head in surrender. "But," she said, popping up again, "I did do something else invisible. I've been leaving money around the place – invisibly."

"Where?" Clare asked, startled. "How much?"

"Envelopes with five dollars in them or even just a dollar coin by itself. Usually in the park or at a shopping centre. I try to make sure no-one sees me do it and sometimes I hang around to see who finds it – without letting them see me watching, of course."

"That is so cool!" Serenity exclaimed.

"What do they do?" I asked curiously.

"If it's a bigger amount of money they usually look around to see if someone dropped it, and then sometimes they stand there, like they're wondering if it's okay to take it, but mostly they just stick it straight in their pocket or bag and keep going. Sometimes the people who find it give this great big smile, like it's the best thing that's happened all day." Nina's own face broke into a smile. "I like that – it feels great."

"Hey, anybody try the 'I Am That' game?" Billy queried, returning with a re-loaded plate of dessert in one hand.

Sandy nearly pounced as he knelt down and began to eat. "Is there more of that pav? I thought it was finished."

"Ah…" Billy said mysteriously. "This is the Very Last Piece. Here – share." He dug his fork into the wobbly pile of whiteness and broke off a piece for her.

"I did," I said. "I Am That-ed a souvenir-seller in Turkey."

"How was it?" Clare asked.

"Uncomfortable," I admitted. "I didn't want to get so, sort of, close to him. But it was a good thing to do. It made me realise how much we separate ourselves from people and do that better-than, worse-than thing. No way we can have peace if we're doing that." I glanced at Serenity.

"I did it too," she said promptly, "with the President of the United States."

"Serious?"

"Yep. Pretty scary, having so many people admiring you and hating you at the same time… And then I did it with a dragonfly; it was so pretty and delicate…"

"Truly?" Clare exclaimed, turning to Serenity in amazement. "I did it with a fly!"

"A fly?" Sandy screwed up her face. "Why would you want to get inside a fly?"

"We were having dinner the other night," Clare explained, "and this fly kept buzzing around my plate and annoying me. Then I remembered the Game and I kind of let myself become the fly for a second, being swatted away and then coming back and being swatted away and coming back again… and I had this really weird second where I felt like *I* was that fly hovering in the air over the food… and I realised he was hungry, just like me!"

"Yeah, of course," Sandy said.

"Well, we had talked about us being, you know, juicy salt bars to flies," Clare said, flushing a bit, "but that was just talking. When I did the Game I actually *felt* his aliveness… It's weird, but he wasn't an annoying pest any more because we were sort of the same – I even kind of cared about him."

"Next thing we'll be giving flies honorary membership to our Mastery Club," Billy said, shaking his head.

"Did you do it?" I asked him. "The Game?"

"Yeah. Sort of. Rick was beating me in every heat so I asked him what he was doing, and he – you tell 'em," he finished, stuffing some more pavlova into his mouth.

"Nice pass," Rick said to Billy, who grinned, almost leaking white stuff. "What I do isn't exactly the same as what you guys are talking about. It's this performance technique to kind of feel your way into someone else's body and mind so you can learn how they're doing what they're doing. My dad coaches athletes and he told me about it, so I've been trying it out on champion racers."

Sandy made a face. "Getting inside someone else – that's a bit creepy."

"Isn't that what you do with acting?" Nina demanded. "Liz does it all the time. One day she copied my exact body posture and then told me what I was thinking. It was freaky."

"It's a bit like an invisibility thing, isn't it?" Clare said; "Stepping out of yourself and into someone else's shoes."

Rosie had been chatting to someone nearby. Now she turned to us. "Are you talking about the 'I Am That' Game? We've been playing it quite a bit since the Conscious Creation course in January, Pete, Neen and I."

Ah. So that was where it came from.

"I did it on the Joker," she said, coming to sit on the floor with us. "You know, from *Batman*? I was so horrified by his cruelty and how easily he could turn his back on people and just, *snap!* get rid of them." She looked at me. "Your pictures of the beggars reminded me. I didn't think I had a single thing in common with that despicable Joker, until I remembered our travels through Europe, and oh, especially last year when we went to India and Nepal. Pete and I have done lots of travelling and you just can't help all the beggars. You have to turn away. So I realised I'd done exactly the same thing. It was *very* uncomfortable, owning that one."

I nodded, remembering. 'Hardening our hearts', Mum had called it, and we'd both hated it. But we'd done it too.

"The more you play the game, the more you find to own," Rosie continued, with a bright-eyed enthusiasm that I was used to seeing in Nina. "Addicts – we often judge 'em but we're all addicts; maybe not to drugs or alcohol but to other things. Did you know that you can even get addicted to your own emotions?"

"How?" Clare asked in alarm.

"Athletes get addicted to that hormone," Billy interrupted, wiping his mouth. "What was it, Rick? The stuff your body produces when you win."

"Dolphins? Dorphins?"

"Endorphins," Rosie grinned. "All emotions release chemicals," she told Clare. "People who get depressed or angry a lot are literally addicted to their own chemicals, which is why it can be hard for them to break the cycle. They're kind of craving those chemicals. Being in love makes your body produce endorphins too. That's what keeps people infatuated with each other in the early stages – their own chemicals."

"Not interested," Sandy said pointedly, and we laughed at her. I butted her with my shoulder. "Seriously!" she protested. "Ugh!" So we challenged her to I-Am-That someone who was in love, and she squirmed.

When everyone had gone Dad said, "Well, so much for small talk!"

Mum gave a half-smile; she was tidying up the last few things with a very preoccupied expression on her face.

Small talk was certainly more restful than these big confronting ideas, I reflected as I wiped the dining room table, but way less interesting.

A Mastery Club Test

1. What is the Law of Polarity?

2. What is the Law of Conservation?

3. Why will life never be 'all nice'?

4. Why/How is that a good thing?

5. What's the difference between setting a fantasy goal and a balanced goal?

6. Explain the Law of Magnetism and the Law of Resonance & Vibration.

7. What is the point of the 'I Am That' game?

Clue: You might have to go backwards or forwards in the book to find the answers...

CHAPTER 49

THE CHINESE CURSE

WINTER HAD REALLY set in while we were overseas. Every day was grey and cold and damp. I shivered at the bus stop in the mornings and found myself spending lunchtimes in the library to keep warm (where I'd often see Mark, reading by himself or playing chess with someone). Miss Walker stopped me in the corridor one day to tell me that she had spoken to the Principal who'd said that setting up more Clubs was 'a possibility' but the schedule was too tightly packed for now. She looked very disappointed. "We'll have to stun everyone with our great results!" she said brightly, "and then they'll be convinced. After all, if students have this information, it supports absolutely everything else they're doing. They can apply it to every other subject." When she had gone, I realised that I was disappointed too.

But perhaps it was just as well. When we had our next Wednesday lunchtime meeting, Holly and Bree weren't there. Apparently they were losing interest. They didn't think this could work. And Tom hadn't spoken to his Mum yet, so his progress was 'on pause'. Petra was quite happy with her next-door pets and not getting around to choosing a new goal, and Kat was being her usual vague and strange self. I wondered if this experiment would have been more successful with Nina at the helm… Maybe I just wasn't up to it.

On Sunday we all gathered at Liz and Nuncle's. It was just like the old days, only this time we had Serenity and Rick as well, and Joel would be arriving later. Liz had made a big pot of vegetable soup for lunch, which we ate with some toasted buttery sourdough bread. The kitchen was crowded, warm and noisy as we tucked in and chatted. There was so much going on that it took me a while to notice that Clare was hardly saying a thing, just eating quietly in a corner.

"What's up?" I asked, dragging my chair closer.

She glanced at me and dipped her bread back into the soup. "Nothing."

"*Clare.*"

Sandy, who had good radar for trouble, noticed us. "What's wrong?" she asked from across the table, and everyone stopped talking and looked.

Clare frowned at her.

"Come on, Clare," Nina encouraged, "we're your friends *and* support group *and* Mastery Club, remember?"

"What's cooking, Clare?" Nuncle asked gently.

Clare had always had a soft spot for Nina's uncle. "I thought it was going to be so good having a Dad of my own," she mumbled. "But now I'm all mixed up. I've been staying at his place and his kids don't like me, and Mum's all by herself at home so I've been feeling guilty and like I'm always in the wrong place. It's all horrible. I just wish it was back like it was!"

"Ah…" Nuncle murmured. "The Chinese Curse."

Sandy was sitting next to him. She tapped him on the arm in her imperious way. "Which is?"

Nuncle pushed his bowl away and looked at each of us. " 'May your dreams come true.' "

"But isn't that what setting goals is all about?" I protested.

"How was your trip?" he replied in answer. "All good or an even balance?"

"An even balance," I said.

"So here's the thing: if we set goals thinking we'll be happier or better off when we achieve them, we're setting ourselves up for disappointment. We'll *always* have a balance of positive and negative, support and challenge."

"The Law of Conservation," Nina chirped.

"I remember when I bought my first sports car," Nuncle smiled. "I was obsessed for months dreaming about it, planning, visiting the car yard, visualising... When I finally got it I was delighted – until I discovered the other side: how much it was going to cost me in upkeep and insurance and parts, the stress about every single little scratch...

"If you had a dream about how wonderful life was going to be when you had your father back, Clare, Life has just been waking you up to the truth: it won't be better, just different."

"That sucks," Sandy said.

"So what's the point of wanting anything?" I asked.

"The adventure," Nuncle said simply. "The growing and the discovery and the waking up."

"Mastery isn't about just having whatever you want or having it all easy and positive," Liz said. "It's about the journey – who you become in the process of going after those things. Look at childbirth: women go back and do that over and over again, even though it can be excruciating, because they want the richness of the mothering journey. They know what they're getting themselves into but they still take it on. I salute them!" And she did.

"Would you go on your holiday again, even though it wasn't

all good?" Nuncle asked me.

I didn't even need to think about that. "Definitely."

Clare looked at Billy. "Have you decided what you're going to do – who you're going to live with?"

"I'm gonna stay with Dad for a while," he answered. "My sister's moving out soon so if we're both gone that will give Mum and Terry some time alone, and Dad could do with some company at the moment. But I'll stay with Mum on weekends and holidays."

"Oh." She ran her finger slowly around the rim of her soup bowl. "So since our parents couldn't get on, we get stuck with all-over-the-place lives. I wish my parents were together like Nat's… or Nina's."

"But not like mine," Sandy muttered.

"*Everyone* has messy stuff in their lives," Nuncle said. "It just takes different forms."

"Yeah? What's yours?" Clare challenged. Sandy and I glanced at each other, realising that she didn't know about Nuncle's son. He told her, and I could see her digesting this information: firstly that her idol had problems, and secondly that it was true – there would always be challenges. Always.

"The thing is," Nina said, "we agreed to be Order Detectives this year. It's like that story about the Man and the Horse from Nuncle's Good Stuff, Bad Stuff Game. You can think something is good or bad but then you get the next piece of the puzzle and you see that it's not; it's both, and the whole thing keeps changing. So unless you deliberately go looking for the Order, most people probably don't get to see it until life eventually gives them a big enough picture, which might not even be till they're about to die."

"Great!" Sandy said sarcastically.

"If we're having a Mastery Club meeting now," I said, "I'd really like some help with my school group. They're all dropping out and not getting their stuff and I don't know what to do."

Nina was beaming, again.

Mastery Club Lesson #28

The Chinese Curse:
"May your dreams come true."

* There will always be an even balance of positive and negative, so...

* when you set your goals, have balanced expectations and

* embrace the whole journey.

CHAPTER 50

Your Goal Wants You – and Nuncle Pulls the Rug Out From Under Us

"Let's do everything!" Nina enthused. "A goals update and help you with your school Mastery Club" (to me), "and find the Order on all the stuff that seems messed up."

"That's no small agenda, Neen," Liz said. "What time is Joel arriving?"

"Three or four. There's heaps of time. Okay with everyone?"

"And we haven't given Rick a chance to set a goal," I said. "So we can do that too."

"He's got it sorted," Billy said. "His dad's a business coach and his mum teaches yoga or something, so he's right on top of all this."

Rick gave a laugh. "I don't know about on top of it, but, yeah. Hey, it's great to find some other kids who'll talk about this stuff and not look at you like you're wacko."

Nina reached out to take his hand. "You are safe now, Comrade," she said. "Welcome to the Mothership."

"What was that you were saying about wacko?" Sandy enquired.

Rick grinned. "Yep. I feel right at home here."

"What does your mother teach?" Liz asked.

"Mindfulness and Pilates. So, yeah, like Bill was saying, I'm into it already. Turns out we were both going for being in the top three at that biking championship."

They gave each other a high five and we got sidetracked congratulating them. Then Rick said, "I've got a different kinda goal. I'd like to raise money to buy bikes for kids in developing countries. A friend of mine is involved in this charity where they provide bikes for kids who have to walk like five, eight kilometres to school, often in really hot weather. Might take them a couple of hours, so by the time they get home there's almost no daylight left and often they don't have electricity so it's too dark to do homework and it's hard to do their chores. With a bike they can be home in twenty minutes. So, yeah, I'd like to see what I can do to help."

Wow. We all looked at him with respect. That was an impressive goal.

"How come *our* goals have all been about ourselves and we haven't thought of helping anyone else?" I asked.

Serenity gave a little cough.

"Oh, well apart from Serenity and Clare's peace goals…"

"To help others you've got to be able to help yourself first," Liz said. "If I'm right, Rick has been playing around with goal-setting for a while."

"Yep. Started delivering newspapers when I was nine because it was a job I could do on my bike. And the goal was to raise money for the exact bike I wanted – and all the accessories. It was a few hundred more than my folks wanted to spend."

"We're going to build up my lawn mowing business," Billy intervened. "I kind of let it go this year but we're going to pick it up again and put some of that money toward the bikes charity. So that'll be my next goal too."

"Sounds like a great venture," Nuncle said. He raised his glass of water in a toast.

"*I* want to do something like that," Serenity announced. "My goal's been a failure so I'm going to start again."

"What was your goal?" Liz asked.

"To be a living example of peace," Serenity said, "by being peaceful in my family." For a moment we almost held our breaths, and then she exploded into laughter. "I know, I know! It was a total disaster. I get it."

"A slightly unrealistic goal," Nuncle smiled. "One that was, I think it would be fair to say, doomed to failure. So... now what?"

"Babies," she said at once. "I'd like to do something for babies. You know, orphaned babies and premmies and that."

"What, you mean raise money?" Liz queried.

"No... something more... hands-on." Serenity frowned in thought, then brightened. "I know! I'm going to learn massage. That'll be my next goal. I've always helped Mum at home with the little kids by giving them a massage to help them go to sleep. She reckons I've got healing hands. So maybe I can do baby massage, and then maybe teach it one day. You know, touch is really important for healing."

"It's everything," Liz agreed with soft eyes.

As I listened to these grand goals I couldn't help feeling quite small. What could *I* do to help the world? But Clare spoke up before I could say anything.

"I'm going to start a blog," she said suddenly. "For kids who've been bullied – and for the bullies. I'm going to write about how it all changed for me, and see if I can help other kids to see it differently."

"Woohoo!" Nina cheered.

"Because, you know, at the start of the year I set a goal for a friend at the new school and I got Serenity. And my maths is going okay and my English is going pretty well. And I got my Dad back, which I kind of secretly wanted, even though that's turned out to be a bumpy ride. And the peace goal was a disaster, as you know. So it's time to choose another thing."

"I feel honoured to be sitting here," Nuncle said, leaning back in his chair and putting his arm around Liz. "We're in very inspiring company, don't you think?"

She nodded, and leaned back against his shoulder.

"Well, it's all downhill from here," Sandy said flatly. "I've done *one* pottery exhibition with my uncle, the one last March that you guys know about, and nothing much since then. Just fight with my parents and run away and be a pest."

"Shocking," Nuncle said, shaking his head. But his eyes were smiling.

"Didn't you say something last year about wanting to be a famous athlete?" Nina asked.

"No. That was Clare's idea. I fluked a couple of medals at the school athletics in Grade Six, that's why. But I'm not into it so much anymore."

Liz leaned forward a little to look across Nuncle's chest at Sandy. "So what *do* you want?"

Sandy shrugged. "I don't dare say peace at home, but I'd sure like less war."

Hearing that gave me a little jolt of surprise. Watching Serenity and Clare try for world peace in their homes was one thing, but it hadn't even occurred to me that Sandy was kind of at war in her home.

"Create conflict somewhere else and you'll have harmony at home," Nuncle proposed.

"What?"

"Seriously. If war and peace are conserved in your life, if you're always going to have both of them, throw yourself into something really challenging somewhere else and you'll find that life at home settles down."

"What? Like pick on my neighbours?"

"Maybe a competitive game of tennis?" he suggested. "Get your ferocious feelings out somewhere safe. If you govern war in your life, you don't have to be at the effect of it. Taking on a big juicy challenge can work, too. You get so busy grappling with all the problems it throws up that you don't need so many problems elsewhere…"

"I want to know why you haven't done any more exhibitions," Nina probed.

"Uncle Brendan's been away and I've lost motivation."

"Gave up the fight, huh?" Nuncle teased, giving her a gentle dig in the ribs with his elbow. "All goals are easy to achieve in our imaginations, kids. In our minds we can have or do anything in an instant, but in matter, in the physical world, it's much harder because it's a slower, denser dimension. And that's where the obstacles turn up, including things like lack of motivation or procrastination."

"Tell me about it," Sandy muttered.

"Why do you want to do the pottery?" Liz asked. "I'm curious."

"She was actually saving money to leave home," Clare chipped in. "Later. When she's old enough."

"Is that really why?" Liz asked Sandy. "That's a very long-term goal. It's hard to be enthusiastic about something so distant and vague. Do you enjoy doing the pottery?"

"I love it," Sandy said. "But I keep not getting around to it when Uncle Bren isn't around and I don't know why."

"Something else is taking priority," Nuncle said. "What's been more important to you lately?"

Sandy's fingers doodled on the table. She shook her head. "Can't think of anything."

"Is there anything else you'd like to focus on?" Liz asked. "Are you going in the school play again this year?"

"I might…"

"Schoolwork?" Rick suggested.

She scowled. "Hate it."

"But she's good at it," I said.

We were stumped. I glanced at Nuncle; he was looking at Sandy thoughtfully, and she was avoiding his eye.

"How are things with Mum?" he asked.

"So-so. A bit better."

Everyone was quiet, waiting.

"This is exactly what's going on with some of the people in the Mastery Club at school," I said. "They don't know what they want or they don't seem to want anything or they can't achieve what they want. Or they don't do what they say they will." I shifted restlessly in my seat. "Me too. I said I'd come up with my A subjects at the start of the year and I still haven't, and part of me is okay with that but another part of me is feeling guilty, like I *should*…"

"People always fulfil their highest values," Nuncle said. "I gather that getting As isn't really important to you."

I made a face. "Not as much as it is to my parents… I'd go for As in Mastery Club stuff, though!"

"There you have it," he nodded. "Most people know what they want; they're just afraid to own up to it or commit to it in case someone else disapproves, or in case they fail."

We all looked at Sandy. She crossed her arms and gave Nuncle a quick sideways glance. He raised his brows and I realised that something was going on between them. Maybe from a conversation they'd had when she stayed the weekend that time.

"Actually," she said suddenly, staring into her empty soup bowl, "there is a goal that I have but I can't say anything about it just yet. I'll know soon."

Nuncle gave a long, slow nod. "All right then," he said.

I was as bemused as everyone else about Sandy, and frustrated that she was so secretive, but it didn't look like any more information was going to be shared just yet.

Nuncle turned back to me. "It's wise to honour your highest values, Natalie, because they're the pathway to your soul. And you know, if you can see how your schoolwork helps you to fulfill those values, you'll transform your results there for sure. So now, tell us about your other goals and those kids in your Club."

"Well, my goal was to keep this Club going, which it is, which is great," I replied. "And the Mastery Club at school just happened out of the blue. I'd been wondering how to make school more interesting and sort of contribute to it a bit more, and then Miss Walker – my teacher – asked me to do the Club..." An image of that first day in Study Room A flashed into my mind. "I was pretty scared about it at first because I don't know as much as Nina about this stuff, but it's turned out to be okay. I guess because even though I only know a tiny bit more than those kids, I *do* know a tiny bit more, and that seems to be enough."

"Everyone is a teacher to someone, and the student of someone else," Nuncle affirmed.

"So yeah, they were all pretty interested in it at first, but lately some of them are starting to give up because they're not achieving their goals. And some of them are just totally unfocused and all over the place."

"The ones who are giving up, do they have a good plan?" Nuncle asked. "Our dreams are mere fantasies without a strategy, and the strategy is all the more important with a big goal."

"Two of the girls are visualising winning their netball matches," I told him. "I don't think they've got any more of a plan than that, other than going to their trainings."

"There are lots of factors when you're dealing with a whole team," Nuncle said, "but the most focused person can influence an entire group. When I was a kid, my brother wanted to go to a particular school. He spent months talking about it, thinking about it, daydreaming about it; he visited the school, made friends there. He was so focused on his intention to be there that in the end the whole family uprooted and moved to the town where that school was…"

Cool. Maybe that story about Nuncle's brother would inspire Holly and Bree to stay committed. I'd tell them next time we met. Especially that bit about it taking months. Maybe they were just giving up too soon.

Liz stood up and began to clear the table. "Something else your girls could do is make an affirmation CD and play it all through the night or just as they're waking up and going to sleep; that sort of thing works for some people. The fact is, it's easy to achieve an easy goal; it's the more challenging ones that call for real commitment."

"Like Thomas Edison getting the design of the light bulb wrong one *thousand* times before he got it right," Nina said, passing her some bowls. "Hey, what's that story about the rocket ship? Oh yeah!" She looked at each of us with bright eyes. "How often is a rocket ship to the moon on track?"

"All the time," Billy said at once. "Otherwise it wouldn't get there."

Nina shook her head. "Nope. Try again."

"Ninety percent," Clare suggested.

"Nope."

"Fifty percent," I said.

"*Three* percent," Nina said.

"What?!"

"It's true. It goes too far this way," she said, doing the trajectory of a rocket ship with her hand towards a fist-moon, "then corrects, then goes too far that way, then corrects… It just keeps going back and forth across its path, over-shooting and under-shooting, and eventually it gets there."

"That overshooting and undershooting is the positive and negative feedback life gives us when we take on any goal," Nuncle agreed. "There's no such thing as straight-line manifesting; in fact, straight lines are an illusion. There will always be curves and detours and delays and unexpectednesses. The main thing is to stay in the process *until* you achieve your goal."

"Christopher Columbus took *ten years* to raise money for his expedition," Nina stated emphatically.

"Which means that your goal has to really *matter* to you," Nuncle added, emphasising the word 'matter', "if you're going to be able to realise it 'in matter' rather than just in your imagination. And you've got to want the journey as much as the outcome. There's no point wanting to be a champion swimmer but hating training. You've got to love the whole package. But, you know," he continued cheerfully, "the good news is that your goal wants you as much as you want it."

"How can a goal want anything?" Serenity objected.

Nuncle picked up the salt and pepper shakers. "Gravity is what's happening when two masses are drawn together," he said, demonstrating. "The closer those two bodies are to each other, the greater the force of attraction between them; it doesn't just go one way. Your goal is kind of a metaphysical mass. It's not a physical body; it's an 'energy body', an idea. The first step you take towards it is always the hardest, because that's when you're moving out of inertia or stuckness, but if you just keep going towards it, you'll build an energy of attraction to it. You've only got to get into motion towards the thing you want and it will be as attracted to you as you are to it because what you seek, seeks you; that's Newton's Law of Inter-attractiveness. He actually called gravity a 'spiritual elastic force' but that metaphysical reference has been cut out of his philosophy."

"Bizarre," Billy said. "So my bike wanted me, too…"

Nuncle threw his hands up in self-defence. "It's pure physics, not a crazy opinion of mine – true!"

"I like it," I said. This was another 'Impossible Idea' – that the things we want, want us too.

Liz sat at the table again and raised her glass. "I'd like to say, 'Well done, Natalie, for taking such a big step out of your comfort zone.'"

I blushed.

"Hear, hear," Nina agreed, lifting hers so suddenly that the water nearly sloshed out. "You keep thinking you're not very powerful and not getting where you *are* powerful."

That was true. It was as if I'd spent my whole life believing that I wasn't capable of anything special and admiring people who obviously were, like wizards… or Nina…

"The quiet achiever," Sandy said, taking me by surprise. I remembered that day in the library when she'd said to me that I wasn't supposed to be Nina, just myself. Maybe I was doing a real 'I Am That'… really owning those leadership qualities… It was an idea that no longer felt so strange.

Nuncle toasted me too. "So what's your next big goal, Miss Natalie?"

"I've been wondering that, too," I said. I wanted to come up with something big… something inspiring… something that would change the world for the better, like Rick's goal… But it had to be something from inside me, not copying someone else…

"For now I'll stick with keeping that school Club going," I decided. "I'm going to do my best to not give up on them and to help them all stick with their goals."

"And our Club," Clare reminded me.

"Of course," I said.

There was a moment's quiet around the table as we sat basking in the afternoon sunshine and thinking about everything that had been said. Nuncle was gazing at each of us fondly.

"What if I told you that your goals don't matter at all?" he said unexpectedly.

"Oh Max," Liz began. "Don't pull the rug –"

"I think they can cope," he said.

"With what?" we asked.

"With the idea that our goals don't actually matter. We're all perfect already, just as we are, and we already have everything we need. We just haven't seen it."

"Okay, that's weird," Sandy said.

"Oh," Nina twigged. "That's because of the Law of Conservation, isn't it?"

"Right; and also the First Law of Thermodynamics, which says that nothing is created or destroyed, it just changes form. Which means that we already have everything we dream of, just in a form we haven't recognised."

"Like Natalie being a leader but not noticing," Nina said.

"Exactly," Nuncle said. "It's like this: we set a goal because we believe that we're missing something that would make life better – you know the expression 'the grass is always greener on the other side'? We think life will be better 'over there', and then when we get there, we find the same old balance of positive and negative. The purpose of the goals journey is to wake us up to that balance, and to take us to ever-higher understanding of our own abilities and potential.

"But it goes even deeper than that because the truth is that if everything is in order everywhere, there's nowhere to go and nothing to fix. It's the divine paradox: to pursue your dreams while knowing that everything is already perfect." He shrugged. "I just think it's wise to occasionally stop and acknowledge that we're all perfect right now exactly as we are."

At that moment there was a distant knock at the front door.

Mastery Club Lesson #29

Your Goal Wants You

✳ The first step out of inertia is the hardest…

✳ but once you've taken it, so long as you stay in motion, Newton's Law of Inter-attractiveness will be bringing it towards you even as you are moving towards it.

✳ That's the 'Gravity of Goal-setting'.

✳ Be clear on what you want, commit to it, and keep correcting all the way to the moon – er, your goal.

CHAPTER 51

JOEL'S JOURNEY

"IT'S JOEL!" Nina leapt out of her chair and ran out of the kitchen. We could hear her feet thumping through the house, and then the front door flinging open and muffled voices.

"I'll put the kettle on," Liz said. "Who wants what?"

We were in the middle of sorting out herbal tea and hot chocolate orders when Nina reappeared in the doorway with Joel. She was smiling and he was standing just behind her, watching us; tall and lanky, just like I remembered him, wearing jeans and a windcheater and a beanie. As soon as we greeted him he smiled, and that dimple appeared in his cheek, transforming his face.

There was a bit of everyone talking at once while space was made at the table for Joel, and drinks and spicy apple cake were served, and then Nina asked the million dollar question: "How did it go with your Mum?"

"Okay," he said. "Pretty good, really."

We waited for more.

"And?" Nina burst out at last.

Joel grinned again. "You want all the gory details, huh?"

"Of course!"

"Always going a hundred miles an hour." Smiling, he gave a little shake of his head and turned to Billy. "Thanks for the messages. Sorry I didn't manage to get back to you. I've been out bush a lot."

"S'okay," Billy replied. "I was just wondering how it was going. Nina said something about your mum kicking you out and going to jail and all that. Pretty tough."

Joel nodded. "But I wouldn't change a thing."

"Liz and I would love to hear the whole story," Nuncle said. "If you don't mind telling."

"I don't mind," Joel said.

I looked at Nuncle and then at the picture on the fridge of his son Josh, both of them dark-skinned with little moustaches and curly black hair... Sandy caught my eye.

"So you know my mother's white and my dad's Aboriginal," Joel began, taking a sip of his drink, "but for years I thought he was African or Maori. Mum wouldn't tell me the truth; just said he was bad news. I felt rejected by him and pissed with her so I started mucking around at school and getting into drugs and alcohol. Just minor stuff, but by the time I was thirteen I was wagging school, nicking things from shops, vandalising buildings... Kids at school were calling me 'abo', which made me furious because it came with such a load of contempt, and anyway, I didn't know...

"Then one day Mum finally told me the truth about my heritage. She said I was turning out just as bad as my old man, and I'd better get my act together or I'd end up in jail like him. I was pretty shocked to find out my father was in prison but when I said I wanted to make contact with him, she wouldn't tell me where he was. I was so angry. Angry with her, angry with him, angry with whites, with the system, with blacks for being hated...

"The only thing in the world I cared about was my pets. Since I was a kid I had an affinity with animals that even I couldn't understand. Mum called me Dr Doolittle – I had a duck, a rat, geckoes, green tree frogs, lizards. My room was literally filled with fish tanks, spiders, scorpions, two pet carpet pythons…

"My favourite pet was a long-necked turtle I was given when I was about nine years old. I always found comfort in talking to my turtle about all the shit in my life. I felt he never judged me and only listened."

Joel's eyes softened at the memory. "That turtle could recognise my voice," he said. "When I came into my bedroom and started speaking he would always climb onto the rocks so I could pick him up and feed him. I reckon he probably kept me alive, because all the times I wanted to give up, my thoughts would be for that turtle – who would feed him?"

"What was his name?" Clare asked.

"Turtle," Joel said. And grinned. "Anyway, Mum and I were fighting more and more and often I wasn't even coming home some nights… I was hardly going to school… Then my turtle died and we had this last horrendous fight and she threw me out. Gave me my grandfather's name and told me to go and live with my lot."

"Man!" Serenity breathed, and I remembered it was the first time she was hearing Joel's story. "How old were you?"

"Fifteen." Joel swiped the beanie off his head and scratched behind his ear. "I lived on the streets with some mates. Someone was always in trouble with the law, so it was a life on the run and on drugs. I hated sobering up because it hurt so much. The higher the better." He was twisting the beanie in his hands and we were listening, spellbound.

"One night," Joel said quietly, "I saw my best friend murdered. He was stabbed in the neck with a broken bottle. I held him in my arms that night and when he died, I declared war on the world. I didn't care for anyone and I had nothing to live for. I just wanted to destroy everything. Me and my friends went out and smashed windows and stole cars and set them on fire, and when a man tried to stop us, we bashed him up too. Then the flashing blue lights showed up... I told my friends to run. I felt I had nothing to live for so I took the entire rap. I got two years juvenile correction."

"Were you scared?" I blurted.

"Nah, I was excited. There wasn't much that scared me, and I could be as mean as anyone else. But it ended up being a turning point; going to jail brought me into contact with other young Aboriginals for the first time. Most of the kids there are Aboriginal, didja know that?" he asked us.

I shook my head. This was all a foreign world for me.

He gave a slow nod. "Yeah... So that was the first time I got to see what and who the Aboriginal people were. It was like looking in a mirror. Suddenly, for the first time, I knew where I belonged. Hearing their stories, I started to understand my own identity. And then, about five months into my sentence, I met my father for the first time." He paused for another sip of his drink.

"How?" Billy asked. "Wasn't he in prison somewhere else?"

"Through the marvels of video conferencing," Joel grinned, "between prison and detention centre. He looked just like me, only with darker skin and older; it was like looking at my future self. I said, 'Dad, what are you in for?' And you know what? My life mirrored his exactly – the drugs, the crime... it was like I was following in his footsteps. My father planted the seed for my life and then disappeared out of it, but my life was following his step-by-step, all of his wounds and all of his addictions. It was really strange."

Nuncle was nodding, as if that made perfect sense.

Joel took another sip. "Dad would get out of jail and it would only be a question of time before he'd be back in. I realised that if

I didn't do something different, that was exactly how the rest of *my* life was going to go.

"The boys in with me were falling into the same pattern as my dad. They would talk about what they were going to do, when they got out of jail, to get back in. Because life's easier in prison – you don't have to think for yourself, take responsibility, deal with a job, renting a place, filling in forms – any of that. It's all done for you. You're told where to go, what to do and when. 'Get up, make your bed, go to breakfast, go to the yard, go to the leather room'.

"But I had dreams that went beyond the walls of the prison. I had wanted to play footy when I was a kid – that was the only thing I ever got praised for. 'Amazing footy player,' they'd say, 'but a bad egg.' When I had money in prison I used it to buy a football instead of a pillow. I used the football as my pillow and I played in the yard with it whenever I could. I started to believe I could get out and have a career in footy."

"Anyway, not long after meeting my father, my grandfather rang. He hardly spoke any English. I was very judgemental of him because all I'd known was the Anglo world. Then he came down from Cape York to meet me. First sight of him – I was gobsmacked. He looked like a caveman, someone off the National Geographic Channel. He was a full-blooded man. Well, he didn't say much. Didn't offer any advice, didn't judge, didn't ask why. Just listened to my gibberish and nodded… I thought he didn't care about me because he never looked me in the eye. I was so used to everyone saying, "Look at me when I'm talking to you, boy!" but Grandfather never did. Later I understood it's our way, the way of our culture. You don't need to see someone to hear them."

"I like that," Liz smiled. "Go on."

"I asked Grandfather later on about that time. He said he was working out who I was and what had to be done to help me; he was getting to know the person I could be if I channelled my energy better… So for three months my Grandfather would visit and just sit with me, listening to me ramble. Not long after that period I was given a conditional parole to go back to the bush with him. I'd done just over a year of my sentence. I thought this was going to be the easy way out." Joel laughed, shaking his head at the memory.

"I had no concept of what the deep bush would be like. I had bushwalked but I'd never been more than five kilometres away from the road – this was going seventy-two kilometres up a tributary into deep bush. There's no phone signal there, no electricity, no running water, no stove; just a tin shed and a mattress on the ground.

"In the juvenile correction facility I had a toilet, a sink, clean sheets, pool tables, pay TV, dinner cooked. But there was nothing here; it stripped me down to this bare reality. I'd come with a bag full of luggage that was useless shit in the bush. When the police dropped by to see where I was going to be, they knew I wouldn't be running away – the sounds in the middle of the day are scary enough; it's even worse at night."

"I wouldn't have wanted to be out there at night by myself," Nina said emphatically. "All those rustlings and rattlings and screeches…" She shivered dramatically.

"More drinks anyone?" Liz asked into the pause. "More cake?" The last few slices were quickly shared out but we were riveted by Joel's story and just wanted him to keep going.

"So you began to rebuild your life," Nuncle said.

"Yeah," Joel agreed. "That's exactly it. The first day I was there my grandfather and uncle took me on a long drive out bush. I hadn't cried for a long time – three years, no tears. As soon as we got out of the truck I burst into tears. My grandfather wiped under his armpits with his hands and then wiped his sweat and smell all over me. It made me mad. I was yelling, swearing, crying.

I threw a rock and cracked the windscreen of the car. Then we drove away.

"I asked that night, 'What was that place?' No answer. My grandmother – Nan – she was beautiful, adorable, everything you'd want a grandmother to be. My grandfather was not very expressive; the best thing you'd get would be a tap on the back. But you could feel his love. It radiated from him. But my grandmother would always give me a kiss on the forehead as she went past. She didn't say anything about what happened at that place either. Just comforted me with a cup of tea.

"The next day we headed off on a different road, a back road, but we ended up in the same place. I burst into tears again. I couldn't understand what was making me cry. I was abusing them for cursing me. I was frightened and blaming. I tried to smash the tracking bracelet off my ankle. Then we got back into the car and drove home again. And Nan gave me tea. And no-one said anything.

"The next day we were back in the car and I knew we were going back to that place. So I prepared myself. What *was* this place? Why was it making me cry? Why was I so mad when I got there? Again as soon as we got there I got out of the car and started wailing. The most unearthly cry you could ever hear. A really deathly wail, like someone has lost a child. There were tears, snot, spit going everywhere. I wasn't angry, just crying.

"This was the first time my grandfather showed any emotion. I was trying to compose myself and get my breath in and Grandfather sat next to me and put his hands on me and said, 'It's okay, my boy, you're home'. He said it first in Aboriginal language. I said, 'What?' and he told me what it meant. Then I asked, 'What is this place?' And he said 'This land was the birthing place of the women of your tribe'.

"The place doesn't look anything remarkable; it was the

vibration of that place – the feeling, spirit. I realised I was standing on the place of something like sixty thousand years of direct blood ancestry. My people had been born, bled and buried here. That was when the significance of the culture dawned on me."

Looking at Joel, I felt that I was starting to understand the stillness inside him. It was a bit like the stillness you felt in a tree. I supposed that a people so used to being on the land came to be kind of like the land…

"In bush medicine-law there are healing ceremonies," he continued. "Grandfather said to me, 'When you feel something call out to you, pick it up. Everything you pick will be a symbol of the pain you have in yourself. Our pain is often not something we can physically see, like a scar. It's a story we have inside ourselves. When you bring that object back to the circle, name it.'

"That's what I did. I named different objects with the pain of seeing my friend murdered, the pain of overdosing – everything that hurt in my life. I built a sacred altar of pain. I turned my pain into something beautiful.

"We went back home to Nan and I started talking with Grandfather and Uncle about the sacred places. Grandfather was always telling stories in language first – for the first half of the day he'd always reply to me in language – so I was starting to make connections between sounds and their meaning. I started seeing miracles too, things I'd only seen on *The Green Mile,* the sort of thing I'd always thought was airy-fairy bullshit. I started following my Grandfather around. I watched him practise his healing and traditional medicine."

"What sorts of things did he do?" Liz asked at once.

"Well, for example, I remember a young girl was having trouble breathing. Grandfather was speaking in language to her. He put his hands over her chest and I watched a pool of water develop on her chest. Then he lit a fire and burnt paper bark over her. We stayed the night there and the next day she was up and running around."

"Cool!" Serenity murmured.

"You could say I was doing my apprenticeship in my culture," Joel said. "I was learning the songs and playing the didgeridoo and doing the healings. Grandfather would say, 'Can you do this?' – he kept inviting me to have a go."

"Did you ever pick up the footy again?" Bill asked.

"Just for fun now and then. My life changed direction when I went into the bush with my grandfather. Now I'm starting to work as a didge player and traditional dancer. I seem to be able to explain our culture in ways that Anglos can understand. My grandfather had tried, but in his broken English the meaning would get lost."

Nuncle stirred in his seat. (We'd all been motionless for ages. I was even beginning to feel stiff.) "So that's what you're doing now? Been doing for the last year or so?"

Joel nodded. "Yeah. And I'm starting to go into juvenile correction centres to tell the youth there about the stability and strength and sense of belonging my culture is giving me. That's my mission now. My grandfather made me look at my pain and begin rebuilding my identity in a way that would give me the skills to walk between the worlds, and maybe build a bridge between them."

"He's got a face paint symbol," Nina interrupted, "of a handprint. It's a symbol of having a hand in both worlds."

"That's me," Joel affirmed. "Walking between the two worlds and finding the balance. There was also a choice I had to make: to stand up and become accountable for my actions and choose a life that would be full of rewards."

"What a story," Liz breathed. "I can just imagine the brain growth that goes on for someone like you who has to make sense of all this stuff and balance two different realities."

"So now," Nina pressed, "how did it go with your mum?"

"Had you seen her since the time you left home?" Liz wanted to know.

"She came to the detention centre after I was sent there," Joel said. "I was mad with her – I refused to talk to her. She'd been relieved when I left, I know that, to be rid of the Joel-problem. But by the time she came to visit me she was feeling guilty and bad about how things had turned out. She wanted to know how my dad was and I just said 'Ask him yourself', and turned away from her. She didn't visit again. So just now, this was the first time in two and half years…" He twisted the beanie in his brown hands and then put it back on his head.

"She's gone on with her life. Got a new man, which is good. If I'd gone back any sooner than this I'd have been fronting up to her full of judgement and abuse. But Grandfather taught me a new way of forgiving. I went there to say 'Thank you for giving me this experience'. If it wasn't for her kicking me out I might never have met my grandfather. I might never have found my life purpose."

"Tough way, but," Sandy said with feeling.

Joel shrugged. "Have a mate who was a drug-runner. He got scared with how deep he was getting into it. Prayed for help and the next day he got caught. Most people would think that wasn't a great answer to his prayer, but it was perfect. Got him out of the game and somewhere safe so he could think it over and have a fresh start."

"Divine Order," Nina remarked. "Looks like chaos but it's all perfect."

"What's your purpose now?" Nuncle asked Joel.

"To help my people reconnect with their dignity," he said simply. "To help them walk between the two worlds."

CHAPTER 52

THE ORDER DETECTIVES GET TO WORK

IT WAS FIVE P.M. and already pretty dark outside but nobody wanted to leave. Some of the parents would be turning up any time now to collect the others, and I should have been leaving to walk home…

Liz put the kettle on again and Nina said, "To most of the world, your story – up to landing in jail – your life looked like a mess."

"Yeah. To me too," Joel agreed.

"You might have…" she drew her finger across her throat with a sinister sound and raised eyebrows. "But who would have known what was just around the corner when you were being slammed in jail? Lucky you hung in there…"

"So that's an example of Divine Order, right?" I said. "When it looks like chaos and disaster but there's blessings in it."

"Exactly," agreed Nuncle.

"I know!" Nina's eyes were shining. "Let's blitz everyone's Order right now before you go." She dragged a chair into the middle of the floor. "Everyone gets to sit there one by one, and the rest of us will be Order Detectives."

Liz glanced at the kitchen clock sceptically.

"Time will stop for this," Nina said confidently. "It's important."

We laughed but she was already tugging Joel out of his seat. "You first, because yours is the best example."

"I thought I was done," he protested, but he shifted seats.

"You're nearly done," she agreed. "We can see that there were hidden blessings in the middle of the horrible stuff – right?" she turned to the rest of us.

"Well…" Serenity hesitated, "but what about the guy you bashed up? He might have died."

"Remember, if you judge that experience from *your* values, it will look bad," Nuncle said. "But who knows what his values were? Maybe life was feeling terrible to him at the time. Maybe he had a desire to go. There are some things that we might never know but if we trust in the Order and Intelligence, we can be sure that that fellow was probably ready to go or questioning his commitment to living for some reason. The more I work with this model, the more proof I get that there is an exquisite degree of Intelligence and Order in the system, but it's not easy to see it at first."

"But we *can* see that through all the hard times there were good things, like the Turtle and playing footy and reconnecting with his culture," Nina said.

"And both those things, the hard times and the Turtle, were love," Nuncle said. "Love in different forms: support and challenge – the two faces of Love."

"In our culture we believe our life was a chosen path before we even enter this physical world," Joel said. "You could say it was my destiny to be born half-half, to suffer and then be reunited with a grandfather whose mission is to teach the value of his culture. If I hadn't gone so far down, I don't think he would have been drawn into my life – and if he had, I probably wouldn't have listened. Having a foot in both worlds, I can carry on that teaching and reach even more people."

"Sounds orderly to me," Liz declared. "Okay. I'm next."

She bounced out of her seat and she and Joel slapped hands as they passed each other.

"Cancer," Liz said, looking at us – and especially, I felt, at me… "What's the Order in that?"

"You've had to grow," Nina said at once. "You've had to clean up your act and change some of your thoughts."

"Yes," Liz agreed, watching me. I shifted in my seat. "So is it a blessing?" she persisted.

"But are you still sick?" I blurted.

"I was never sick," she said gently. "My body was just giving me messages that it was time to make some corrections. That's how a healthy system works: it gives you feedback when you need to change. I got some feedback and I'm changing. The cancer was the symptom of a system that's working *properly*. It woke me up to how mad I was with my Dad and how guilty I was feeling about taking Max away from his family… It invaded me to show where I was feeling invasive… That sounds orderly to me."

"Another expression of love," Nuncle said.

Illness as an expression of love was a bit different… but it made sense, put like that.

"And maybe, through making these changes to my lifestyle and in my thinking, I'll end up living much longer and healthier than I might have if it had never happened," Liz said. "Besides, it's given me my next purpose, which is to take the self-care message into the modeling world."

"You finished? My turn," Clare said. She and Liz swapped seats.

"What's the apparent chaos?" Nina asked, holding a pretend

microphone to Clare's mouth.

"Hm. My mum being alone and dad causing heaps of problems by turning up."

"Answering your prayers and turning up!" Nuncle interrupted with a broad smile.

She grinned. "Yeah. Chinese-cursing me."

"What's the blessing in Mum being alone?" he asked.

"More time with me," she said at once. "Dad's place is so full-on. There's people everywhere."

"Ah… And what's the blessing in Dad messing everything up?"

"I got to meet him at last."

"And something else," he said.

"You got to find out that he's not the all-good fantasy dad you were imagining," Sandy pronounced. "You got a reality check."

"Yeah, that's true," Clare agreed.

"I always thought a father should be your greatest role model," Joel said, "and my father was: he was the greatest role model I had for the sort of man I did *not* want to become. I'll always be grateful to him for waking me up."

"My turn," Serenity said, standing up. "Are you done?"

"This is the fastest Divine Order game I've ever played," Liz remarked to Nuncle.

"We're in a time warp," Nina said briefly.

"Hold on! One last question," Nuncle said, and Clare froze with her bum inches off the seat. "When Dad appeared to be missing, who was playing his role in your life?"

She looked at him uncertainly for a moment, sinking back into the chair.

"Who was protecting you, being a father-figure?"

Clare's gaze went straight at Sandy, who said, "What, me? I wasn't trying to be your dad!"

"Maybe not trying to be, but you sure were," Clare said.

"Thanks, Daddy." She blew Sandy a kiss and surrendered the hot seat. Sandy looked disgusted.

Serenity slipped into the vacant seat while the rest of us were laughing.

"And what's *your* illusion?" Nina asked with the pretend microphone, which was now a banana.

"That there can be world peace," Serenity said. "I still really want world peace."

"Do you get the value of conflict?" Nina quizzed.

"Yes. I guess."

"I'll be straight with you," Nuncle said, and Serenity nodded, meeting his gaze. "The very people who want peace on earth will never find it because they're trying to change things. When you really do 'get' Divine Order, you don't need to change anything or anyone – not even those war-ish people – because you see the perfection… The old paradox strikes again: when you want peace you can't have it and when you don't need it, you can… It's the ultimate cosmic joke."

"But you said there'll never be peace," I objected.

"Oops," Nuncle grinned. "You're right, Natalie; we'll always have both peace and war, support and challenge, right into infinity because it's a Universal Law –"

"Which means everywhere, throughout Universe, and through all time," Nina sang out.

"Yes. But there is a kind of inner peace where you see the Order and balance and you appreciate all of it."

"Serenity," Liz said, "I understand your dilemma. I struggled with the idea that we're not evolving towards a one-sided heavenly kind of state or place too. It was so obvious in *my* life that I'd achieve peace on one issue and at the same time be experiencing conflict or anxiety over something else – but understanding that that dynamic goes on forever, at ever higher levels, was difficult at first."

"The Law of Conservation," Billy and Clare said together.

"Jinx!" he grinned, and she made a face.

"Jinx! I haven't heard that in ages," Liz laughed.

"Who do we think we're teaching?" Nuncle asked Liz, smiling. "They get this; they understand that the Order is in the balance of the whole."

"Yep," Nina confirmed.

"I know; very switched on," Liz agreed. "Do you guys mind if I share an insight I've had? You're aware that I've been thinking a lot about health this year. Well, I've been reflecting on how often people separate cause and effect, like thinking sickness just 'happened to us' rather than it following on from our own actions, or thinking that someone attacked us and we had nothing to do with it – we're the innocent victim! Anyway, I realised that life appears to be crazy and unfair and chaotic when it looks like the things happening are outside of us, but when we can see our part in them, that's when we begin to see the Order, because then we're bringing cause and effect together. End of lecture," she finished, with a bob of her head.

"But what have *I* done to cause war in the Middle East, for instance?" Serenity pouted. I was pretty keen to hear the answer to that one too.

"Well, for one thing, the Law of Polarity means you're directly involved," Nuncle said. "Every person on earth who's committed to peace-without-war births someone who is equally committed to war-without-peace because every extreme position has a 'partner', just like every particle has a corresponding anti-particle. Get off *your* hobby horse and they can get off theirs."

Serenity frowned. She was wearing a rainbow tie-dyed t-shirt over a blue long-sleeved top and pants. She looked like a little bit of clear blue sky that had just clouded over.

"Then," Nuncle went on, "take responsibility for where you

act the victim or the aggressor in *your* life. Recognise the Order there. Own your power if you've been playing the victim. What's happening out in the world," waving in the direction of outside, "is just a big mirror to our little dramas."

" 'For things to change, first I must change'," Nina quoted solemnly.

At that moment the phone began to ring somewhere in the house. "Be the change you want to see in the world," Nuncle said, standing up, "because we're entangled with everyone else. The best way to change somebody else is to change yourself, because your perception of them as anything but perfect just the way they are is an illusion. And if you see them as perfect you don't need to change them. The other side of the cosmic joke that works in our favour," he added from the doorway, "is that the second you love them enough to see them as perfect, they spontaneously change. Back in a minute!" And he dashed away in the direction of the pealing phone.

"Who knows," Rick said as Nuncle left, "maybe you're going to be the next world leader? If this bugs you so much, maybe you're going to find a way of really selling the idea to the whole world that we're one human family."

"I like that," Serenity said.

"Bucky called our planet Spaceship Earth. We either all win or all lose because our fates are all tied together. Hey, have you guys seen that story about the corn farmer? It's been going around on emails."

"Yes, that's a good one," Liz said. "Why don't you tell it?"

"If I can remember it…" Rick tipped his chair back for a moment and then landed back on all four legs with a jolt. "I can only remember the punchline."

"I'll start you off," Liz offered. "The punch line is the bit I often forget. Okay… the story is about a farmer who enters his corn in the state fair and wins awards each year. One year a newspaper reporter interviews him and discovers that this farmer always shares his seed corn with his neighbours."

"Oh yeah," said Rick.

"So he asks the farmer why he shares his best seed corn with his competitors," Liz continued. She held her hands out to Rick as if she was directing the spotlight to him; "And the farmer goes…"

"'Didn't you know?'" Rick made his voice really deep and spoke in an American accent. "'The wind picks up pollen from the ripening corn and swirls it from field to field. If my neighbours grow inferior corn, cross-pollination will degrade the quality of my corn. If I am to grow good corn, I must help my neighbours grow good corn.'"[28]

We applauded and he bowed.

"I like that story," Serenity said. She looked at Liz. "I really want to see the world working together."

"If that's what you'd love, that's what you're here to do," Liz said. "Just remember there'll always be a balance of support and challenge, and there'll always be people with different values to yours, so you'll never get everyone doing the same thing all at once."

"Support and challenge: the two faces of love," Clare reflected.

"That's right. If you can appreciate the whole dynamic and see that everything is always love in some form, you'll be a power to be reckoned with."

"Okay. I'm done," Serenity said. She hopped off the hot seat and we looked at each other. Who'd go next?

Sandy glanced towards the door, as if she was waiting for Nuncle to come back before she sat there.

"I'll go," Billy said. He tapped Clare on the head as he went past, unjinxing her with the words, "Clare, Clare, Clare."

She rolled her eyes.

Straddling the chair, he said, "I think for me it's falling into

---

28   author unknown

place. I was pretty crook with my parents for splitting up last year, but now I can see how it's all kind of working out. Terry's much more involved with the family than Dad ever was, so I get what Mum was wanting. And Dad did need a wake-up call because he was just buried in his work…"

"What's the next bit of chaos look like then?" Nina asked.

"Survival," Billy said simply. "My father can't cook to save his life."

We all laughed at that, and Sandy stood up suddenly.

"Okay. I'll face you Detectives," she said. As soon as Billy had moved, she plumped onto the seat and crossed her arms, like she was waiting for judgement.

"Uncross please," Liz said with a half-smile, bobbing her head in the direction of Sandy's chest.

Sandy let her arms drop and sat there looking more vulnerable.

"What's the deal?" Nina asked. She thrust the banana microphone in front of Sandy's face.

"War at home."

"Where's the peace? There always has to be a balance, right?"

"Mum. She's the peace-maker."

"And who's been supporting you?"

"My uncle Bren – and Mum."

"What's the blessing in the war?" Clare asked, almost gleefully – probably because she was remembering all the times Sandy had tried to coach her to stand up to bullies at primary school.

Sandy scowled at her. "Getting stronger."

"You say that every time," I said. "What else?"

She looked at me in surprise and I felt surprised myself. I hadn't felt that coming.

For a moment they were freeze-framed: Sandy sitting wordless in front of the banana, and Nina standing there, one hand on her hip. I felt, rather than saw, Nuncle appear in the doorway, where he stopped.

"Okay," Sandy said slowly. "I didn't like you too much when you turned up," looking at Nina, "because I thought you were so pushy. Like my dad… and me," she added, flushing. "I didn't like that quality but I know now that it's helping me. It's finally getting me to speak up and ask for what I want instead of just complaining about things." She glanced across at the doorway, and I saw Nuncle smile at her, a warm smile that spoke of the secret between them. "I've asked Mum and Dad if I can go and do a pottery-on-the-wheel class next term with Uncle Bren, and they said yes. And now that I'm not feeling so angry with Dad, I seem to be getting on better with Mum, too."

"Is it my turn?" Nuncle asked. And coming across the kitchen, he gave Sandy's shoulder a loving squeeze as he passed her.

"Okay, what's your drama?" Nina demanded with her banana mike.

"Not getting to raise my own son," he said. And even though he wasn't specifically looking at me or Clare or Sandy, I reckon we all felt looked at.

"So what's the blessing in that?"

"Well, he was raised by an even more committed mother and her family and friends. And all the love I couldn't give to him, I gave to those around me – like you, Madame Detective."

Nina blew him a little kiss and then grew stern again. "Very good. You get the hardest questions, so be serious. How was he always in your life even when it looked like he wasn't?"

Nuncle smiled and touched his heart. "Always in here. On the fridge," with a jerk of his head towards that photo. "In my thoughts, driving me to be more conscious. And just now," he looked around at all of us with a radiant smile, "on the phone. That was Josh."

Liz started. "Josh?"

"Yes," Nuncle said, and his eyes were moist. "That was Josh. He's ready to have us over."

"Oh my God," said Liz. She clapped a hand to her mouth. "What happened?"

"Pure synchronicity," Nuncle said. "He's been running into Maxes and references to Australia constantly the last few months. He finally decided to stop resisting. And his mother, bless her fiery heart, gave him the letters I've been posting that she's been sitting on for years. All my emails were going into his junk mail."

"Well!" said Liz. "I'll be…"

Outside, a car came crunching up the drive.

Nina glanced at the clock. "Come on, Nat, quick. Before the time warp magic runs out."

Nuncle popped out of the hot seat to wild applause and catcalls (Sandy), and I gave him a quick delighted hug before I took the spot. It was toasty warm.

Nina stuck the banana in front of my mouth and asked me what my perceived disorder was. I could have said it was feeling inadequate but I'd always feel that way to some degree, I saw that now – because there'd always be someone in my life inspiring me to greater things. For the last year or so it had been Nina and her family; most recently Miss Walker – and Rick with his big vision, and before all of them, my stories about magic. Feeling inadequate drove me to grow and stretch. I'd always be both friend and foe to myself, encouraging myself when I felt bad, and disapproving of myself when I needed to be humbled.

I could have said it was my mother's criticism that unsettled me but I could see how that was a blessing too. I wasn't supposed to just swallow all these ideas whole, without thinking about them and testing them. My mother's doubts flushed out my doubts and made me examine things harder and stick with things till they made sense to me. Like that business about 'you can't create your reality'. Well, she was right about that. For exactly the reasons that Nina and Nuncle had taught me: nothing is created or destroyed; it's all already here. It just changes form, and we're in charge of the forms by how we think and what we choose. Nothing gets 'blinked' into existence like magic just because you've been visualising a bit; it all works through matter, like Nuncle said, and the results are scored by the people who are most focused and most committed.

I could have said that I didn't know what my next challenge was going to be or how I was going to keep the Mastery Club at school going or how I was going to answer those kids' questions. But I could see that everything would unfold in perfect Divine Order and Timing, whether it looked like it was or not. I couldn't fail. Just like they taught us in science: there's no such thing as a failed experiment. The experiment is successful because it tells you how something doesn't work, which is also important information. If I trusted inside-me, I'd find my right way forwards.

I sat there wordless, grateful, feeling tears sprouting in the corners of my eyes.

"I think she's got it," Nina smiled.

Footsteps approached the kitchen door.

"What about you?" I asked, wiping a hand across my nose. "And Rick."

"I'm good," Rick said. "Next time."

Nina dropped into the seat that I had just vacated. "I used to feel lonely," she said solemnly. "But now I know that wherever I am, I Am there."

There was a knock at the door. Liz stood up.

"What sort of airy-fairy bullshit is that?" Sandy snorted.

Nina giggled. "I designed that statement especially for you, Sandra Jones." As Billy's mother and stepfather Terry, entered, she stuck her finger in her mouth, and gaped, like a fish on a hook.

Sandy threw a tea towel at her and in the background we heard Cathy saying cheerfully, "This looks like a lovely, cosy, afternoon tea party."

Mastery Club Lesson #30

Masters look for the Hidden Order

* No matter how it looks, everything is in perfect Order according to the Laws of a vast Intelligence that some call the 'Grand Organising Design(er)'.

* Our job is to find the Order.

* The two faces of Love are support and challenge, and, no matter how the situation looks, they're both always there.

* The proof that you've seen the Order is when you feel grateful. When you can say 'Thank you for giving me that experience,' you are experiencing Love and Divine Order. You are in the zone.

CHAPTER 53

THE FINAL QUESTION

AS THE DAYS grew colder and greyer, I realised that it was just over a year since I had met Nina. Boy, had my life ever changed. I couldn't look at the world the way I used to anymore, thinking that things just happened to me. And I also couldn't believe that mastery was about just waving your wand – or saying an affirmation – anymore. I'd been shocked into realising that masters don't have fantasy-perfect lives; they have as many challenges as everyone else, but they respond to them differently. Masters work at deliberately manifesting what they love instead of what they fear, and at the same time they love and appreciate *whatever* manifests because they respect that it's there for a reason. And actually everyone's a master because *everyone's* making their own beliefs true all the time, just like magic. (Although we didn't always want to own up to what we were manifesting…)

I came downstairs to breakfast one school morning not long after the slide show day to find Dad in staying-at-home clothes and Mum nowhere to be seen.

"She's sick," Dad told me, squeezing orange juice, "so I'm

working from home today."

The newspaper was spread out on the kitchen table. A headline caught my eye: 'Hollywood: the land of dreams and the entrance to hell'. I had to smile at the balance in that description. My eye wandered to an article about how democracy was on the increase in the Middle East, while government rules and regulations were chipping away at it in the West. I guessed that was the Law of Conservation at work. Amazing how the balance and Order were there when you knew what to look for...

"Mum wants you to do an errand on your way home tonight," Dad said, pouring the juice into glasses. "Go ask her about it."

I found Mum lying in bed leaning against a stack of pillows and looking bleary-eyed and miserable. "How are you feeling?" I asked. Dumb question.

"Terrible," she croaked. "I'b subbosed to bick up a package frob subwud today. Could you do dat for be od your way hobe?"

"Sure," I said.

"Dak you." She blew her nose. "Her dabe is Gloria. Here's the address. Apparrotly she has a geedius brother. He's ad artist or subting. But dot all there."

"Okay, no worries."

Mum looked at me thoughtfully over the hankie. "You've really cub out of yourself dis year. Dey say idderdashodal travel is good for kids, so I guess dat's it."

That, and perhaps leading my own Mastery Club.

It turned out to be my day for meeting new people. Miss Walker gave our Mastery Club a challenge: to go and ask three strangers a question.

"Now I trust you to not follow strangers into their cars or approach anyone too weird," she said, ("As if!" Holly muttered), "but I do hope you take this on. I want you to ask three people what is the main lesson their life so far has taught them."

"Like, just front up to three strangers and ask them 'What's your main life lesson?'" Bree demanded, taken aback. "They'll think we're headcases!"

"Tell them you're doing a school project if you have to," Miss Walker replied. "Now, here's the clincher: I bet you that whatever they say will be relevant to you. You'll each be given a piece of wisdom that is tailor-made for *you*, in your life, right now."

"Sounds freaky. Why?" Holly wanted to know.

"Just to explore and prove to yourselves a little fact about us and this universe we inhabit: the fact of its entanglement – the interconnectedness of everything."

"Ah!" Mark said. "I've been reading about that. Did you know that particles are conscious of being observed? Did you know that matter has *no independent existence from us?*"

"Exactly," beamed Miss Walker. "The observer is engaged in the process. We are literally co-creating our world in every moment."

Holly and Bree exchanged sceptical looks.

"But some of us have been thinking these affirmation things and they're not working," Kat drawled.

"It's always working," I said at once. "It just depends what you're talking about. If you say the positive affirmation a few times and a negative affirmation a few hundred times, which one do you think is going to come true?"

She shrugged, feigning disinterest, but I reckon I nailed her there. 'We get what we *are*, not what we want,' Nina had said to me once. It had taken a while for me to understand that 'we are' meant what we tell ourselves, since that decides who we become. (If that makes sense.)

"And did you know that scientists are working on how to make things invisible and how to do time travel?" Mark continued, startling me.

Tom pricked up his ears at that. "For real?"

"Yes." Miss Walker looked a little troubled. "Here's hoping the military doesn't get hold of those discoveries."

"That's probably who's funding them," Mark said knowingly.

I told the netball pair what Nuncle had said about the most focused person influencing the whole group. They exchanged looks again, and I wondered if they wanted it enough to really commit. Mark was apparently steadily winning chess tournaments, but it looked like Petra was satisfied with her mouse and still not in a hurry to choose another goal, and I wasn't sure that Tom would ever get around to doing anything. Maybe they would drop out. As for Kat...

When everyone had left, Miss Walker told me that she was still working on the school principal – she wasn't going to give up! This was *her* goal. But in the meantime she just wanted to say how much she felt I had grown this year. I'd been very meek and retiring when she first met me, and now look at how confidently I spoke up.

I felt myself swelling a little, with pride. Yes, she was right, I had grown. First Mum had noticed it, and now Miss Walker.

On my way out, I stubbed my toe on the door. Wincing and hobbling, I had to laugh when I realised that the universe was bringing me back to centre...

I told Sandy about our strange Mastery Club homework on the way home in the bus.

"Interesting," she said, but she didn't seem to be paying too much attention. She was smiling to herself and bobbing her head slightly, as if she was listening to music.

"What's going on?" I asked suspiciously. Sandy doesn't smile without a reason.

She looked at me almost in surprise. "Uh... something. I'm going to tell everyone tonight. On Skype."

"Oh, tell me now," I pressed, "go on."

But she refused to say.

I left the bus stop and walked up the street that was parallel with my usual route home to pick up the package for Mum. I thought about The Question as I walked. It was going to feel really weird 'fronting up to a total stranger', as Bree had said, and asking this deep question. It was all very well to ask a stranger the time but 'What's your biggest life learning?' They would surely think I *was* a headcase…

As I trudged along the unfamiliar street, my schoolbag heavy on my back, I noticed a magnificent elm tree on the nature strip. My gaze wandered to the garden behind the low stone wall. It was lovely – a profusion of greens and rainbow colours. There were creamy white magnolias in front of the house, purple and blue hydrangeas along the driveway, beds of golden marigolds and crimson poppies… A plump, oldish woman in a flowery apron was sweeping the driveway.

"You have a beautiful garden," I called to her.

"Thank you," she answered in an elegant English sort of accent. She paused and looked at the garden herself. "It just grew."

My face must have shown my thoughts because she laughed and said, "Of course it grew! What I mean is that it used to be a very boring expanse of grass and weeds. Bit by bit, I've been planting things. And now it's quite transformed." She chuckled. "They even put a picture of my little garden in the local paper – imagine that!"

"Congratulations." I took a deep breath and plunged in. "If you don't mind me asking – it's for a school project I'm doing – what would you say is your biggest life lesson so far?"

"Goodness." The woman didn't seem at all put out by the question. She crossed her plump arms across her chest and frowned slightly in thought. "Well, dear, I would say it is to just get on and do what you love and not compare yourself with other people. I have a very clever older brother who has done all sorts of exceptional things with his life, you see, and it seemed to me that all I did was get married and have children. And of course the children are terribly important to me, but they're all grown up and off living their own lives now. Whenever I compared myself with my brother I felt that I hadn't accomplished much in my life… And then one day I decided that I would dig up some of the couch grass over there," she pointed, "and plant a little tree. And then a little later I planted another. And then some shrubs. And before long all this just… appeared – like magic!"

"Do what you love," I repeated, "and don't compare." Bingo. That was definitely for me.

"Yes. I always felt that one had to have a big vision, a grand vision. But one doesn't. One can start small. So very many people aren't happy in their lives, and all it takes is that first step. I'm almost dangerous now!" She came closer and elbowed me conspiratorially. "I've got plans for the backyard too!"

"I'm sure it will be wonderful," I grinned. "Thank you."

"Oh, you're welcome, dear. I hope that helps."

"It's perfect," I told her warmly, and went on my way.

"So take my advice!" she called after me merrily, beginning to sweep again. "Do what you love! Believe in yourself!"

There was a little park on the corner of this street and Marriott Way, where the package-person lived. A man in a business suit was sitting by himself on a bench with a briefcase at his feet, tapping a message on his phone. As I came closer, I noticed that he had a diamond stud in one ear; odd for a businessman. He glanced up and gave a little nod, then turned back to his phone. I had no intention of speaking to him, but even as I was thinking that, I had this sinking feeling as I approached him like I was not in control of myself and the words just came tumbling out of my mouth.

"Excuse me, sir, but do you mind if I ask you a question?"

"What's that?" he replied with a slight frown, as if I'd disturbed him in the middle of something very important. (I probably had.)

"I'm doing a school project and I have to ask three people what they've learnt from life. The main thing," I said awkwardly.

"You're not as good as you think," the man said abruptly. And then quickly, when I stepped back; "Not you; that's what I've learnt."

"Oh."

A little muscle was working in the side of his jaw, which was clenched tight. "Is that all you need?"

I hesitated.

"You know what? I'm going to give you another bit for free. Two bits of advice – you're in luck, girlie." He shook his head with a dry half-smile and took a packet of cigarettes out of the inside pocket of his jacket. He lit one, then continued. "I was really up myself when I was, oh, late teens. Drinking. Yahooing. The usual brainless stuff. I caused the death of a mate. It wasn't anything I could be convicted of in a court of law, but I know it was my fault." He blew out some smoke and stared off into the distance for a moment, then back at me. "So that's where the first bit of advice comes from. Don't get up yourself. You're not as good as you think.

"Here's the second bit – the free bit. Any limitations you feel you have are a reflection of your conditioning, not your potential. Face your fears. Give any project two years minimum before you give up on it. Think about everything that could go wrong and plan how you're going to deal with it. Keep your feet on the ground. Specialise in creative thinking and overcoming obstacles. When you start cruising, you're on your way down."

Phew. "Thank you," I said, digesting that lot.

He gave another short nod and turned back to his phone. I walked on thoughtfully, smoke in my nostrils. I was beginning to enjoy this exercise. It was like being sent on a quest, say to find the Holy Grail, and these ordinary-looking people were actually significant characters on my journey. They might *look* like housewives and businessmen, but really they were powerful magicians with mysterious messages…

I wondered who I would be drawn to ask next and what I would be told…

I arrived at the address on my scrunched up bit of paper and headed up the pebbled driveway. The door was answered by Mum's client, Gloria, a very masculine-looking woman with broad shoulders, wearing a lemon-coloured suit. Her voice was quite deep too, when she greeted me. A thin balding man hovered behind her; he took my hand enthusiastically as soon as I stepped into the hallway.

"Hello, hello," he babbled, holding onto my hand, "who are you? I'm Will – resolute, determined. Will Bedford Holmes, 48 Marriott Way, Blackburn, Melbourne, Victoria, Australia, Southern Hemisphere, Earth, Milky Way, Universe. What's your name?"

"Natalie," I said, a little taken aback.

"Natalie. You're Natalie. That means birthday, did you know that?"

"All right, Will," Gloria said. "Don't overwhelm her. I'll be right back with the package for your mum, Natalie."

"Birthday, birthday," Will was muttering. "You can be born physically but also other ways – mentally, spiritually, emotionally. Happy birthday! Pleased to meet you," he enthused, pumping my arm. "Welcome to the world! Happy birthday!"

He touched my schoolbag and then began to unzip it, rambling all the while. "Can I look in here? Anything interesting?" And without waiting for my answer he began to move everything around inside my bag! I stared at him in utter amazement. "Books,

books… pencil case. Can I look in here?" Before I could say a word he had begun to unzip my pencil case. "Pens, pencils, erasers… You see this one? HB. That's good, that's fine. B2 is darker but easier to erase. I'm an artist. Paintings all over the world, all over the place – Paris, London, New York, Milan, Tokyo… Canada, Holland, Africa, Germany, Russia… it's a big world."

He dug more deeply into my bag. "Anything else? Nothing interesting. Don't be rude. Don't overwhelm her. Where do you live? I live here. Let me show you around." He slung my bag over his shoulder, seized my hand and dragged me after him. "This is the living room of course; dining room here… kitchen… Would you like to see my bedroom? I'll show you –"

From somewhere in the house Gloria called out, "Stay in the living room, Will! I'll just be a minute, Natalie."

Will led me back to the living room, still talking. "Stay in the living room, Will. Do you know what you're going to do for a career? Never mind. Later. You're still young, still young. What's your mother's name? Beth? Oh that's my mother's name! Beth, Elizabeth. It means consecrated to God. Consecrated means sacred…"

Back in the living room he stopped suddenly and just stood there, holding my hand between his and still talking non-stop. "There's a scratch on your leg. Not bleeding," as I glanced down, startled. He was right, there was – I hadn't noticed it.

"Never mind. It's not important. What's your father's name?"

"Charlie."

"Charlie, Charlie. Charles, to be correct. Prince of Wales. How's your Charlie then? Is he a Prince? Means strong and manly. Is he strong and manly? Hm?" Before I could say anything – although, what do you say when someone describes your father as strong and manly…? – he was off again.

"What's your best friend's name? You can learn a lot about

someone from their friends… Nina? Nina. Means girl, daughter, beautiful eyes, powerful, friend. Rhymes with bambina."

"How do you remember what all those names mean?" I asked, amazed. (Not only by his memory, but also by how accurately Nina's name described her.)

"Eidetic memory. Means photographic. Always had it. It's a brain thing. I remember everything – everything! You can't erase my memory. No, no, no. It's all in here," tapping himself on the side of the head. Then he started tapping *me* on the side of my head. "All in here. Yes, yes-yes."

Gloria's footsteps came clattering along the hallway.

"Will you visit again?" Will asked in a rush. "Do visit again. We like visitors, don't we, Gloria? Very important, visitors; keep you sane."

"They certainly do," she agreed heartily, passing me a neatly-wrapped parcel. "Thanks for this, Natalie. Tell your mum it should all be there. She can give me a call if anything's missing."

"Okay," I said.

"Keep you sane, keep you sane," Will was mumbling. "Goodbye, birthday girl, goodbye. Come again." He wrapped his long arms around me in a hug and pressed flat lips to my cheek in a sort-of kiss.

"Okay, Will," Gloria said, taking his hand and drawing him away. "Let her go. She has to go now."

"Has to go, has to go. Of course. Back to your busy life. Thanks for visiting – come again!"

I might not have asked him my question, I reflected, walking to the end of Marriott Way, but I'd certainly been given some sort of message. 'Do what you love/Follow your heart/Don't compare yourself to others' from the gardening lady; 'Don't get cocky and stay committed' from the businessman, and 'Happy birthday' from Will! Which I guessed could mean that no matter what went wrong, I could always start again – I could be 'born again'. Or maybe Will's message was that everything had a hidden meaning, just like our names did. And maybe, if I rolled all the messages together, they were saying that we *are* our choices, and to build ourselves a great life, a life that we will love.

After all – and I found myself stopping in my tracks on the street as this thought burst into my mind – it wasn't about everyone becoming a Nina or a Nuncle. We didn't need a world full of Ninas and Nuncles or of any one-sort-of-person, even if that person was a master. We needed the mad, mixed-up, fascinating variety that we already had. Just like Nuncle had said: nature was healthiest when there was diversity, and farms that were planted with just one thing were way more susceptible to pests. We needed faithful fathers and wandering ones, times when we tuned into Nature and did Medicine Walks and times when we plugged into technology; we needed sickness and health, old wise cultures and brave new ones that broke all the rules.

This quest was a bit like a medicine walk. As I turned into my street, I wondered what sorts of answers the others would be getting. Would they be captivated by the mysterious, magical side of this exercise? What if all people went through their lives consciously, taking everything as a message, looking past the appearance of ordinary old conversations to something deeper and more significant…?

As soon as I had that thought, I realised it would be impossible because the other side of being conscious was being *un*conscious, and life was fifty-fifty. The Hidden Order was always there, whether we saw it or not.

THE END... OR NOT

THE LAUGHTER OF THE GODS

WHEN I ARRIVED HOME, Evan was squatting in the driveway, a look of sheer concentration on his face as he whittled away at a piece of wood with some sandpaper. He and Dad were making a toy plane, he informed me without stopping, and it was his job to make the rough wood smooth. Which he had to do with rough paper. You couldn't make rough wood smooth with smooth paper, he explained seriously.

Of course. How many clues did we need?

I gave the parcel to Mum who thanked me and asked me to check what Katie was up to – and to switch off the TV if she was watching it, which of course she was. It was a cartoon about kids who didn't realise that milk came from cows and not the supermarket. The cartoon kids were guzzling milk and tossing the empty plastic bottles over their shoulders into a rapidly growing heap of rubbish. A villainous character rubbed his hands and cackled in the background. "Hehe! My evil plan is succeeding!"

"What plan, Master?" asked his stupid-looking henchman.

"My plan to destroy the world!" the villain said gleefully. "So long as humans don't figure out where things come from or where they end up, I will be victorious!"

"You're so clever, Master!" the henchman said, though he obviously didn't have the first clue what his boss was on about.

"Mum said to switch it off," I told Katie, ignoring the grizzle. "Have you had a snack?"

Over our mashed banana sandwiches, I quizzed her to make sure that *she* knew where milk came from and how bad it was for the earth if everyone just kept buying stuff and throwing the rubbish away. We couldn't bemoan a polluted earth if we had caused it.

"I know that," Katie said, rolling her eyes. But then Dad came in and she started working on him to talk Mum into letting her have a new outfit for her barbie doll. I was about to say something sharp when I remembered my insight about variety, and I thought, yep, the world needs people like Katie too, so I should just shut up.

I took my snack over to the computer because it was nearly time for our Skype call. I wanted to tell everyone about the school Mastery Club task – especially Nina, because I knew she'd love it. And I was busting to hear Sandy's news.

We'd finally figured out how to get more than two computers connected on Skype so we didn't all have to be in front of one little screen. When we started dialling in, I found that Clare was at Serenity's place, Rick was with Billy – and Sandy was at Nuncle's!!!! *What was she doing there?!*

"I'll go first," Sandy said with a bit of a smirk, "because I know you're all wondering why I'm here."

"Yeah, why are you there?" Nina demanded. "Hi Nuncle!"

"Hi Neen," he replied with a wink. "Hi Natalie, Clare, Serenity, Billy and Rick!"

"Because I had to give your uncle the news first," Sandy told Nina.

"What news?" we asked.

"Dad's been assigned a new job… overseas," she announced.

"Overseas! Where?" I squeaked.

"Malaysia."

"When?" Clare asked.

"Soon. In a few months."

"So… you'll be moving?" Nina voiced the question on all our minds.

Sandy grinned. "Nope. Staying here."

"How?"

"With my uncle. He's going to look after me while they're away. It took ages to get Mum and Dad to agree, but when I said I didn't want to interrupt my schooling –" she chortled – "they had to give in."

"Man. So you got your goal that was going to be for years later," Clare marvelled.

"Which goal?"

"You know, to move out. Only you're going now."

I was struck by a sudden thought. I grinned. "So what's the bad side of your dream life going to be? Just so you don't fall for the curse!"

Sandy made a face. "Food," she said. "Uncle Bren's on this health kick at the moment – to lose weight. So… no chips, no sausages, no junk food…"

"Oh my!" It was Nina's turn to chortle.

Sandy changed the subject by asking me if I was going to tell the others about my Three Questions Mastery Club homework. I did, and they were fascinated.

"I'm going to do that tomorrow!" Nina declared. "You just ask three people what was their biggest life lesson, right?"

"Yes."

"Tough thing for that guy," Billy said, "the one who reckons he killed his mate. Must be hard to live with that."

"A lot of things are hard to live with when we don't have a big enough picture," Nuncle reminded us. "In fact, the Ancient Greeks tell stories of the gods up on Mount Olympus looking down on all the loss and pain and death down here, and laughing their gigantic heads off – they called it *asbestos gelos*, the unquenchable laughter of the gods."

"That's a bit mean!" Serenity exclaimed.

"It sounds like cruelty," Nuncle agreed, "but that's not the whole story. The gods are only metaphors for our higher selves, our potential, and the reason they were laughing was because they knew none of it could really hurt us – the undying part of us – and because they'd been through it all themselves, and because they knew that one day we'd all be up there *with* them, laughing down at the next worldful of students in the school of life going through exactly the same lessons to wake them up to their own divinity. You have to really love someone to let them go through what they need to, to wake up."

For a moment I imagined myself up there in the clouds, looking down and smiling and loving all the little people below living their lives so earnestly, and suddenly my heart felt like it was swelling inside my chest with this incredible feeling of understanding.

Liz's face appeared next to Nuncle's. She waved to us and perched on his knee, and he drew her close, looping an arm around Sandy as well so they could all be seen.

"The thing is," Liz said, looking radiant in a knitted yellow jumper, "even though nothing down here can harm us, we have to believe in it and take it seriously or we won't get the lesson. A scary movie isn't any fun if you know what's coming or don't get involved in it, and life is just the same – a really big, scary, beautiful, wise, wonderful movie that never ends."

"I suppose that's what happened for you with the cancer," Clare said.

"Yes. Scary and kind of a game at the same time."

"Hey, you know," Nina said, "someone who did a pretty roller coaster life is that Buckminster Fuller guy you and your dad talked about at Natalie's slide night, Rick. I've been reading about him and he has a pretty outrageous story, doesn't he?"

"Disaster after disaster at first," Rick nodded. "A stack of business failures, and he blew family money in a big way and was kicked out of college *twice.*"

"And then the really worst thing – well, from a human point of view," Nina conceded; "he had this sick little daughter and one day he was going to a fair and she asked him to bring home a cane for her and he promised that he would, but he forgot because he was a bit of a party boy and a drinker. By the time he got home a few days later his daughter was sicker than ever and really weak, but as soon as she saw him she whispered, 'Did you remember my cane?' and he had to own up that he'd totally forgotten – and she died in his arms."

"Oh how terrible," I said, and then echoed Nina, "from a human point of view…"

"So listen to this!" Nina continued, breathless, "this is where it gets amazing! He's feeling like such a total failure and no-hoper that he goes walking out to Lake Michigan, planning to throw himself into it and drown, and he's standing there at the edge of the water when suddenly he has this revelation moment. It was like time stopped, and he heard a voice saying, *"You do not have the right to eliminate yourself. You do not belong to you. You belong to Universe."*

I felt chills as Nina said this. The others were very still too.

"And then," she went on in a hushed tone, "he gets this message that he'll never know exactly why he's here on earth but he can assume he's on track if he turns all of his life experiences into things that will be of service to the rest of the world. What do you think of that?"

"Why wouldn't he ever know why he's here?" Serenity objected. "Lots of people reckon they know what their purpose is."

"Well, it says in the book that you can't ever see your true purpose because it's always at a ninety-degree angle from you. Like a honey-bee that thinks its purpose is to get nectar, which is straight in front of it, but its real purpose is to pollinate the plants it's flying over." She demonstrated a right angle with her hands and then rushed on excitedly.

"Remember when we were talking about doing Six Impossible Things before breakfast?"

"Yeah."

"Well, Bucky totally got busy inventing things and he created this car that's like a Chitty Chitty Bang Bang – it can fly and go on water and everything! And these houses that get flown to sites and you drop a bomb to make a hole and then plant the house into it like a tree."

"That sounds crazy!" I exclaimed. My mind wandered to my bookshelf of fantasy books.

"He was just so far ahead of the rest of the world. His inventions have won a stack of awards and stuff for being really useful and practical – his trump card was copying nature to find the most efficient ways of doing things. He just decided he would devote himself to doing everything he possibly could for humanity in ways that would work for the earth as well, and he wouldn't let anything stop him."

Maybe *this* was the third message, I thought. That it was time to let my imagination run wild too… If things only appeared to be solid, and life only appeared to be chaotic, then why should *anyone* live a small life…? I tuned back into the conversation in time to hear Nuncle saying something about how humans only used about three percent of their genetic potential. Wow. Imagine if we used all of it – we'd be G.O.D.s…

As I sat there smiling at these special friends who were sharing this incredible, mind-opening journey with me, I thought of Joel and the beggar kids in Greece, and of the whole world in all its perfect imperfection, and suddenly the lights came on for real! I got a glimpse of a BIG idea, a real deep-sea whale that would take us completely beyond anything we'd done before – and I had to tell them about it straight away.

ANOTHER BEGINNING

GLOSSARY

goog — slang for egg

jail — gaol

caf — short for cafeteria (kiosk)

mo — moment ('back in a mo')

sook — Australianism for a sulky, cry-baby person

good on you — Australianism for 'well done'

queue — a line or sequence of people (or vehicles) awaiting their turn to be attended to or to proceed *

dodgy — unreliable, dishonest, a bit shady, potentially dangerous…

billy lids — 'little kids'; it's Australian rhyming slang

rapt — very happy

kilometres — a kilometre is approximately 0.62 of a mile

premmies — abbreviation for premature babies

wagging school — playing truant

nicking things — stealing things

gecko — a small lizard

didgeridoo — (or didjeridoo) an Australian Aboriginal wind instrument in the form of a long wooden tube, traditionally made from a hollow branch, which is blown to produce a deep, resonant sound, varied by rhythmic accents of timbre and volume *

headcase — a crazy person

Source: Websters Online Dictionary

Timeless Wisdom

"Zeus has ordained that there be summer and winter, plenty and poverty, virtue and vice and all such opposites for the sake of the harmony of the whole." — Epictetus

"Remember that there is nothing stable in human affairs; therefore avoid undue elation in prosperity and undue depression in adversity." — Socrates

"He who wants to know the greatest secrets of nature should regard and contemplate the minima and maxima of contraries and opposites." — Giordano Bruno, Italian philosopher, mathematician, astronomer and friar.

"There is nothing absent (or lacking), everything is present, already in potential." — Lopon Tendzin Namdak, Tibetan monk and philosopher

"Unity is not something one is aiming at. It is something which one may experience every moment in every action."

and

"Even the most terrible events contain hidden blessings. The masters know this truth and remain undisturbed while those of lesser wisdom swing from elation to depression as they move through positive and negative events on their way to understanding."
— Dr John Demartini, Human Behaviour Specialist

. . . .

If the idea of Order intrigues you, do check out *The Breakthrough Experience, a Revolutionary New Approach to Personal Transformation,* and the other books and programs of Dr John Demartini: www.drdemartini.com

From the Author

YES, this is a big book...

When I wrote *The Mastery Club* I felt as if I had just scratched the surface of some big, magnificent ideas. I wanted to explore them further, hence this sequel. In the process of writing it, many of my beliefs were challenged – but in a good way! I hope you enjoy the deep dive into these thought-provoking ideas.

Where is The Hidden Order in our current challenging times?

- There is *always* a balance of positive and negative.
- Every positive holds the seed of a negative, and vice versa.
- An essential step along the road to maturation and mastery is to own one's shadow, which means embracing our positive *and* negative aspects.
- It also means owning the reflection that the world holds up for us, which, in confronting and difficult times, requires humility and courage.
- Even the darkest days present us with opportunities and benefits.

My novel *Power of the Light* directly targets the issue of dark times through a story about illness and government control. In this book 13-year-old Nathan grapples with his father's cancer diagnosis. His dreams take him into an alternate world where a new breed of 'Reactors' are taking over, and a small group of rebels are choosing to deliberately Create their reality rather than fall for appearances. (*More info on the Products Page.*)

I love to hear from readers. You can reach me at hello@lilianegrace.com.

Acknowledgements

I'm grateful to Jeremy 'Yongurra' Donovan for allowing me to base the Aboriginal character of Joel on his life story. I encourage you to visit Jeremy's website for more information about his programs. *[www.jeremydonovan.com]*

I was absolutely captivated by Jeremy's presence and message when I heard him speaking at an event. I contacted him many months later and asked if he would allow me to base Joel's character on his life story. He agreed, and generously shared more of his personal life with me so that I could ground the Joel character in reality rather than in my imagination. Jeremy shares from his heart with great humility and power; he has a mission to inspire his fellow Aboriginals, especially the youth, with the strength of their culture, and to encourage the rest of us to understand the original culture of Australia. I feel sure we will be hearing more about Jeremy Yongurra Donovan.

All of the Aboriginal stories in *The Hidden Order* are true. A little artistic license may have been employed with regard to time frame or location, but they were all the authentic, first-hand experiences of a number of friends and acquaintances, and I am privileged to have been permitted to share them. I would like to thank Helen and Clive Benoy, Hannah Belfrage, Mary Whiting, Jenny Day, Yvonne Green, Esther Blanquet and Biljana Torbakova for sharing their experiences and resources with me. I'm also grateful to the many authors whose books about Aboriginal culture provided background and insights.

Thank you to Dr Kristian Ronacher for his wise words regarding health in the second Foreword. It has long been important to me to eat a largely unprocessed diet, and I have learnt many gems from Don Tolman, the 'Whole Foods Cowboy'. I met Dr Ronacher at one of Don's events. Don Tolman's many extraordinary stories of health breakthroughs (and alarming stories of mis-information and intervention), and his sheer passion where personal responsibility, common sense, and respect for our bodies and earth are concerned, have greatly inspired me. The journey with cancer described in this book is inspired by his stories and research. *[www.thedontolman.com]*

I would particularly like to acknowledge and thank my daughters and sisters and my close women friends for the 'Red Tent' rite of passage experiences we have shared together, which provided rich material for that part of this book. Thank you, also, to shaman and author, Susan Oliver, for conversations at her 'Little Jaguar Mystery School', and for her input regarding medicine walks.

Natalie's Greek Islands trip is based largely on my adventure with my daughters in Europe in 2010. This was a goal I re-set many times and finally achieved. Act on your dreams! It was a fabulous experience.

Heartfelt thanks to Timothy Marlowe, my very knowledgeable and dedicated editor. Tim spent countless hours with me working through the manuscript at a metaphysical level, a characters-and-story level, and at the level of language and expression, and it is a much finer work now than it was when I first posted it to him. Tim's own book, *Way of the Wealthy*, is now available. Visit his website to order and to explore some of the many other services Tim offers in his role as a Demartini Facilitator. *[www.demarlowe.com.au]*

Originally *The Mastery Club* and *The Hidden Order* both had striking front covers illustrated by my niece Jessica Hall, who captivated many readers with her portrayal of the green-haired Nina. However it was time for a more contemporary set of covers. The new edition of *The Mastery Club* was illustrated by Jacob Harnwell and *The Hidden Order* by Kimberly Djehanian, who did a marvelous job of aligning her cover art with Jacob's. You'll find her on Instagram at kimberlys.illustrations, where you will be impressed by the skill of this enterprising young woman.

It has been a long journey since I wrote *The Mastery Club* in 2005. There have been many ups and downs and a huge learning curve for me encompassing self-publishing, book launches, websites, public speaking, publicity, marketing, program development, business administration, sorting though a plethora of opportunities, audio and video recording (and editing!), and international programs. With regard to the latter, I would like to express my love and profound thanks to all The Mastery Club® Facilitators, especially Tess Day, Diane Price and Nicola Unite.

A number of international leaders have acknowledged my work – Jack Canfield, co-creator of *The Chicken Soup for the Soul*® series and

The Success Principles, Ken Pierce (Psychologist and Co-Author of *The Dance of Bullying – a breakthrough tool for teachers and parents*), Brandon Bays (The Journey®), William Tiller (Emeritus Professor in Bio-Energetics, Stanford University), Jon Gabriel (The Gabriel Method), Joane Goulding (The Goulding Institute/SleepTalk® for Children), and, of course, Dr John Demartini, to whom I have dedicated this book. All of these personal and spiritual growth teachers have delighted me by praising my work.

Finally, a huge thanks to all the people in my inner circle who quietly and steadfastly support me: my son, Jeremy Strong (Shevek Creative), who variously manages my website, prepares my books for printing/production and helps with technical issues – he stepped into the big shoes of my ex-husband/'Tech Support', Derek Rawson. Thanks to my daughters, Lesley and Emma, who provide me with honest feedback and so much love; and to my husband, Albert Tapper, whose head is probably still spinning since meeting me. Thank you for your love, belief in me, and generous support.

There are too many friends, fans, allies and colleagues to name you individually but you are all deeply appreciated.

And you, the reader of my books, without whom I could not do this work I so love – thank you.

PRODUCTS AND PROGRAMS
available at https://lilianegrace.com/store

THE MASTERY CLUB® – *See the Invisible, Hear the Silent, Do the Impossible* tells the beginning of this story when Nina turns up

at Natalie's school with the intention to form a 'Mastery Club'. Natalie and her friends are swept up and their worlds are turned upside down as they grapple with new ideas, meet Nina's colourful family and tackle a variety of goals.

The Mastery Club is available in paperback and ebook formats, and as an audio download.

THE MASTERY CLUB® 10 LESSONS POSTER

A 300mm x 420mm full colour and laminated poster.

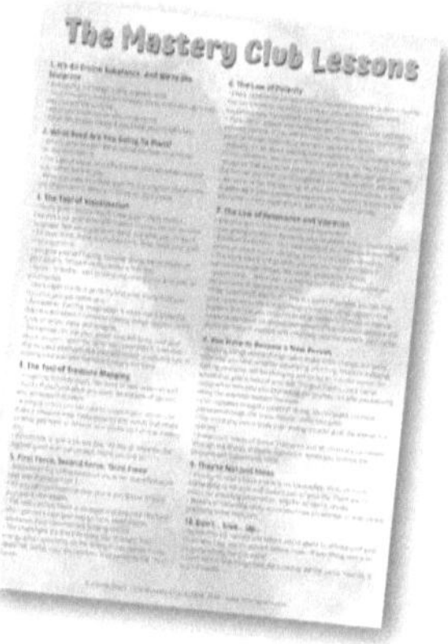

THE MASTERY CLUB® 'MASTER YOURSELF & YOU CAN MASTER ANYTHING'

PROGRAM guides students through the 10 Lessons, teaching each principle through games and activities, and providing opportunities for application to the students' own goals. To enquire about either the Program or the Facilitator Training: hello@lilianegrace.com.

SET UP YOUR OWN MASTERY CLUB OR JOIN

MINE! A Dominican University Study found that just having a goal in your mind is hardly effective at all. But if you write it down, tell a friend, make up an action plan, and agree that the friend can stay on your case about it, you're much more likely to achieve it. That's a Mastery Club! To participate, email hello@lilianegrace.com.

TALK. LISTEN. RESOLVE. REPEAT.

Let's make Communication and Conflict-Resolution Skills core-curriculum subjects and assist children to consciously and deliberately 'skill up'. Bullying in one form or another has been around forever and always will be. Universal laws explain why. But we don't have to be at the effect of it; both the perpetrator and the target can learn the lessons bullying offers and transform the situation. Ask me more! hello@lilianegrace.com

POWER OF THE LIGHT

How do you finish a stuck story and solve your biggest problems? Do you use cunning, force, luck, magic or... 'the Power of the Light'? Nathan's adventures in a fantasy world give him the answers that he and his sick father need.

20% of the profit from each sale of this book is donated to Farmer's Footprint.

QUEST FOR RICHES – *Four teenagers discover the keys to wealth and prosperity*

Discover the four 'money personalities' (which one are you?) as teenagers Toni, Eric, Jackson and Brooke attempt to raise funds for a school-organised trip to India. In the process of a colourful and confronting journey, they learn the principles of sound money management.

This book was written in collaboration with 'Money Mastery For Teens'.

THE CHAMPION SERIES

The Champion Series are fully illustrated children's picture books about real people who followed through on their childhood dreams.

The Boy Who Barked tells the inspiring story of Dr John Demartini, labelled 'learning disabled' as a child and now a leading Behavioural Educator and multi-bestselling author.

The Boy Who Found His Pulse introduces you to Don Tolman, whose childhood desire to outsmart and out-

wrestle his brothers sent him on a quest to find an ancient recipe for a sacred meal that builds strength and restores health.

The work of these two men is transforming lives around the world. Both books written by Liliane Grace and illustrated by Yvette Bentata-Moore.

WANTED: GREENER GRASS – *a novel about love, envy and a crazy kind of courage*

Mia and John's relationship has become flat and boring and she's over her job, so when John heads overseas for his father's funeral, she feels relieved and excited and ready to explore new options. He returns prepared to commit more deeply, but something isn't right... This 'conscious chick lit' novel explores the issue of personal and relationship fulfilment and the Hero's Journey.

MASTERY CLUB WORKSHOPS

"Master yourself and you can master anything."

The 10 Lessons in *The Mastery Club* come to life in a 10-session program in which your child or student can learn to apply these empowering principles while developing practical skills in a supportive group.

Watch your child

- gain confidence and choose an empowering attitude;
- develop great character qualities such as patience, persistence, resilience and resourcefulness;
- take responsibility for his or her results;
- give and receive support.

Fun and Inspiring!

"In a world where the peer group is all too often seen a crusher of dreams and an enforcer of mediocrity, The Mastery Club is an uplifting peer group where the young are encouraged to aim high and stretch themselves to realise their goals." – Dr Peter Ellyard, *Designing 2050 - Pathways for Sustainable Prosperity on Spaceship Earth.*

Make a difference to a child's life – and to yours!

For more information:
hello@lilianegrace.com

- Facilitator Training
- In person and online
- School / group / family programs
- Or set up your own Mastery Club!

"Move over Harry, there's a new wizard in town and her magic isn't confined to fantasy." **– Sunday Star Times, New Zealand**